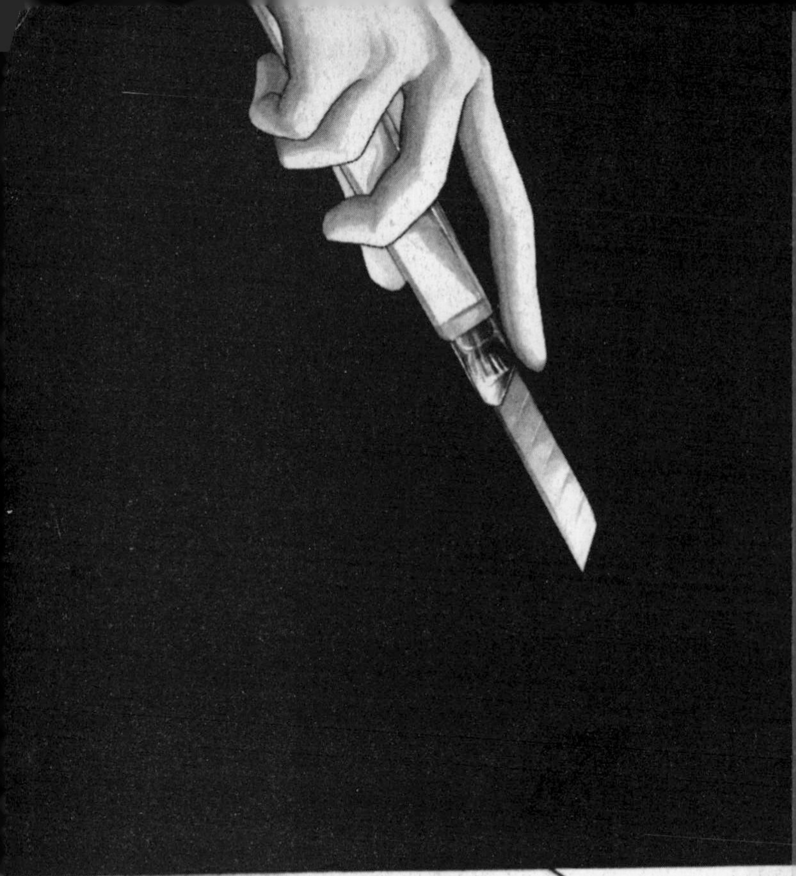
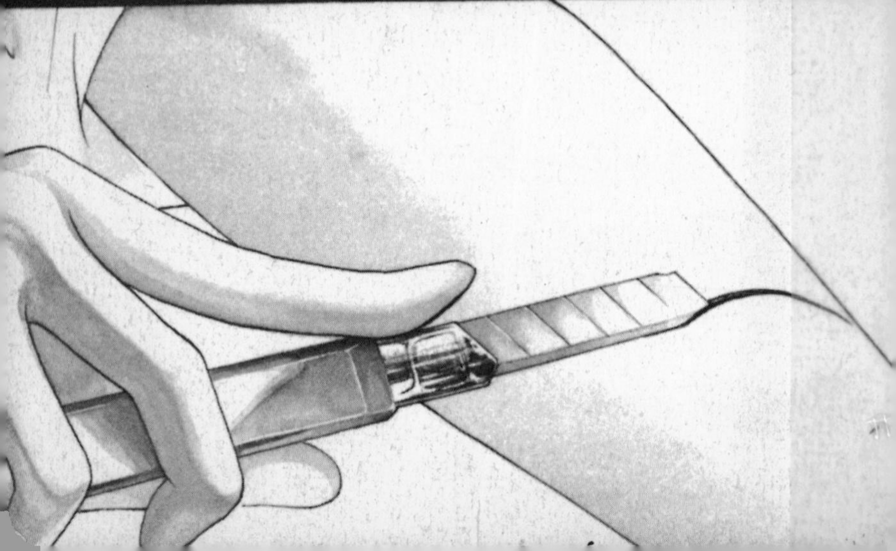

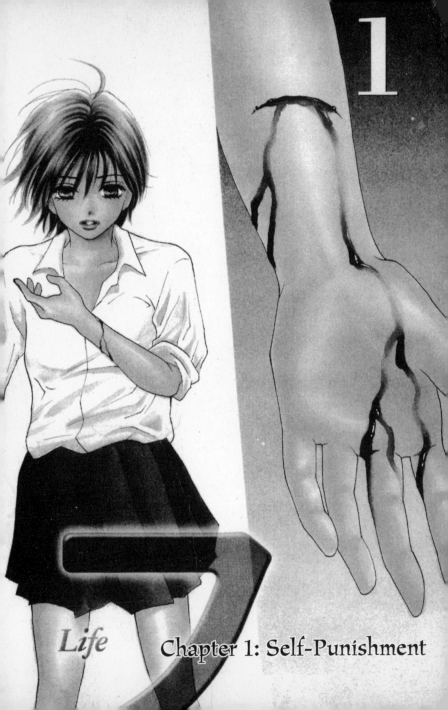

Life

Chapter 1: Self-Punishment

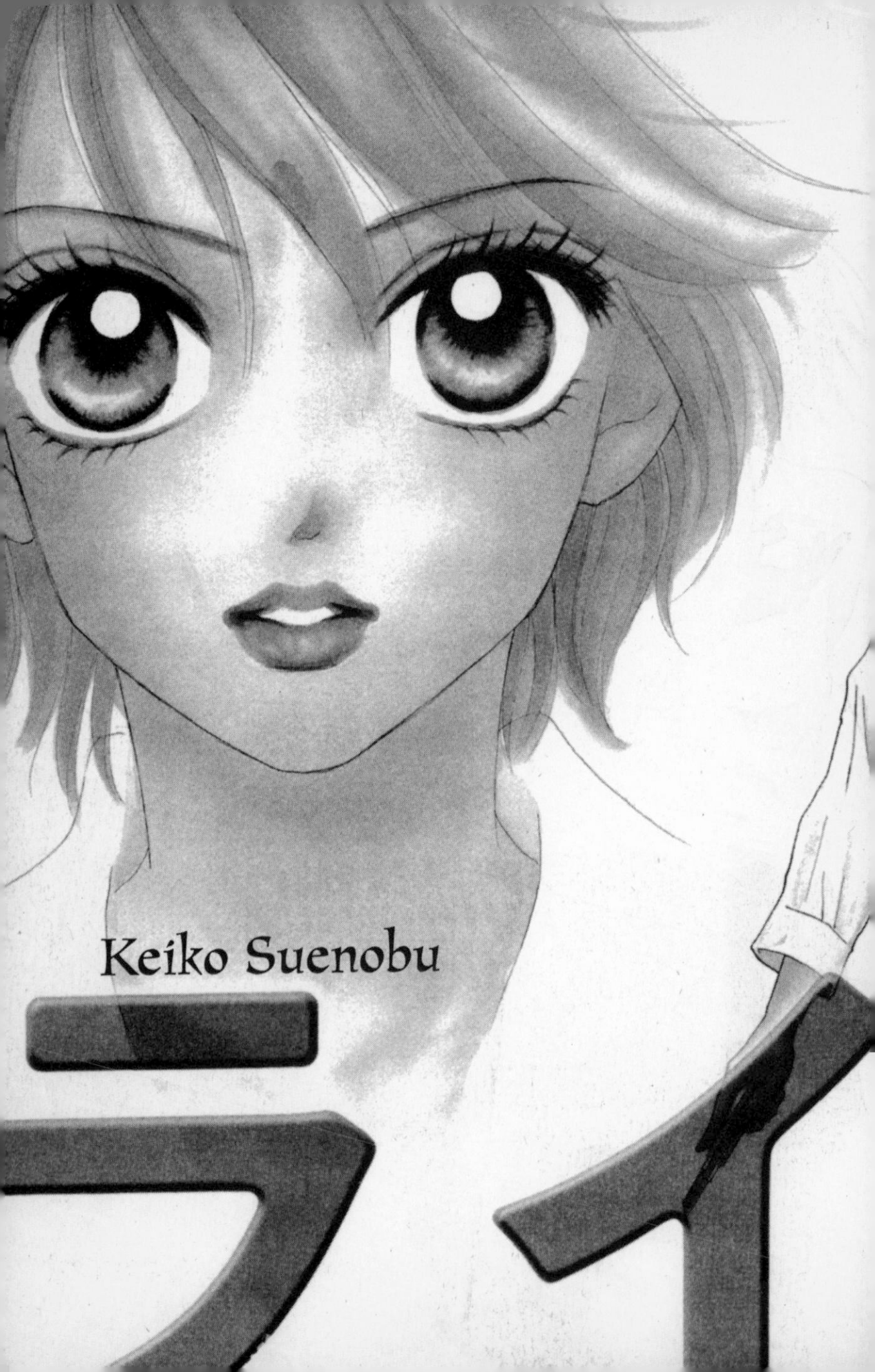
Keiko Suenobu
ライ

ライフ
Life

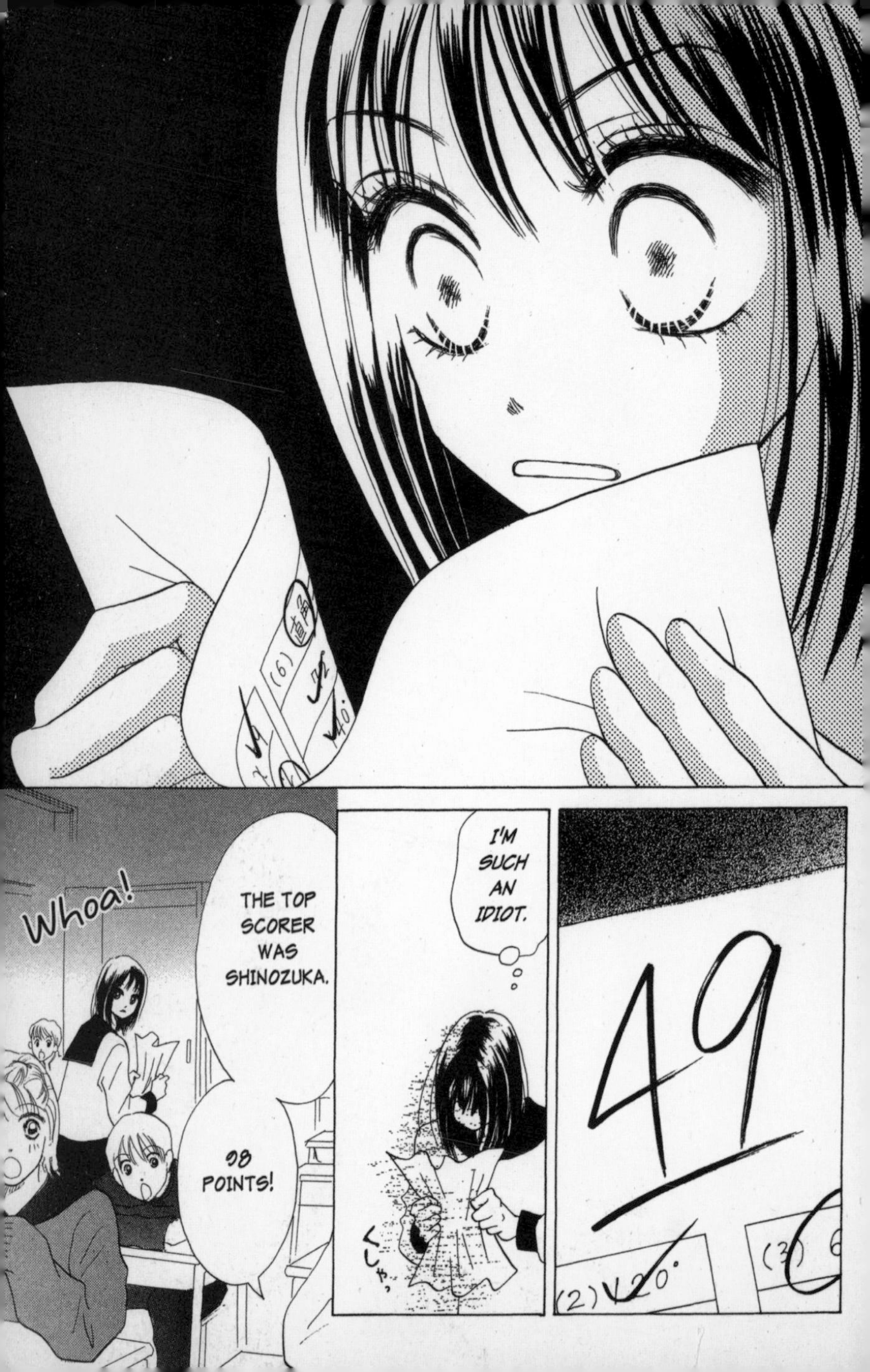
49
I'M SUCH AN IDIOT.
くしゃっ
THE TOP SCORER WAS SHINOZUKA.
Whoa!
98 POINTS!

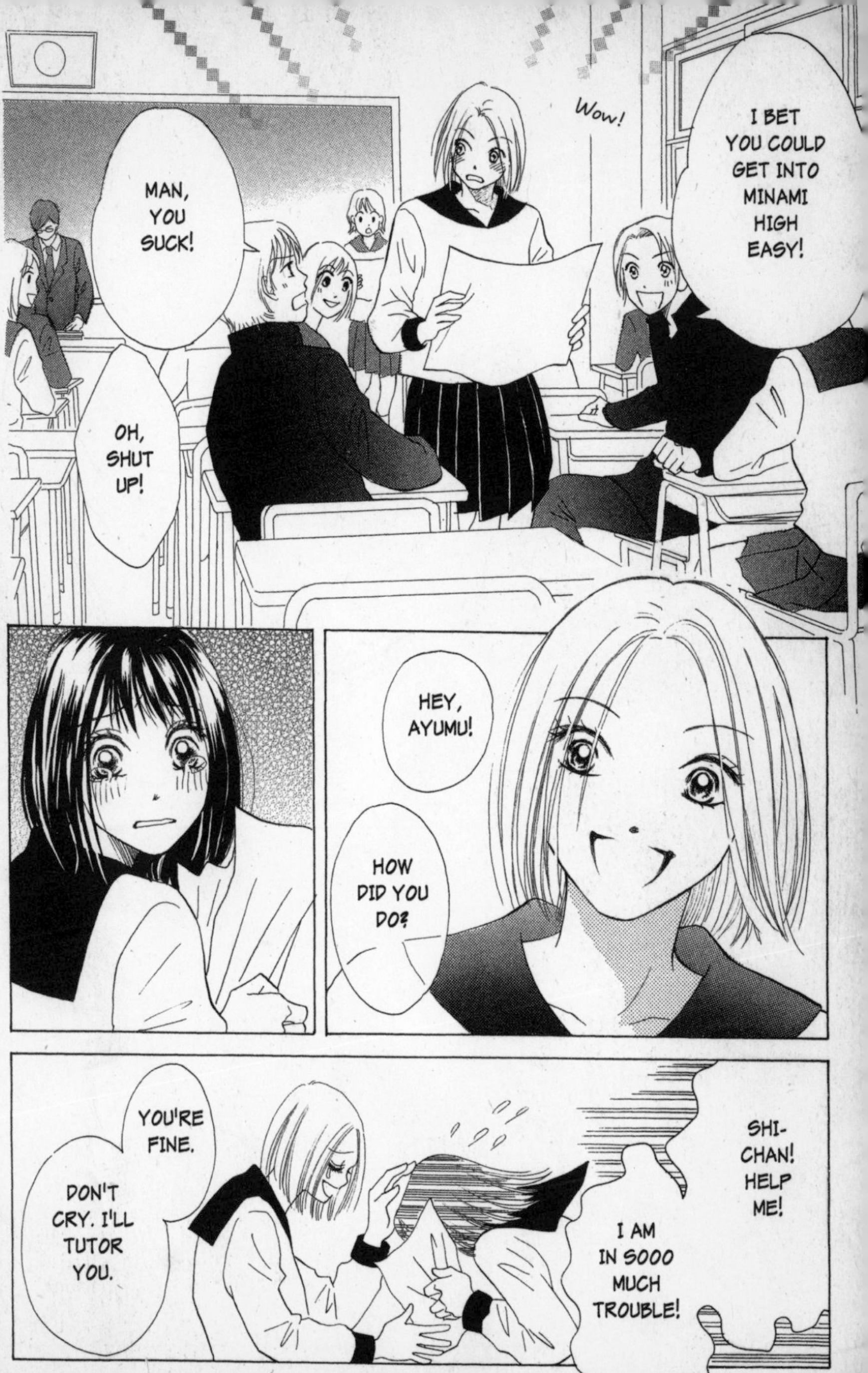
I BET YOU COULD GET INTO MINAMI HIGH EASY!
Wow!
MAN, YOU SUCK!
OH, SHUT UP!
HEY, AYUMU!
HOW DID YOU DO?
SHI-CHAN! HELP ME!
I AM IN SOOO MUCH TROUBLE!
YOU'RE FINE.
DON'T CRY. I'LL TUTOR YOU.

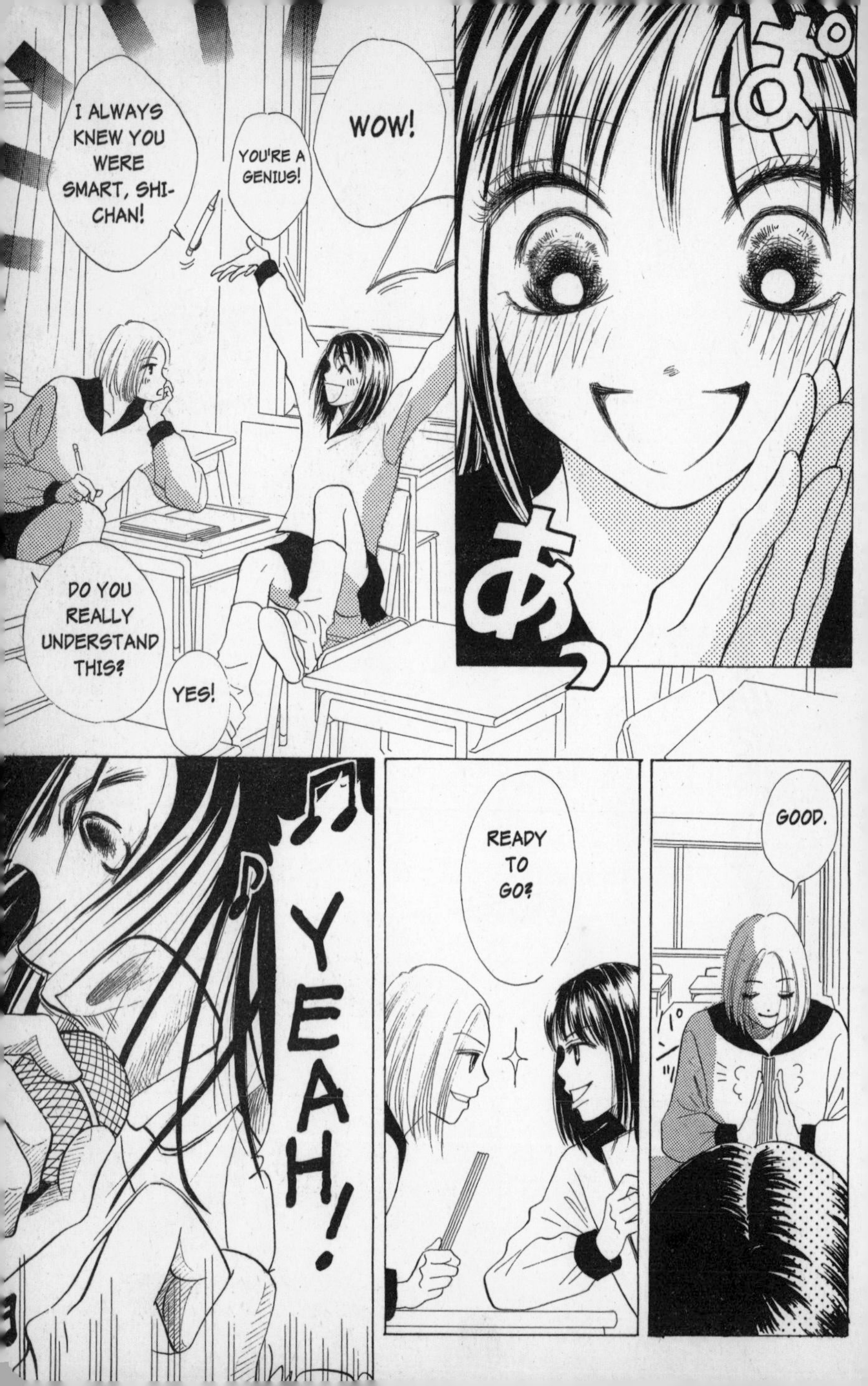
ぽ
あっ
WOW!
YOU'RE A GENIUS!
I ALWAYS KNEW YOU WERE SMART, SHI-CHAN!
DO YOU REALLY UNDERSTAND THIS?
YES!
GOOD.
READY TO GO?
YEAH!

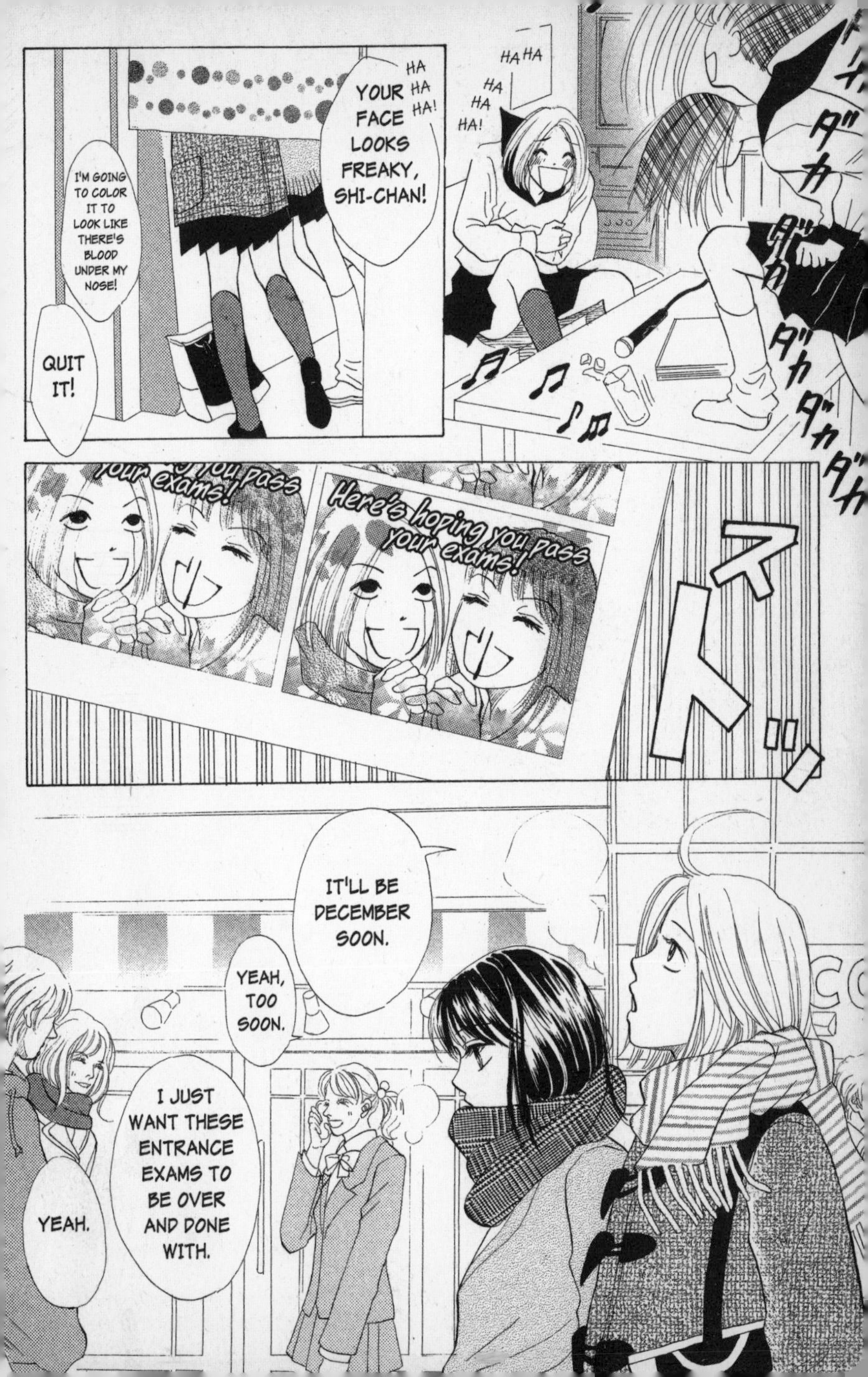
HA HA
HA HA HA!
HA HA HA!
YOUR FACE LOOKS FREAKY, SHI-CHAN!
I'M GOING TO COLOR IT TO LOOK LIKE THERE'S BLOOD UNDER MY NOSE!
QUIT IT!
Here's hoping you pass your exams!
your exams!
IT'LL BE DECEMBER SOON.
YEAH, TOO SOON.
I JUST WANT THESE ENTRANCE EXAMS TO BE OVER AND DONE WITH.
YEAH.

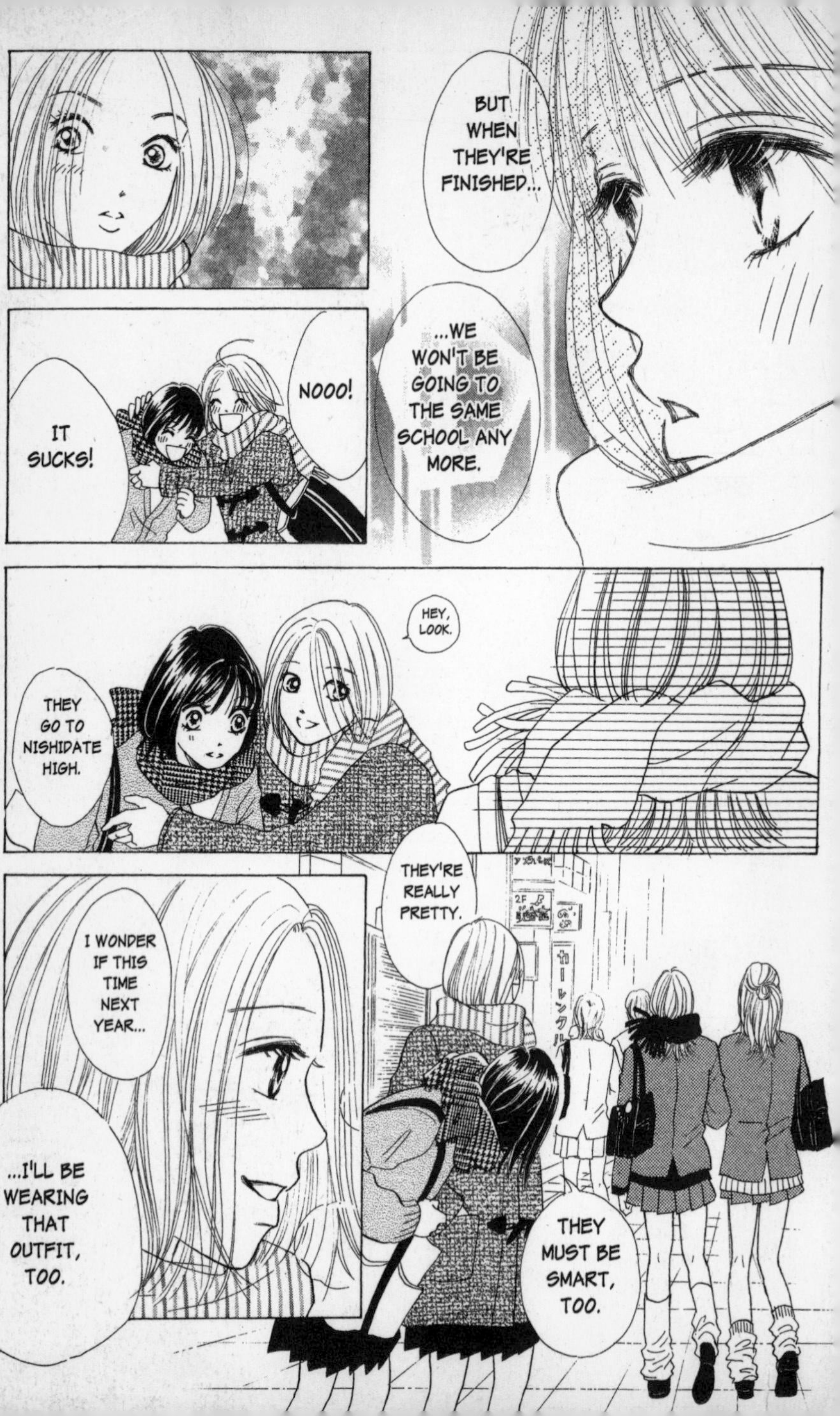
BUT WHEN THEY'RE FINISHED...
...WE WON'T BE GOING TO THE SAME SCHOOL ANY MORE.
NOOO!
IT SUCKS!
HEY, LOOK.
THEY GO TO NISHIDATE HIGH.
THEY'RE REALLY PRETTY.
THEY MUST BE SMART, TOO.
I WONDER IF THIS TIME NEXT YEAR...
...I'LL BE WEARING THAT OUTFIT, TOO.

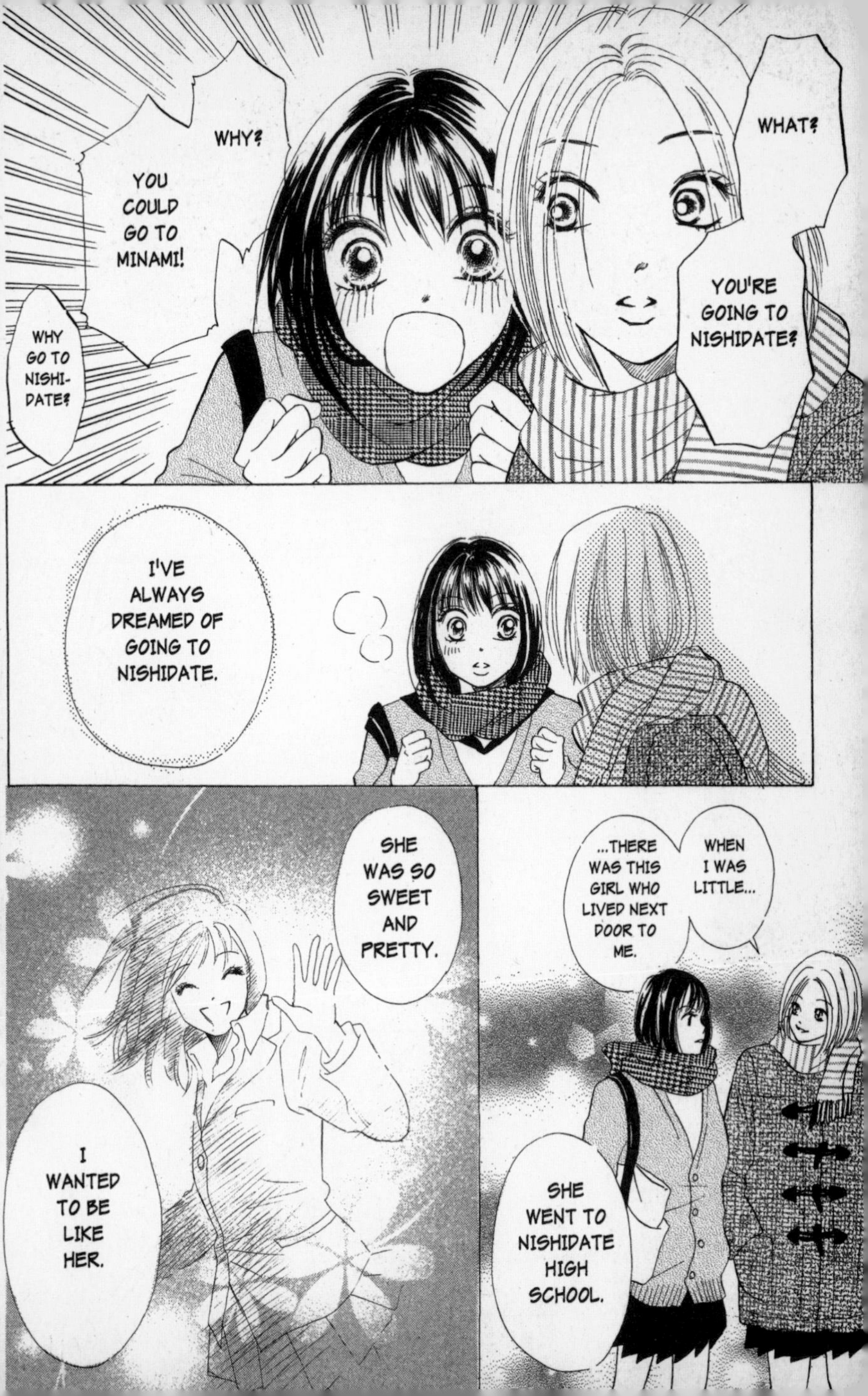
WHAT?
YOU'RE GOING TO NISHIDATE?
WHY?
YOU COULD GO TO MINAMI!
WHY GO TO NISHI-DATE?
I'VE ALWAYS DREAMED OF GOING TO NISHIDATE.
WHEN I WAS LITTLE...
...THERE WAS THIS GIRL WHO LIVED NEXT DOOR TO ME.
SHE WENT TO NISHIDATE HIGH SCHOOL.
SHE WAS SO SWEET AND PRETTY.
I WANTED TO BE LIKE HER.

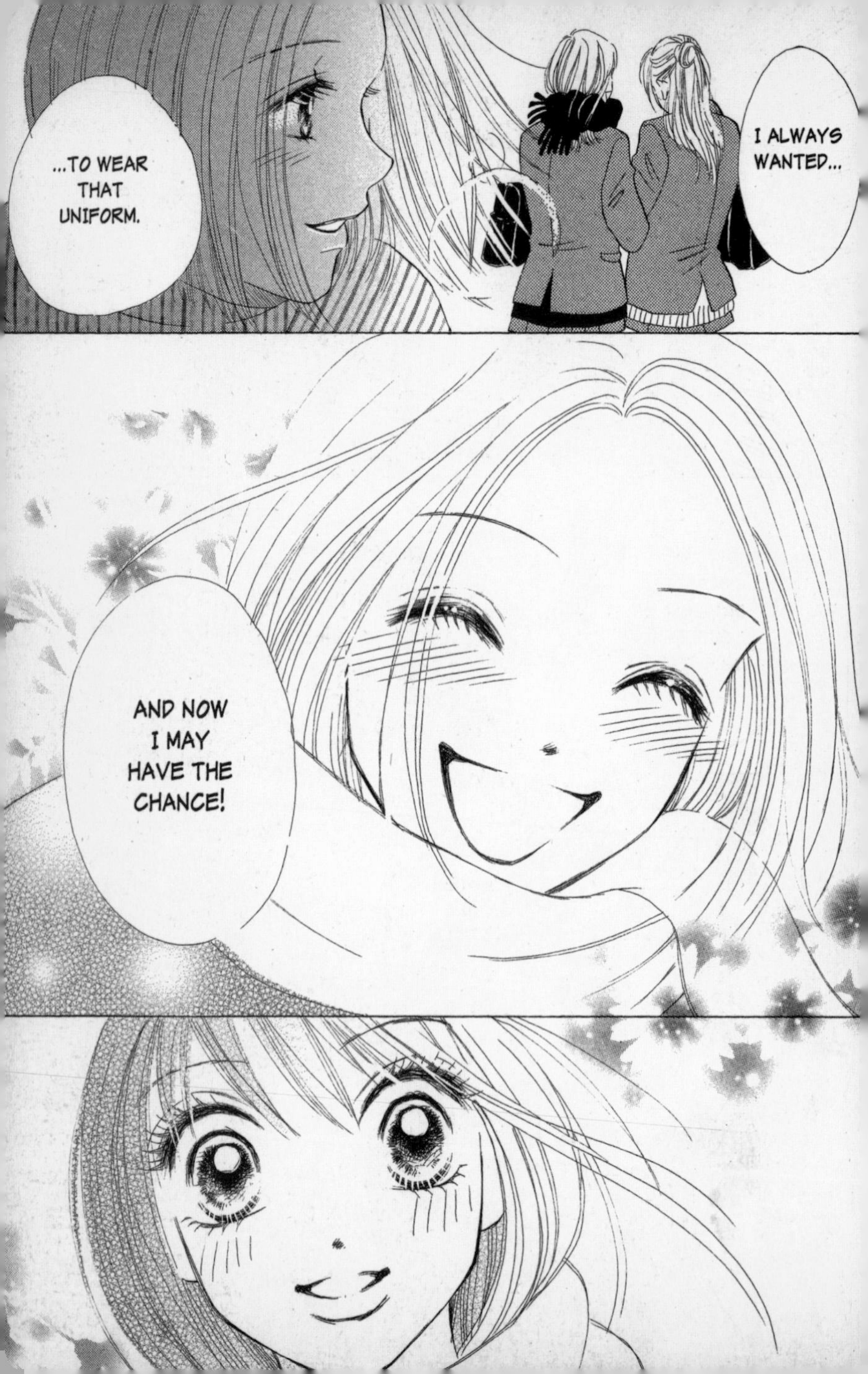
I ALWAYS WANTED...
...TO WEAR THAT UNIFORM.
AND NOW I MAY HAVE THE CHANCE!

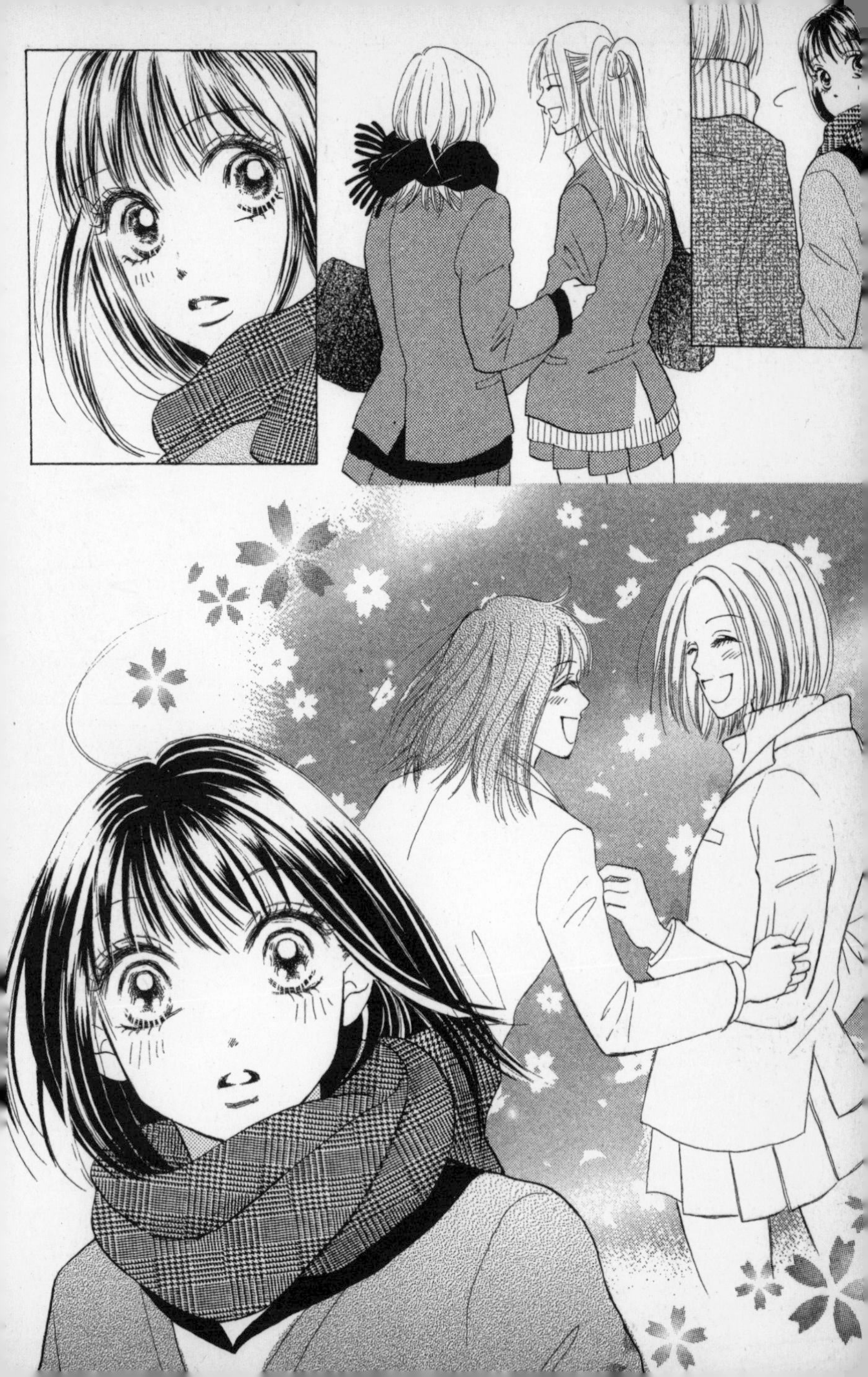

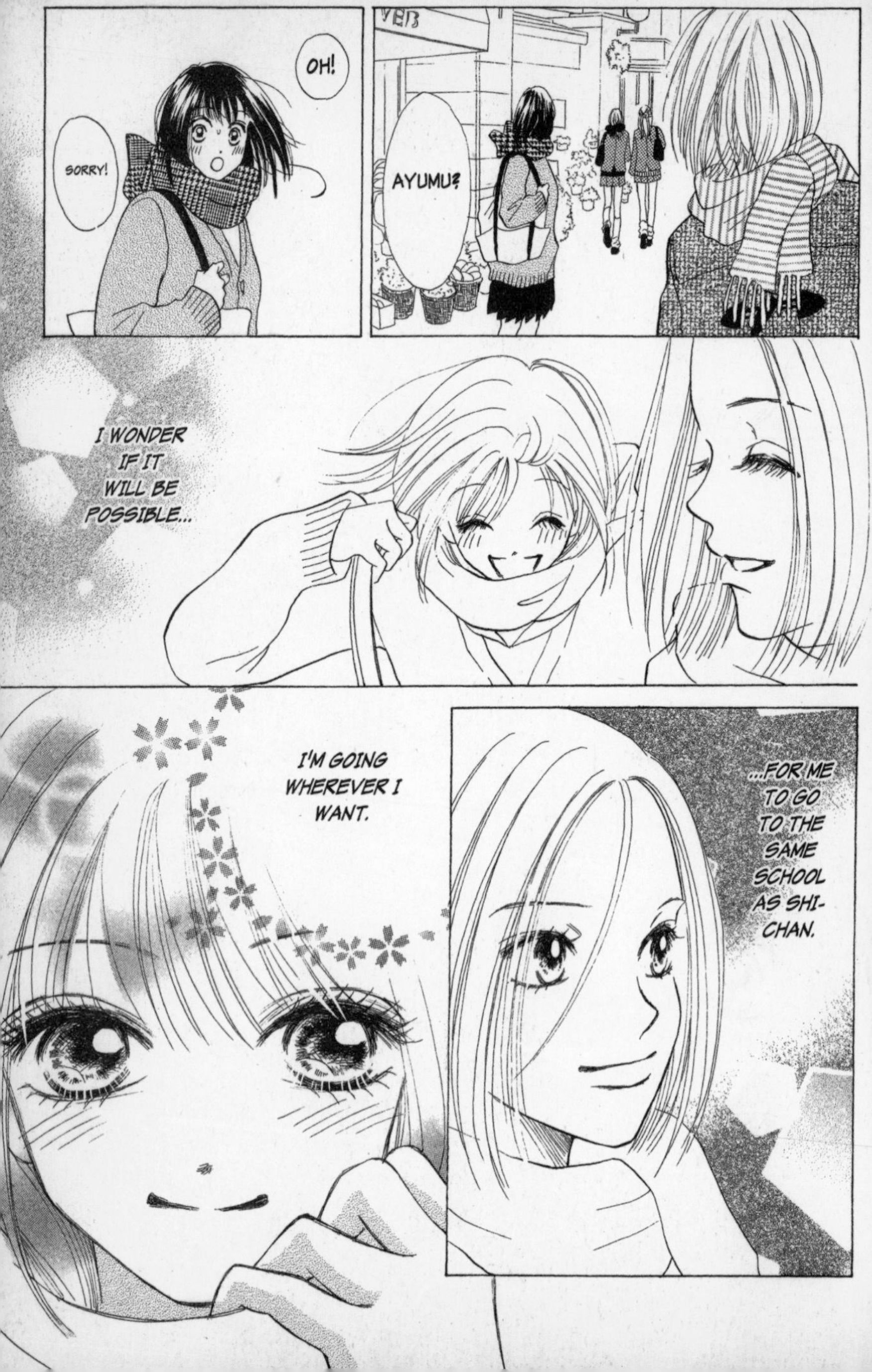
AYUMU?
OH!
SORRY!
I WONDER IF IT WILL BE POSSIBLE...
...FOR ME TO GO TO THE SAME SCHOOL AS SHI-CHAN.
I'M GOING WHEREVER I WANT.

I FEEL...

...LIKE I'VE
SEEN THE
LIGHT.

LIGHT...

DARKNESS...

	Grade
Nishidate High School	D
	B

ARE YOU
TRYING TO
GET INTO
NISHIDATE,
TOO?

AYUMU...

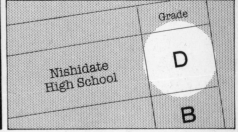

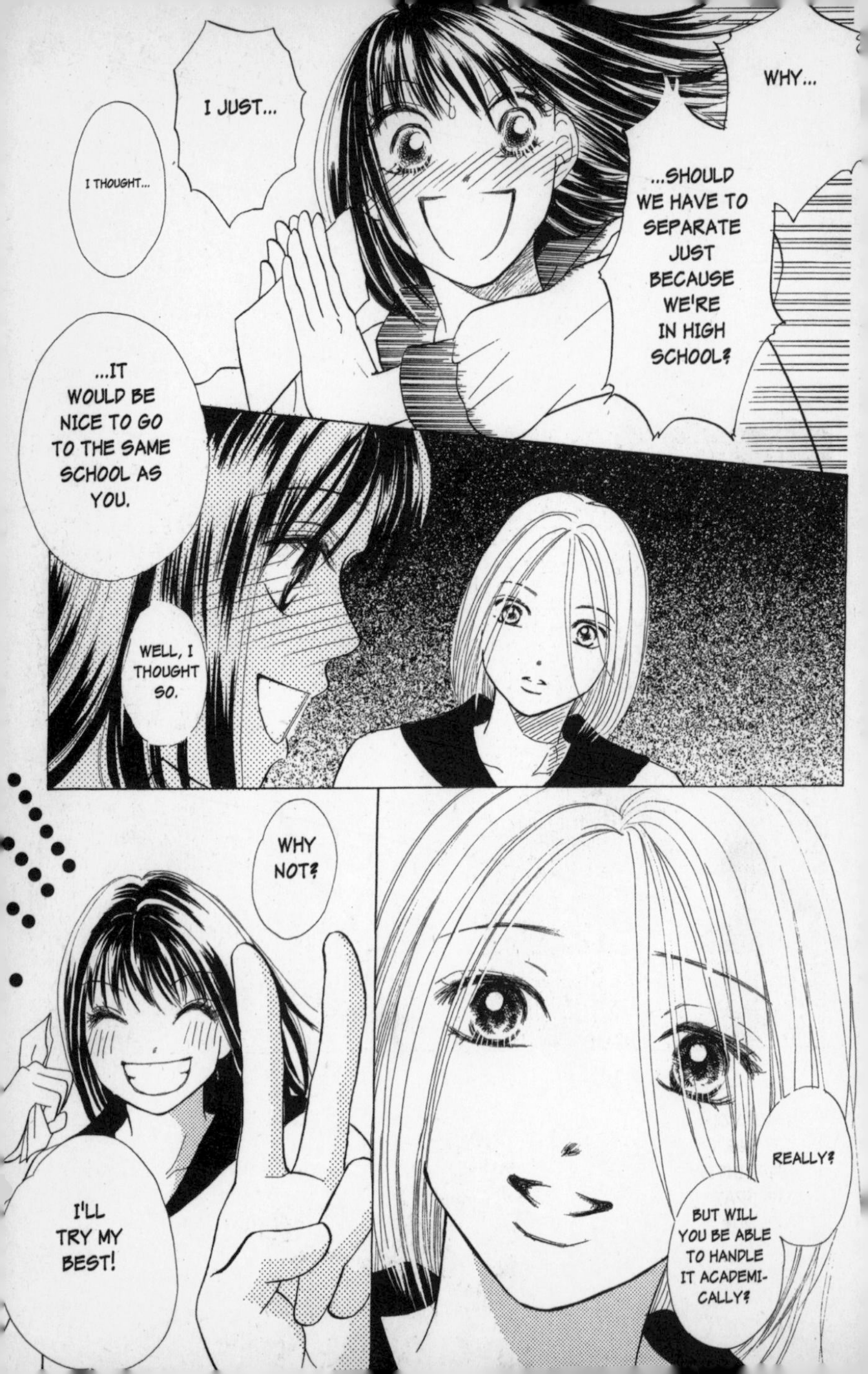
WHY...
...SHOULD WE HAVE TO SEPARATE JUST BECAUSE WE'RE IN HIGH SCHOOL?
I JUST...
I THOUGHT...
...IT WOULD BE NICE TO GO TO THE SAME SCHOOL AS YOU.
WELL, I THOUGHT SO.
REALLY?
BUT WILL YOU BE ABLE TO HANDLE IT ACADEMI-CALLY?
WHY NOT?
I'LL TRY MY BEST!

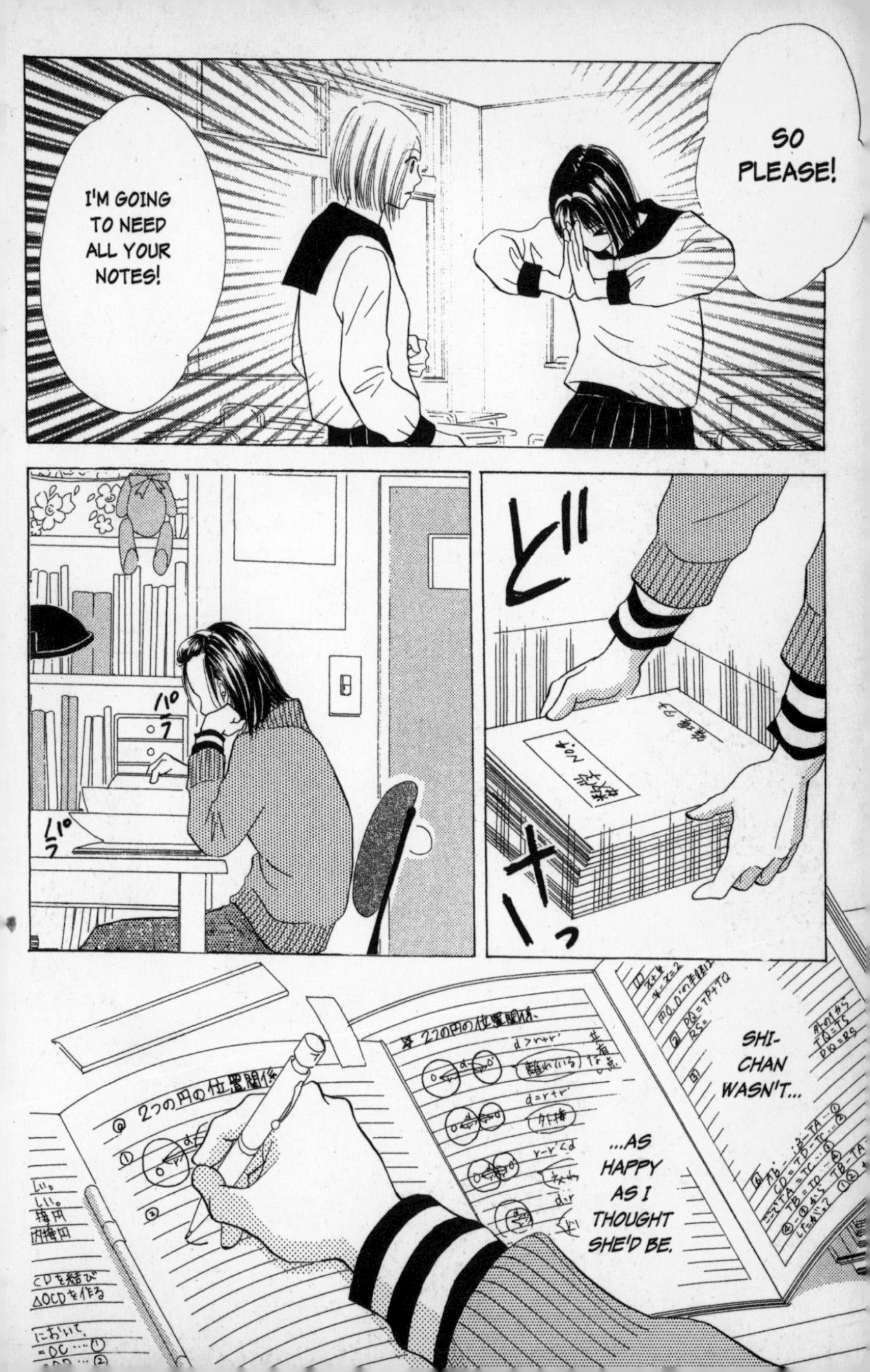
I'M GOING TO NEED ALL YOUR NOTES!
SO PLEASE!
どサッ
パラ
パラ
SHI-CHAN WASN'T...
...AS HAPPY AS I THOUGHT SHE'D BE.

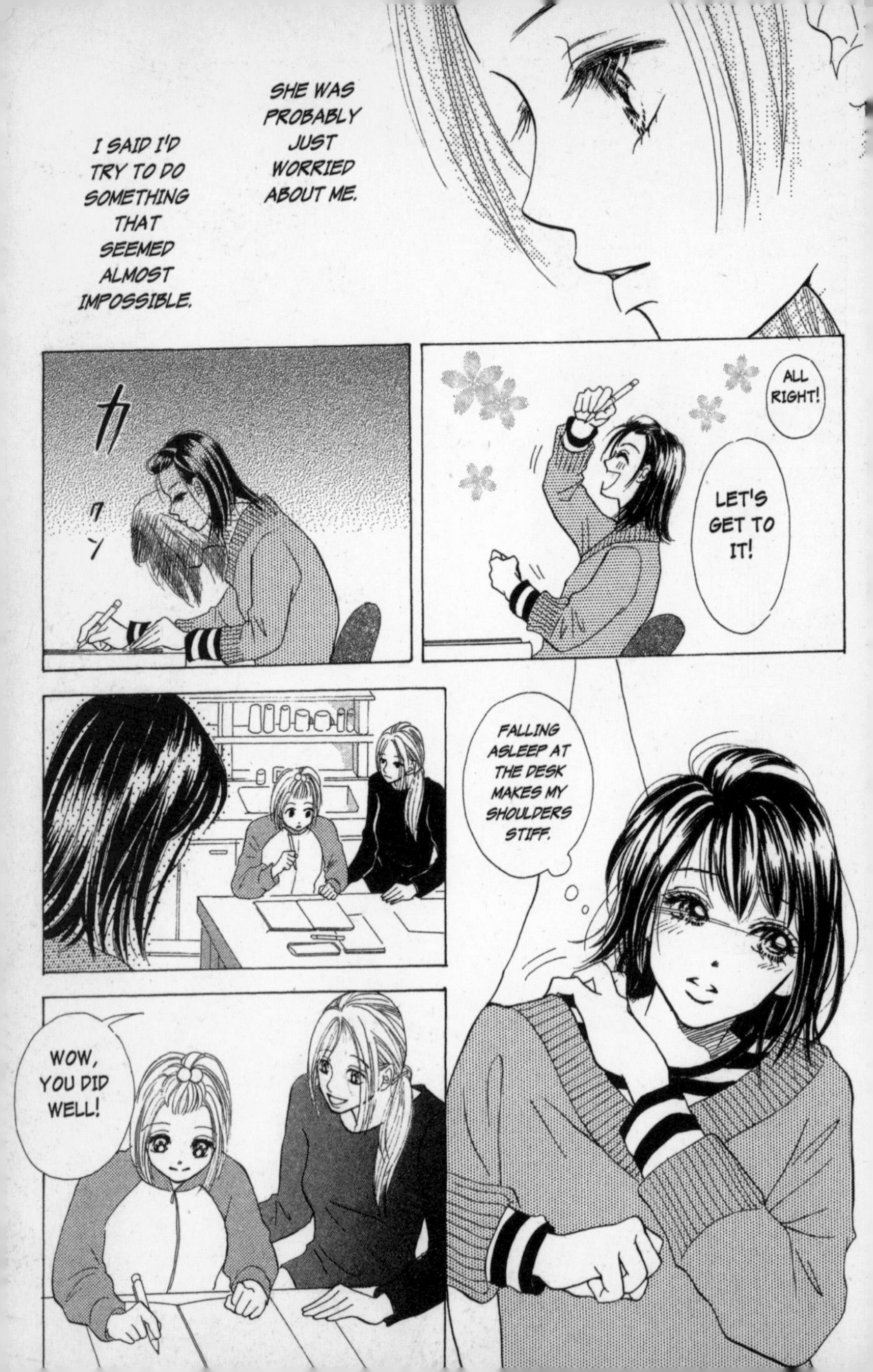

SHE WAS PROBABLY JUST WORRIED ABOUT ME.
I SAID I'D TRY TO DO SOMETHING THAT SEEMED ALMOST IMPOSSIBLE.
ALL RIGHT!
LET'S GET TO IT!
カクン
FALLING ASLEEP AT THE DESK MAKES MY SHOULDERS STIFF.
WOW, YOU DID WELL!

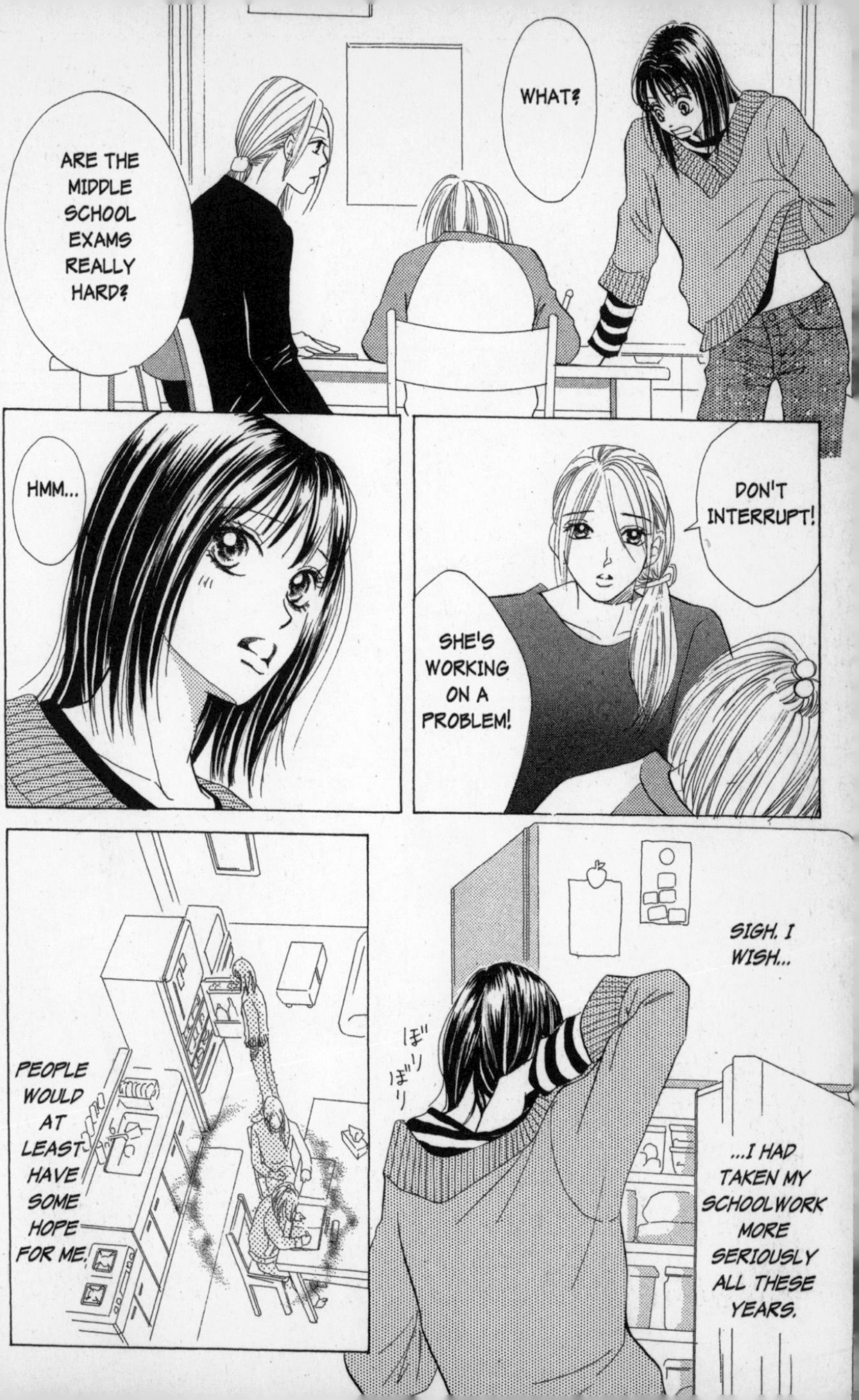
WHAT?
ARE THE MIDDLE SCHOOL EXAMS REALLY HARD?
DON'T INTERRUPT!
SHE'S WORKING ON A PROBLEM!
HMM...
SIGH. I WISH...
ぼりぼり
...I HAD TAKEN MY SCHOOLWORK MORE SERIOUSLY ALL THESE YEARS.
PEOPLE WOULD AT LEAST HAVE SOME HOPE FOR ME.

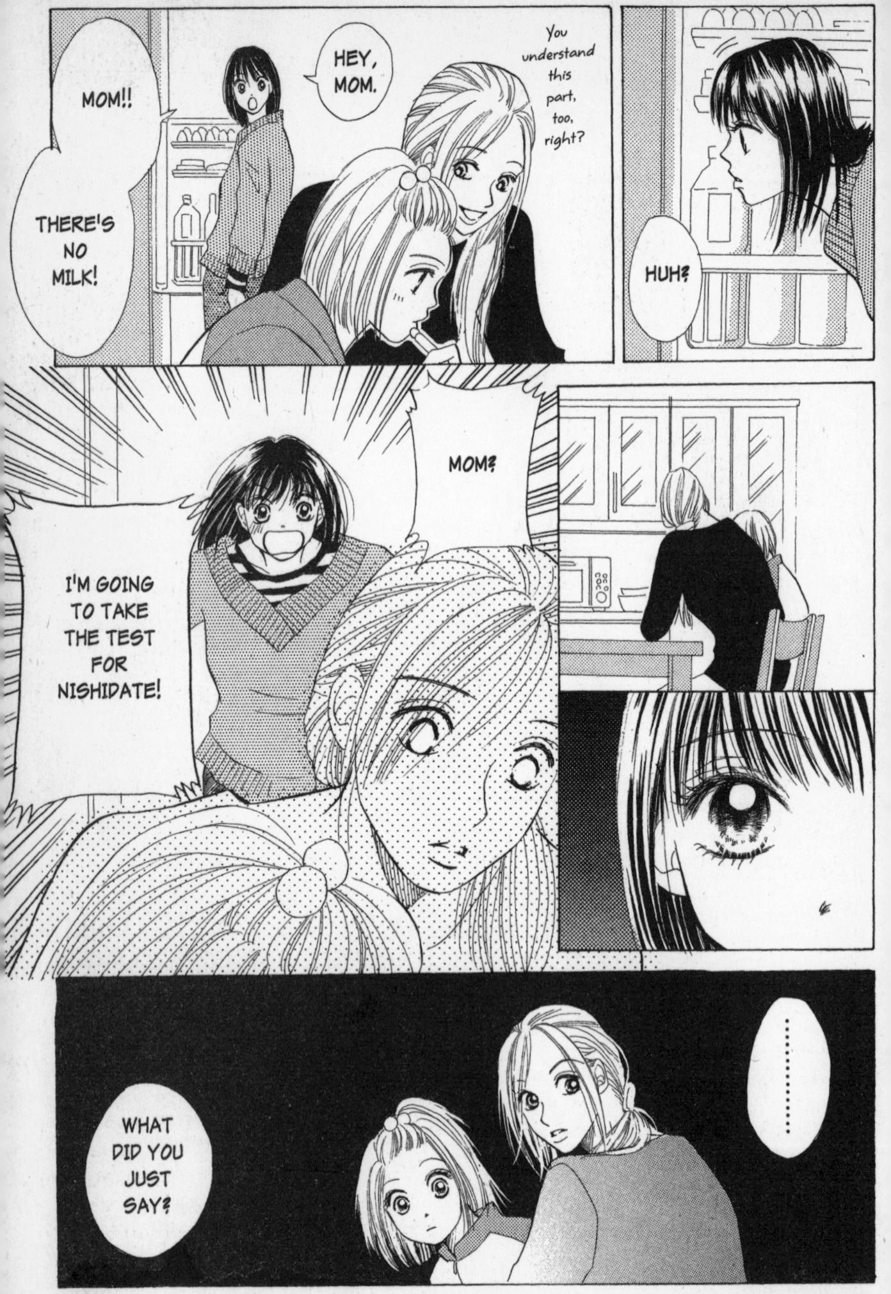
HUH?
You understand this part, too, right?
HEY, MOM.
MOM!!
THERE'S NO MILK!
MOM?
I'M GOING TO TAKE THE TEST FOR NISHIDATE!
......
WHAT DID YOU JUST SAY?

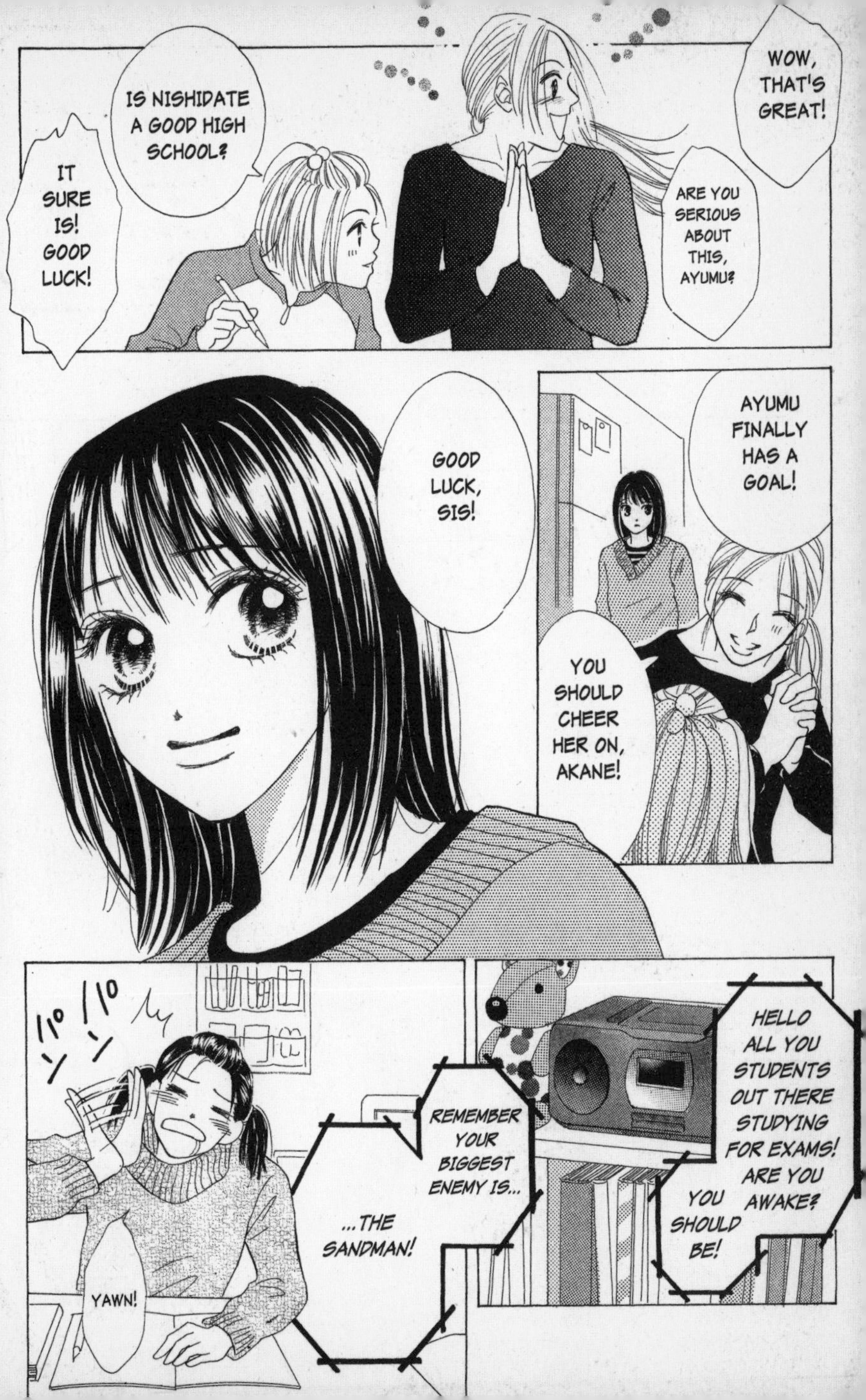
WOW, THAT'S GREAT!
ARE YOU SERIOUS ABOUT THIS, AYUMU?
IS NISHIDATE A GOOD HIGH SCHOOL?
IT SURE IS! GOOD LUCK!
AYUMU FINALLY HAS A GOAL!
YOU SHOULD CHEER HER ON, AKANE!
GOOD LUCK, SIS!
HELLO ALL YOU STUDENTS OUT THERE STUDYING FOR EXAMS! ARE YOU AWAKE?
YOU SHOULD BE!
REMEMBER YOUR BIGGEST ENEMY IS...
...THE SANDMAN!
YAWN!

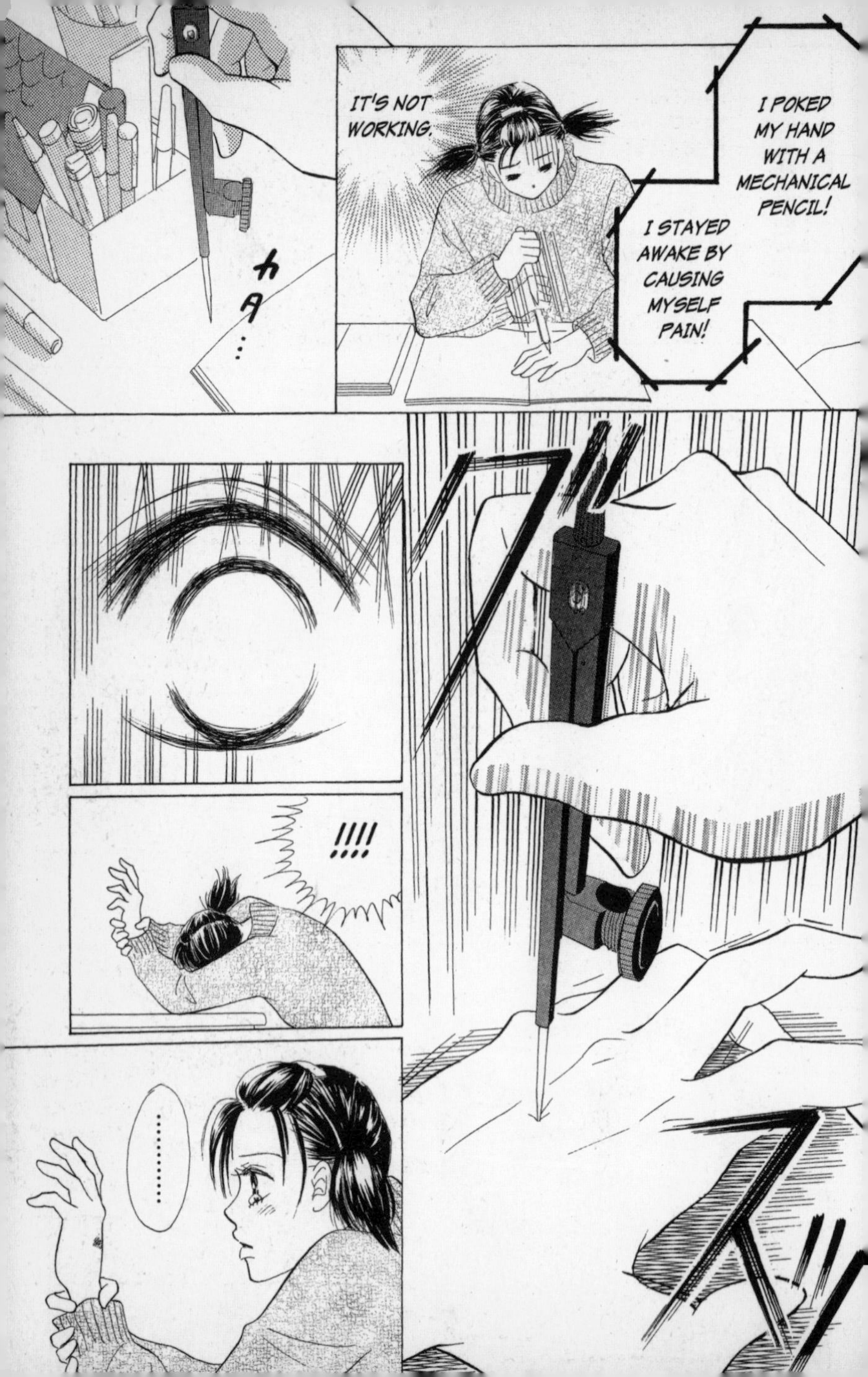
I POKED MY HAND WITH A MECHANICAL PENCIL!
I STAYED AWAKE BY CAUSING MYSELF PAIN!
IT'S NOT WORKING.
カタ…
!!!!
……

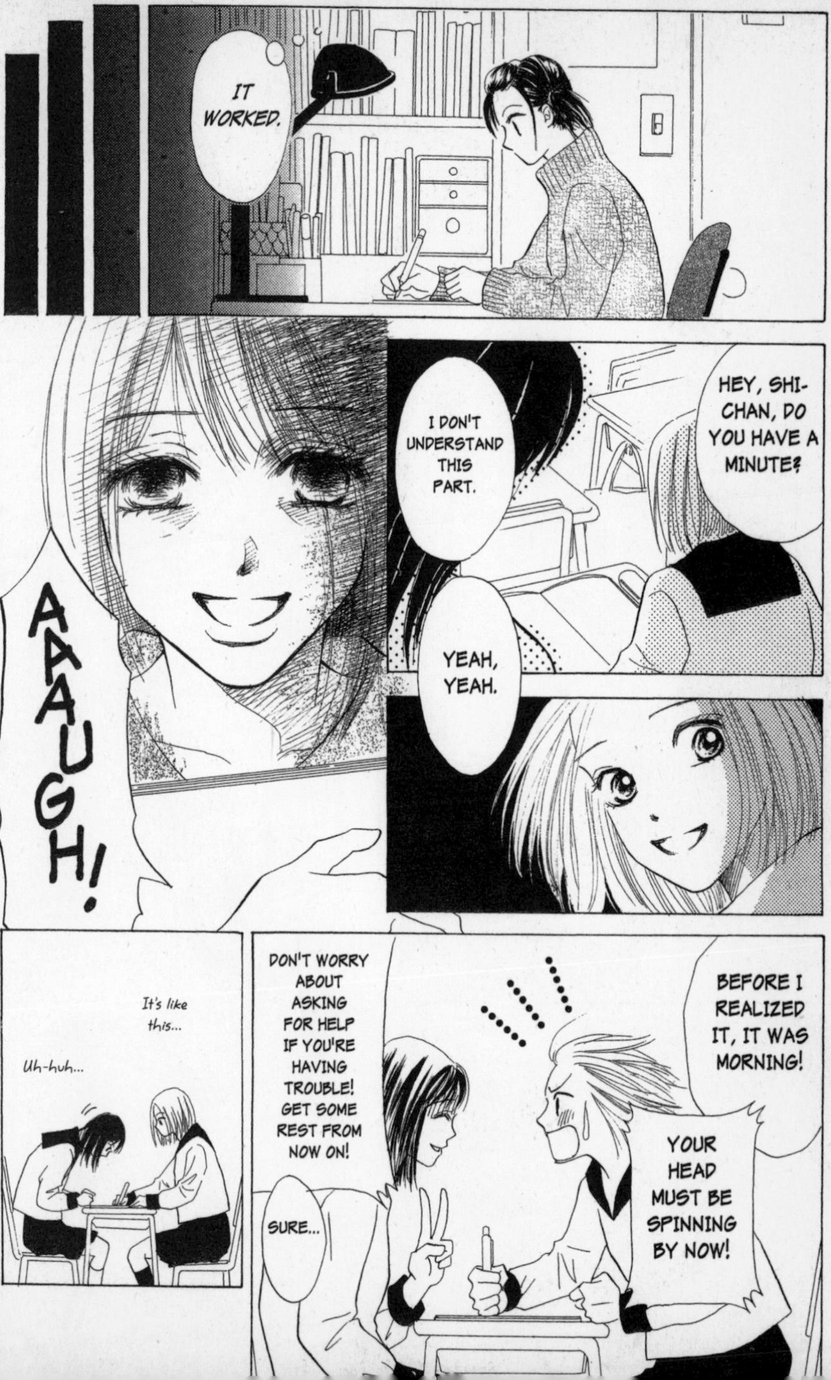
IT WORKED.
HEY, SHI-CHAN, DO YOU HAVE A MINUTE?
I DON'T UNDERSTAND THIS PART.
YEAH, YEAH.
AAAUGH!
BEFORE I REALIZED IT, IT WAS MORNING!
YOUR HEAD MUST BE SPINNING BY NOW!
DON'T WORRY ABOUT ASKING FOR HELP IF YOU'RE HAVING TROUBLE! GET SOME REST FROM NOW ON!
SURE...
It's like this...
Uh-huh...

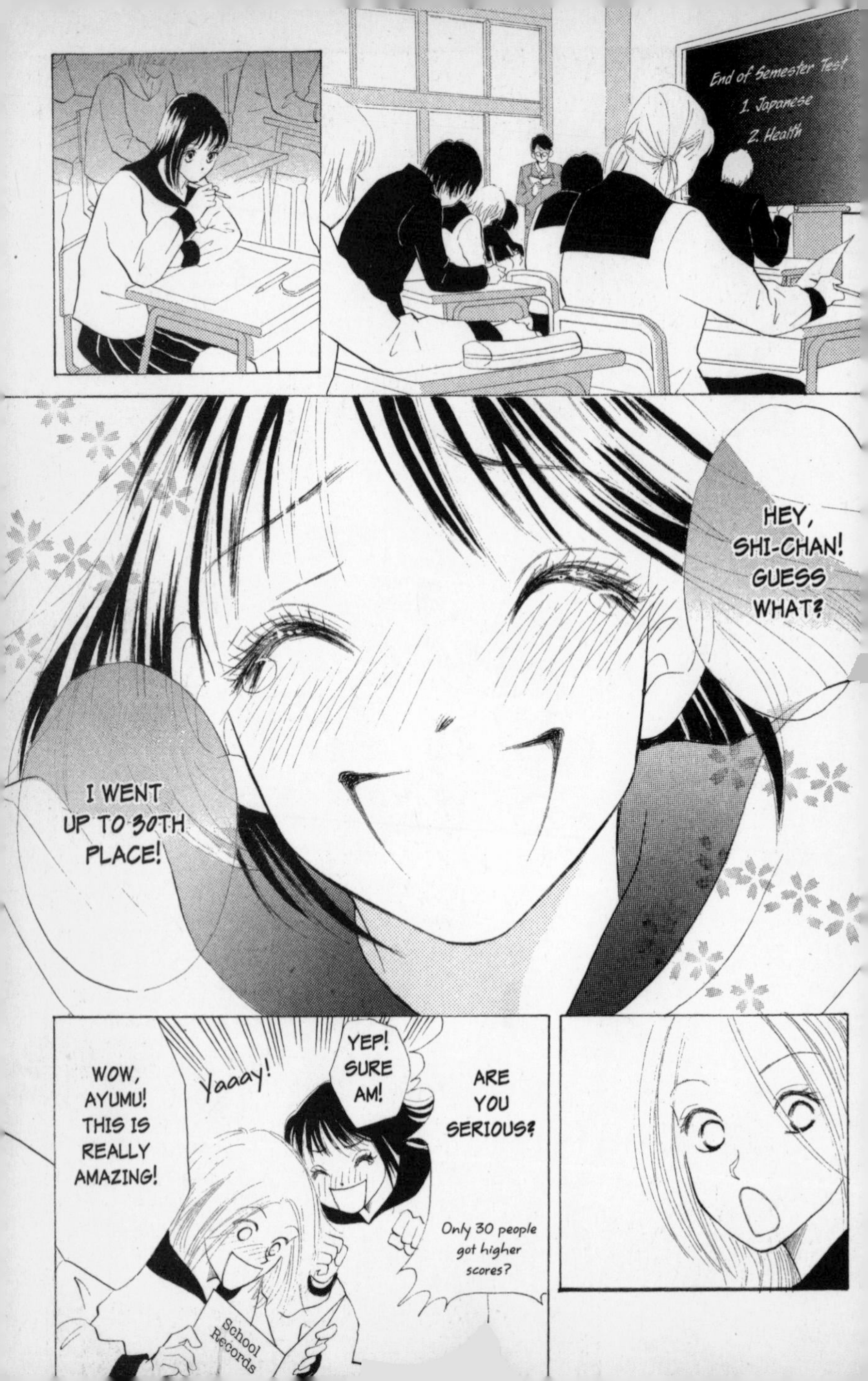
End of Semester Test
1. Japanese
2. Health
HEY, SHI-CHAN! GUESS WHAT?
I WENT UP TO 30TH PLACE!
ARE YOU SERIOUS?
Only 30 people got higher scores?
YEP! SURE AM!
Yaaay!
WOW, AYUMU! THIS IS REALLY AMAZING!
School Records

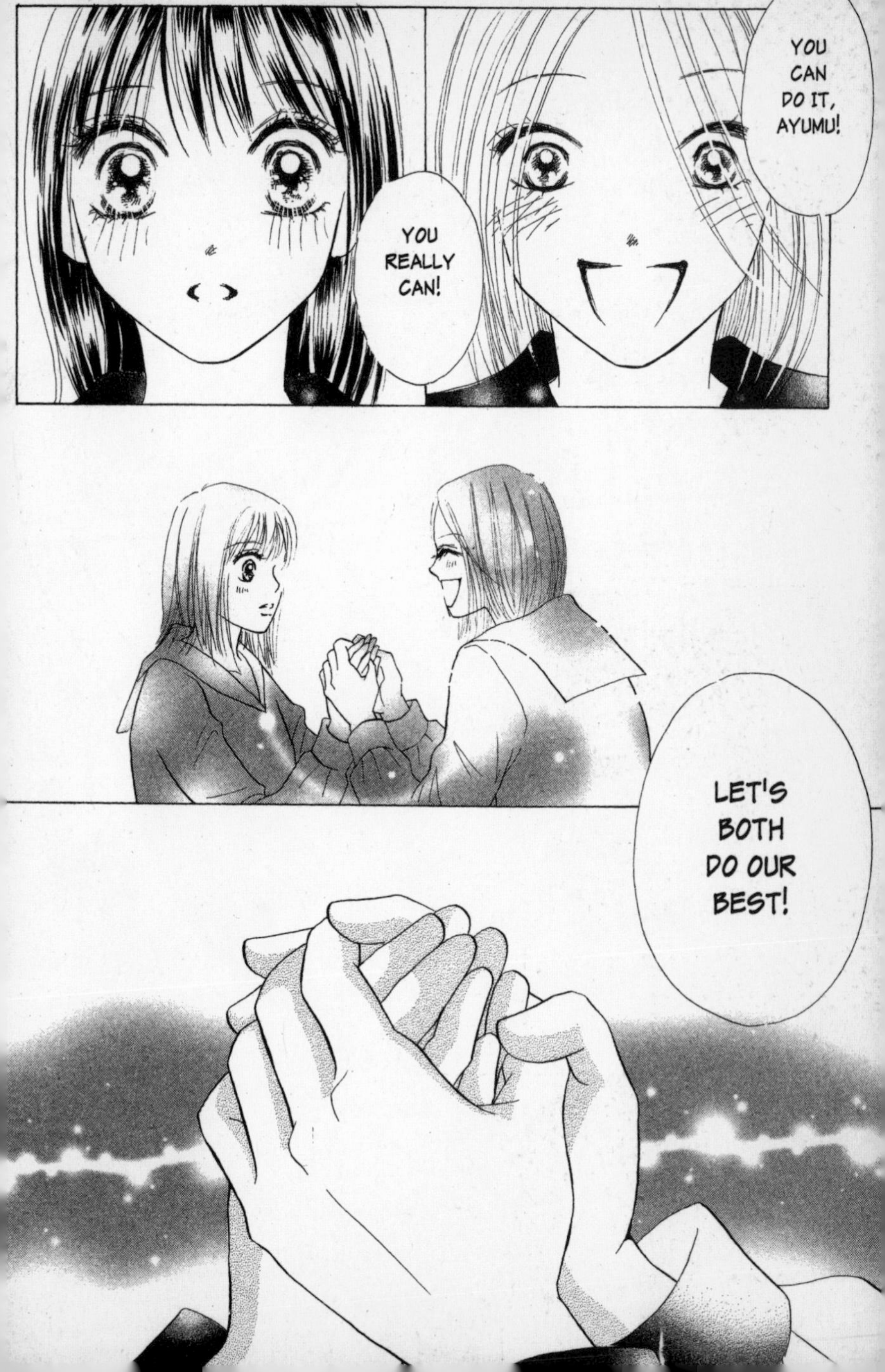
YOU CAN DO IT, AYUMU!
YOU REALLY CAN!
LET'S BOTH DO OUR BEST!

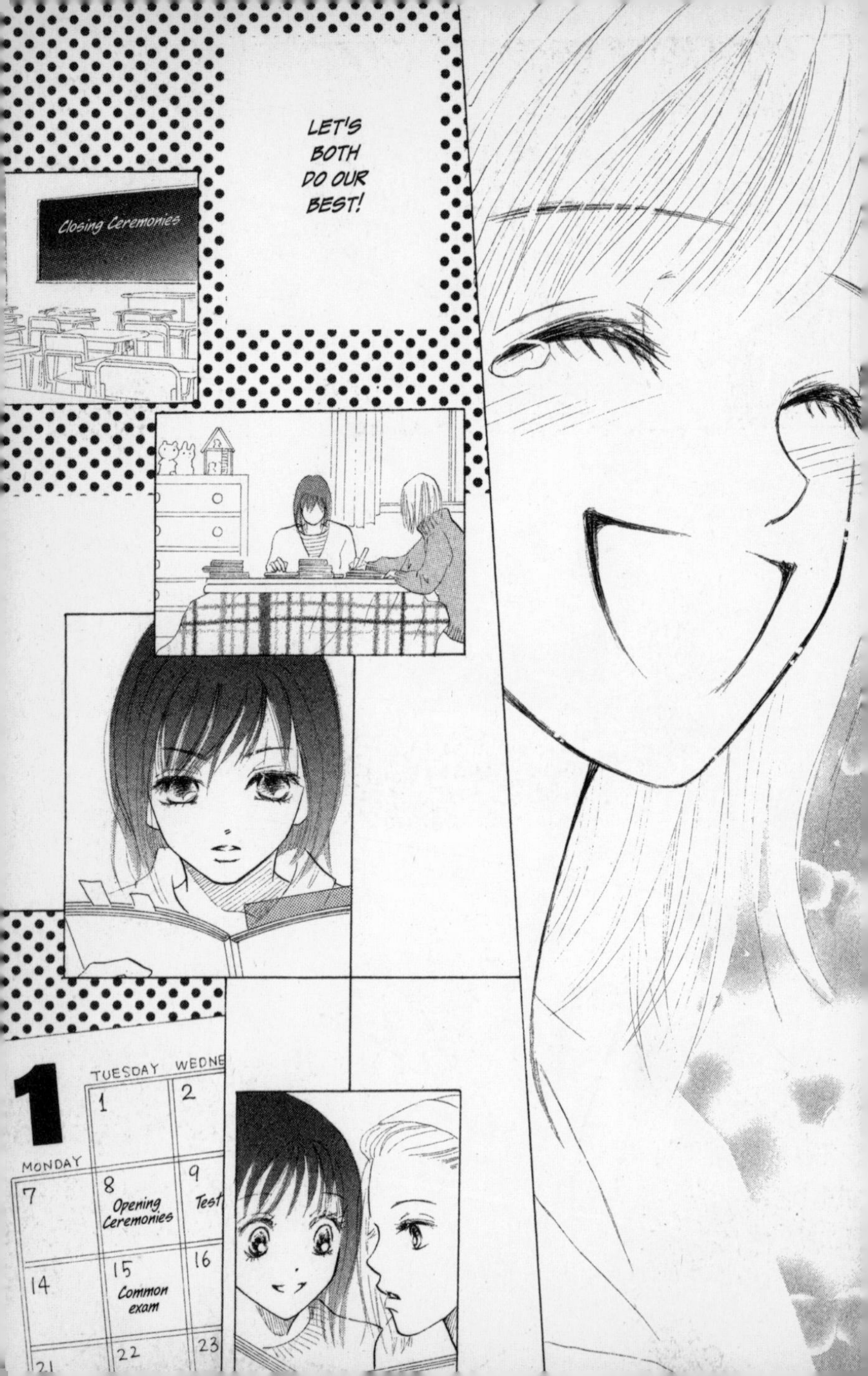
LET'S BOTH DO OUR BEST!
Closing Ceremonies
1
TUESDAY
WEDNE
1
2
MONDAY
7
8
Opening Ceremonies
9
Test
14
15
Common exam
16
21
22
23

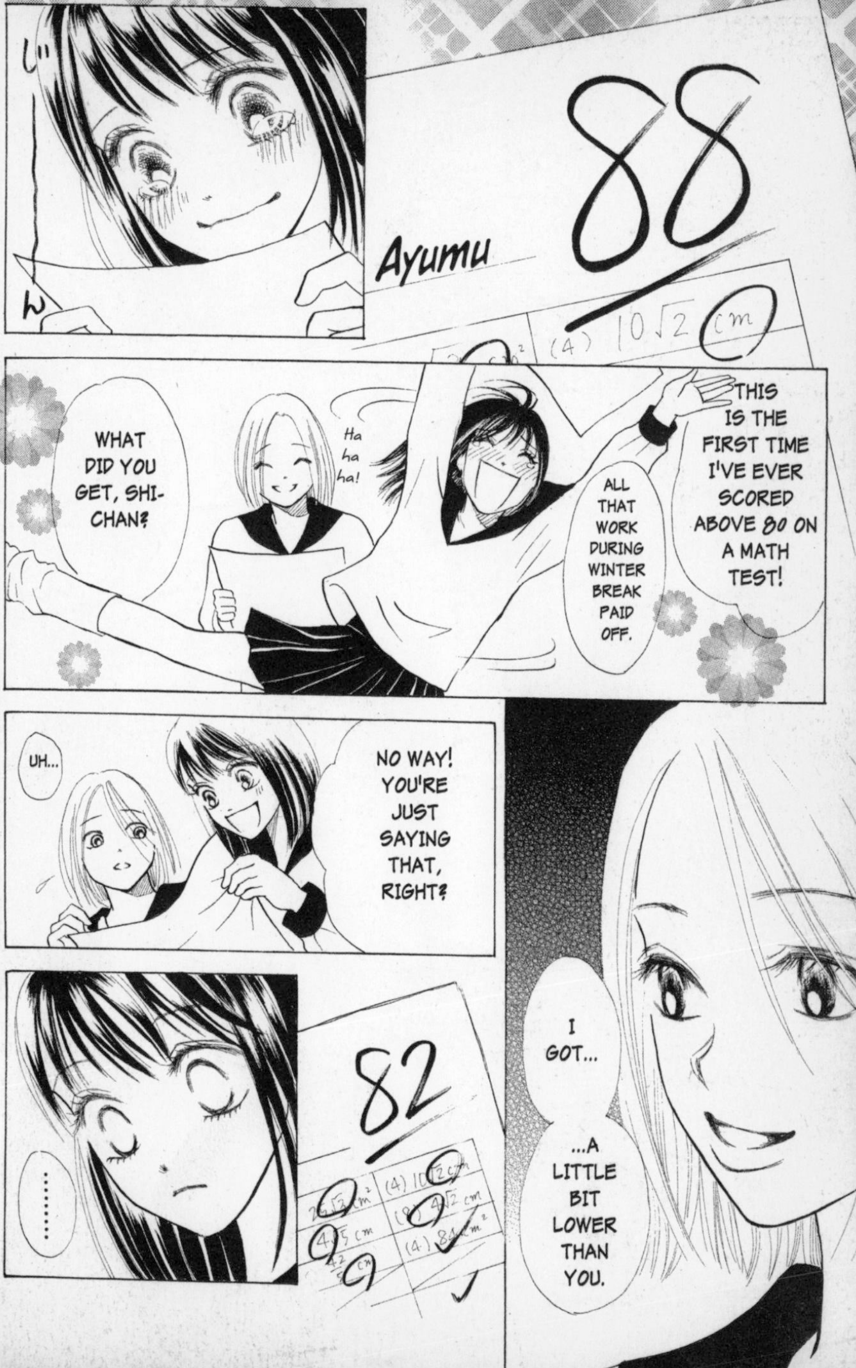
88
Ayumu
(4) 10√2 cm
THIS IS THE FIRST TIME I'VE EVER SCORED ABOVE 80 ON A MATH TEST!
ALL THAT WORK DURING WINTER BREAK PAID OFF.
Ha ha ha!
WHAT DID YOU GET, SHI-CHAN?
I GOT...
...A LITTLE BIT LOWER THAN YOU.
NO WAY! YOU'RE JUST SAYING THAT, RIGHT?
UH...
82
....

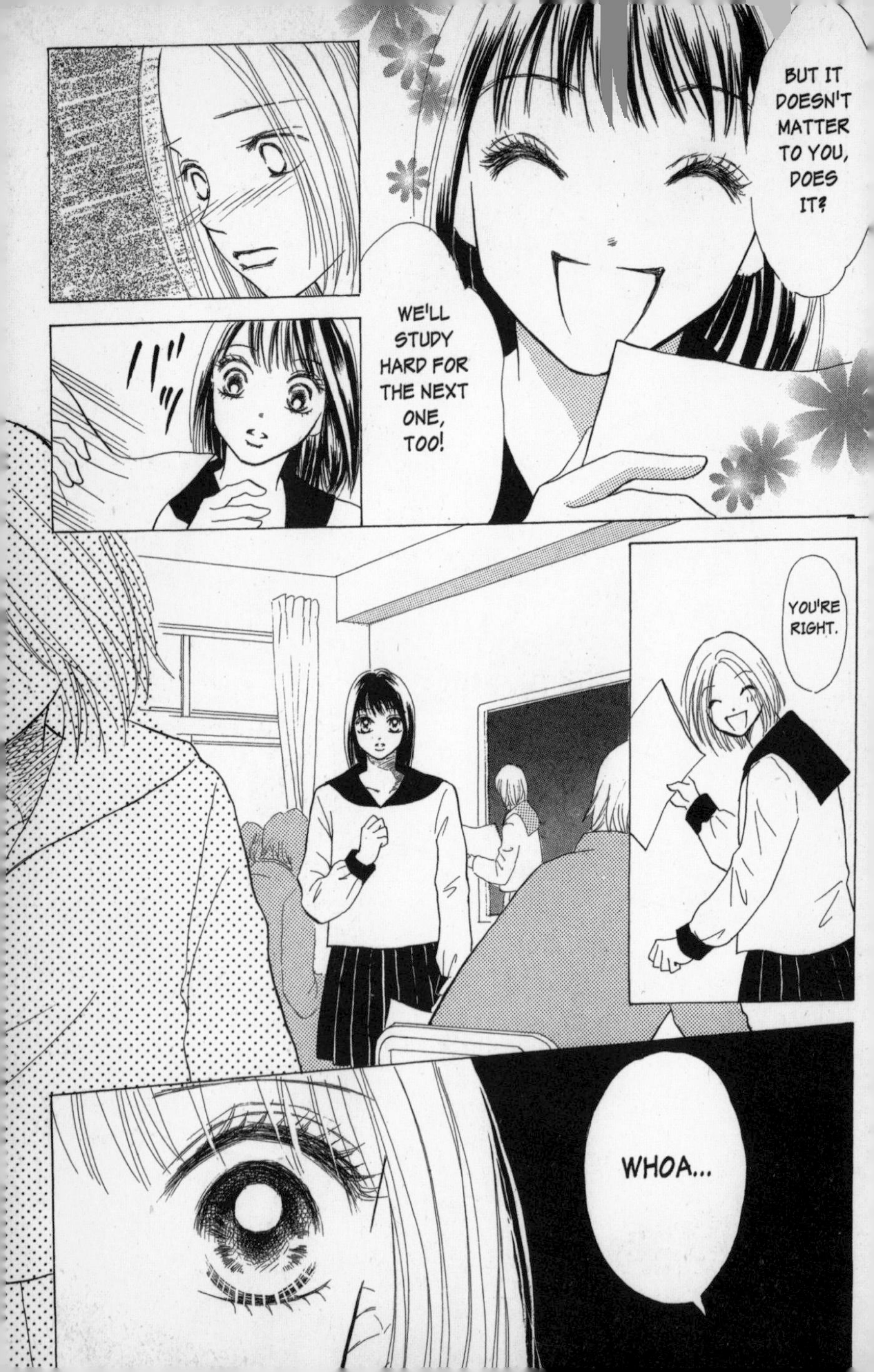
BUT IT DOESN'T MATTER TO YOU, DOES IT?
WE'LL STUDY HARD FOR THE NEXT ONE, TOO!
YOU'RE RIGHT.
WHOA...

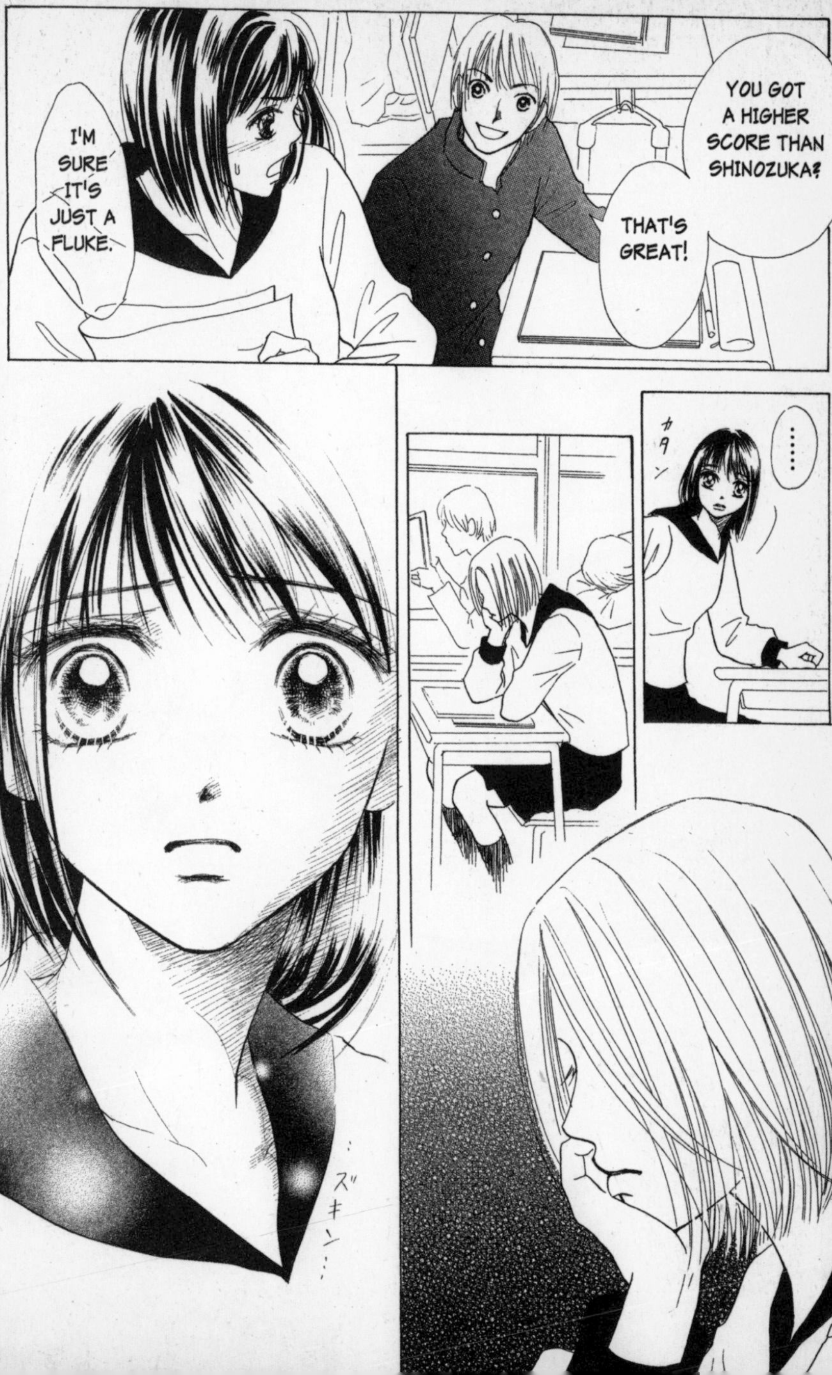
YOU GOT A HIGHER SCORE THAN SHINOZUKA?
THAT'S GREAT!
I'M SURE IT'S JUST A FLUKE.
カタン
......
ズキン...

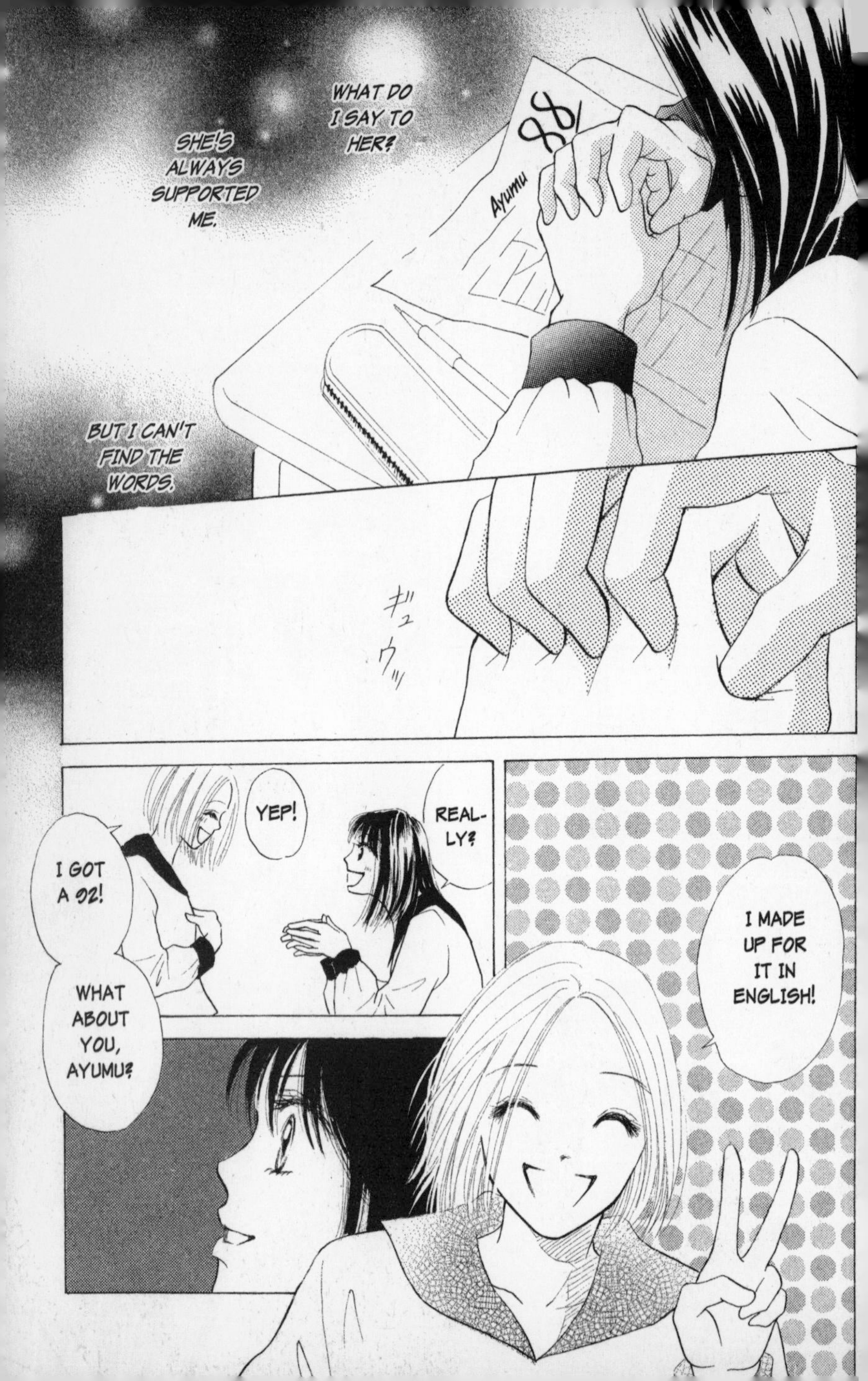

WHAT DO I SAY TO HER?
SHE'S ALWAYS SUPPORTED ME.
88
Ayumu
BUT I CAN'T FIND THE WORDS.
ギュウッ
REAL-LY?
YEP!
I GOT A 92!
I MADE UP FOR IT IN ENGLISH!
WHAT ABOUT YOU, AYUMU?

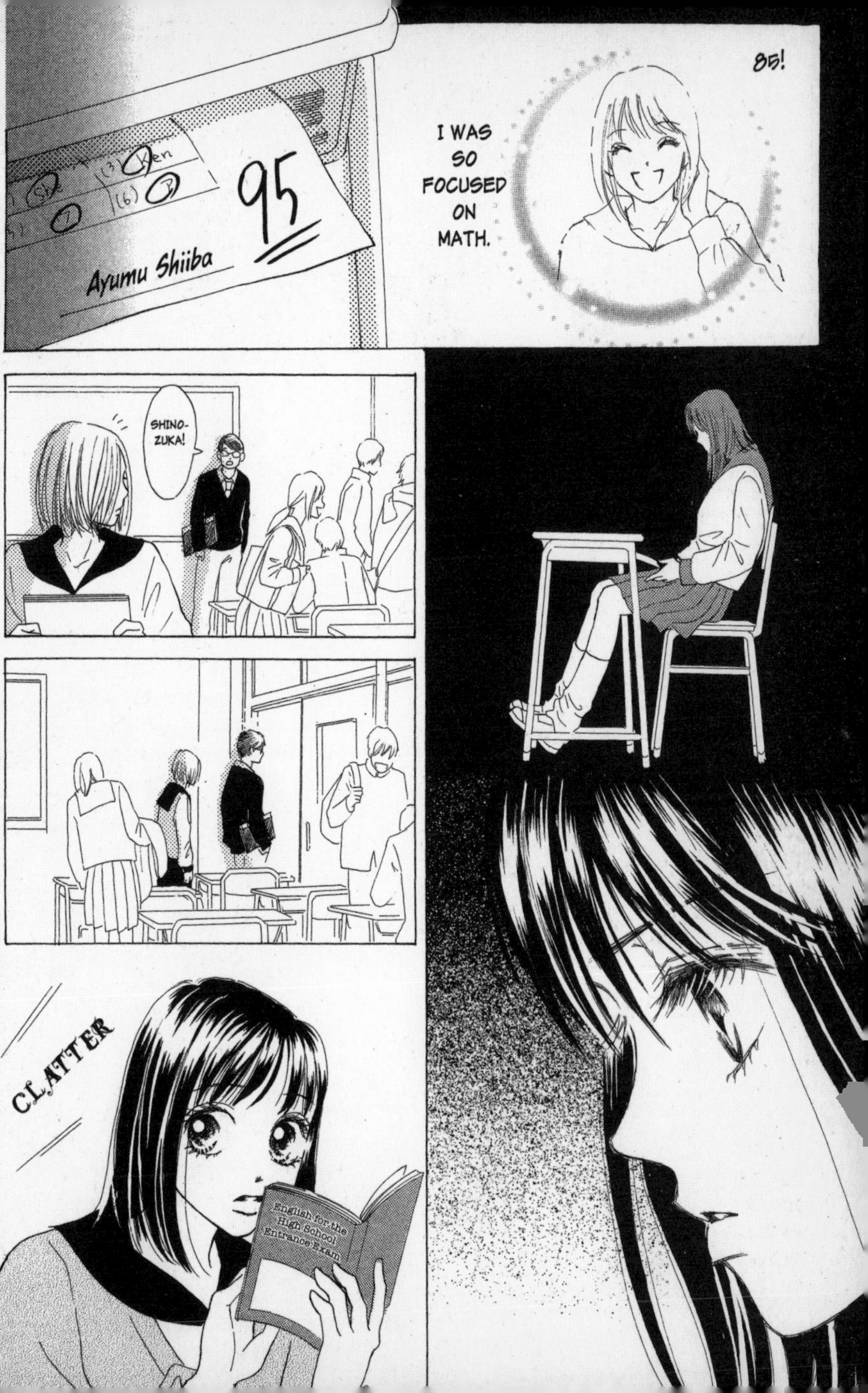
85!
I WAS SO FOCUSED ON MATH.
Ayumu Shiiba
95
SHINO-ZUKA!
CLATTER
English for the High School Entrance Exam

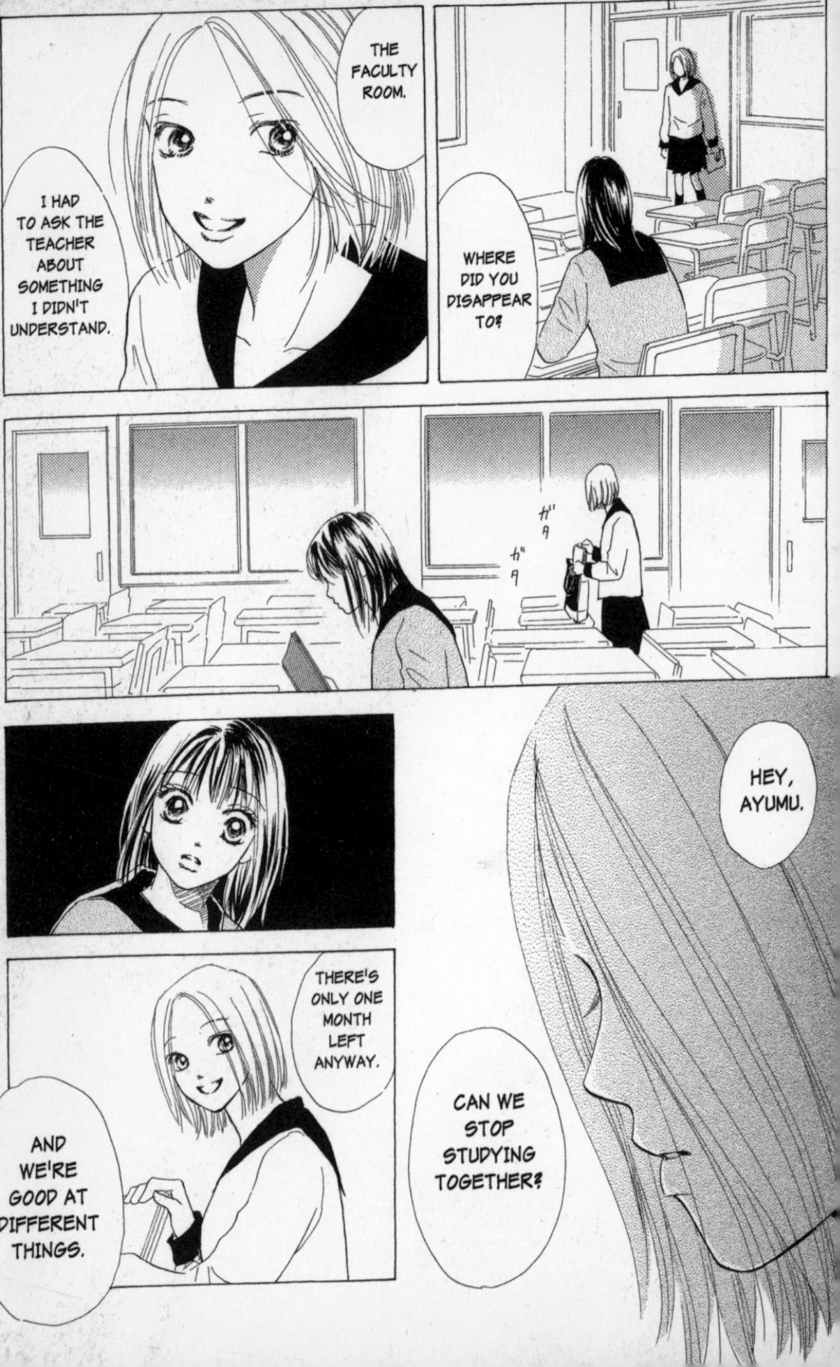
WHERE DID YOU DISAPPEAR TO?
THE FACULTY ROOM.
I HAD TO ASK THE TEACHER ABOUT SOMETHING I DIDN'T UNDERSTAND.
ガタ
ガタ
HEY, AYUMU.
CAN WE STOP STUDYING TOGETHER?
THERE'S ONLY ONE MONTH LEFT ANYWAY.
AND WE'RE GOOD AT DIFFERENT THINGS.

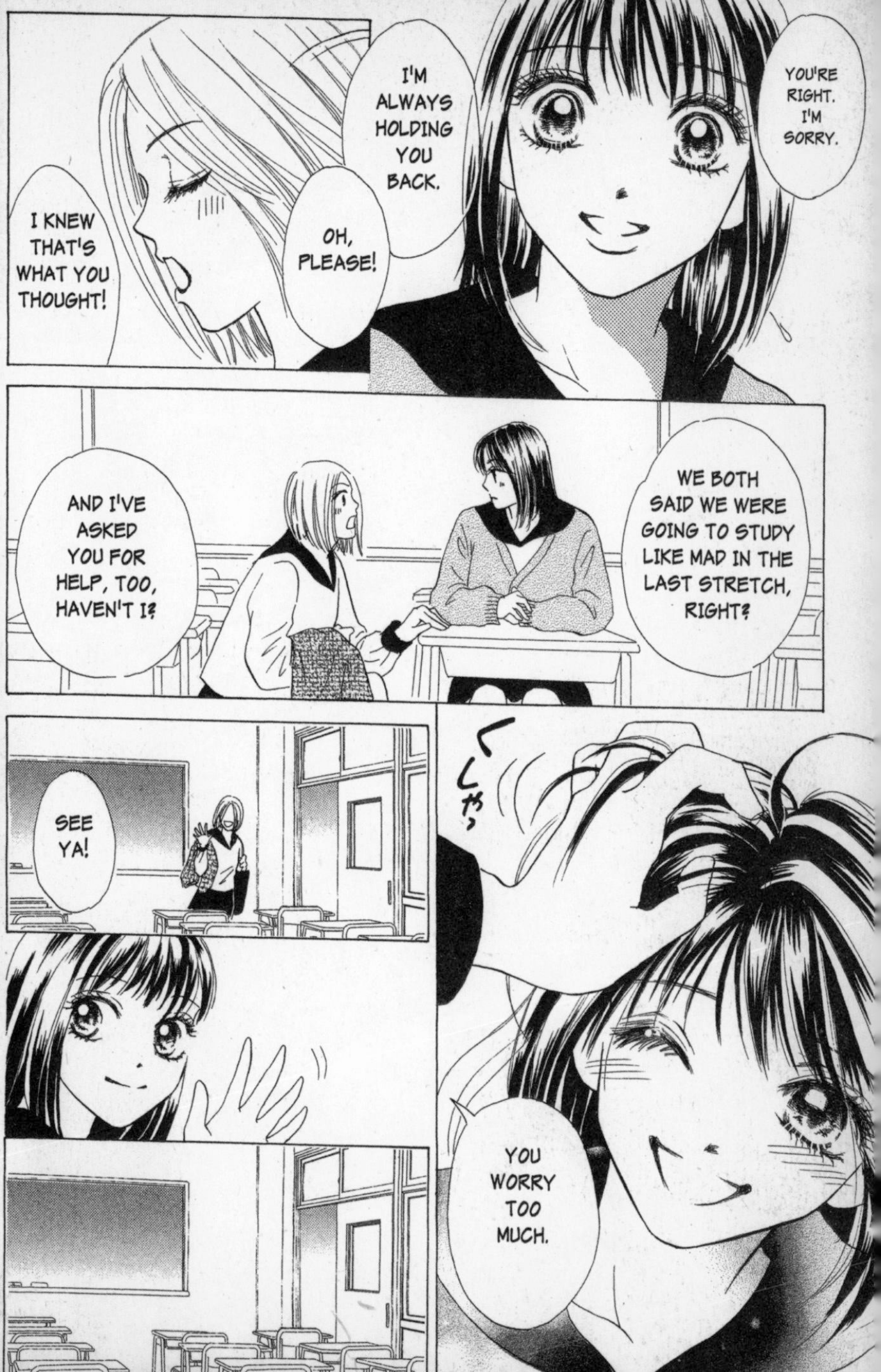
YOU'RE RIGHT. I'M SORRY.
I'M ALWAYS HOLDING YOU BACK.
OH, PLEASE!
I KNEW THAT'S WHAT YOU THOUGHT!
WE BOTH SAID WE WERE GOING TO STUDY LIKE MAD IN THE LAST STRETCH, RIGHT?
AND I'VE ASKED YOU FOR HELP, TOO, HAVEN'T I?
くしゃ
YOU WORRY TOO MUCH.
SEE YA!

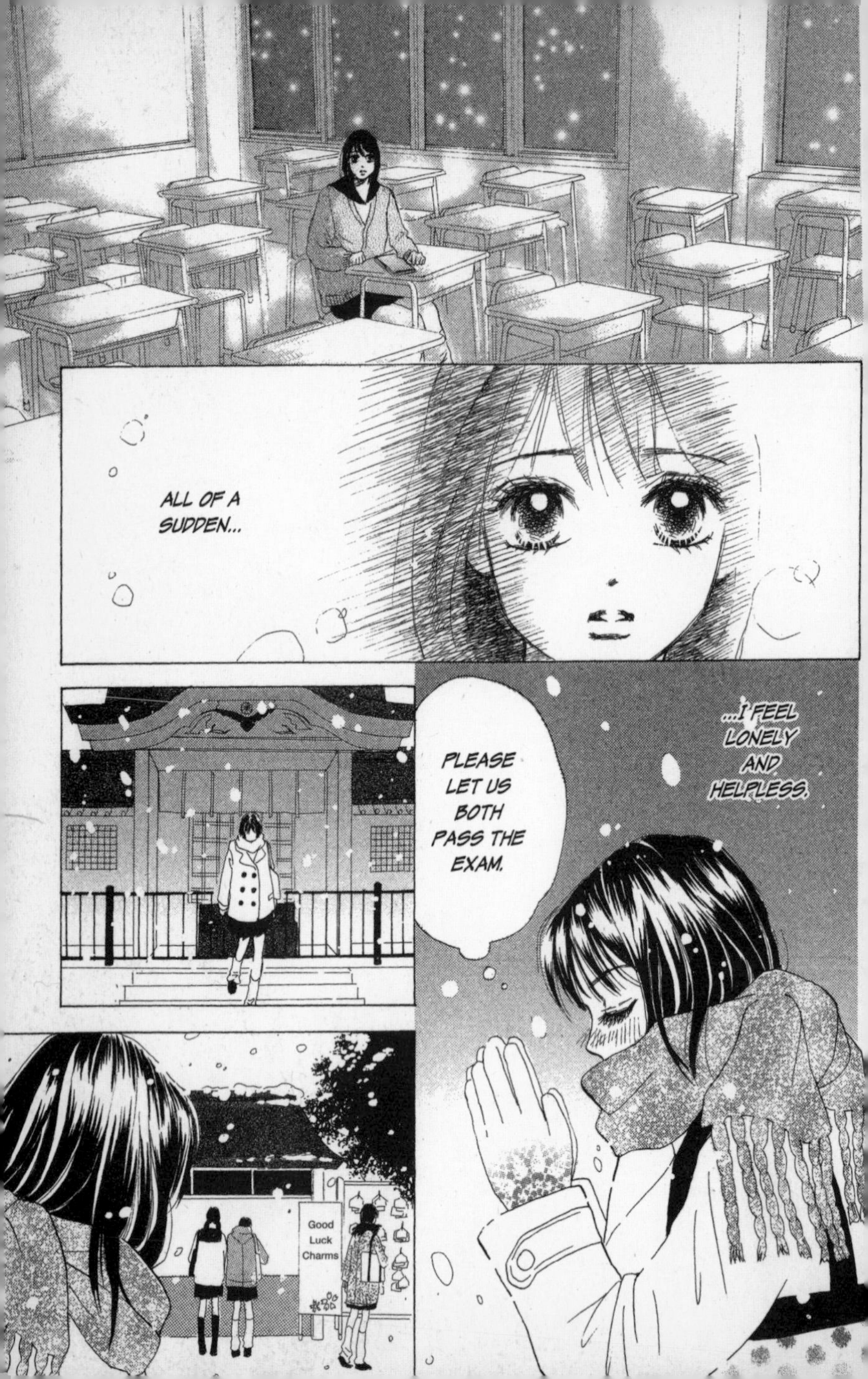
ALL OF A SUDDEN...
...I FEEL LONELY AND HELPLESS.
PLEASE LET US BOTH PASS THE EXAM.
Good Luck Charms

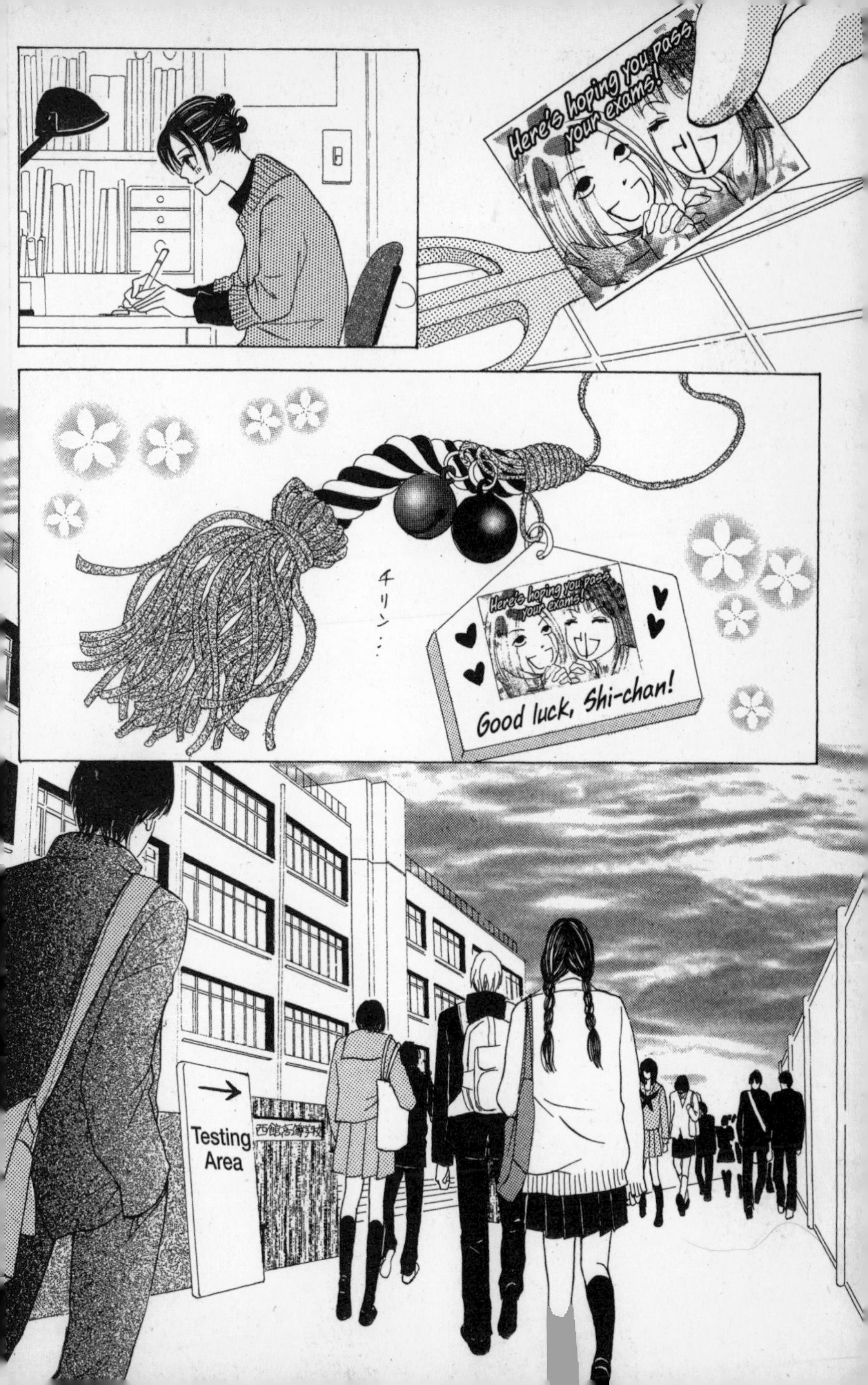
Here's hoping you pass your exams!
チリン…
Here's hoping you pass your exams!
Good luck, Shi-chan!
Testing Area

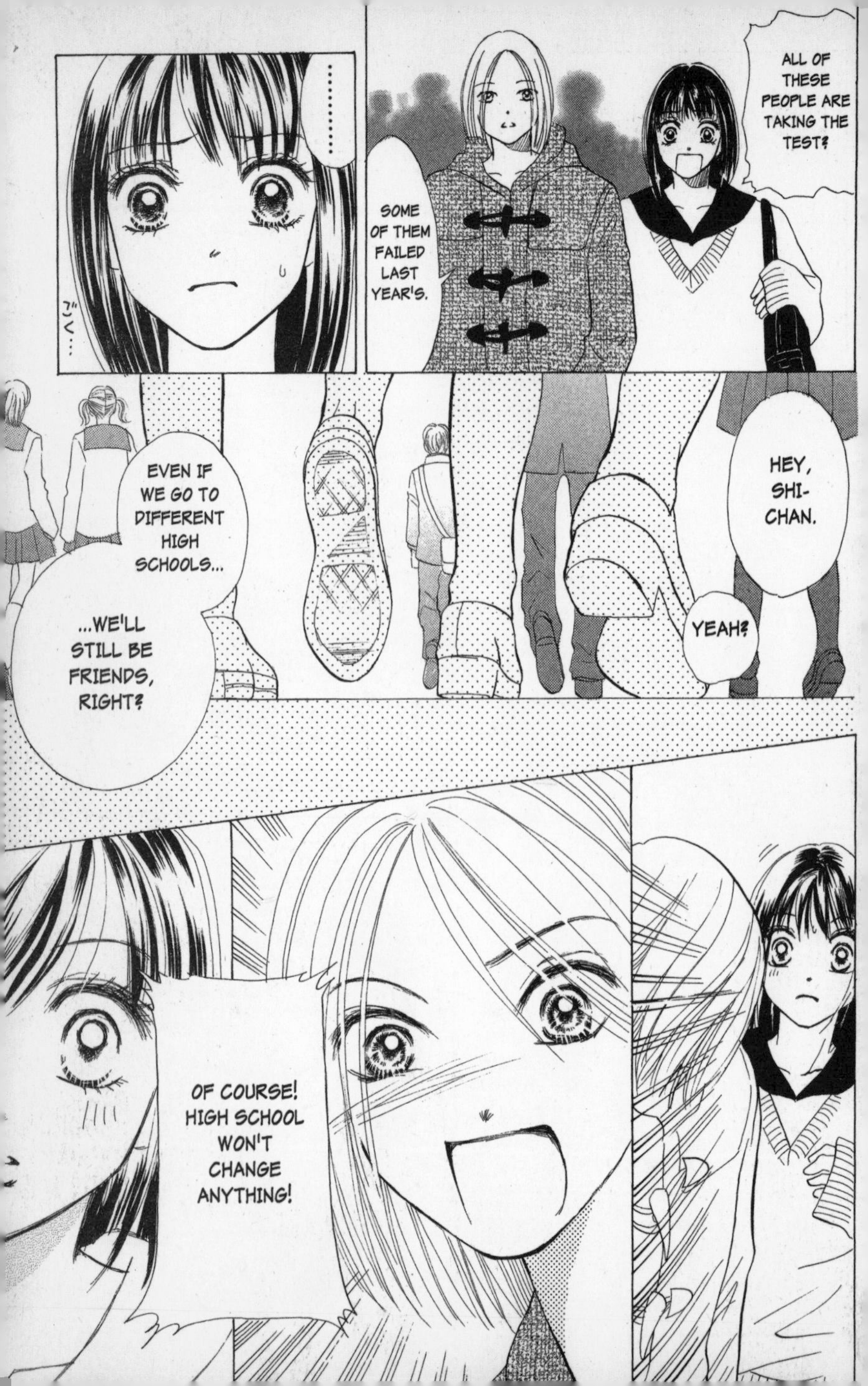
ALL OF THESE PEOPLE ARE TAKING THE TEST?
SOME OF THEM FAILED LAST YEAR'S.
......
ごく…
HEY, SHI-CHAN.
YEAH?
EVEN IF WE GO TO DIFFERENT HIGH SCHOOLS...
...WE'LL STILL BE FRIENDS, RIGHT?
OF COURSE! HIGH SCHOOL WON'T CHANGE ANYTHING!

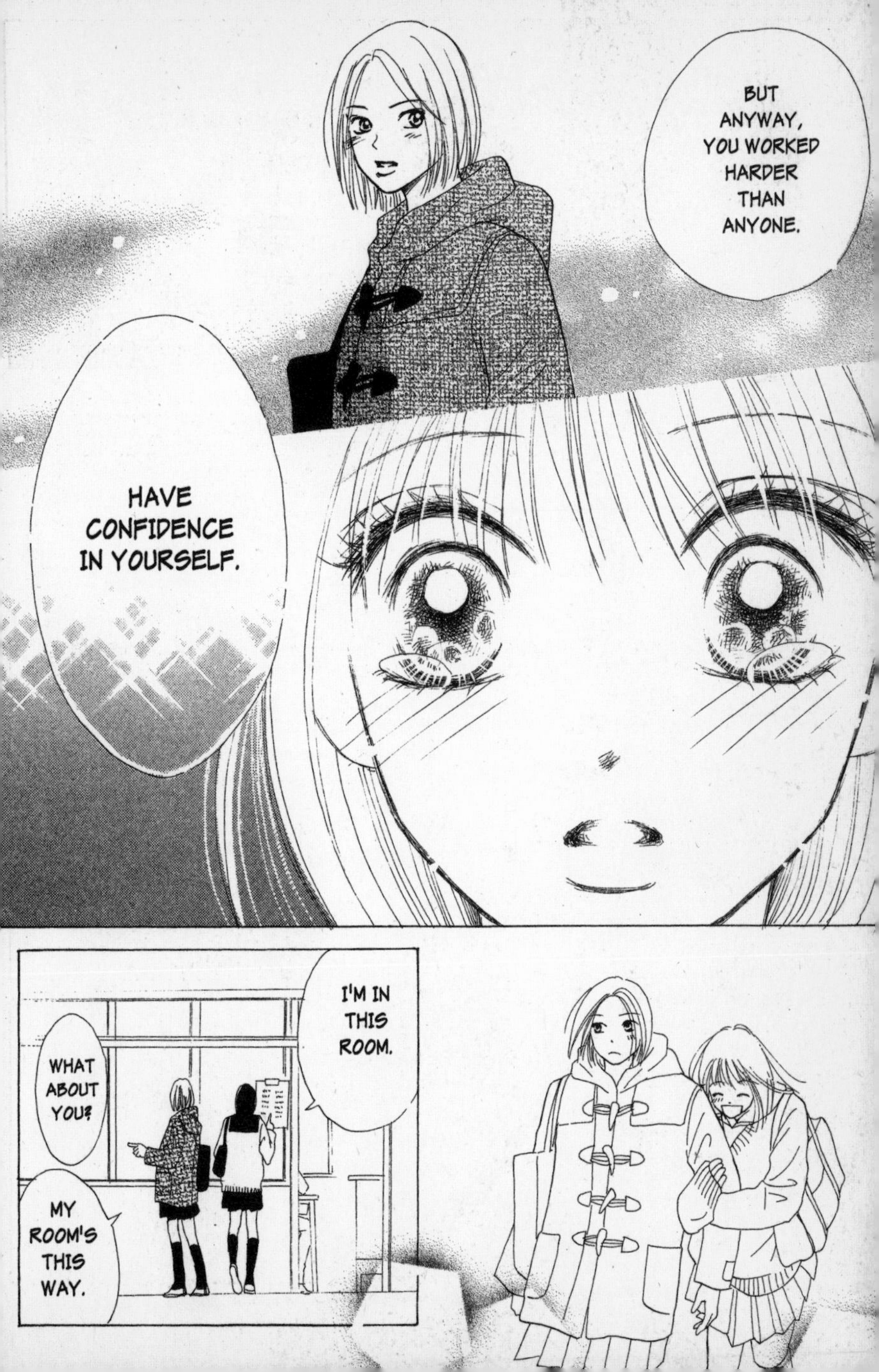
BUT ANYWAY, YOU WORKED HARDER THAN ANYONE.
HAVE CONFIDENCE IN YOURSELF.
I'M IN THIS ROOM.
WHAT ABOUT YOU?
MY ROOM'S THIS WAY.

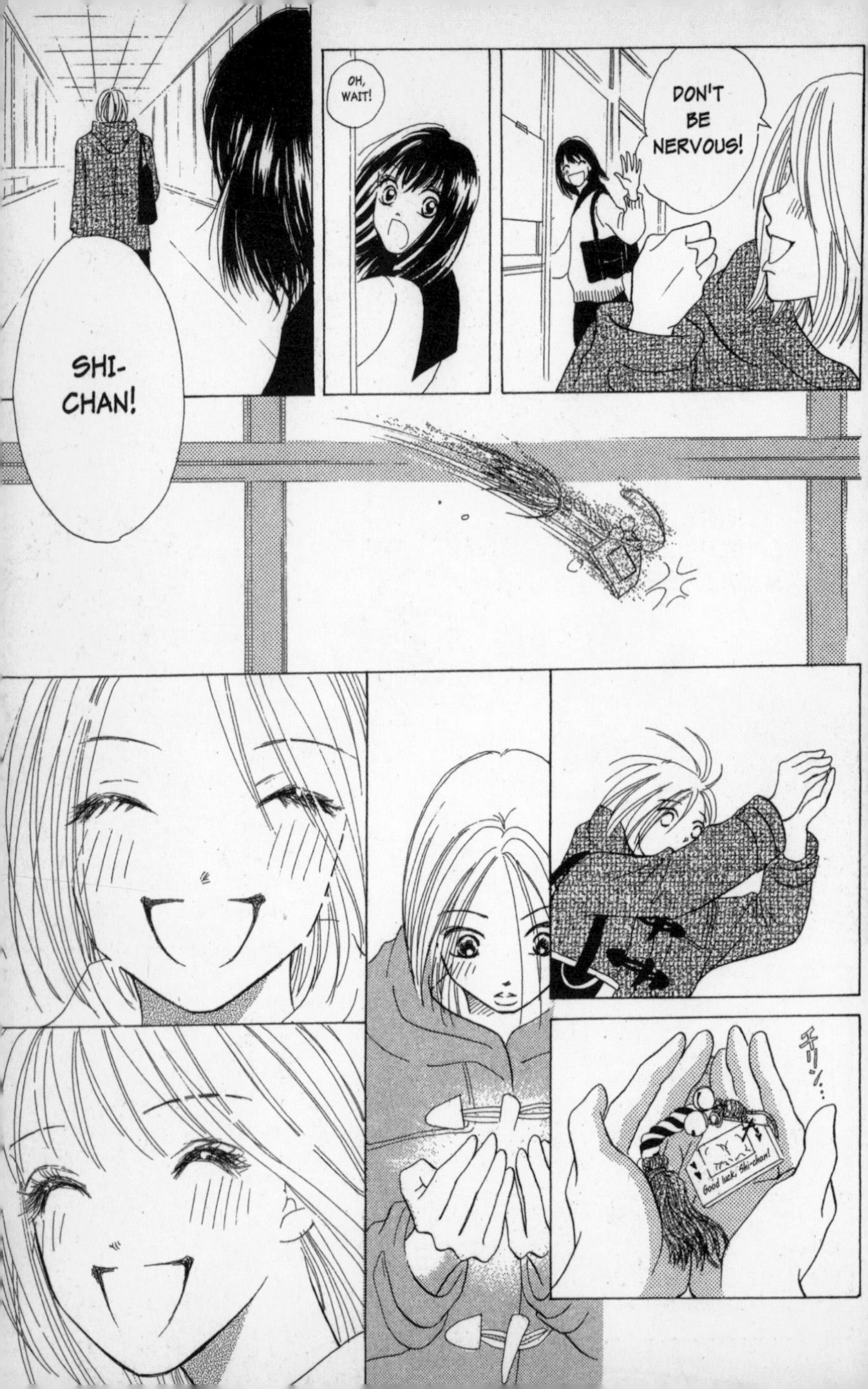
DON'T BE NERVOUS!
OH, WAIT!
SHI-CHAN!
チリン…
Good luck, Shi-chan!

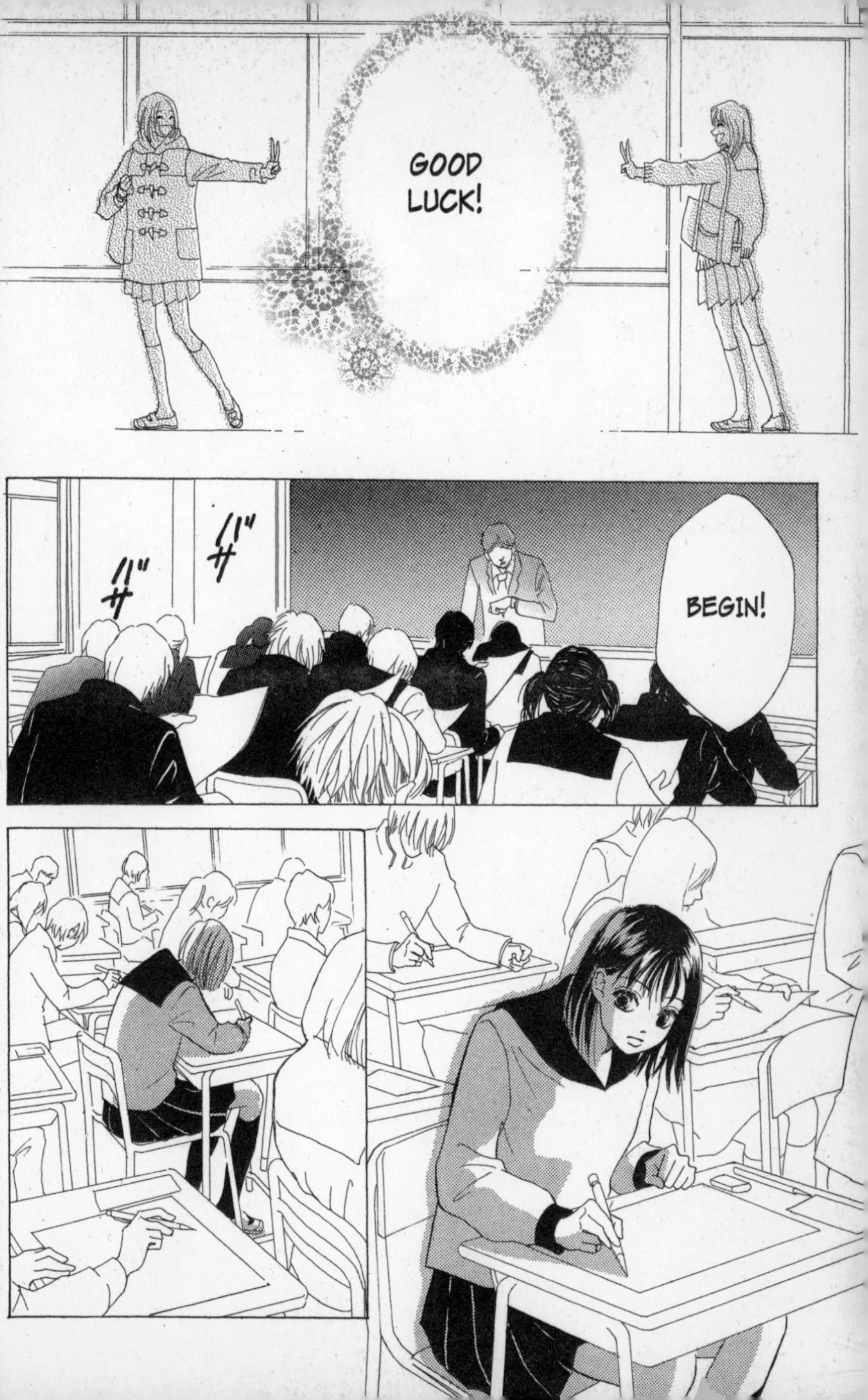
GOOD LUCK!
BEGIN!
バサ
バサ

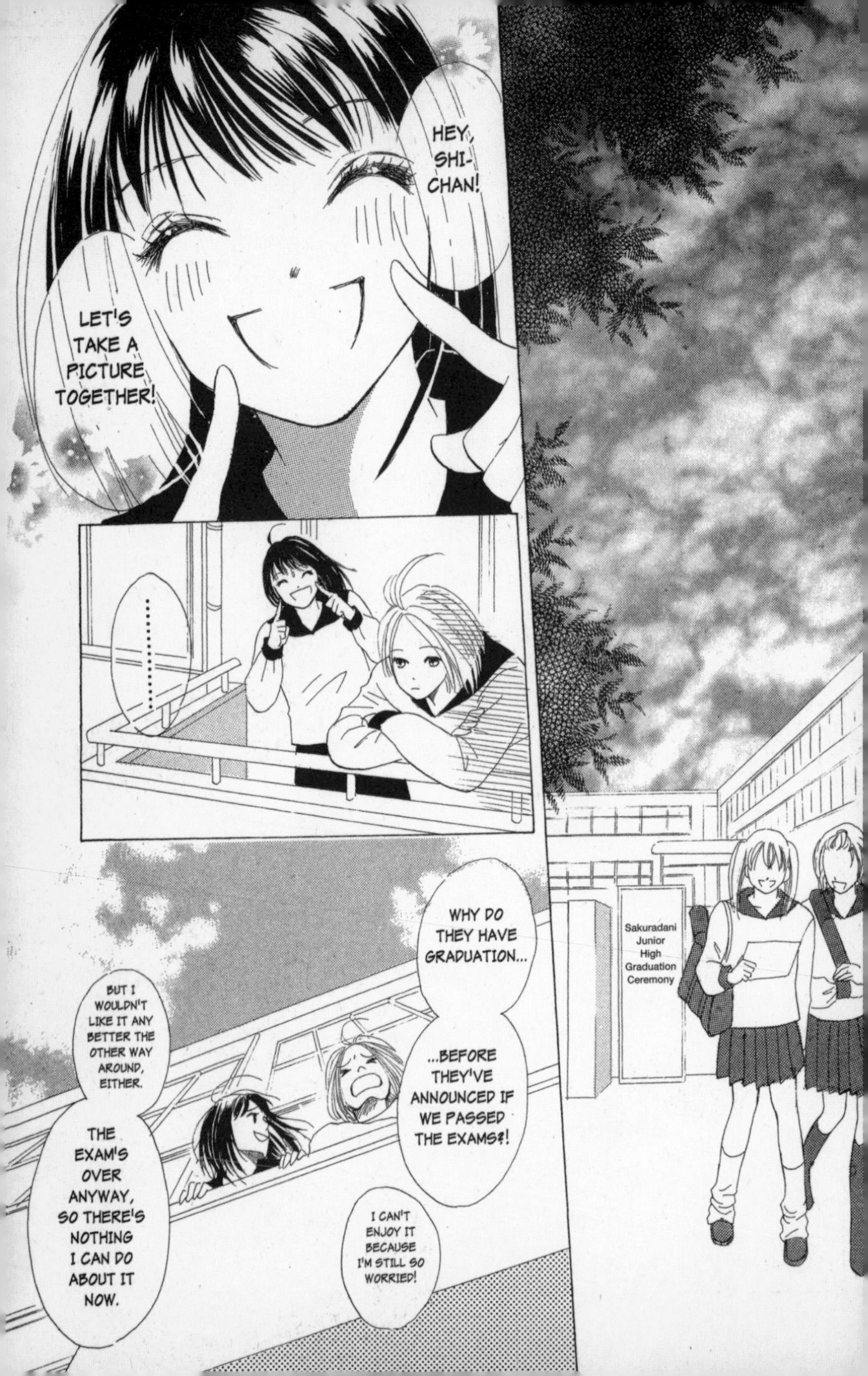
Sakuradani Junior High Graduation Ceremony
HEY, SHI-CHAN!
LET'S TAKE A PICTURE TOGETHER!
....
WHY DO THEY HAVE GRADUATION...
...BEFORE THEY'VE ANNOUNCED IF WE PASSED THE EXAMS?!
I CAN'T ENJOY IT BECAUSE I'M STILL SO WORRIED!
THE EXAM'S OVER ANYWAY, SO THERE'S NOTHING I CAN DO ABOUT IT NOW.
BUT I WOULDN'T LIKE IT ANY BETTER THE OTHER WAY AROUND, EITHER.

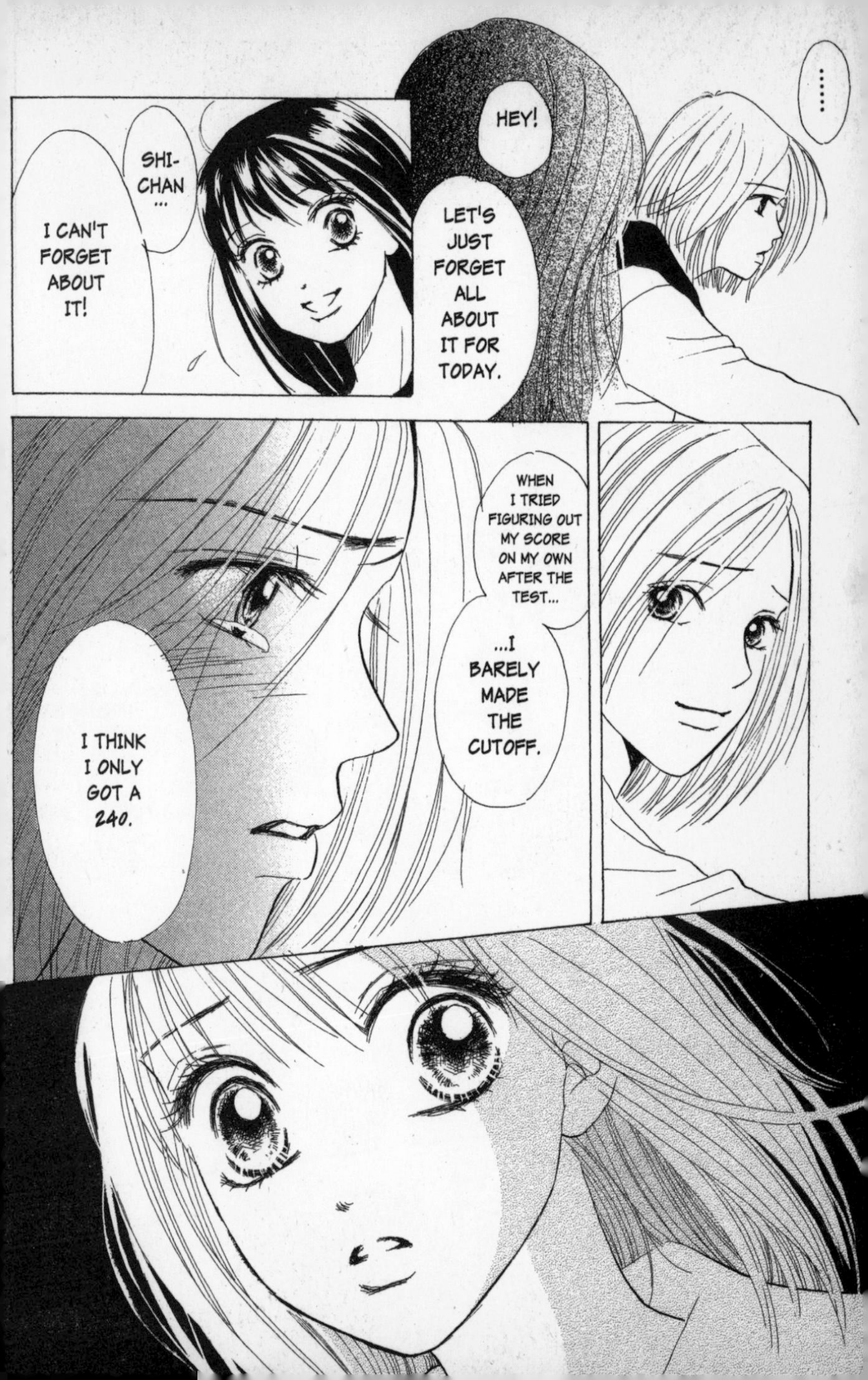
……
HEY!
LET'S JUST FORGET ALL ABOUT IT FOR TODAY.
SHI-CHAN ...
I CAN'T FORGET ABOUT IT!
WHEN I TRIED FIGURING OUT MY SCORE ON MY OWN AFTER THE TEST...
...I BARELY MADE THE CUTOFF.
I THINK I ONLY GOT A 240.

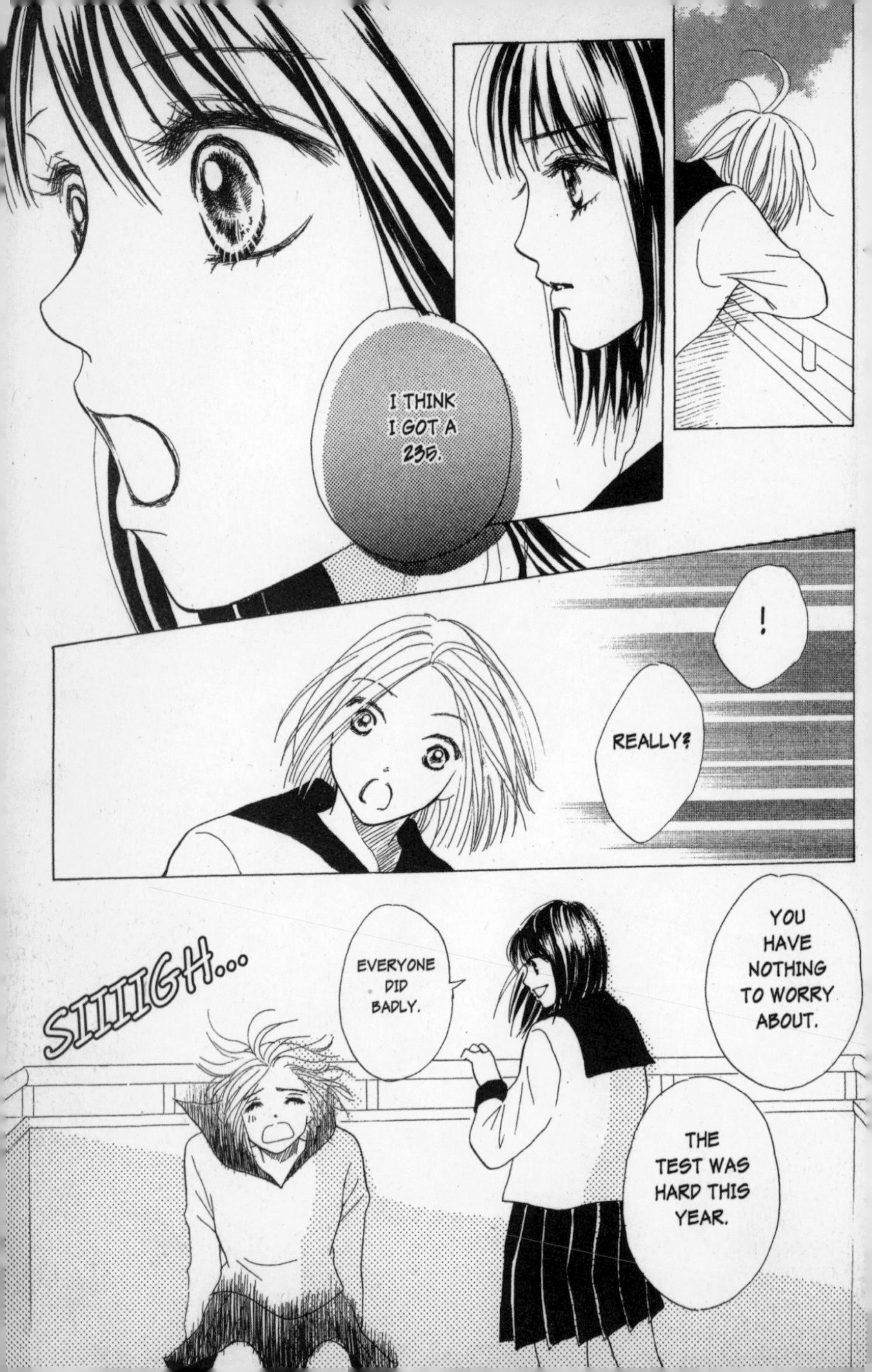
I THINK I GOT A 235.
!
REALLY?
YOU HAVE NOTHING TO WORRY ABOUT.
THE TEST WAS HARD THIS YEAR.
EVERYONE DID BADLY.
SIIIIGH...

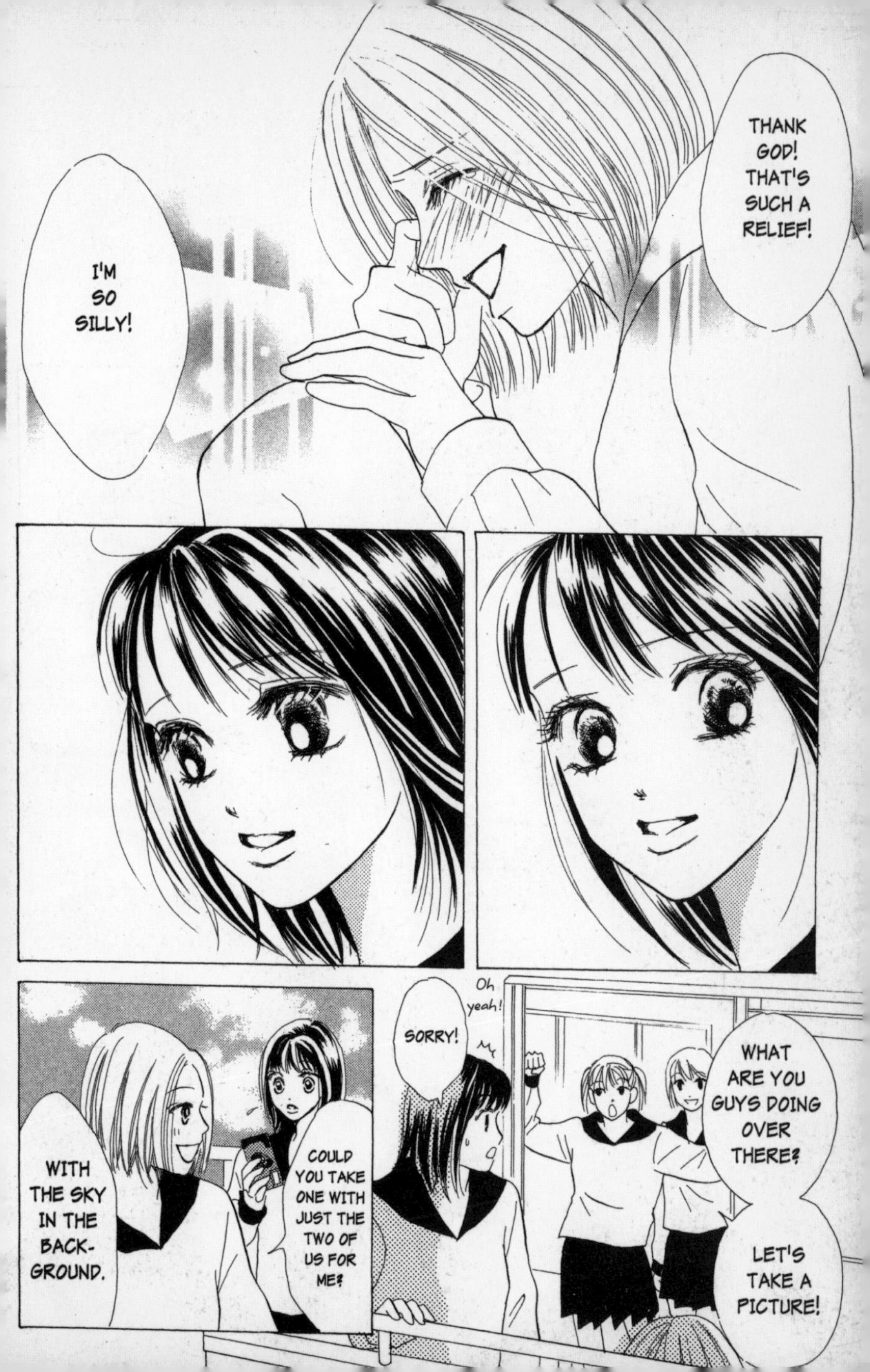
THANK GOD! THAT'S SUCH A RELIEF!
I'M SO SILLY!
WHAT ARE YOU GUYS DOING OVER THERE?
LET'S TAKE A PICTURE!
Oh yeah!
SORRY!
COULD YOU TAKE ONE WITH JUST THE TWO OF US FOR ME?
WITH THE SKY IN THE BACK-GROUND.

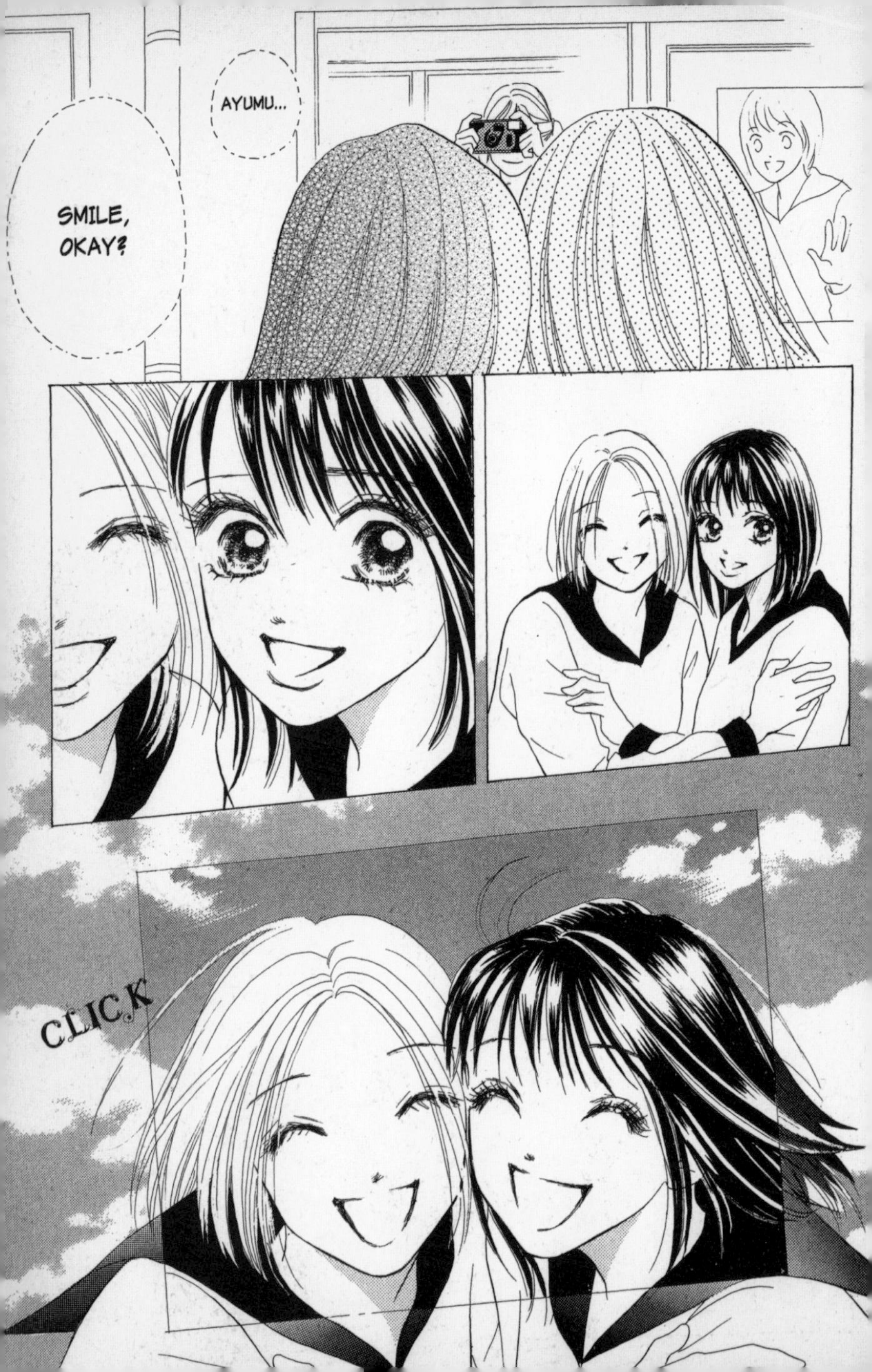
AYUMU...
SMILE, OKAY?
CLICK

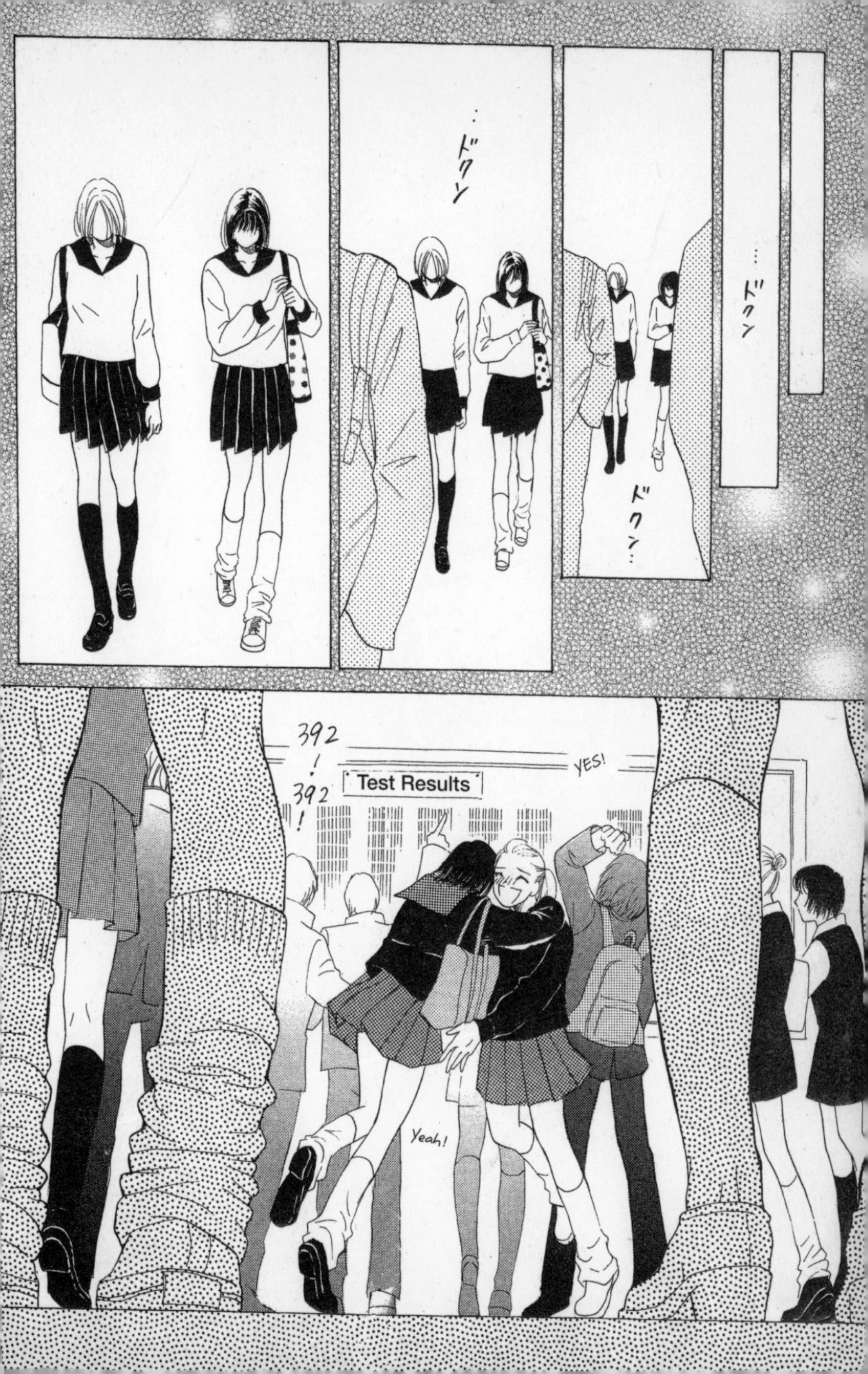
…ドクン
ドクン…
…ドクン
YES!
Test Results
392!
392!
Yeah!

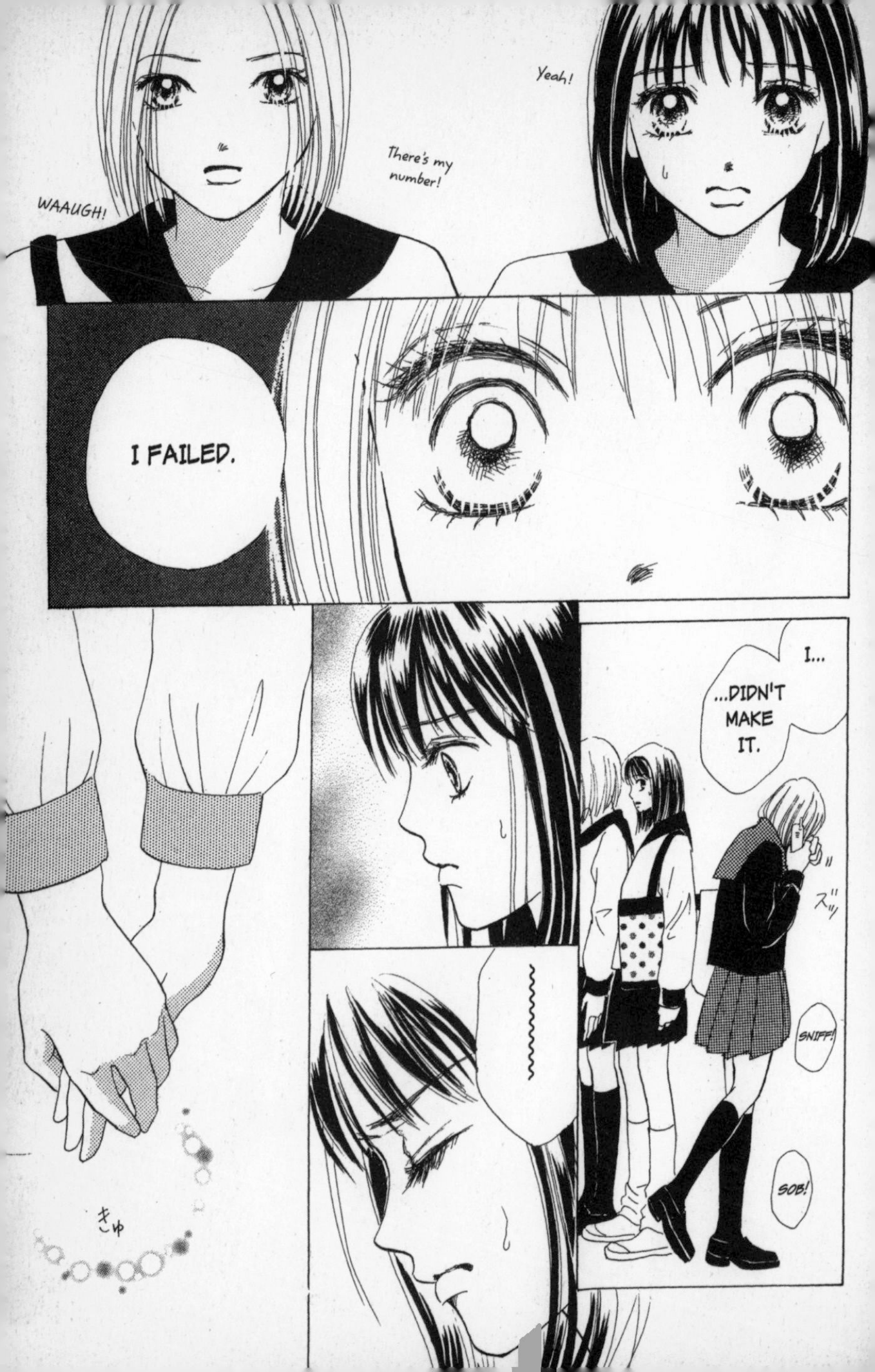
Yeah!
There's my number!
WAAUGH!
I FAILED.
I...
...DIDN'T MAKE IT.
ズッ
SNIFF!
SOB!
きゅ

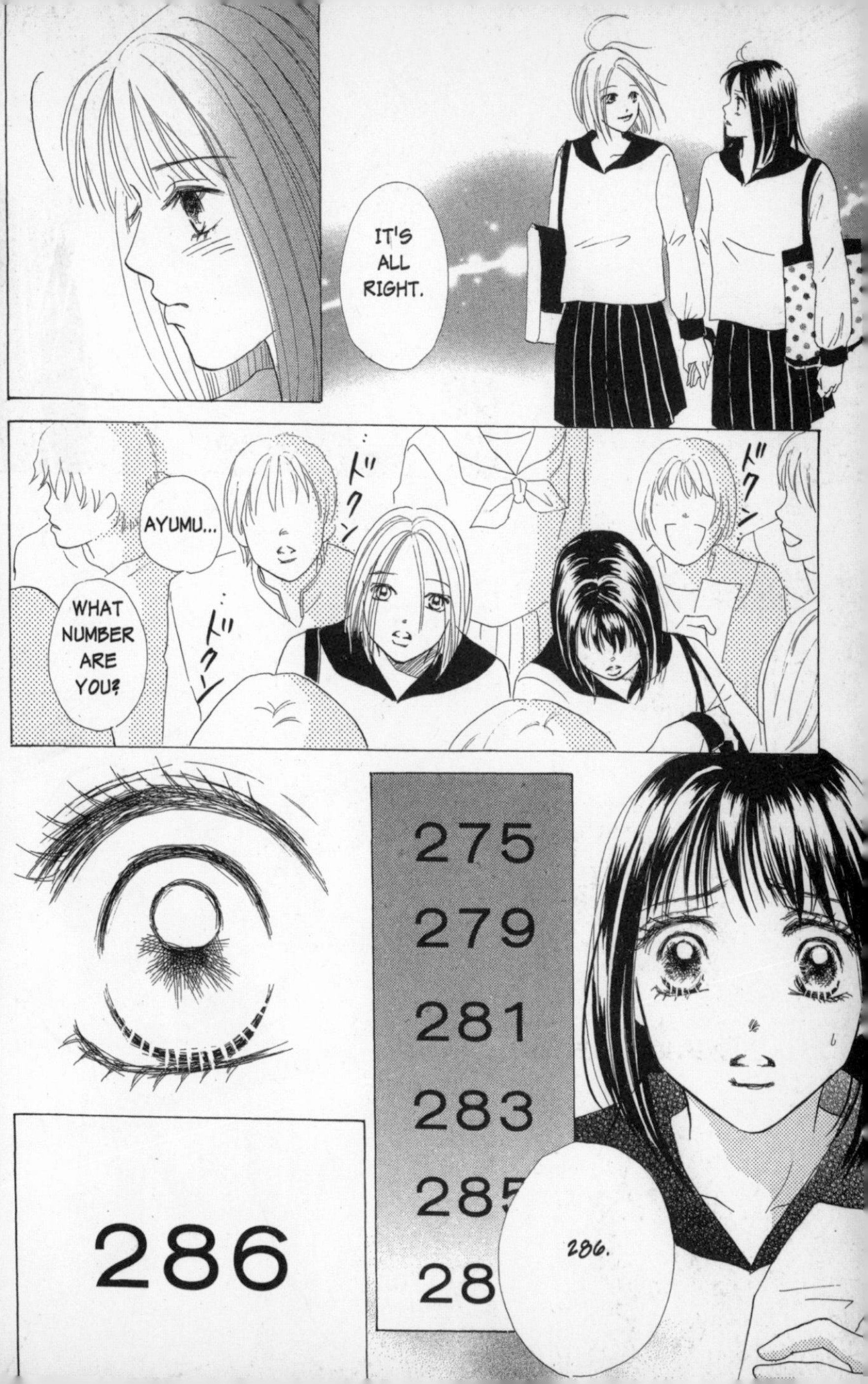

IT'S ALL RIGHT.
ドクン
ドクン
AYUMU...
ドクン
WHAT NUMBER ARE YOU?
286.
275
279
281
283
285
28
286

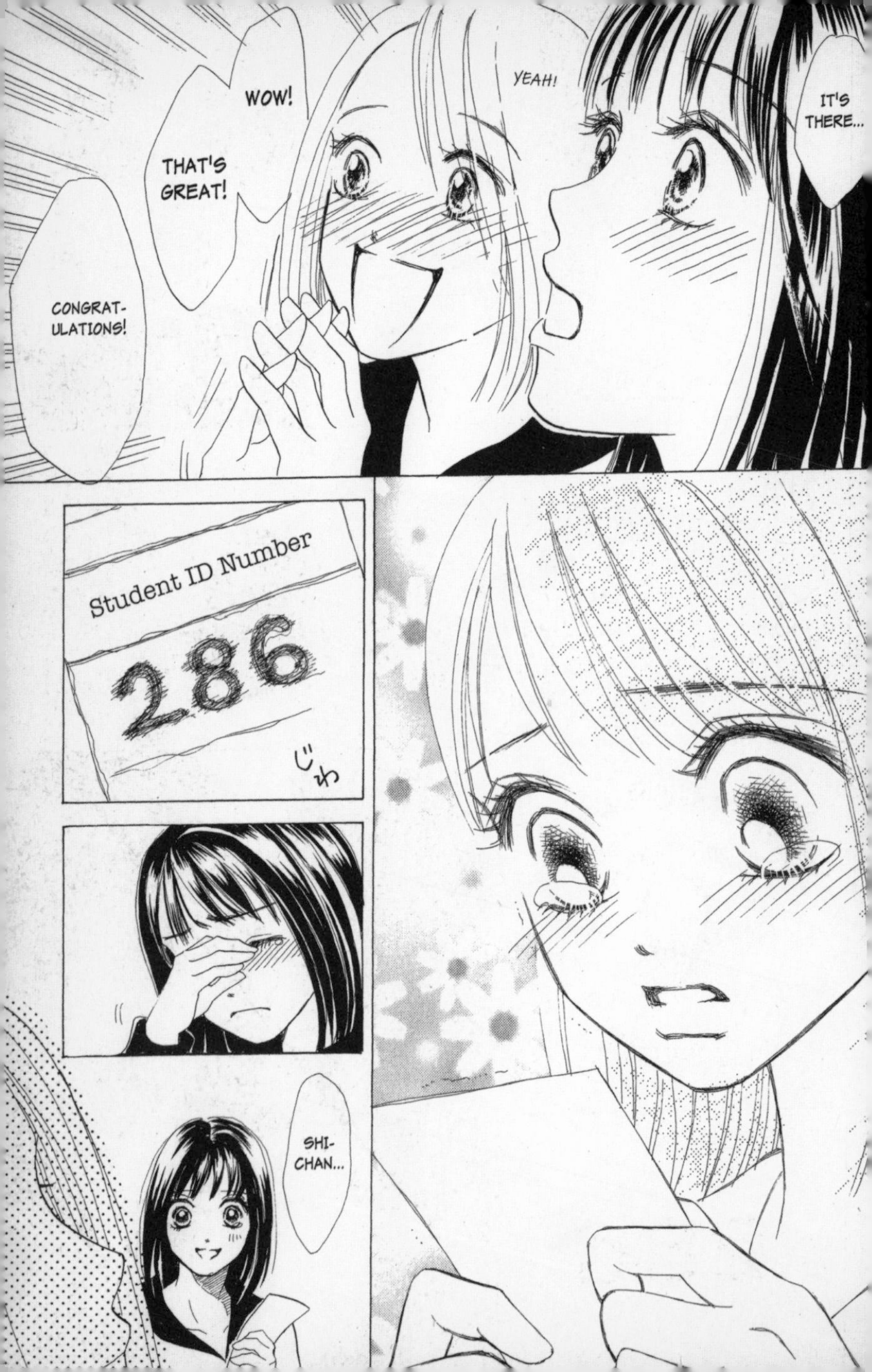
IT'S THERE...
YEAH!
WOW!
THAT'S GREAT!
CONGRAT-ULATIONS!
Student ID Number
286
じわ
SHI-CHAN...

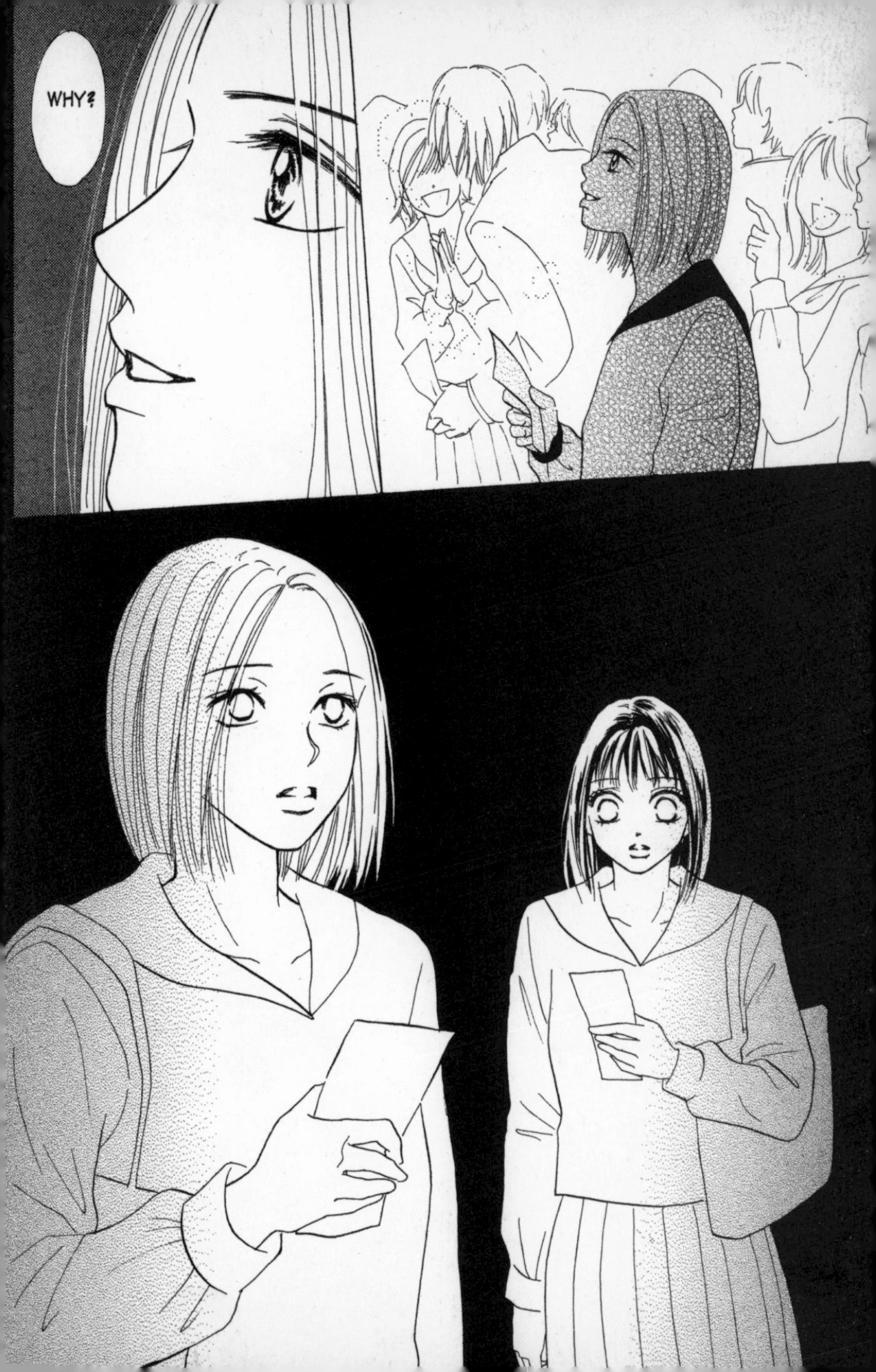
WHY?

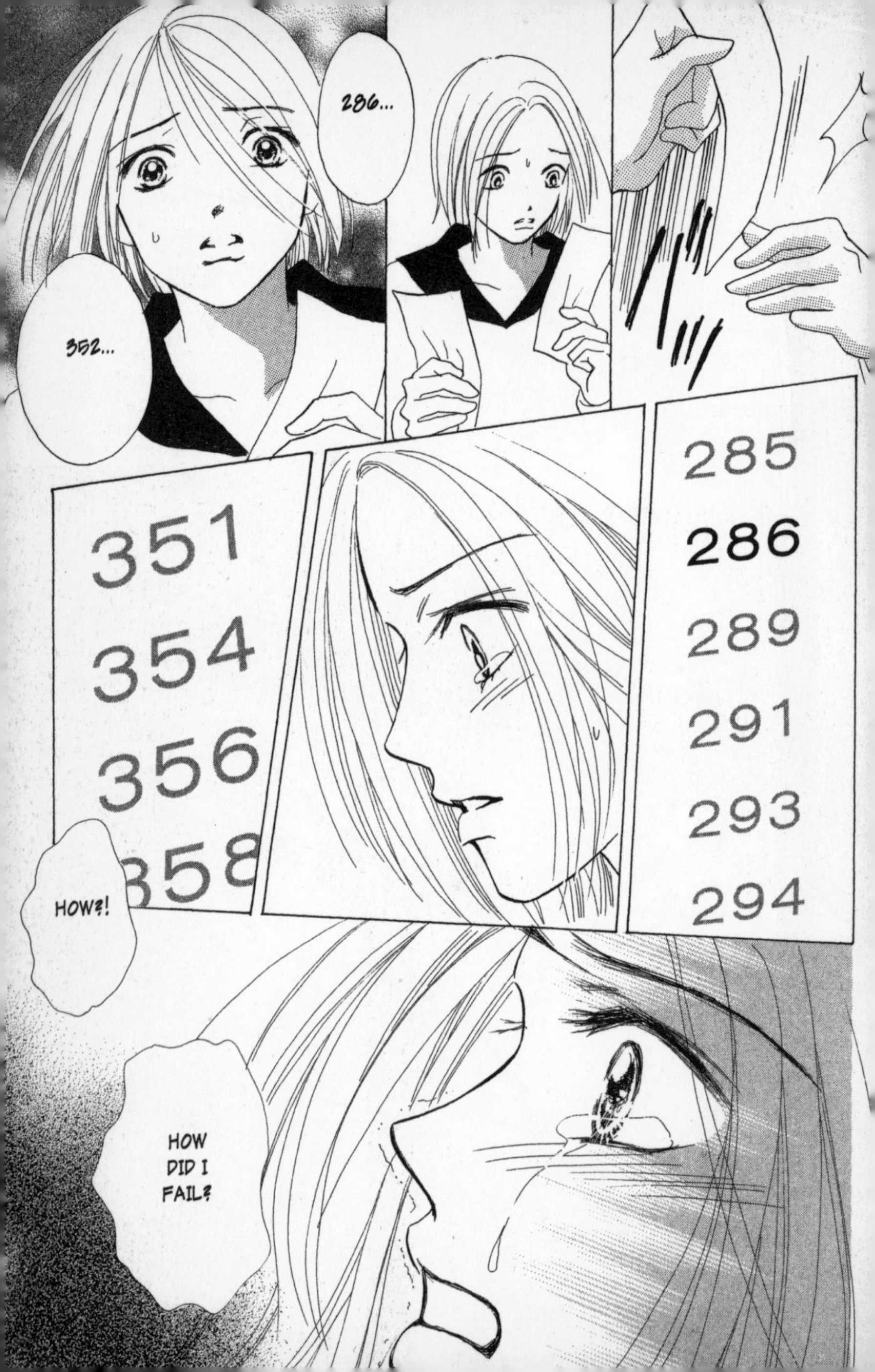
286...
352...
285
286
289
291
293
294
351
354
356
358
HOW?!
HOW DID I FAIL?

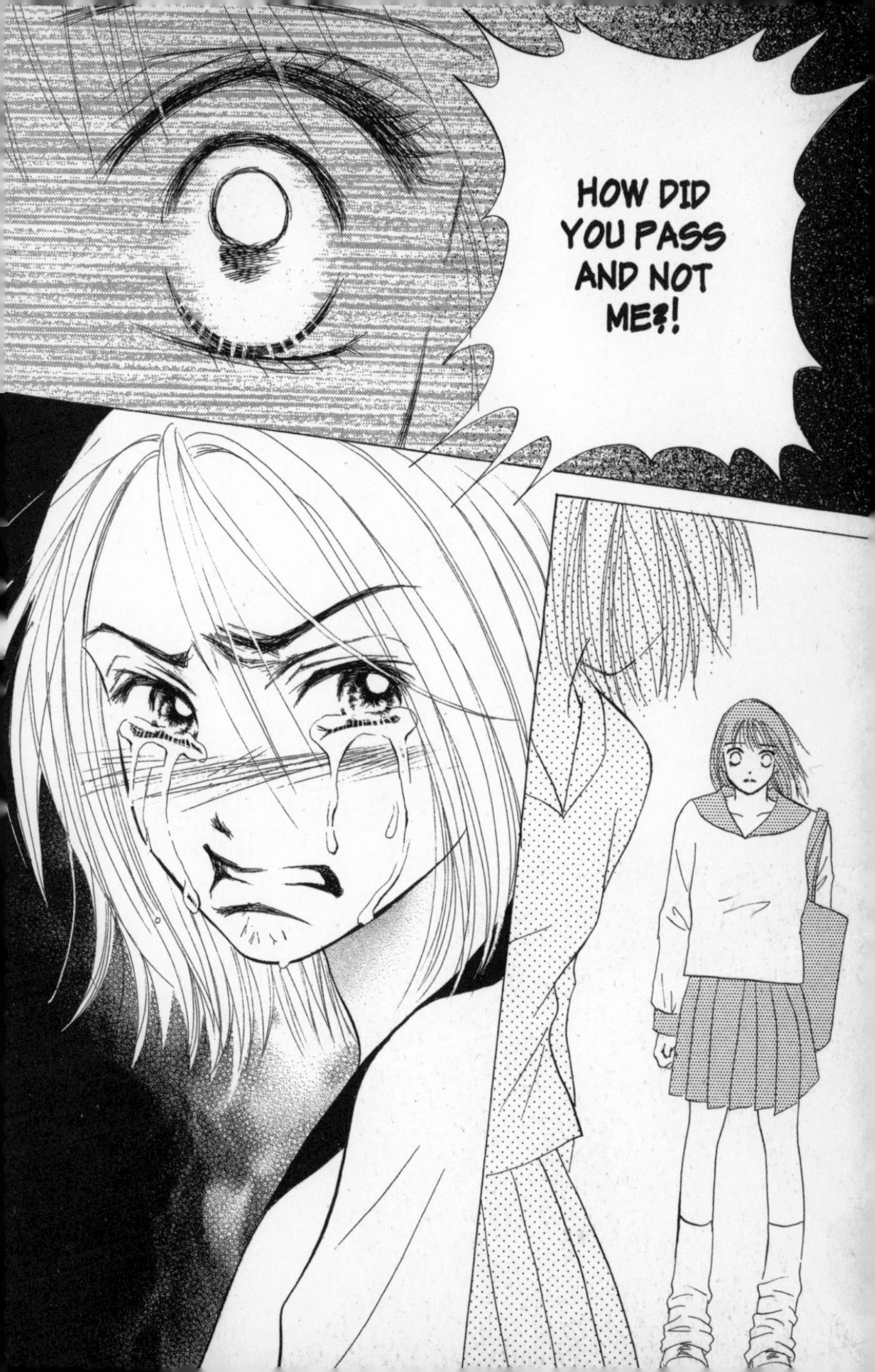
HOW DID YOU PASS AND NOT ME?!

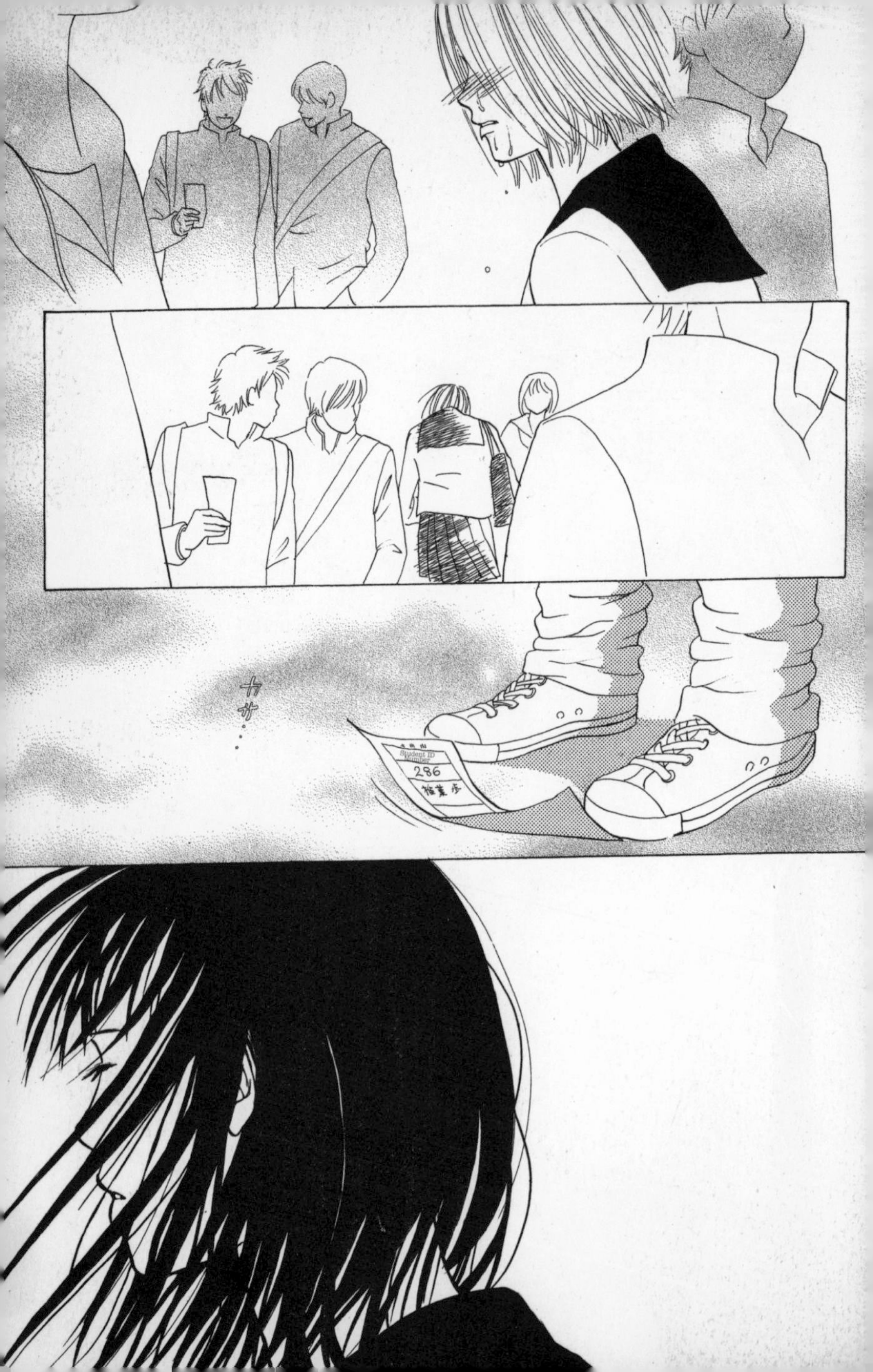
カサ…
Student ID Number
286
稲葉歩

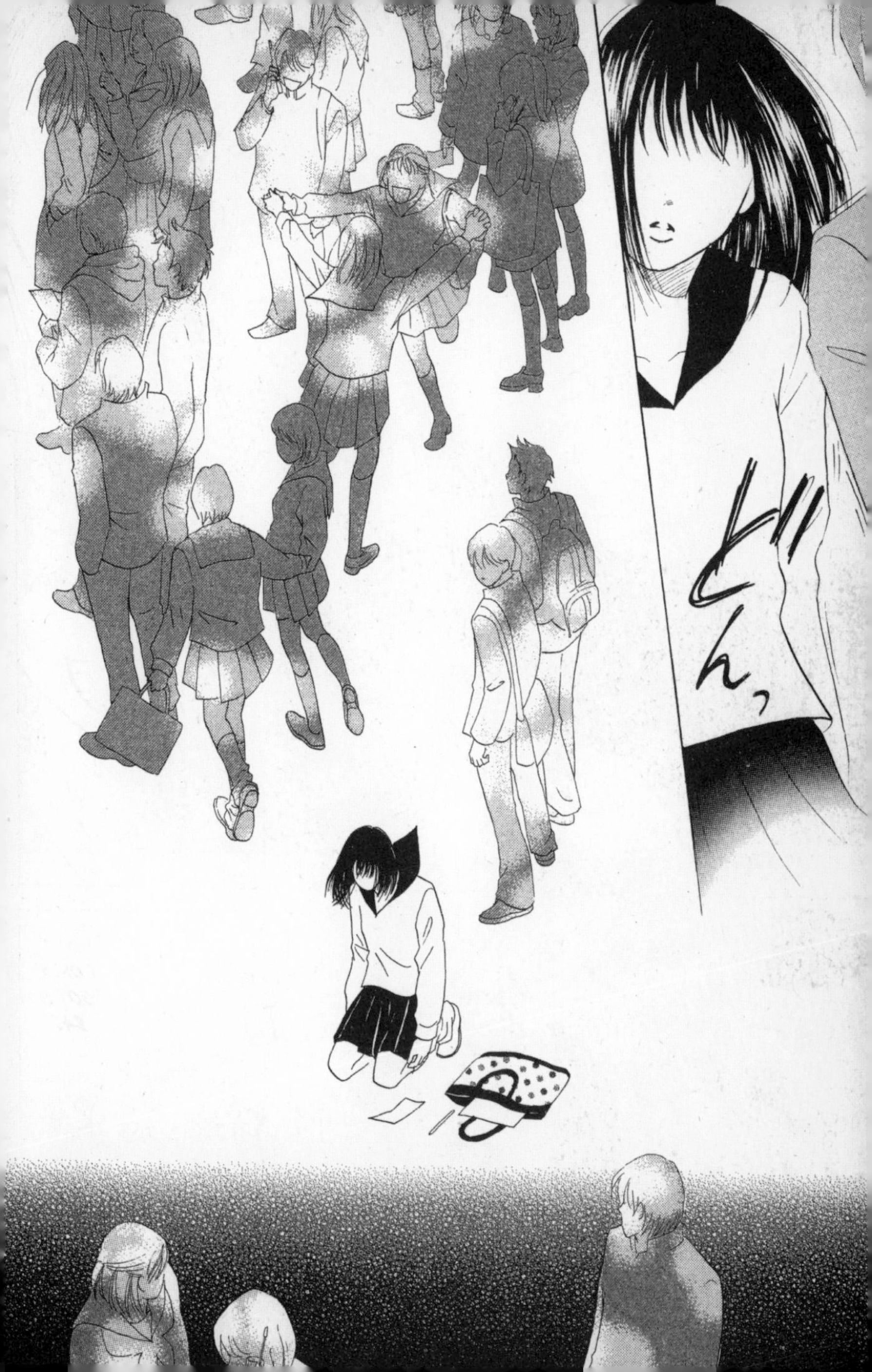
どんっ

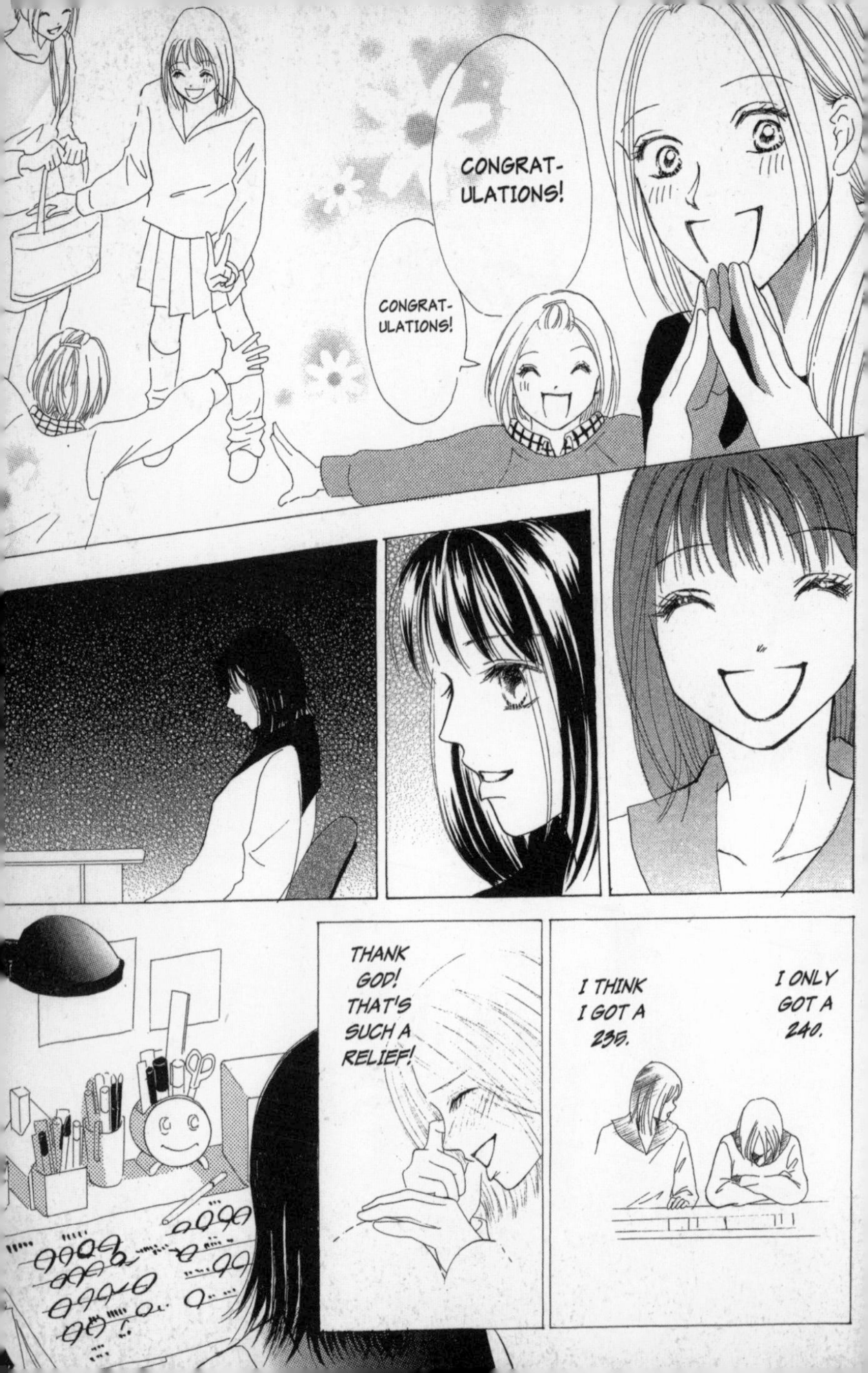
CONGRAT-ULATIONS!
CONGRAT-ULATIONS!
I ONLY GOT A 240.
I THINK I GOT A 235.
THANK GOD! THAT'S SUCH A RELIEF!

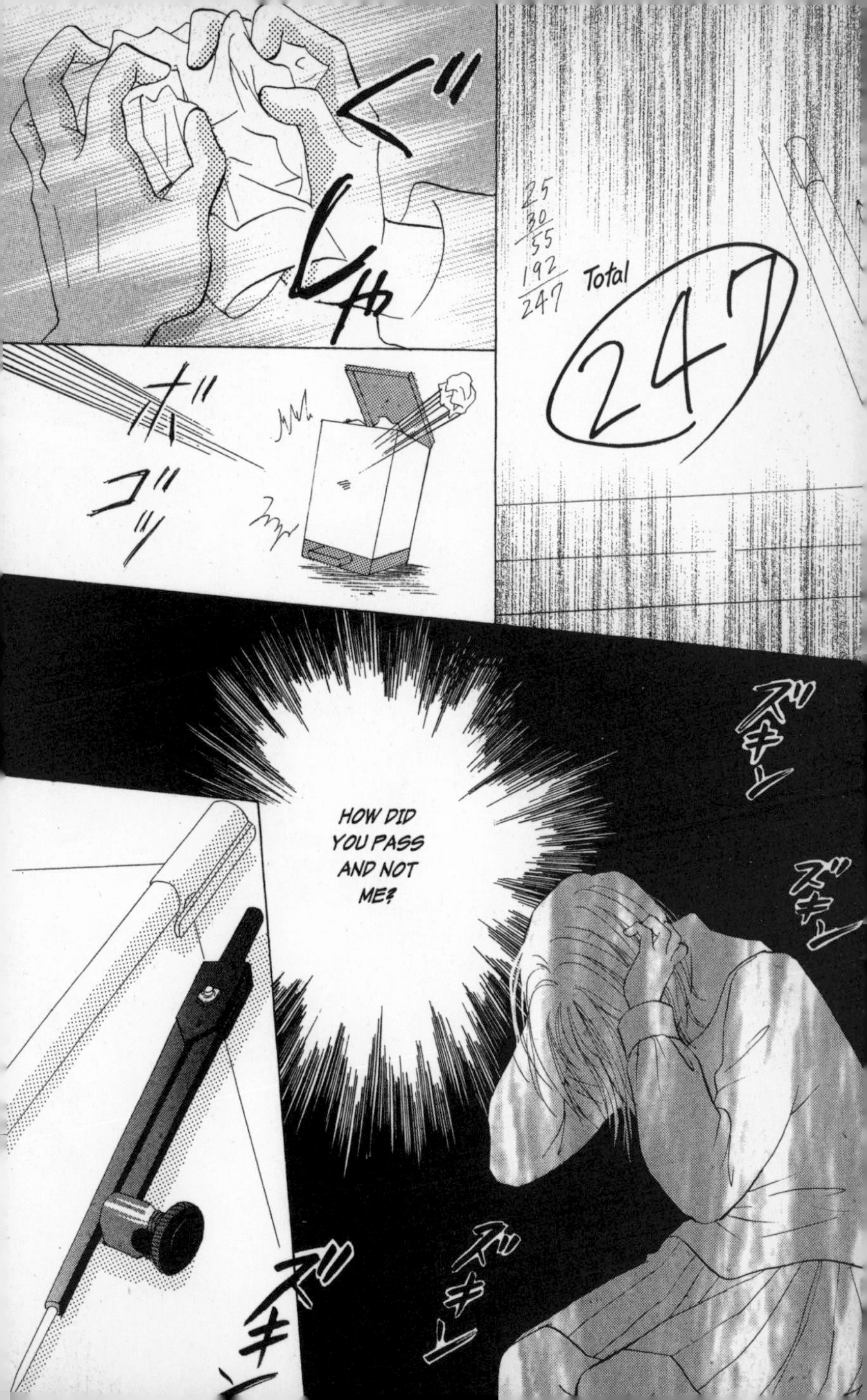
25
30
55
192
247
Total
247
ぐしゃ
HOW DID YOU PASS AND NOT ME?
ズキン
ズキン
ズキン
ズキン

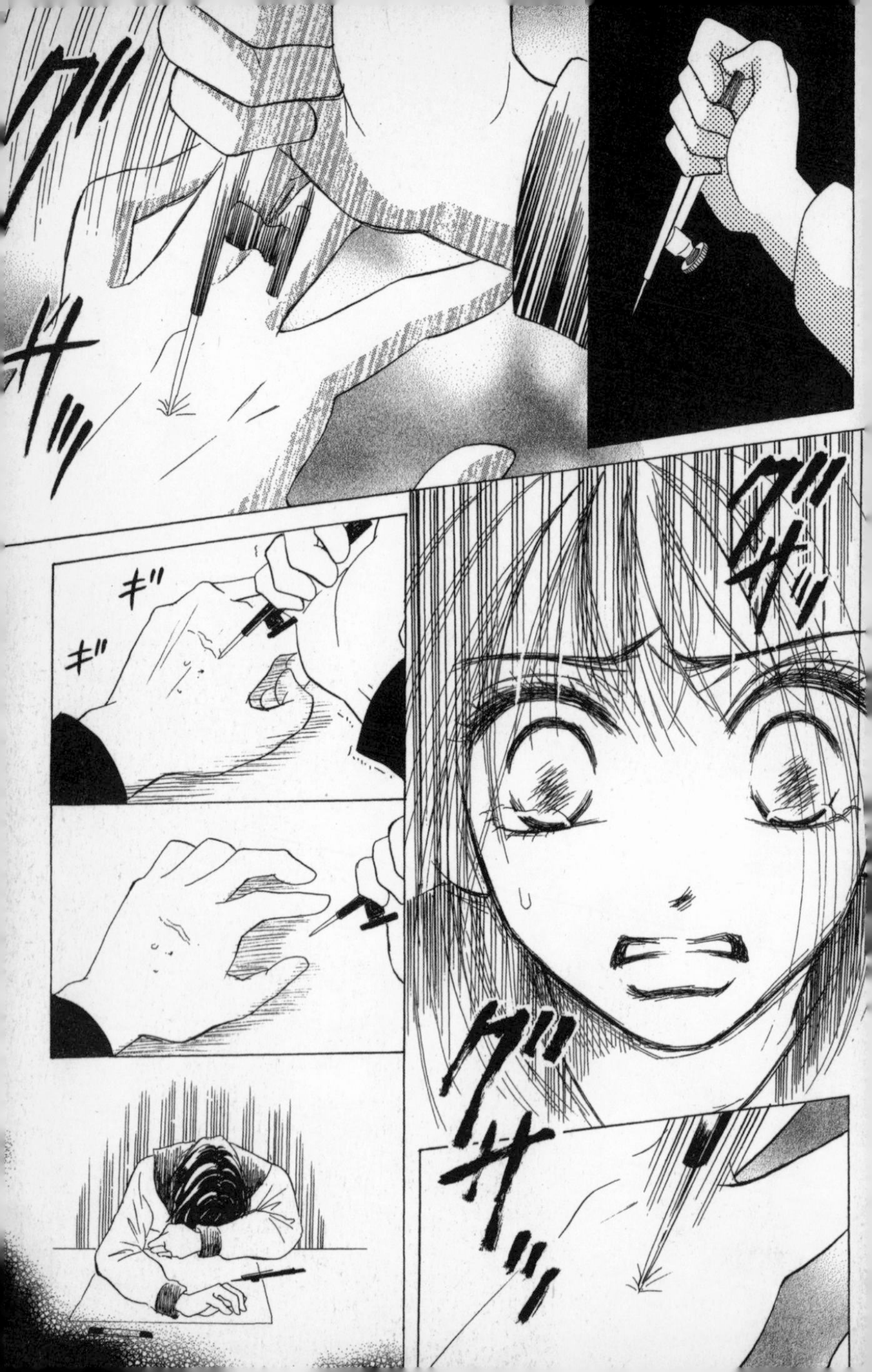

グリ
ザッ
グザッ
グザッ
ギ
ギ

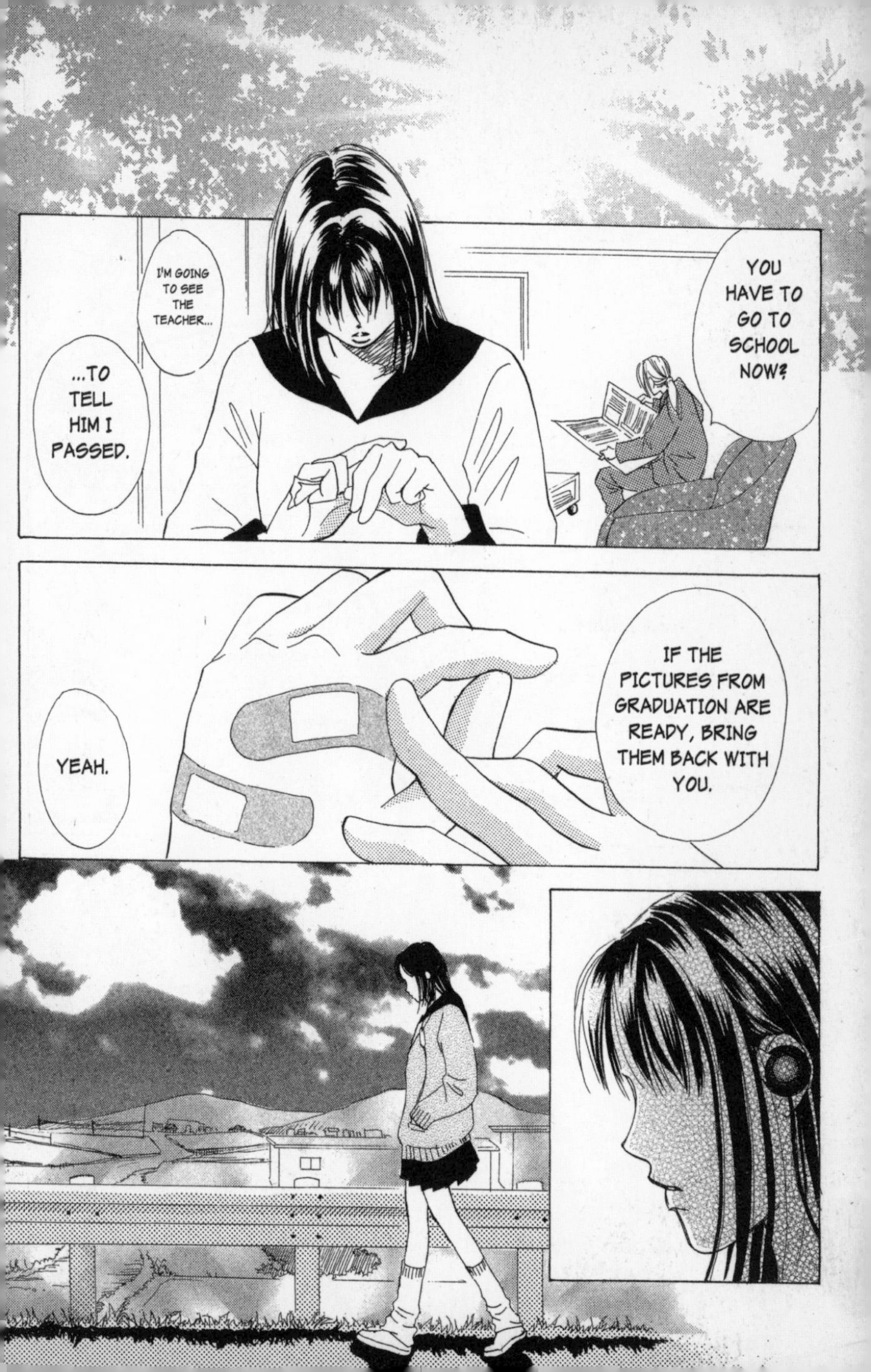
YOU HAVE TO GO TO SCHOOL NOW?
I'M GOING TO SEE THE TEACHER...
...TO TELL HIM I PASSED.
IF THE PICTURES FROM GRADUATION ARE READY, BRING THEM BACK WITH YOU.
YEAH.

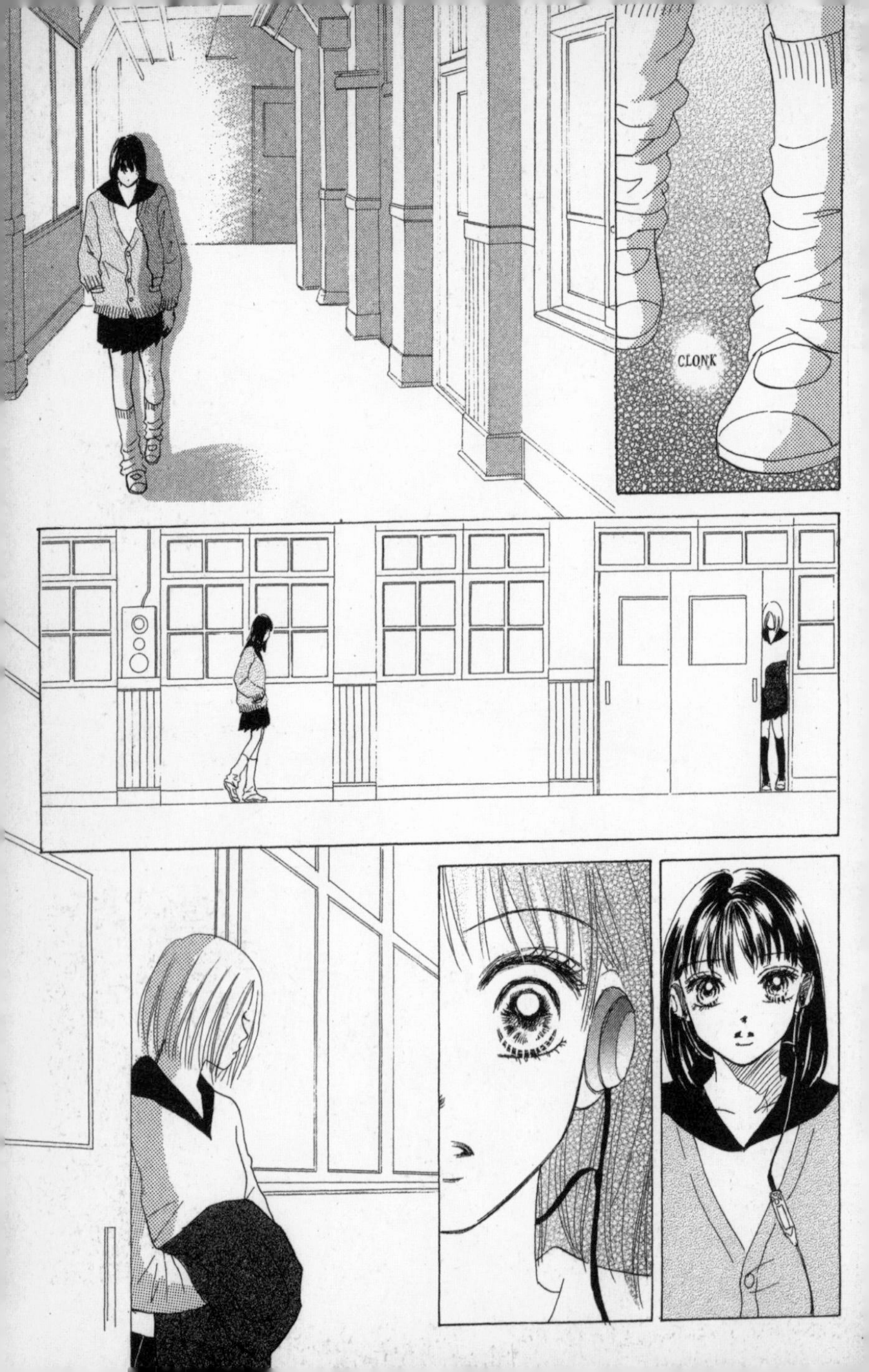
CLONK

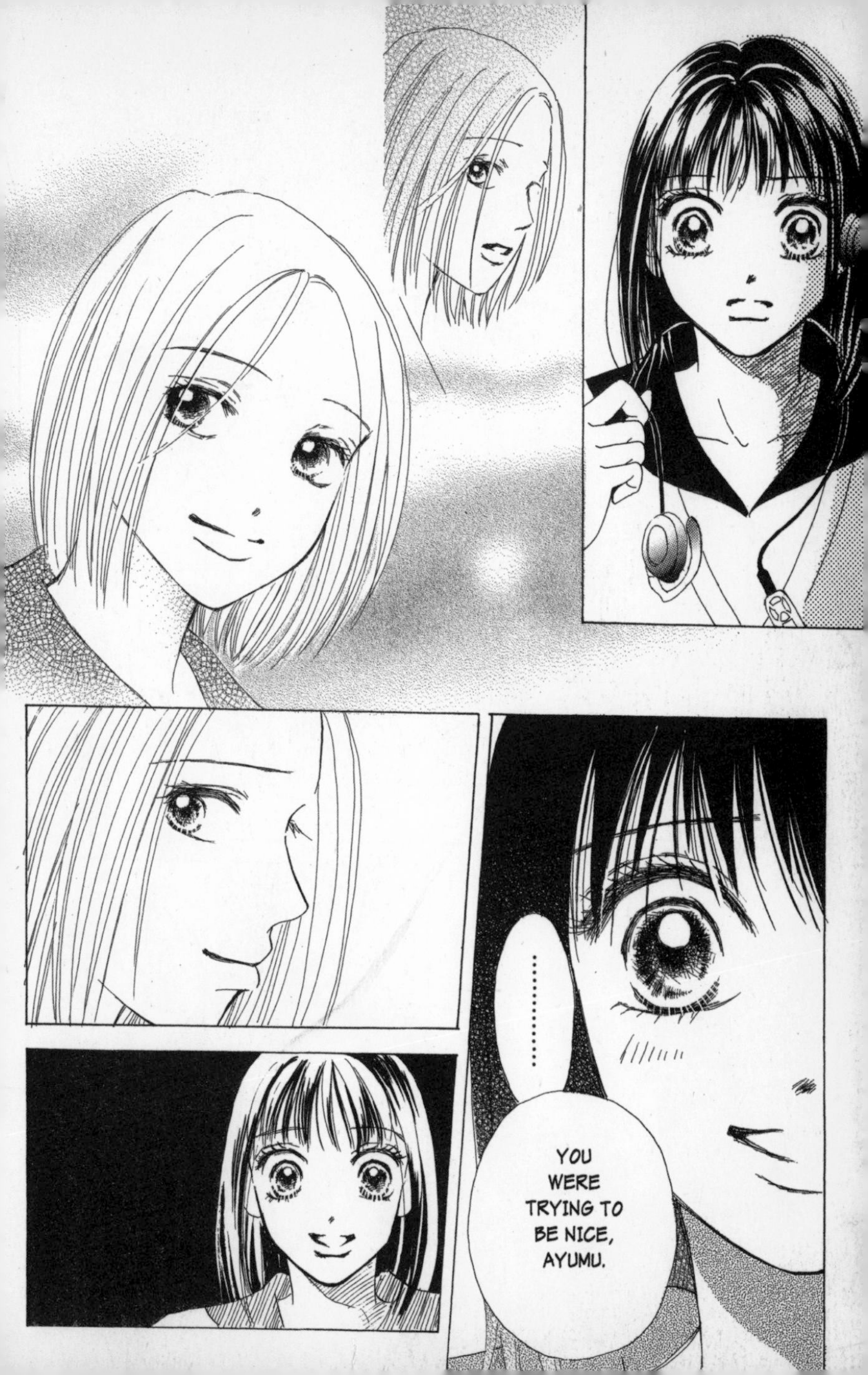
......
YOU WERE TRYING TO BE NICE, AYUMU.

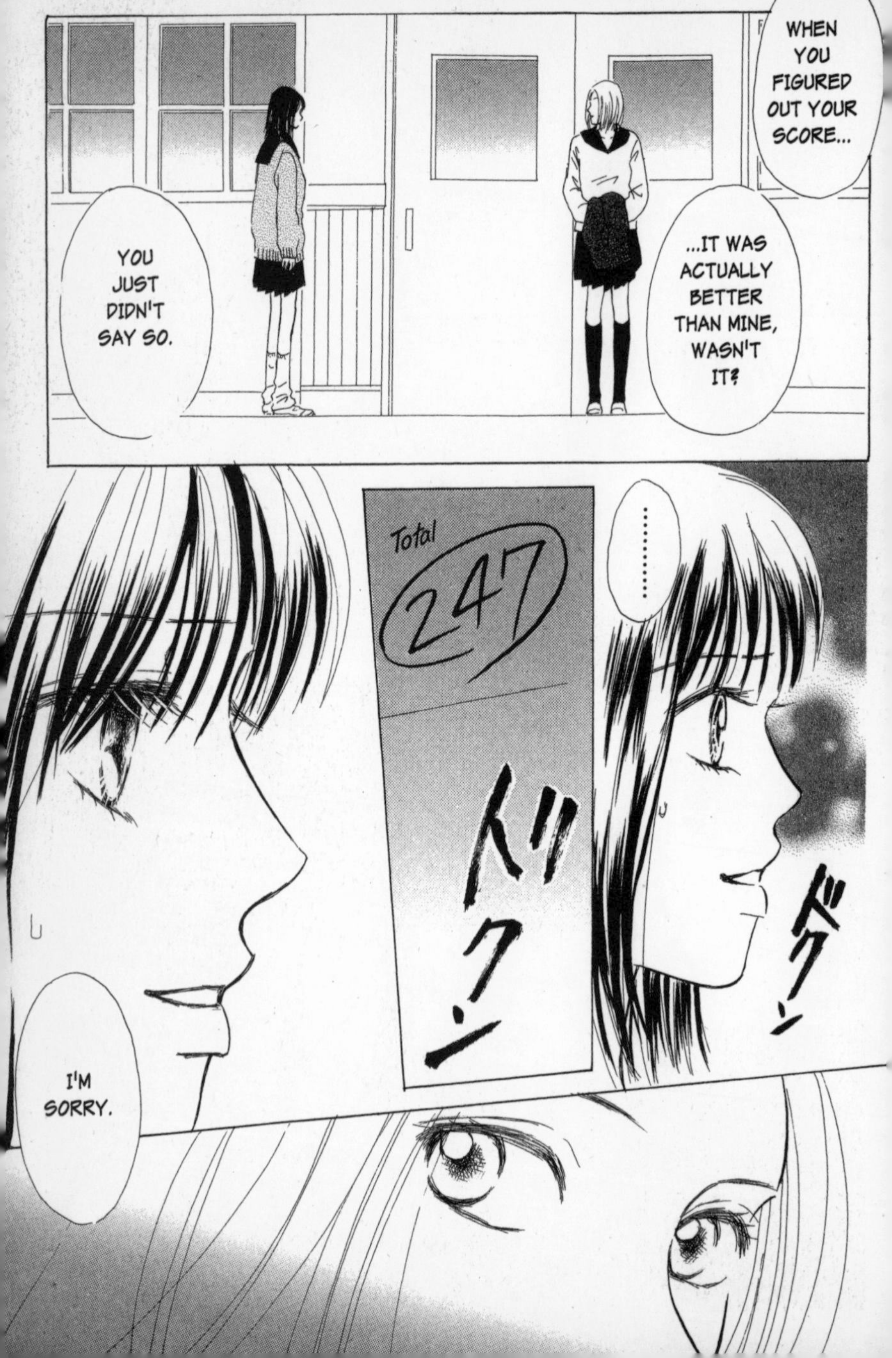
WHEN YOU FIGURED OUT YOUR SCORE...
...IT WAS ACTUALLY BETTER THAN MINE, WASN'T IT?
YOU JUST DIDN'T SAY SO.
......
Total
247
ドクン
I'M SORRY.

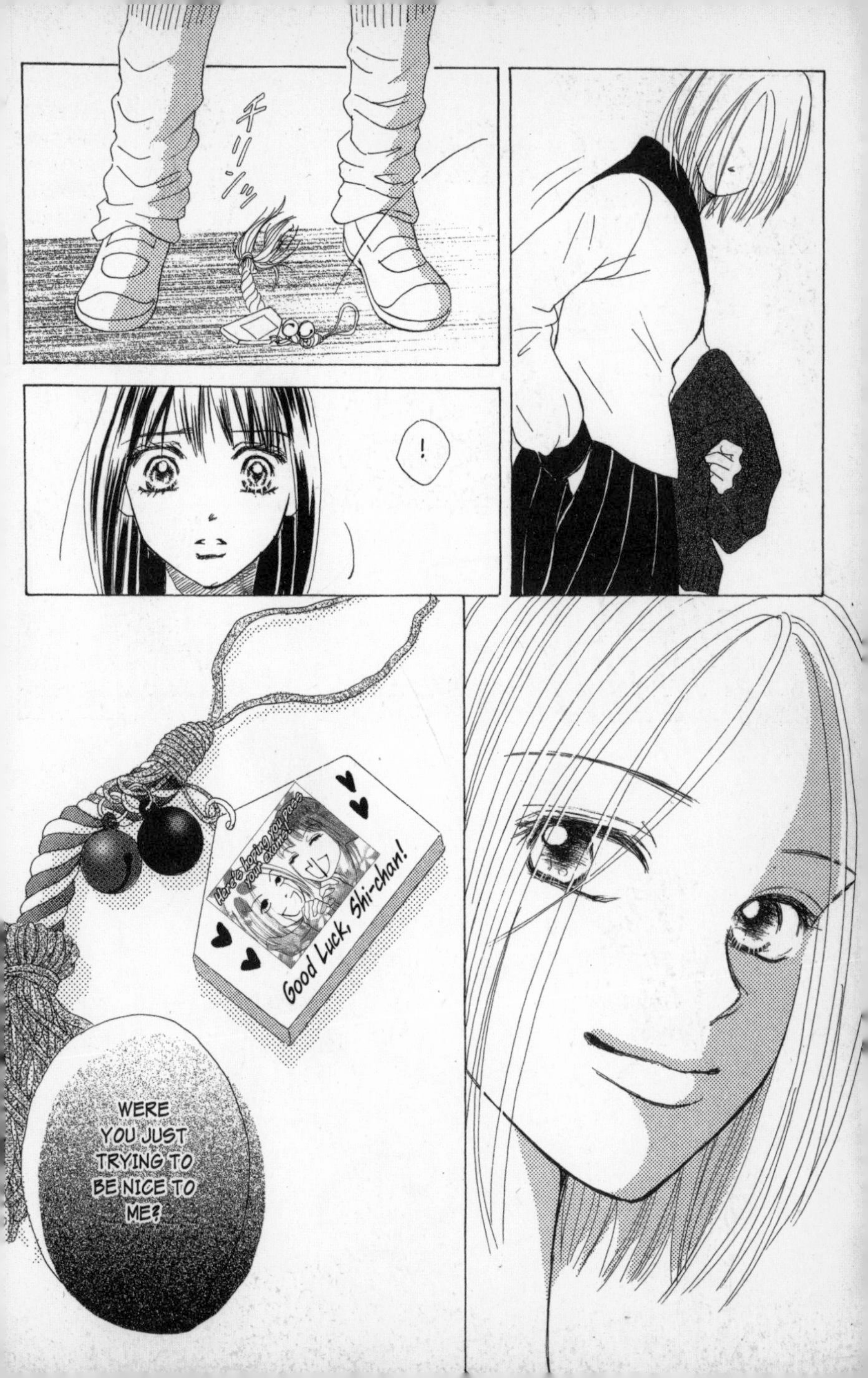
チリンッ
!
Good Luck, Shi-chan!
Here's hoping you pass your exams!
WERE YOU JUST TRYING TO BE NICE TO ME?

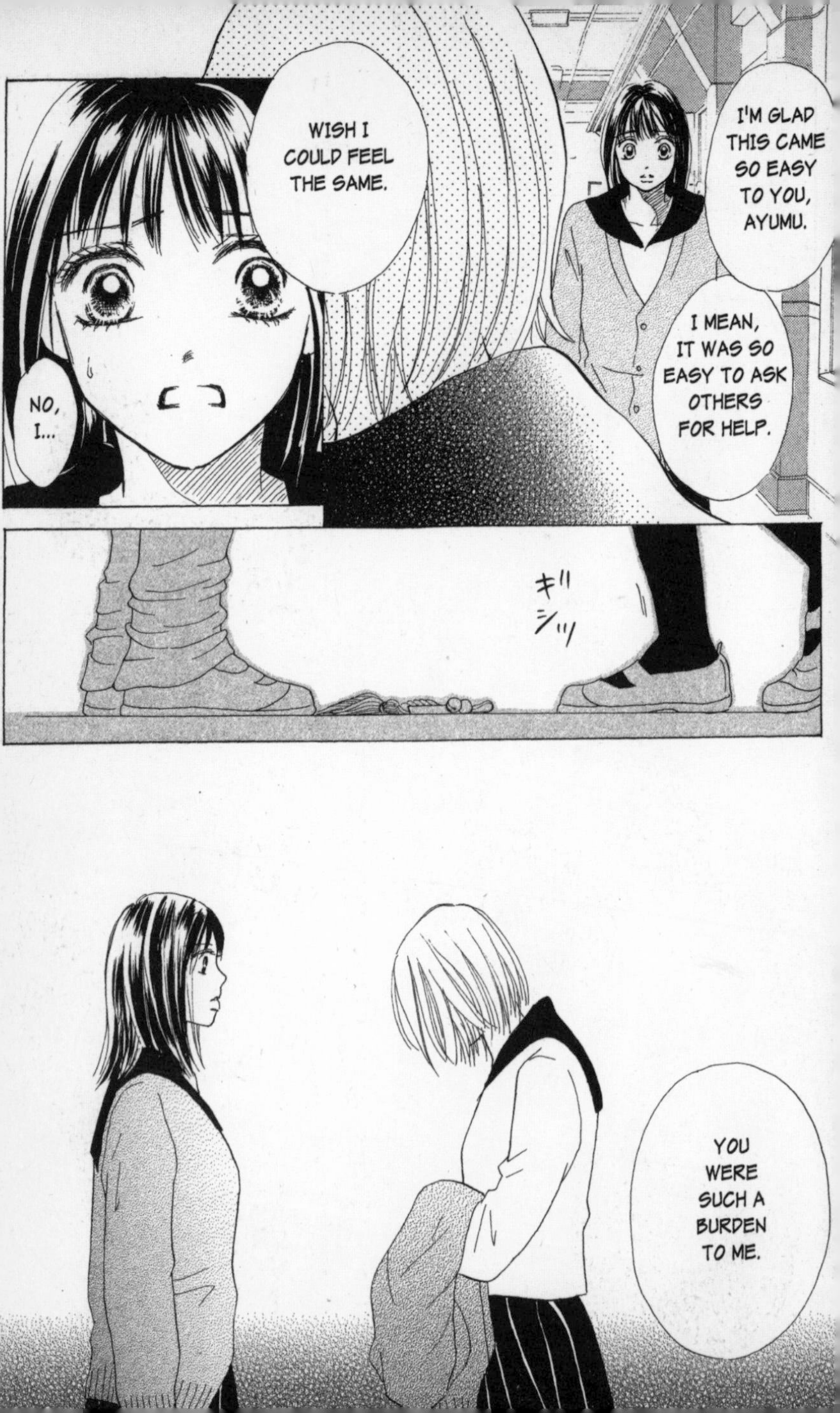
I'M GLAD THIS CAME SO EASY TO YOU, AYUMU.
I MEAN, IT WAS SO EASY TO ASK OTHERS FOR HELP.
WISH I COULD FEEL THE SAME.
NO, I...
ギリシッ
YOU WERE SUCH A BURDEN TO ME.

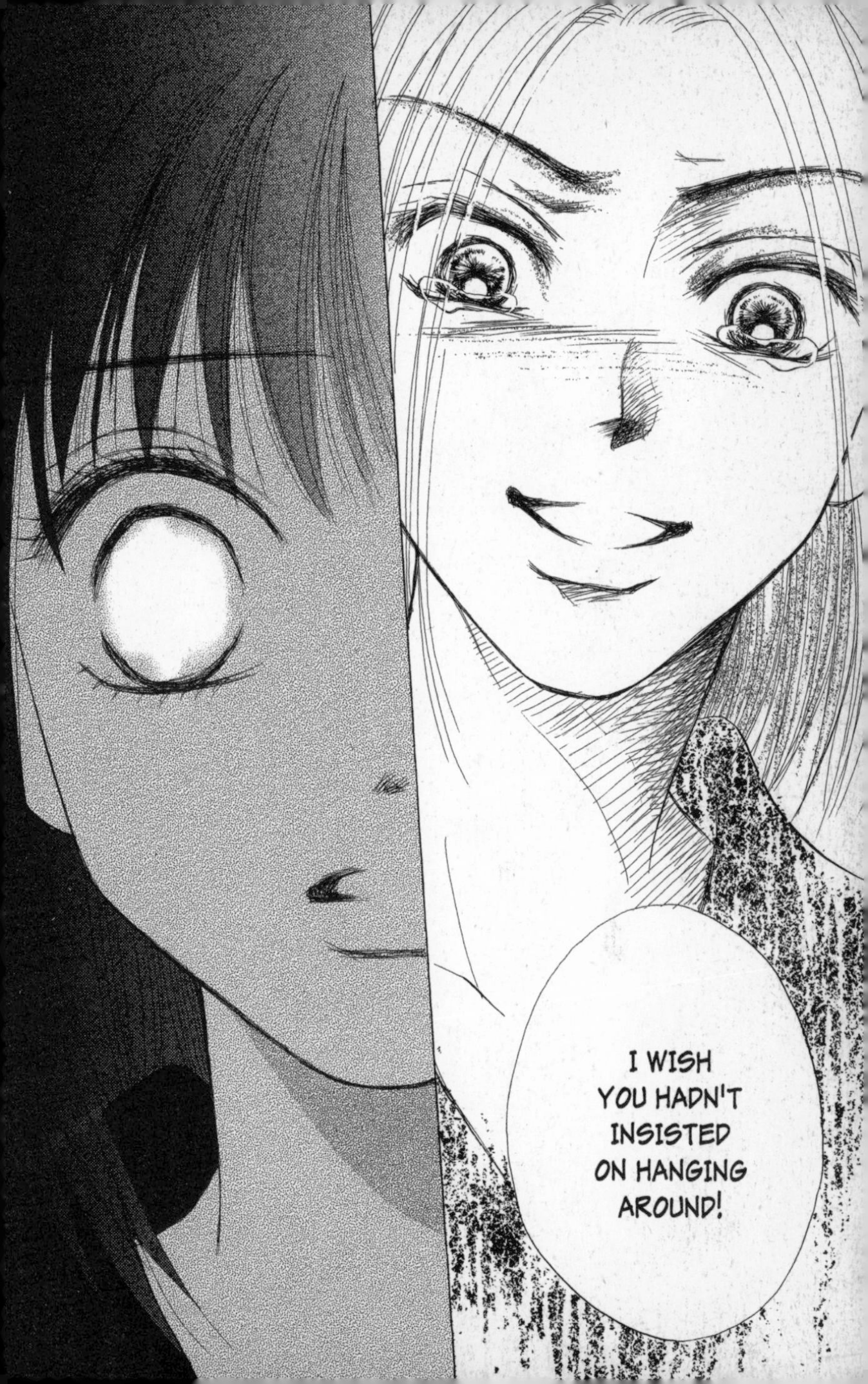
I WISH YOU HADN'T INSISTED ON HANGING AROUND!

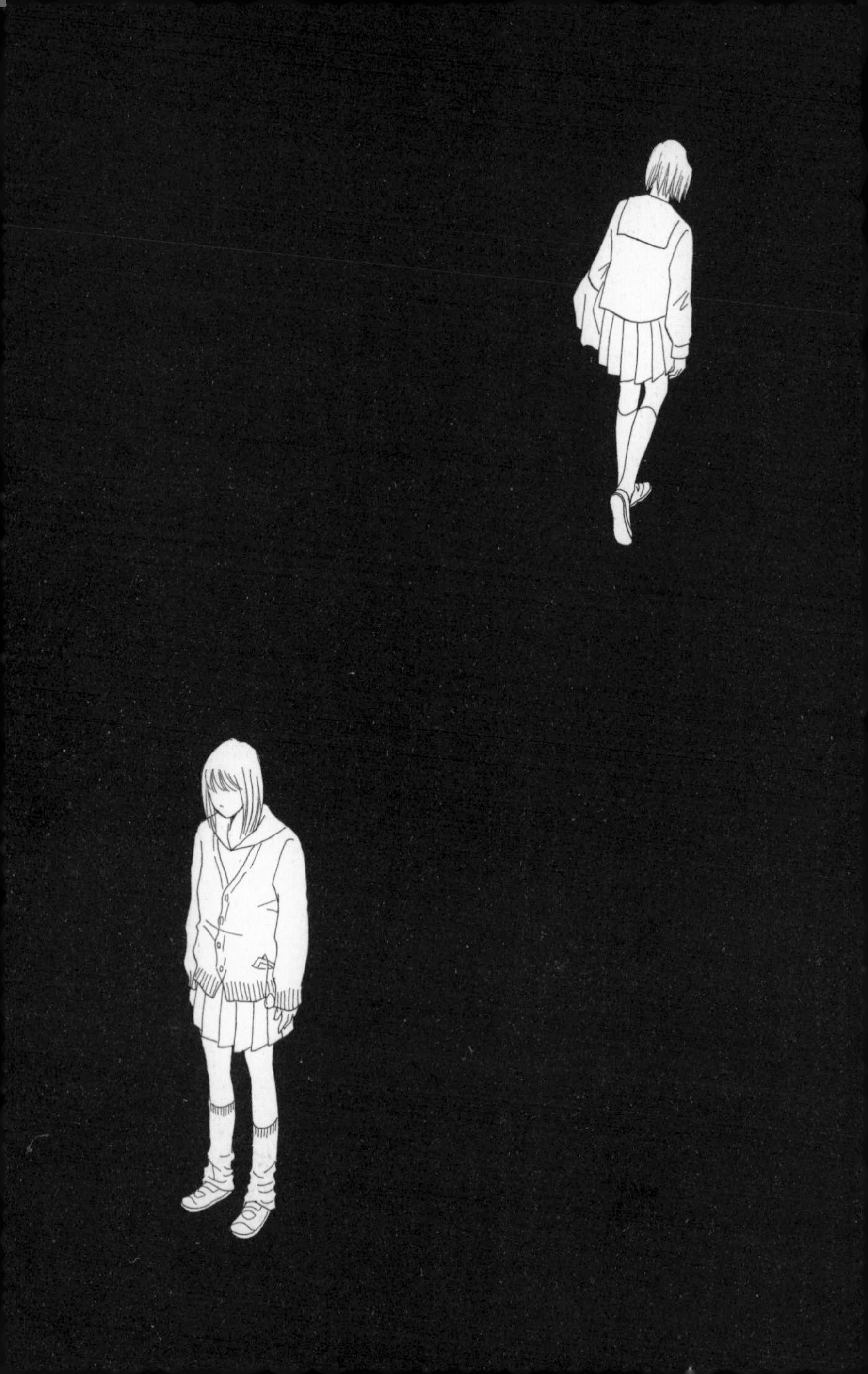

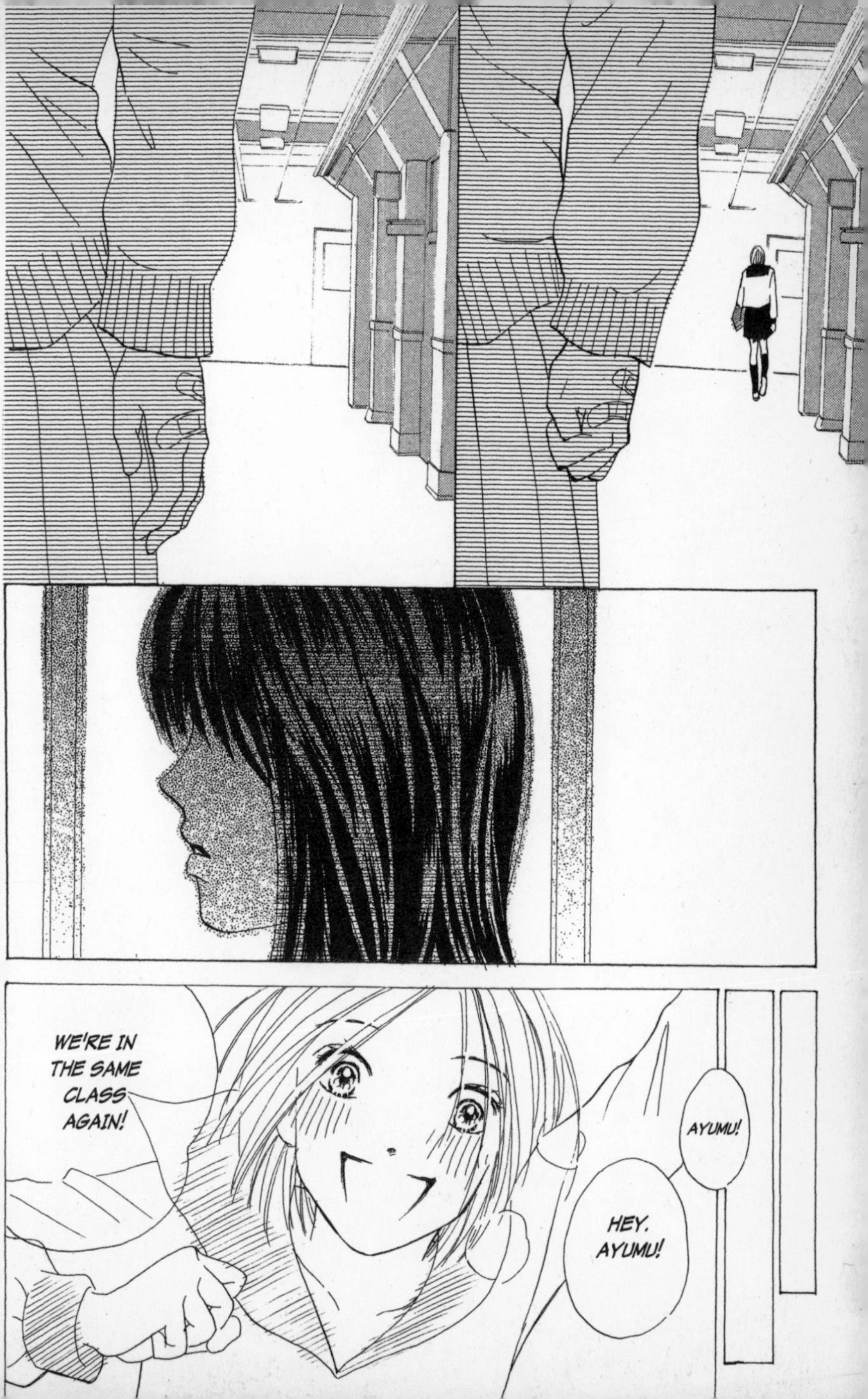
AYUMU!
HEY. AYUMU!
WE'RE IN THE SAME CLASS AGAIN!

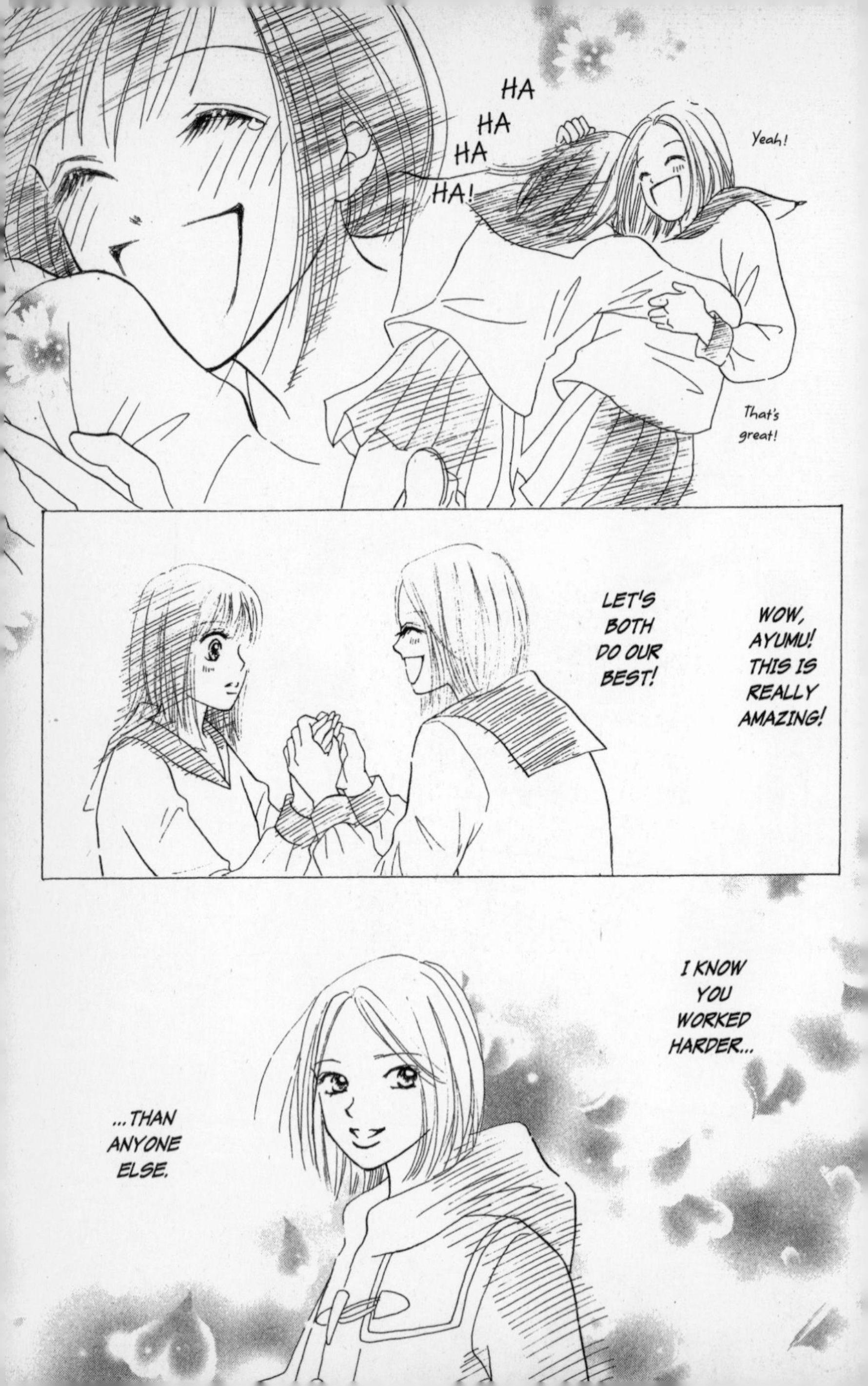
Yeah!
That's great!
HA HA HA HA!
WOW, AYUMU! THIS IS REALLY AMAZING!
LET'S BOTH DO OUR BEST!
I KNOW YOU WORKED HARDER...
...THAN ANYONE ELSE.

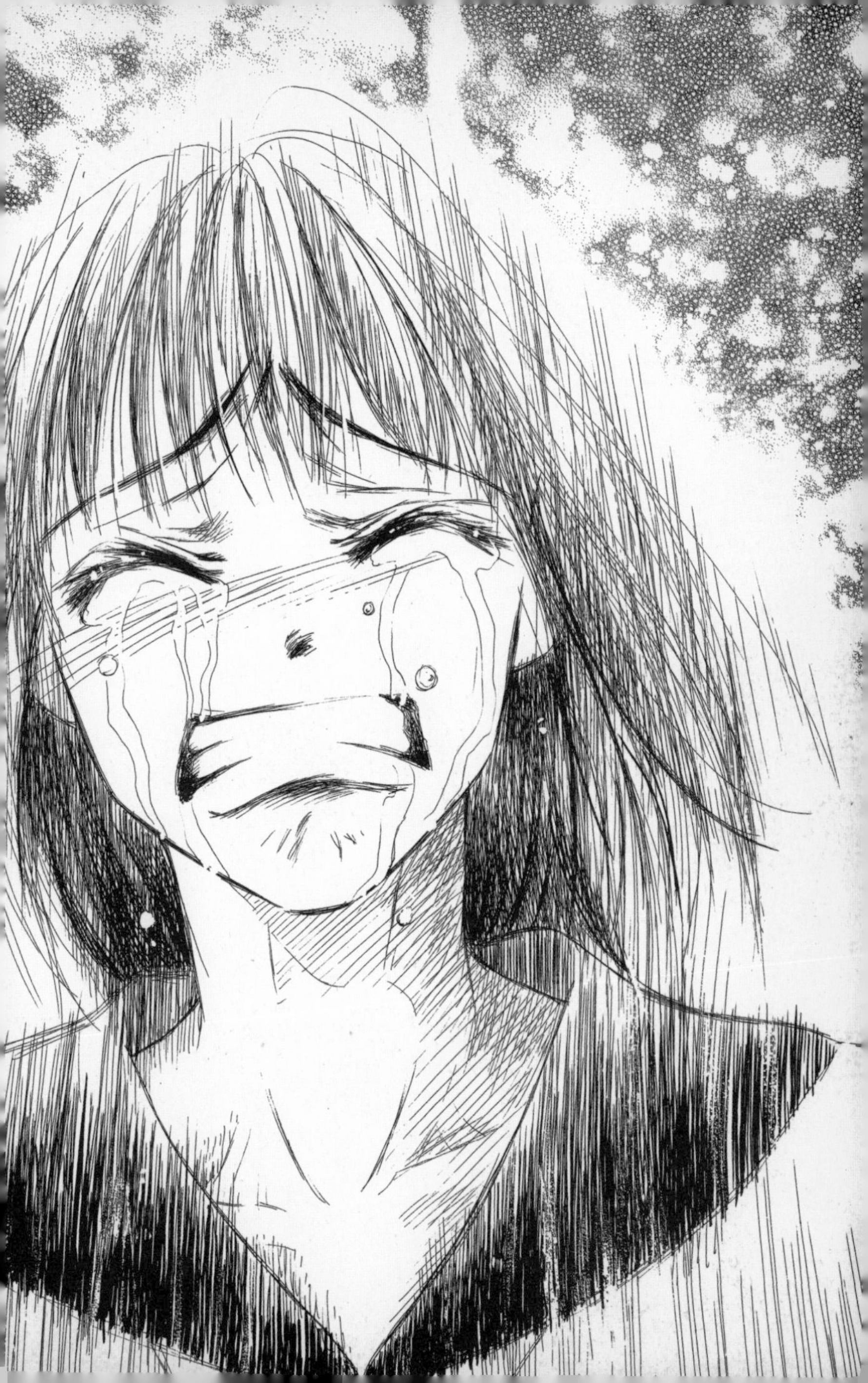

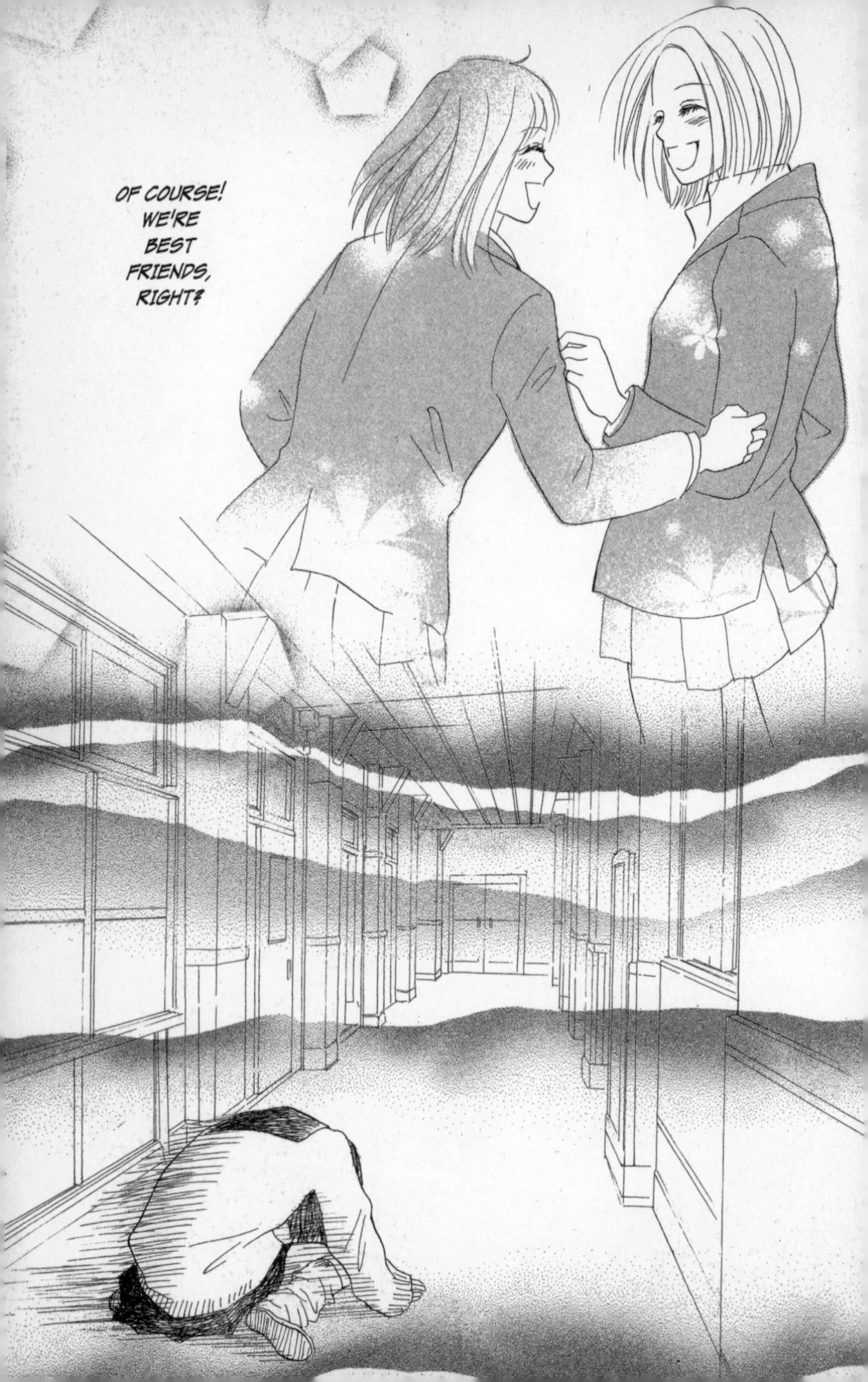
OF COURSE! WE'RE BEST FRIENDS, RIGHT?

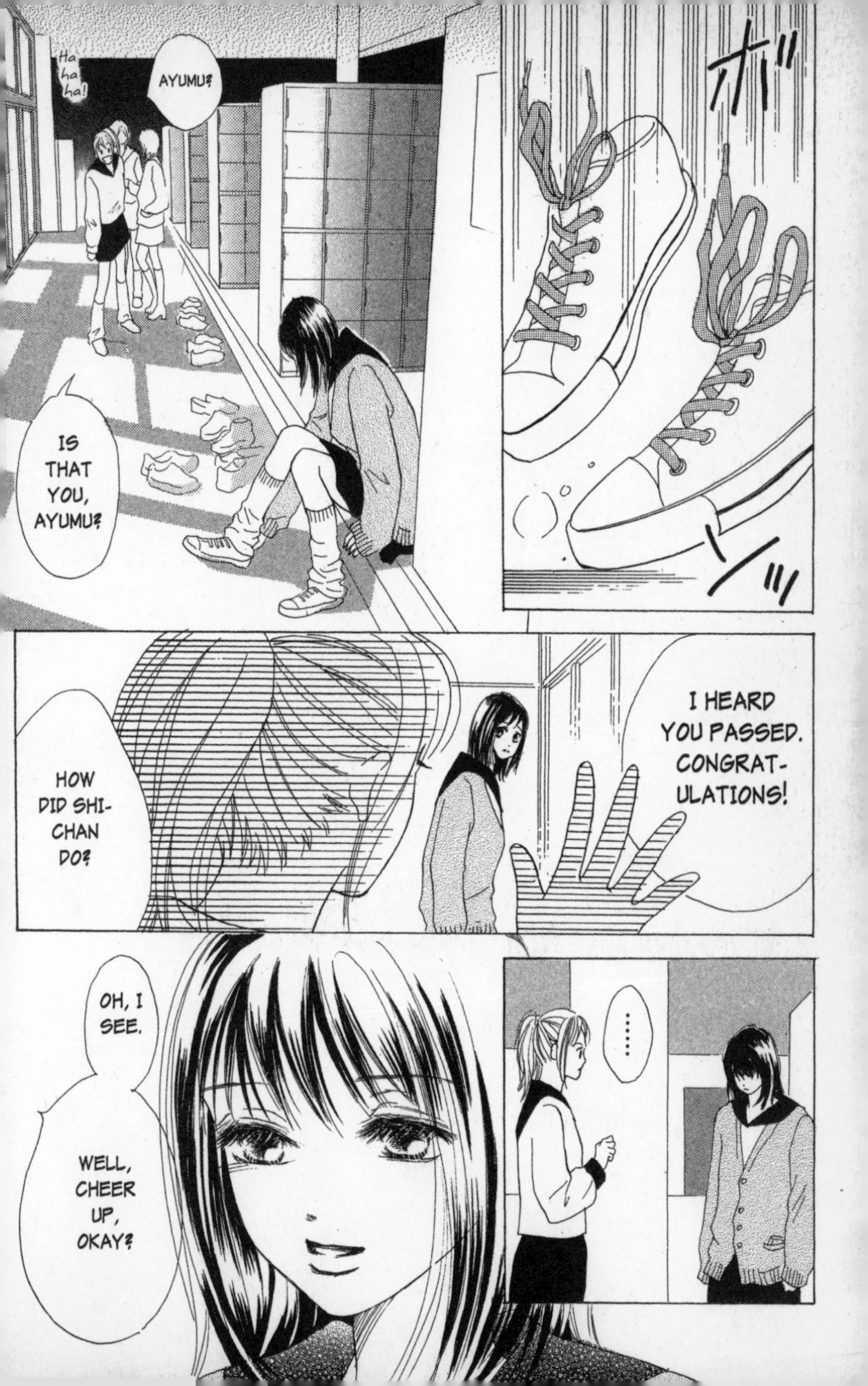
AYUMU?
Ha ha ha!
IS THAT YOU, AYUMU?
I HEARD YOU PASSED. CONGRAT-ULATIONS!
HOW DID SHI-CHAN DO?
......
OH, I SEE.
WELL, CHEER UP, OKAY?

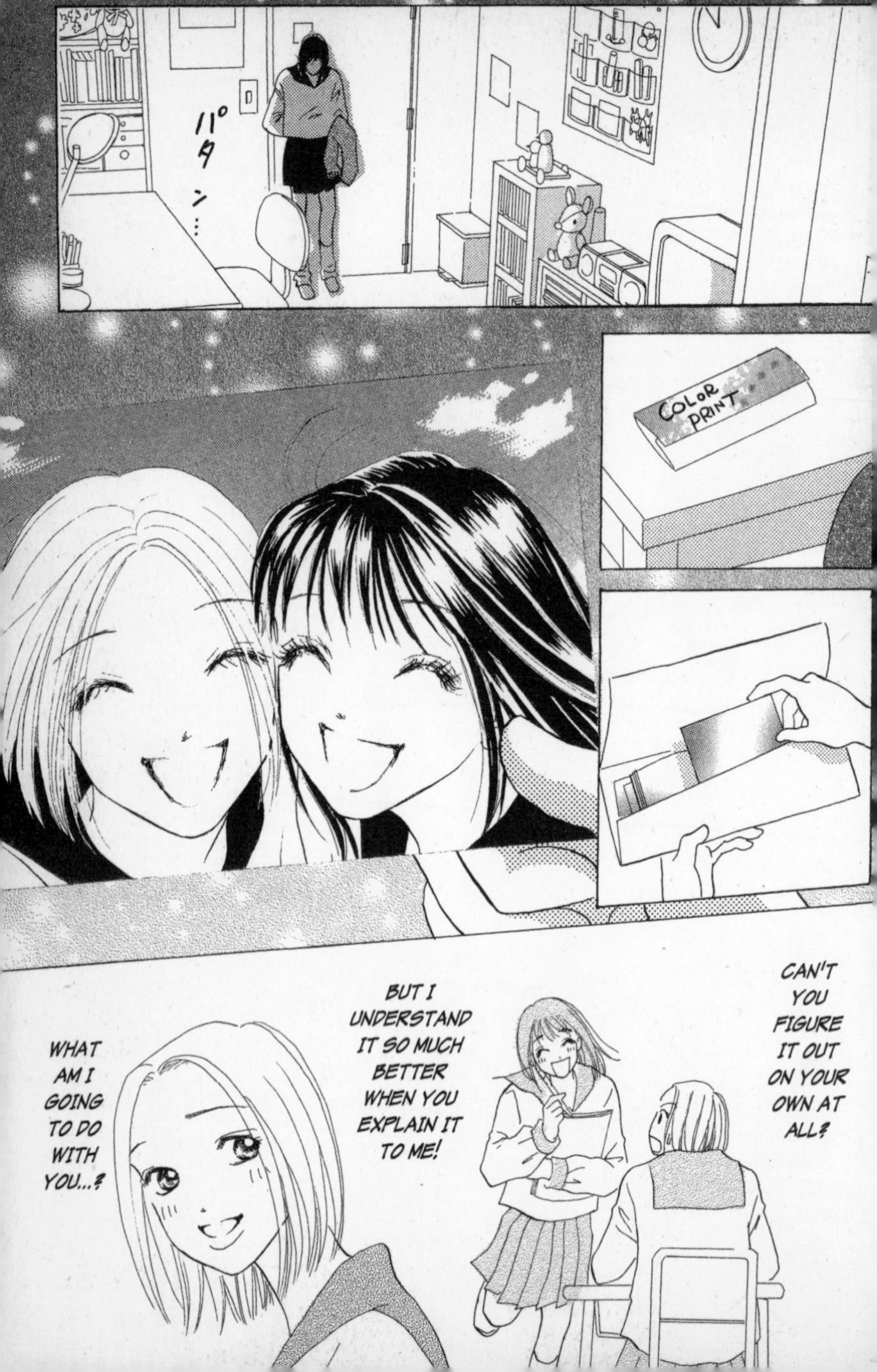
パタン…
COLOR PRINT
CAN'T YOU FIGURE IT OUT ON YOUR OWN AT ALL?
BUT I UNDERSTAND IT SO MUCH BETTER WHEN YOU EXPLAIN IT TO ME!
WHAT AM I GOING TO DO WITH YOU...?

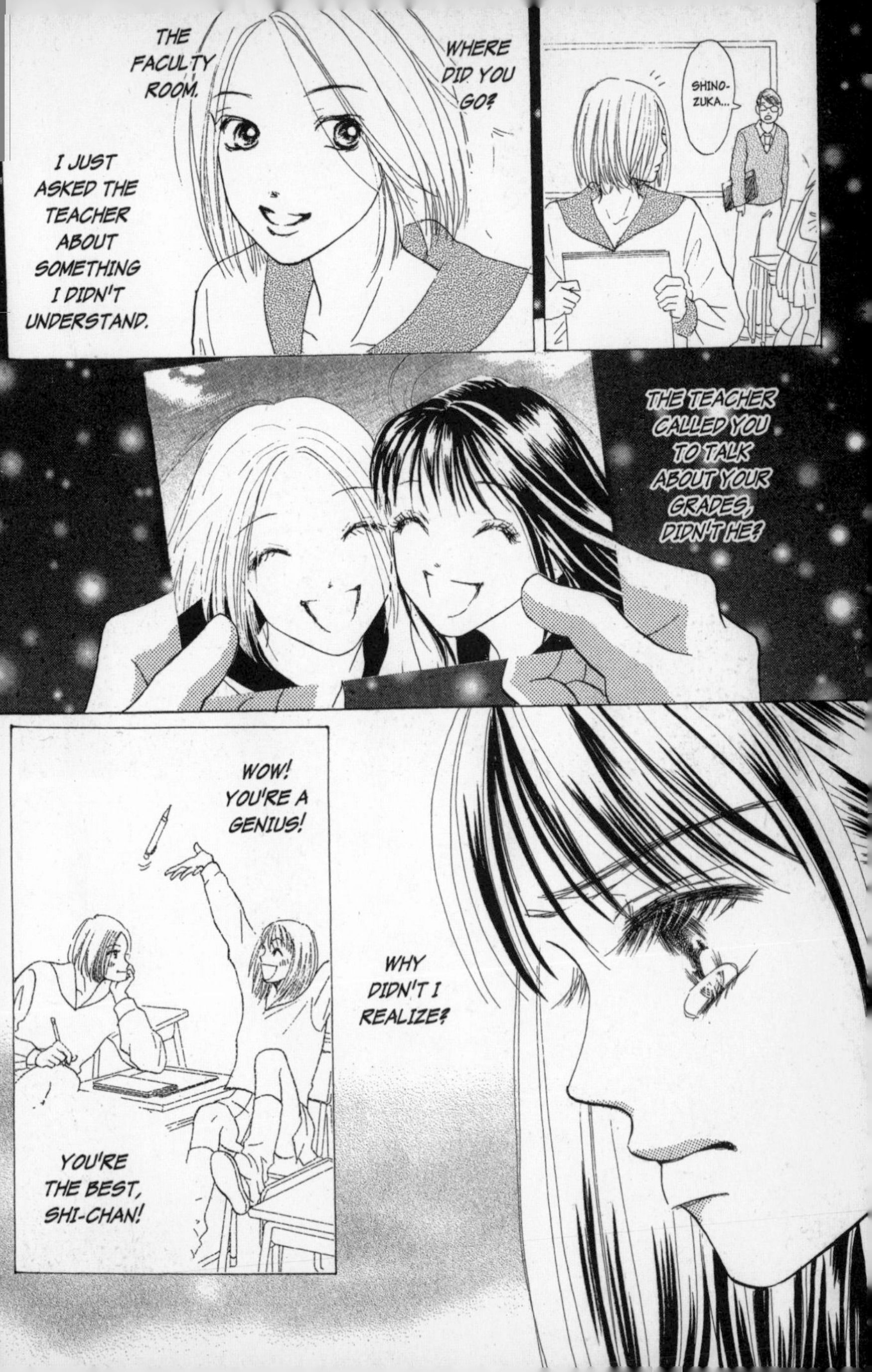
SHINO-ZUKA...
WHERE DID YOU GO?
THE FACULTY ROOM.
I JUST ASKED THE TEACHER ABOUT SOMETHING I DIDN'T UNDERSTAND.
THE TEACHER CALLED YOU TO TALK ABOUT YOUR GRADES, DIDN'T HE?
WHY DIDN'T I REALIZE?
WOW! YOU'RE A GENIUS!
YOU'RE THE BEST, SHI-CHAN!

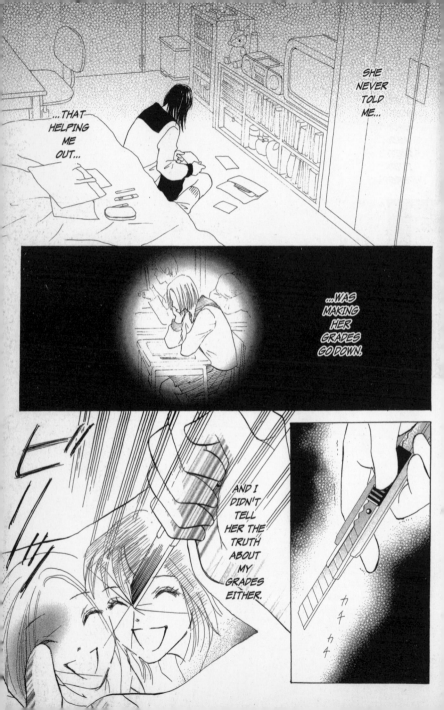

SHE NEVER TOLD ME...

...THAT HELPING ME OUT...

...WAS MAKING HER GRADES GO DOWN.

AND I DIDN'T TELL HER THE TRUTH ABOUT MY GRADES EITHER.

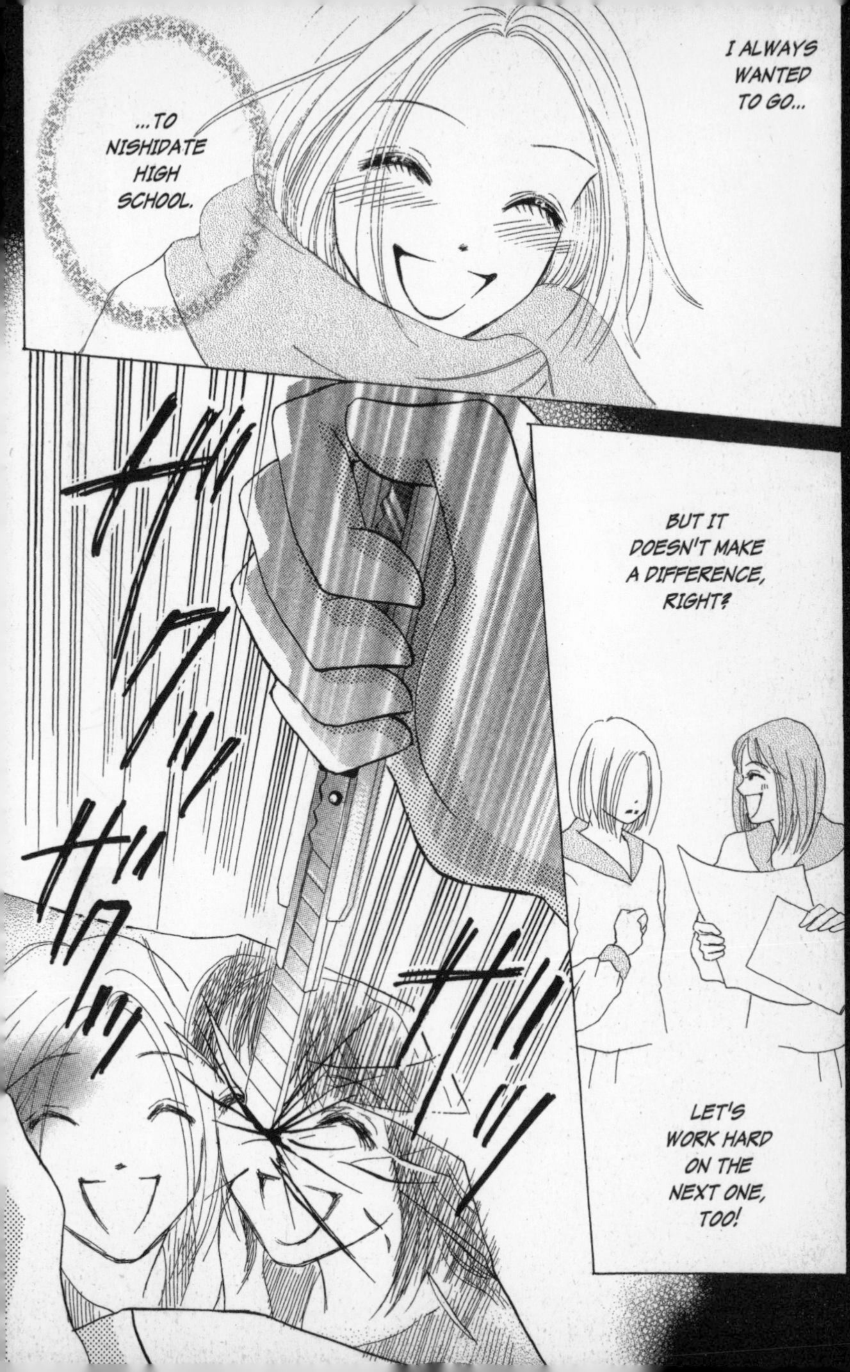
I ALWAYS WANTED TO GO...
...TO NISHIDATE HIGH SCHOOL.
BUT IT DOESN'T MAKE A DIFFERENCE, RIGHT?
LET'S WORK HARD ON THE NEXT ONE, TOO!

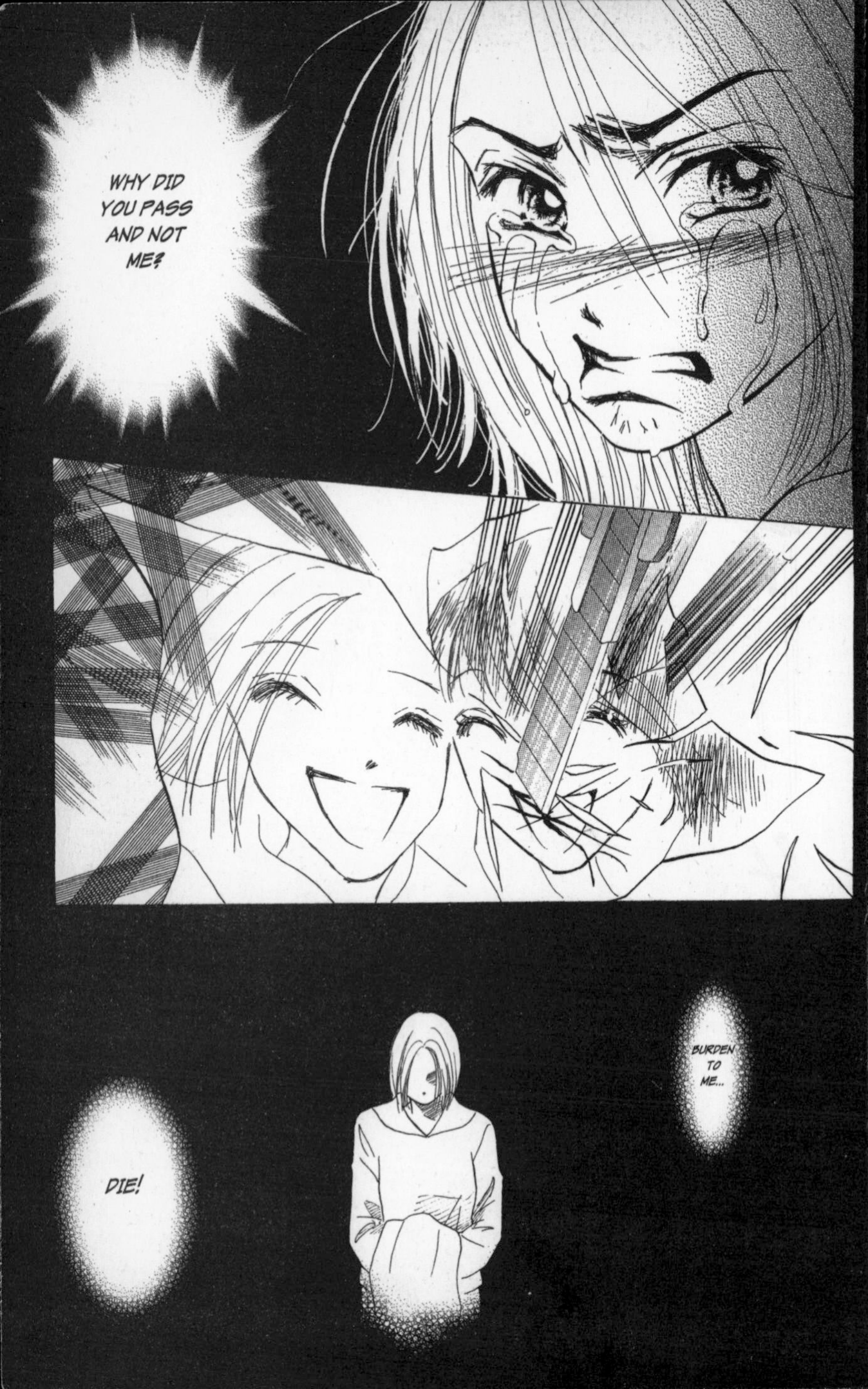
WHY DID YOU PASS AND NOT ME?
BURDEN TO ME...
DIE!

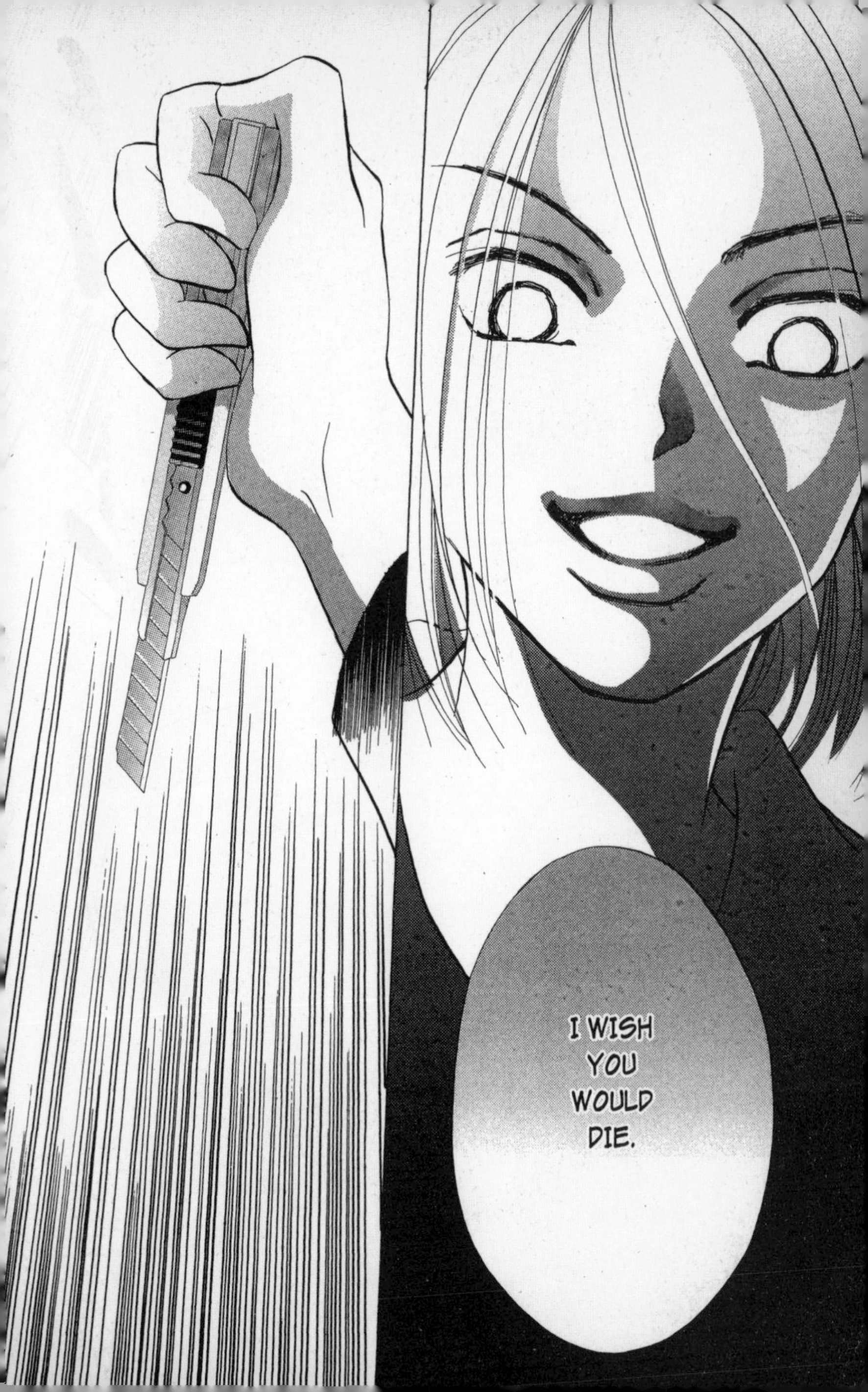
I WISH YOU WOULD DIE.

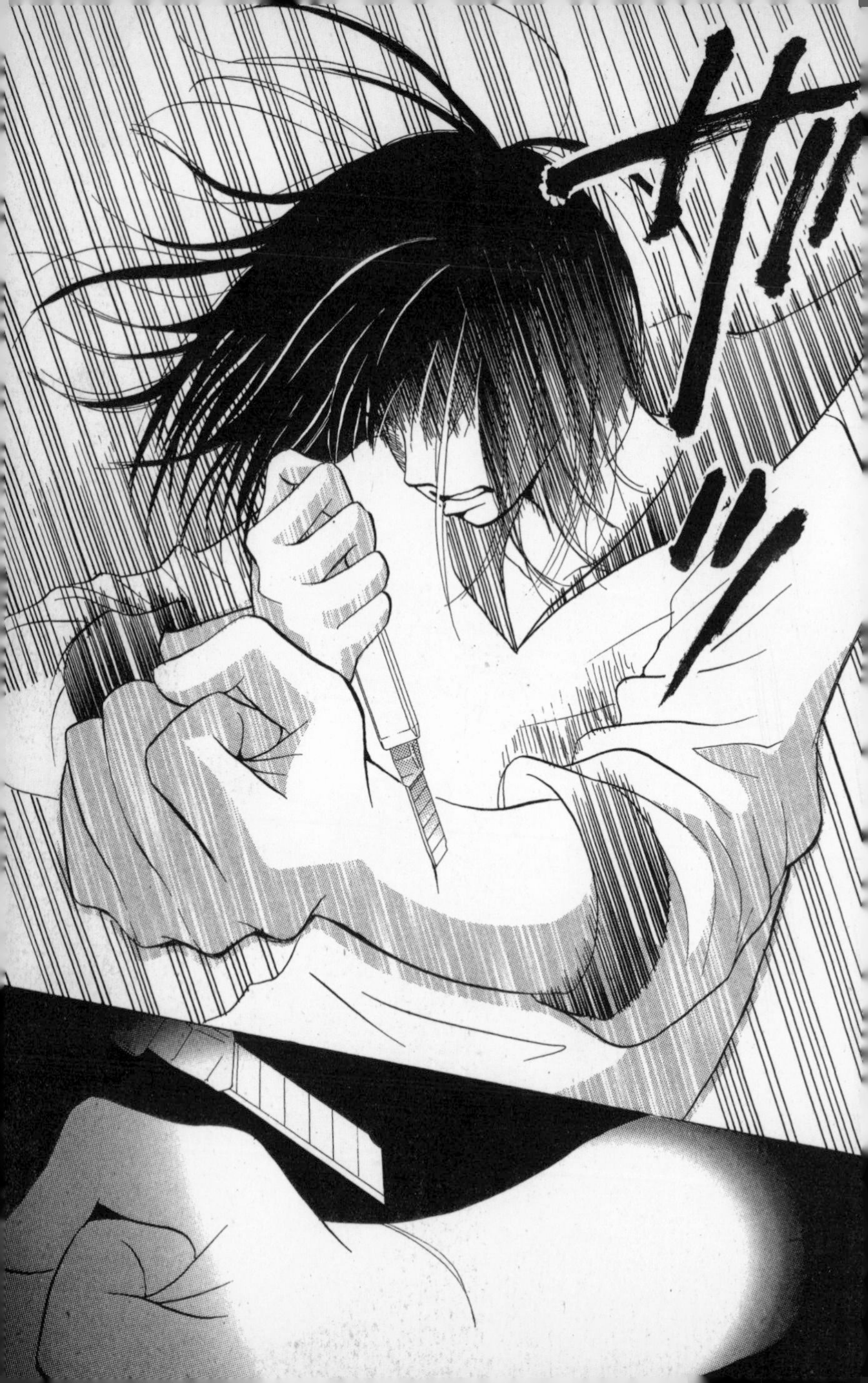

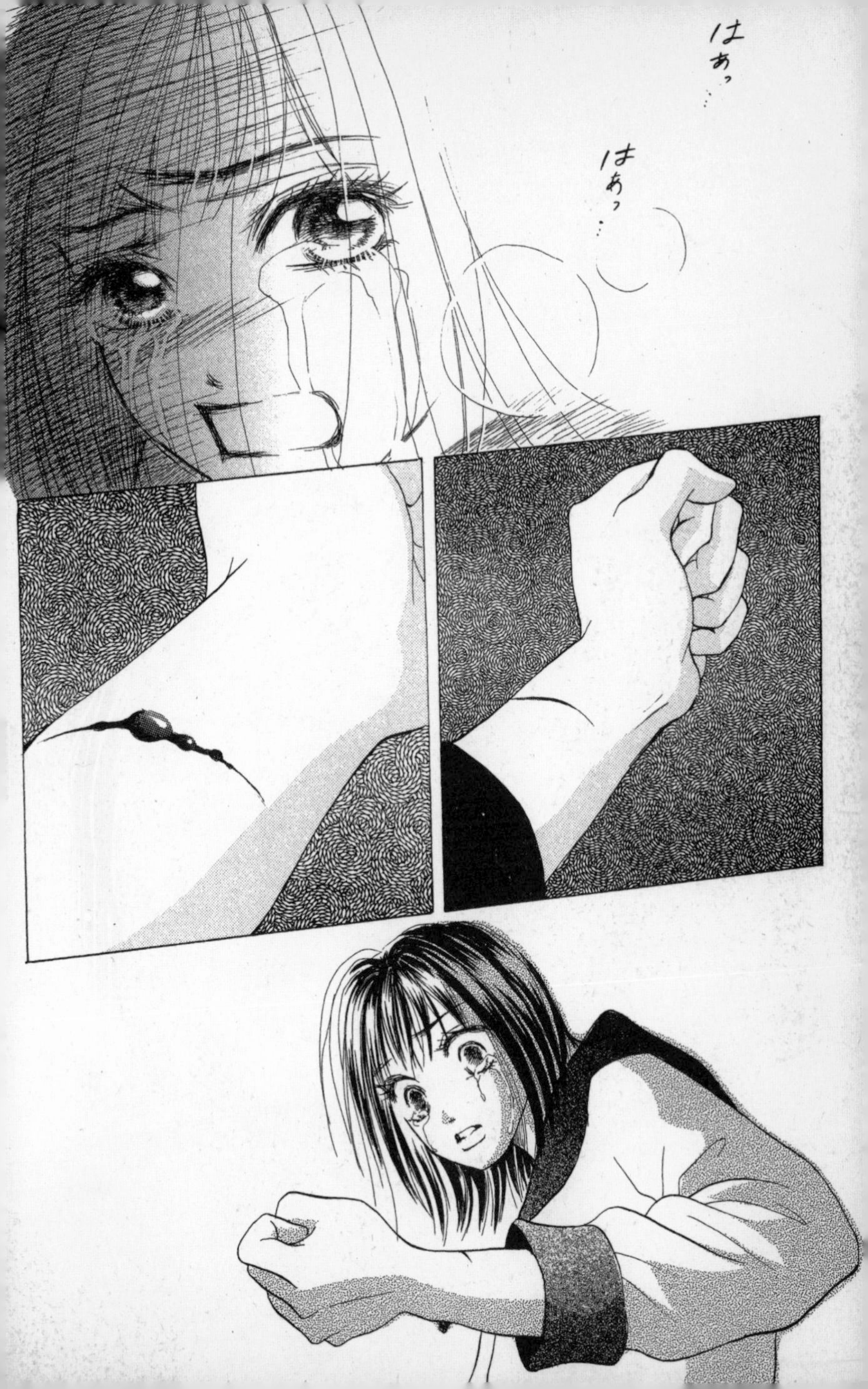
はあっ…
はあっ…

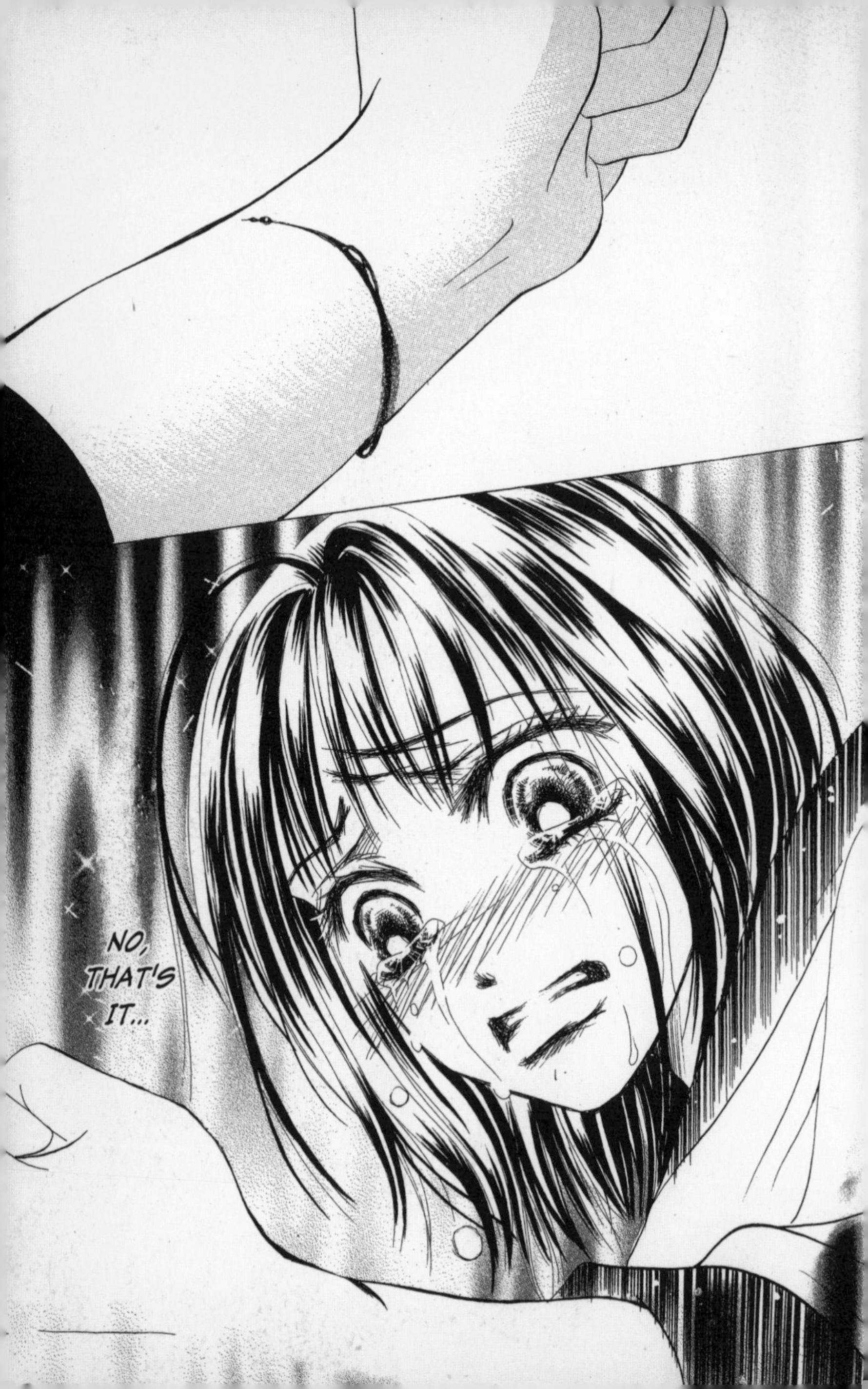
NO, THAT'S IT...

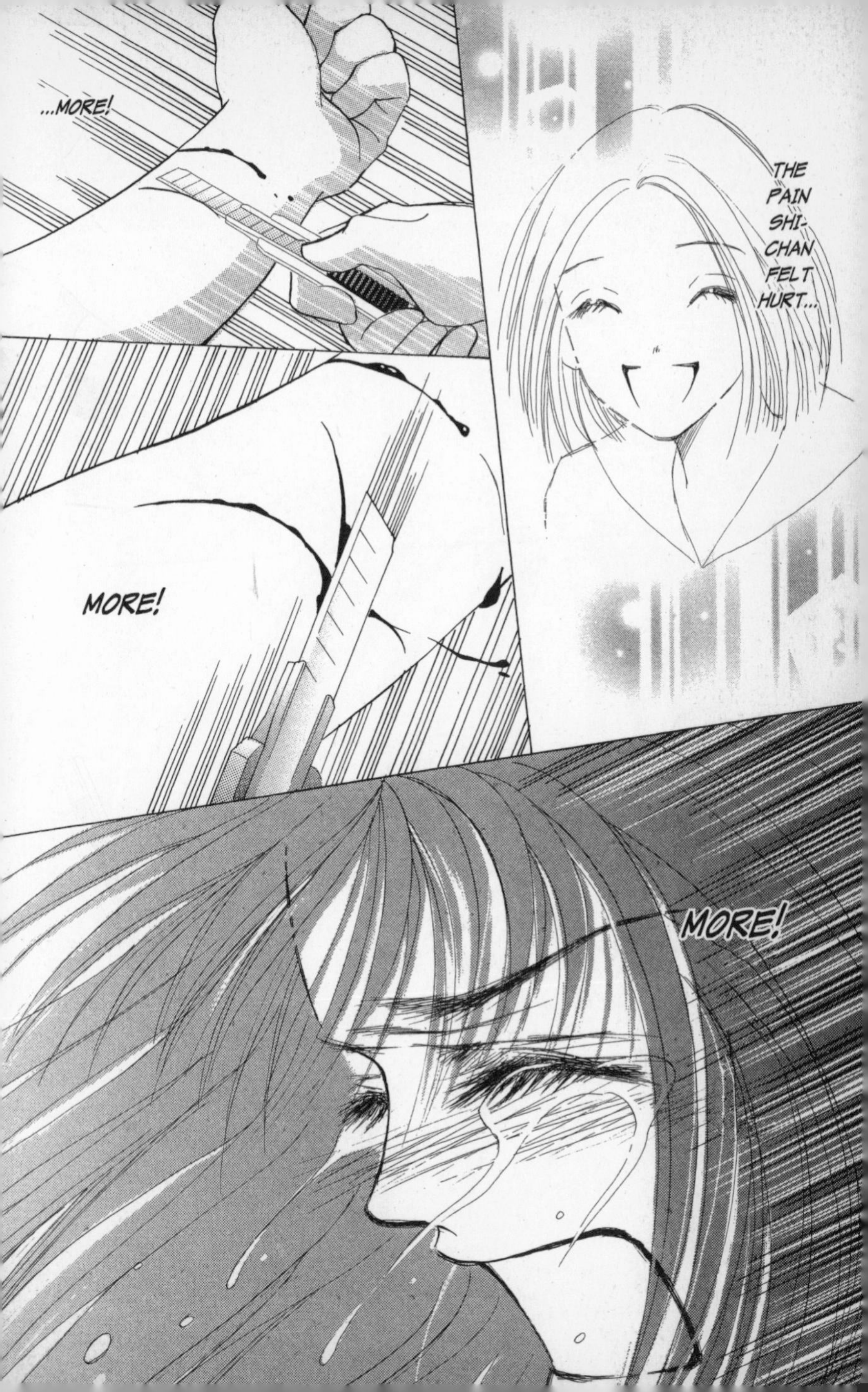
THE PAIN SHI-CHAN FELT HURT...
...MORE!
MORE!
MORE!

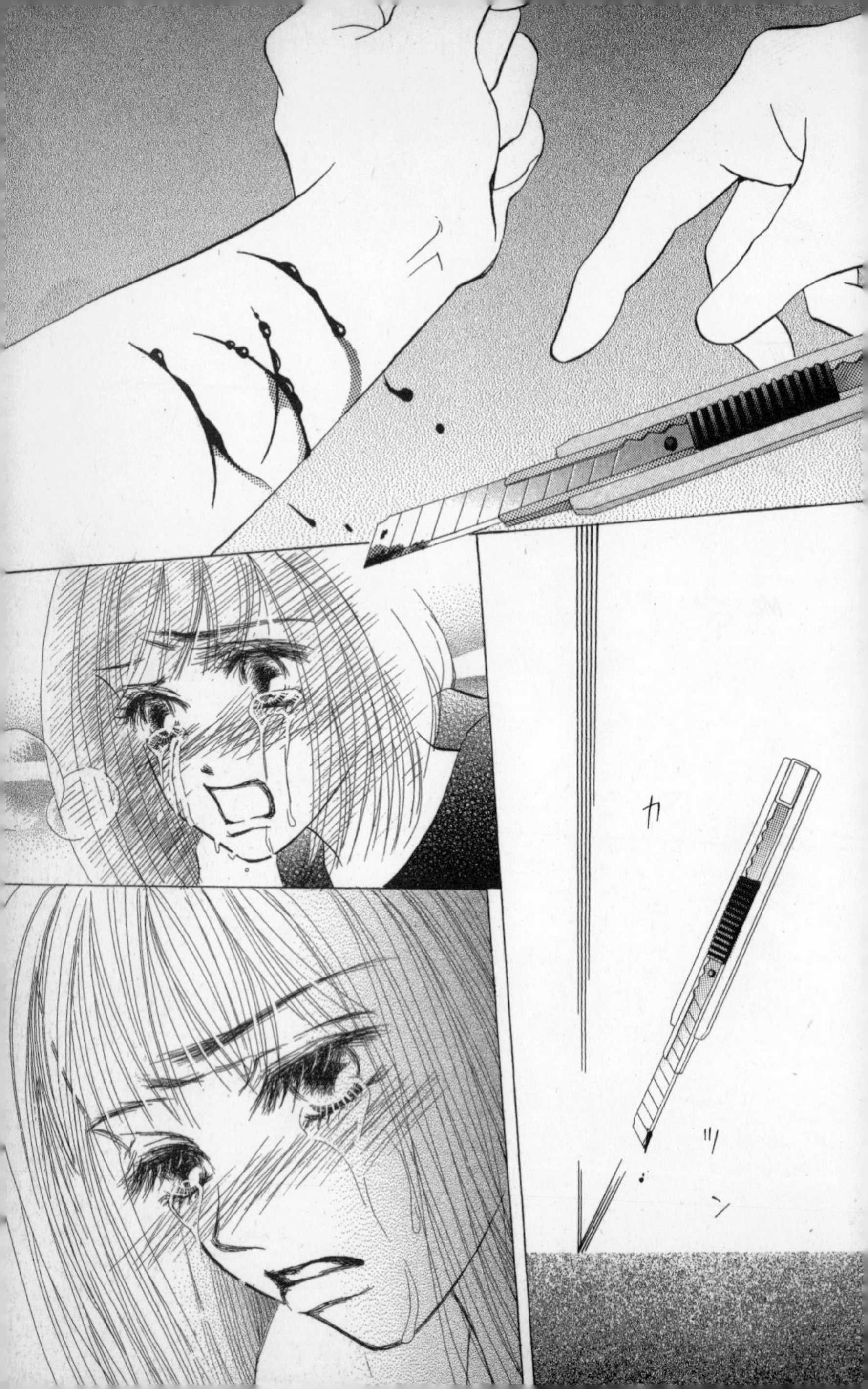
カ
ツ
ン

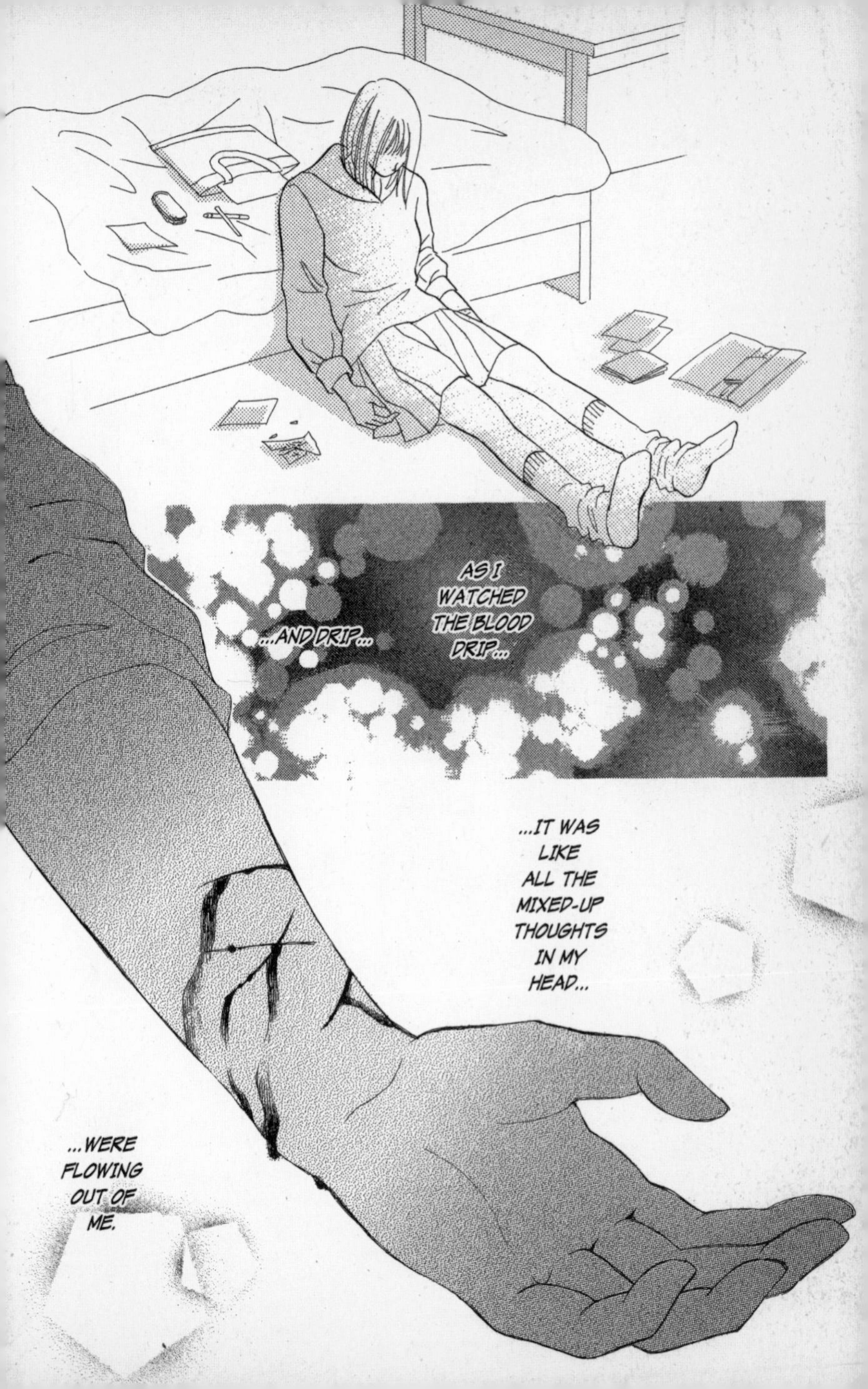
AS I WATCHED THE BLOOD DRIP...
...AND DRIP...
...IT WAS LIKE ALL THE MIXED-UP THOUGHTS IN MY HEAD...
...WERE FLOWING OUT OF ME.

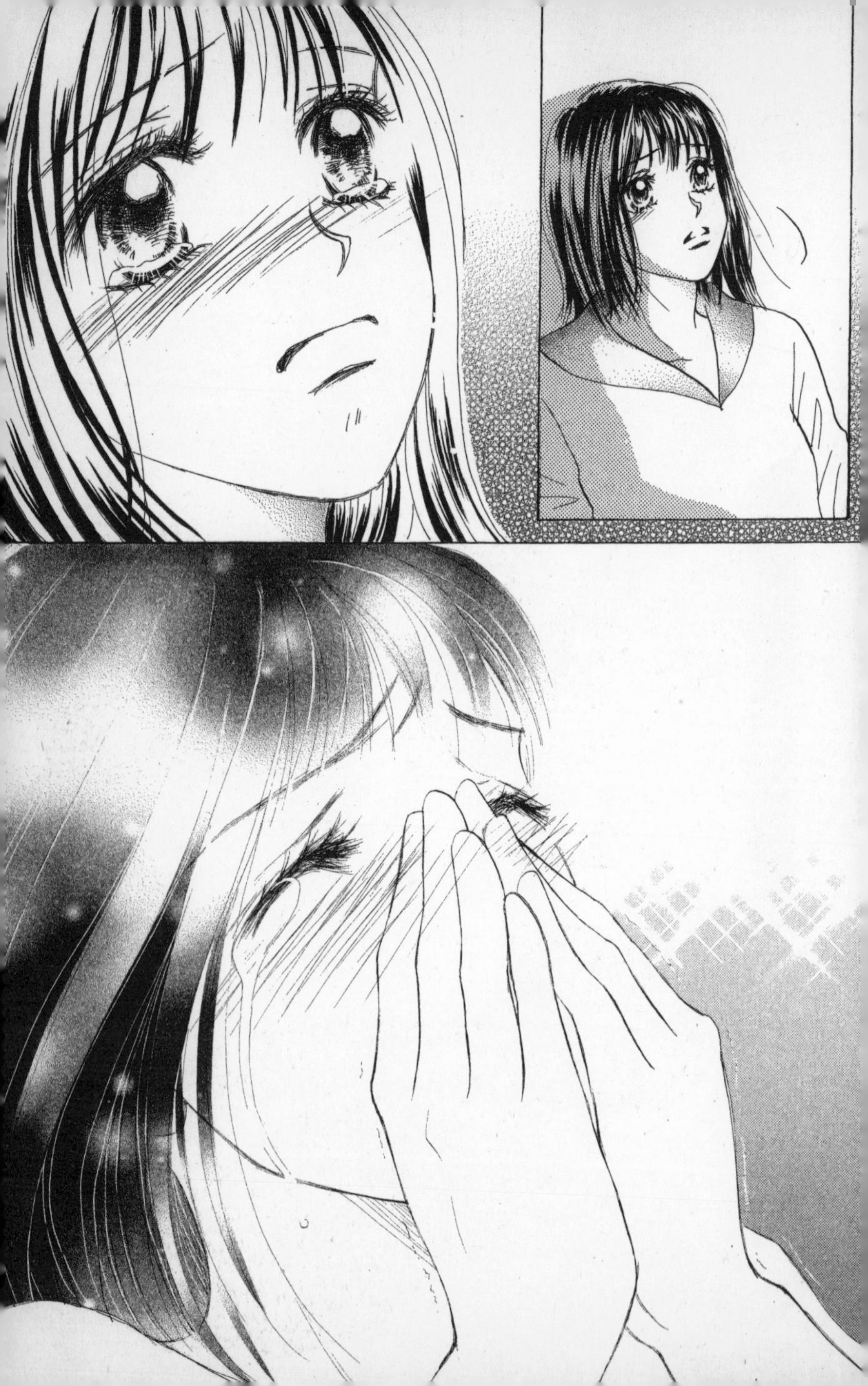

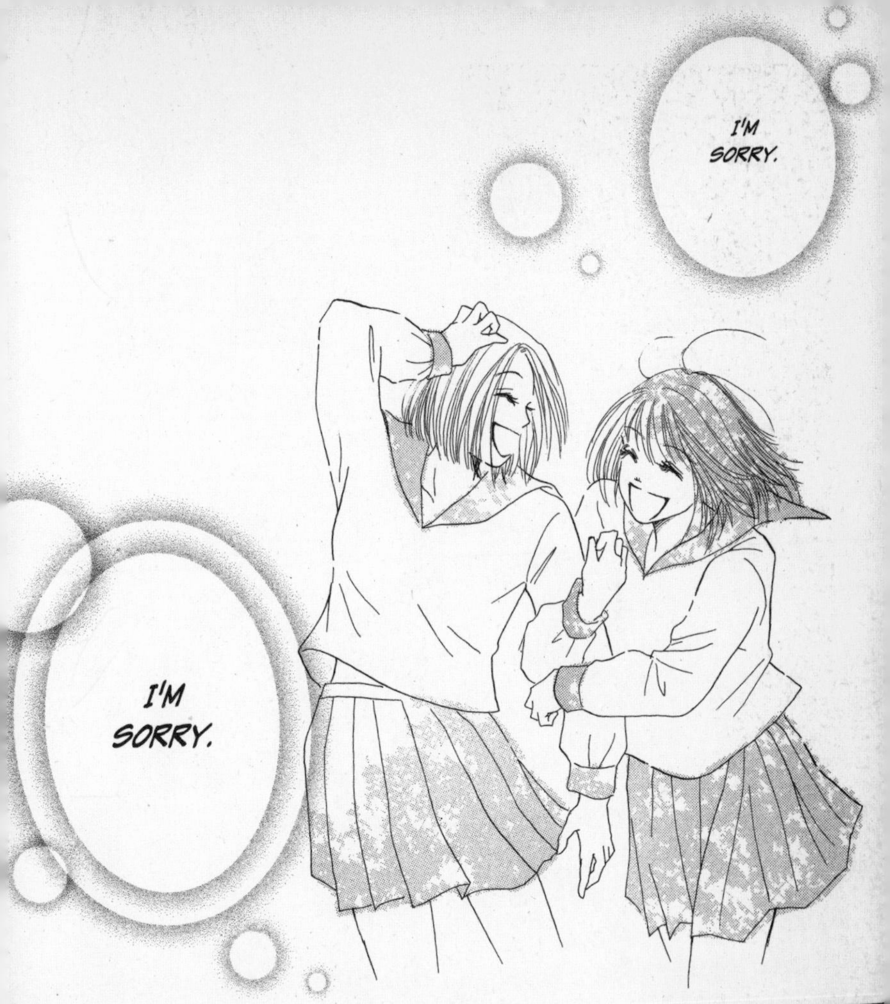
I'M SORRY.
I'M SORRY.

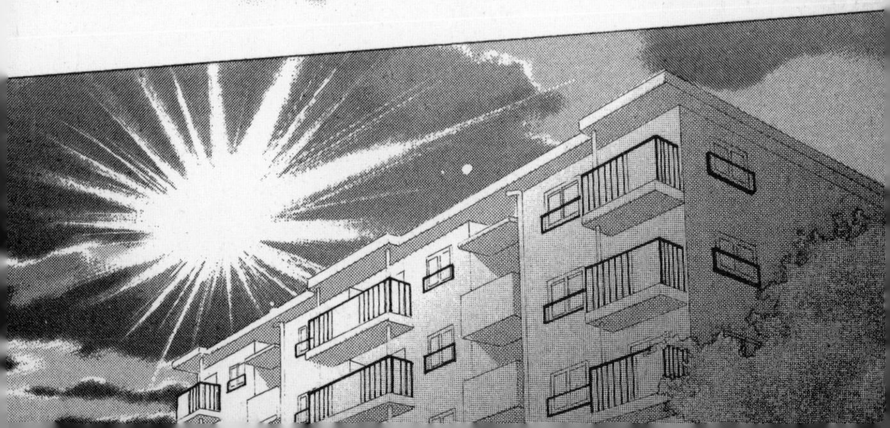

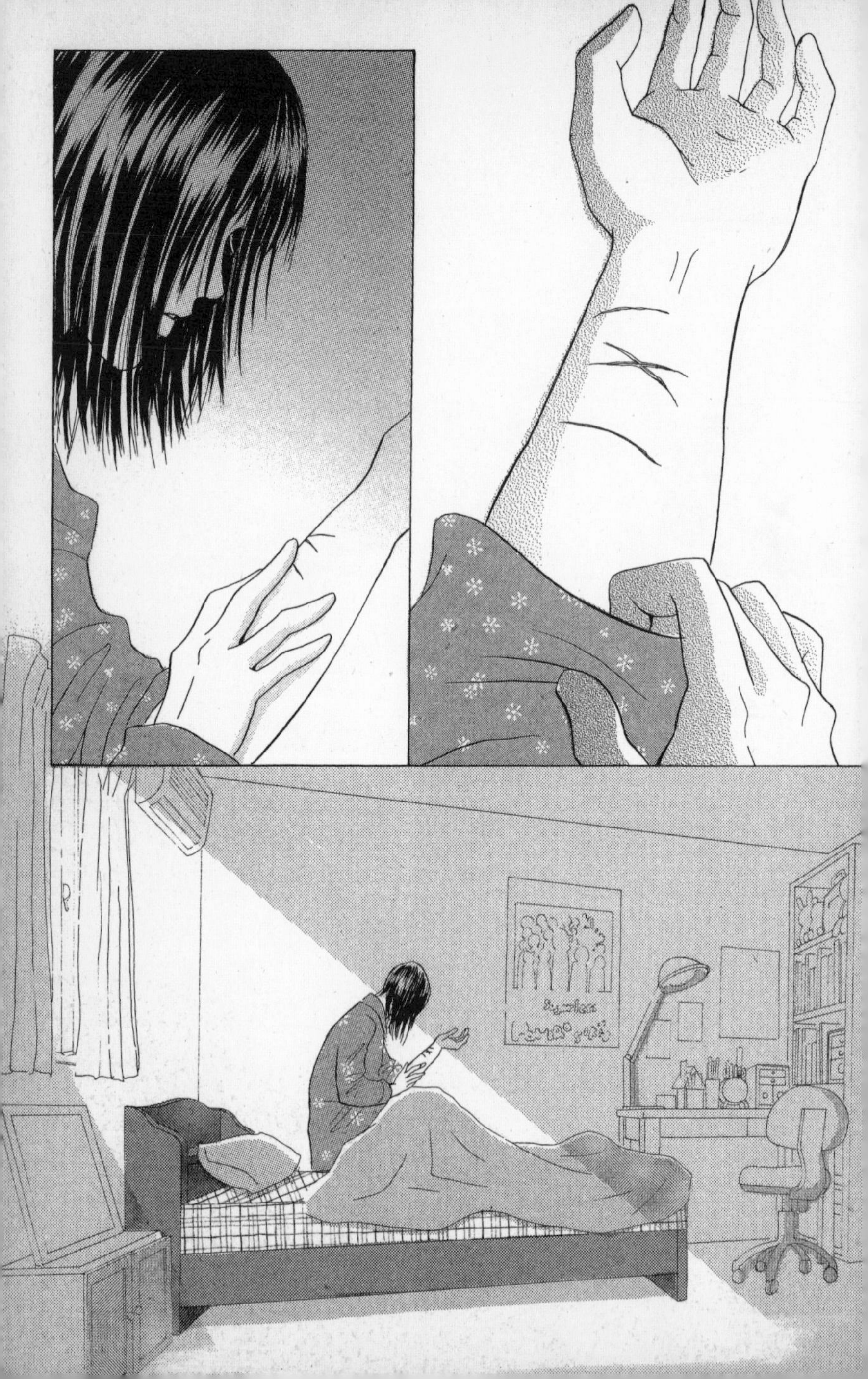

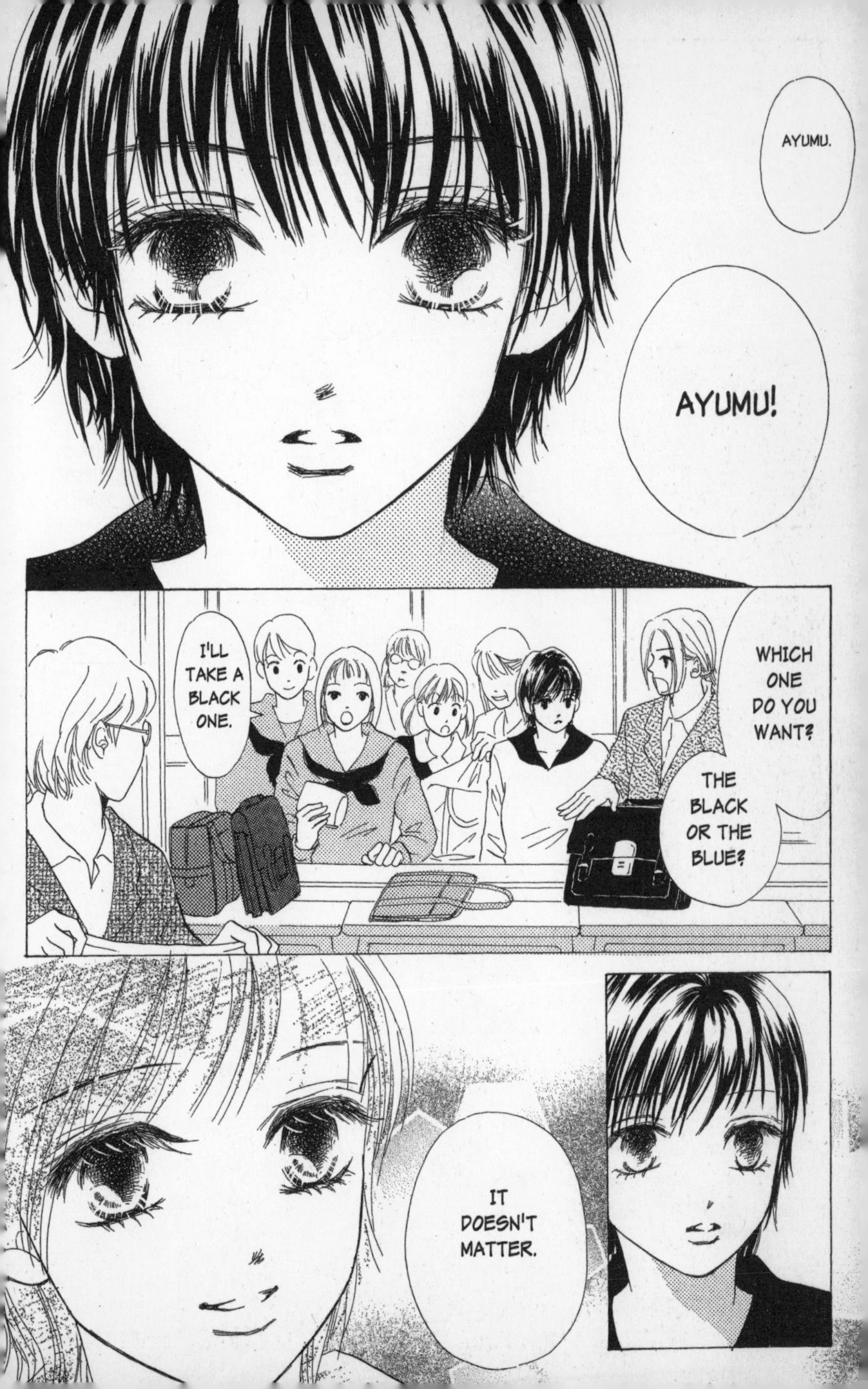
AYUMU.
AYUMU!
WHICH ONE DO YOU WANT?
THE BLACK OR THE BLUE?
I'LL TAKE A BLACK ONE.
IT DOESN'T MATTER.

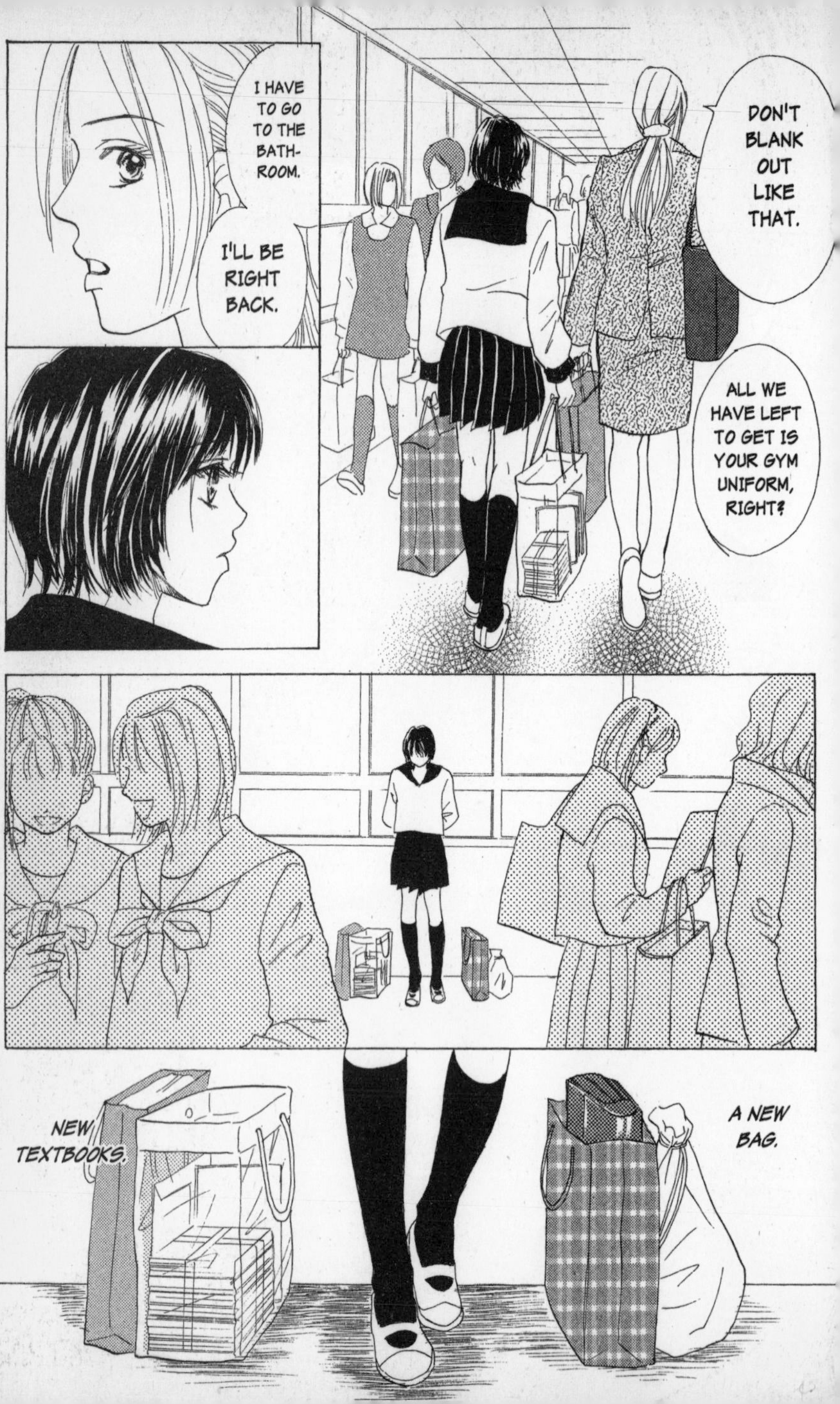
DON'T BLANK OUT LIKE THAT.
ALL WE HAVE LEFT TO GET IS YOUR GYM UNIFORM, RIGHT?
I HAVE TO GO TO THE BATH-ROOM.
I'LL BE RIGHT BACK.
A NEW BAG.
NEW TEXTBOOKS.

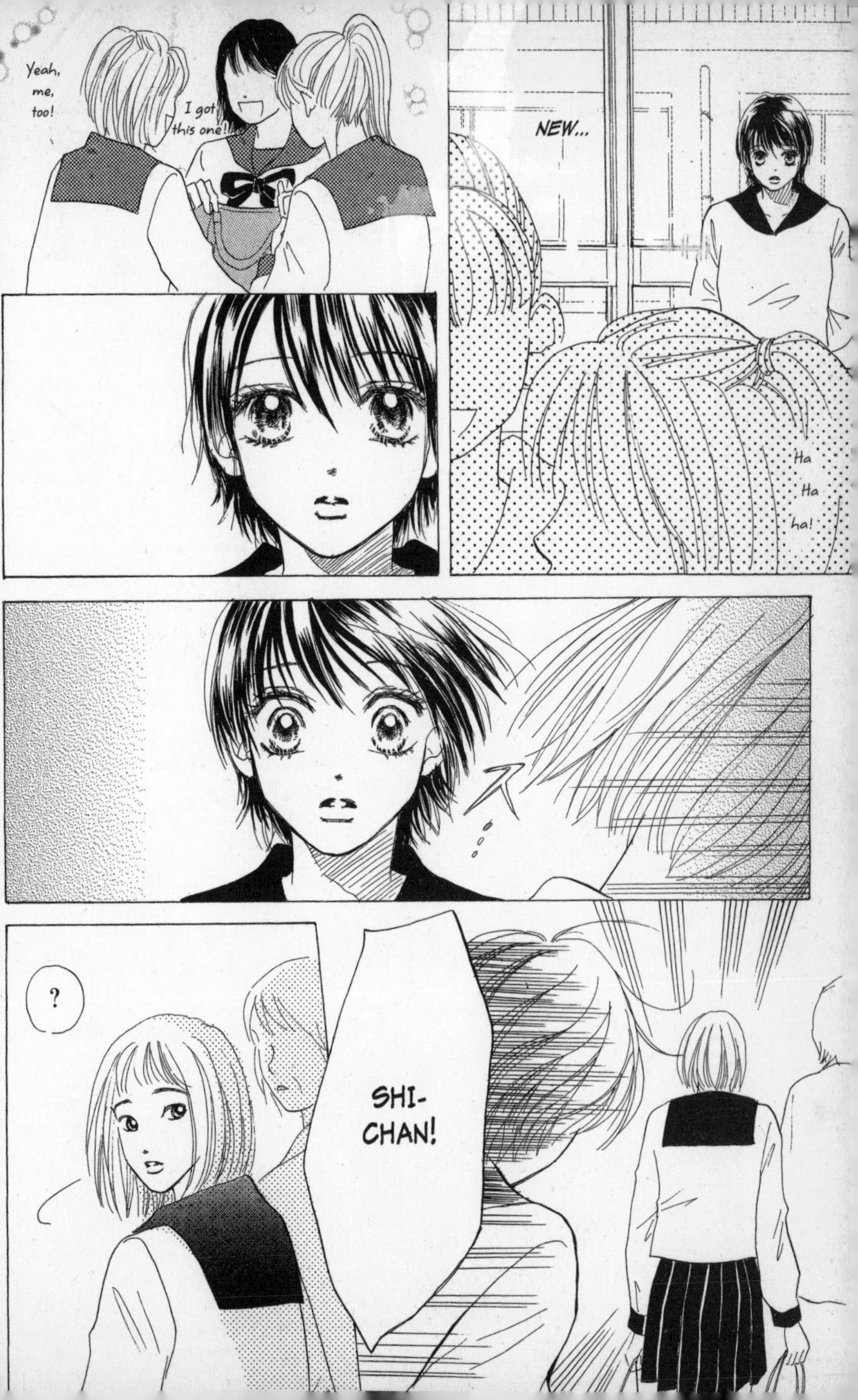
NEW...
Yeah, me, too!
I got this one!
Ha Ha ha!
SHI-CHAN!
?

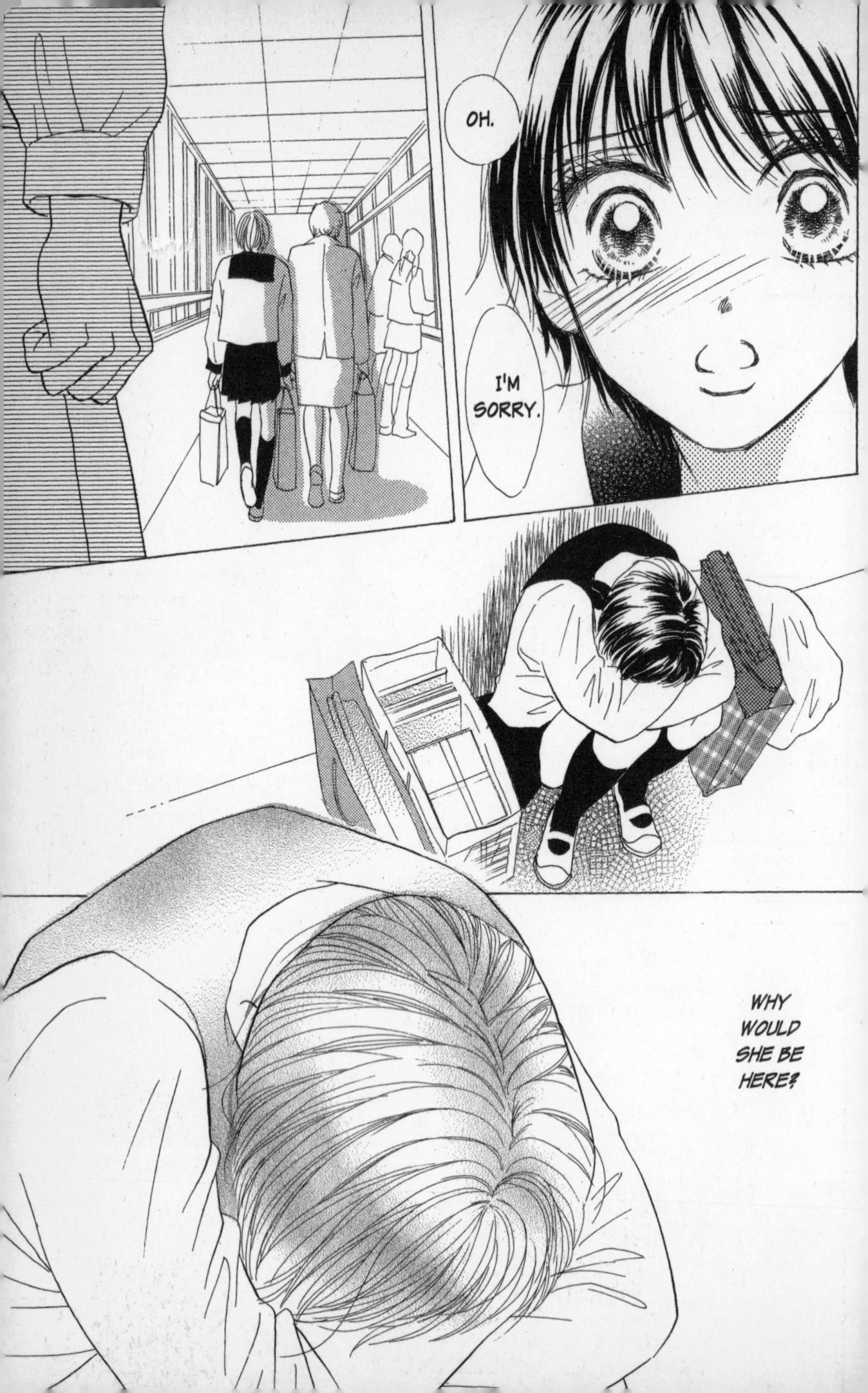
OH.
I'M SORRY.
WHY WOULD SHE BE HERE?

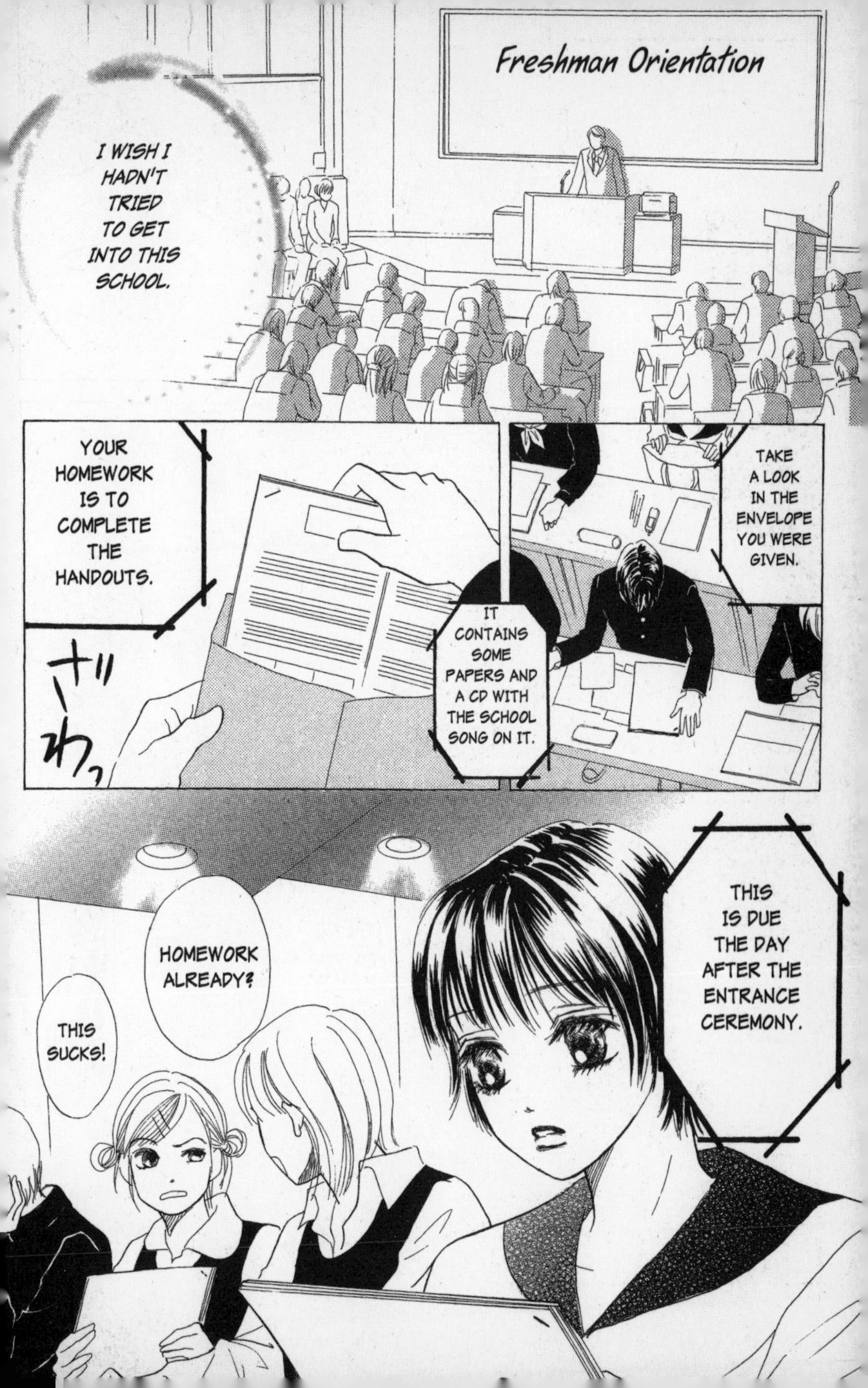
Freshman Orientation
I WISH I HADN'T TRIED TO GET INTO THIS SCHOOL.
TAKE A LOOK IN THE ENVELOPE YOU WERE GIVEN.
IT CONTAINS SOME PAPERS AND A CD WITH THE SCHOOL SONG ON IT.
YOUR HOMEWORK IS TO COMPLETE THE HANDOUTS.
サッ
わっ
THIS IS DUE THE DAY AFTER THE ENTRANCE CEREMONY.
HOMEWORK ALREADY?
THIS SUCKS!

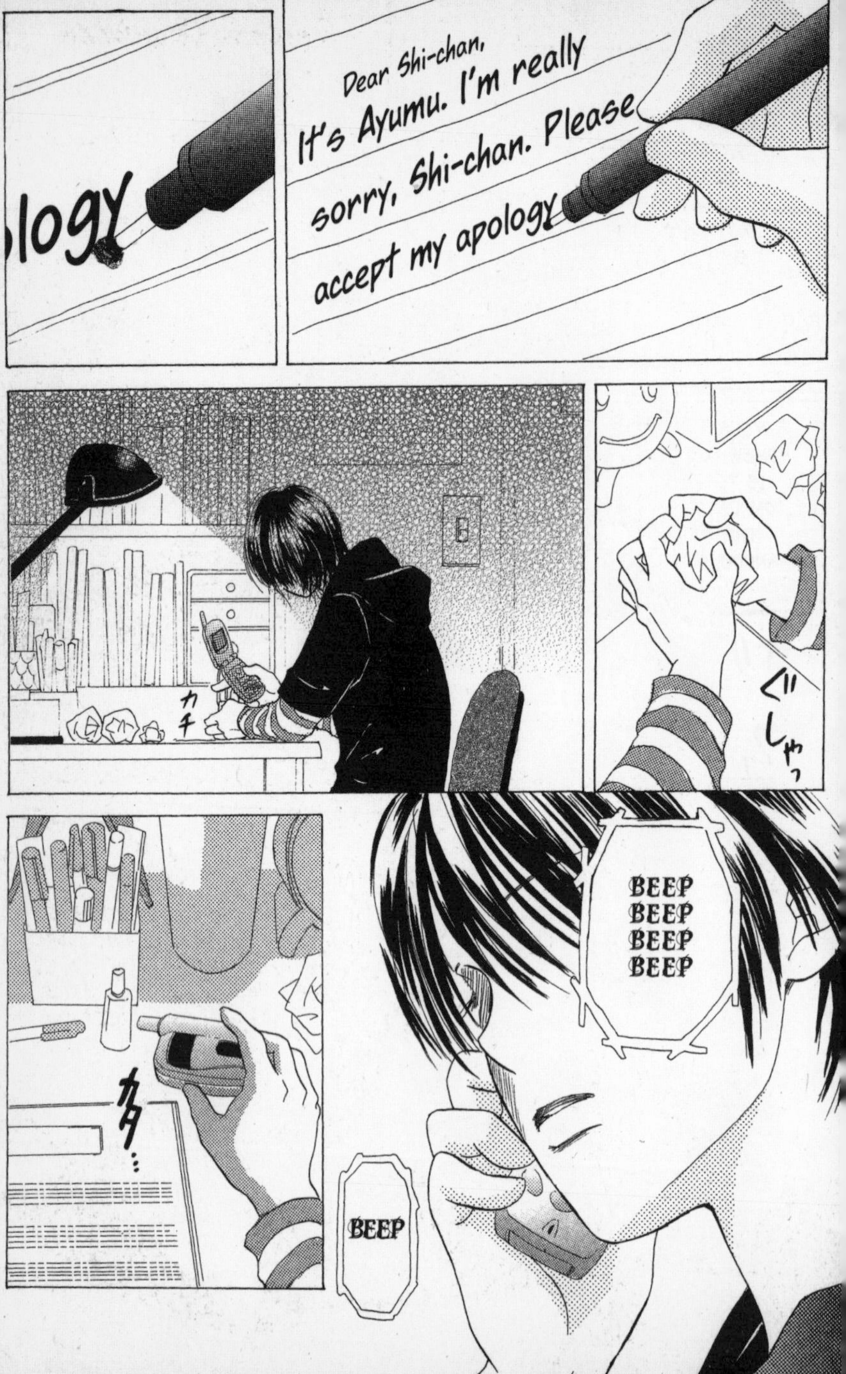
Dear Shi-chan,
It's Ayumu. I'm really sorry, Shi-chan. Please accept my apology
logy
ぐしゃっ
カチ
BEEP BEEP BEEP BEEP
BEEP
カタ…

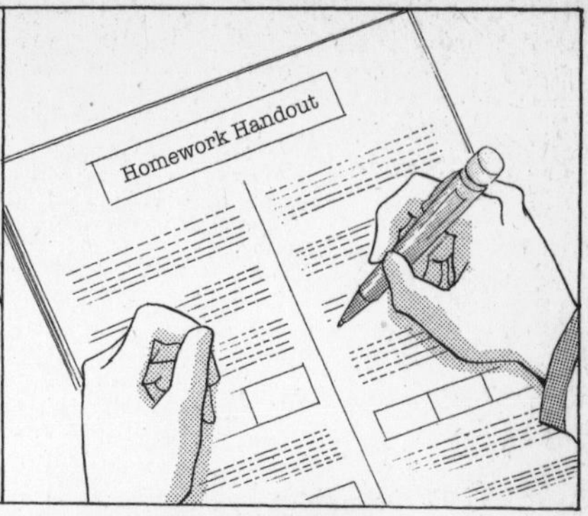
Homework Handout
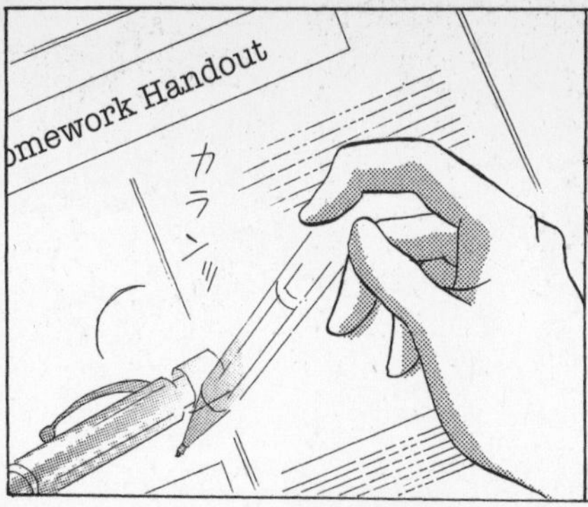
omework Handout
カランッ
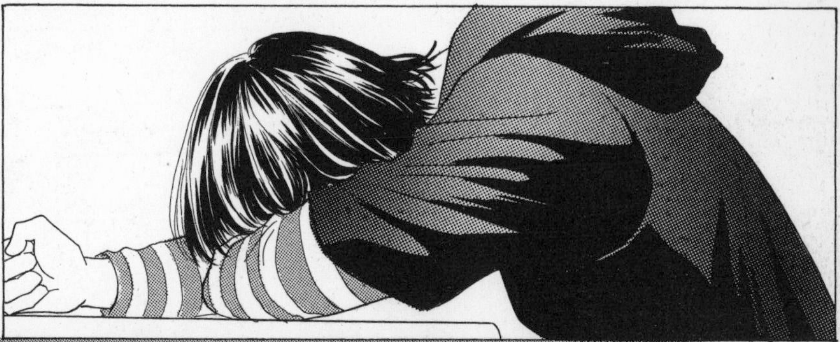
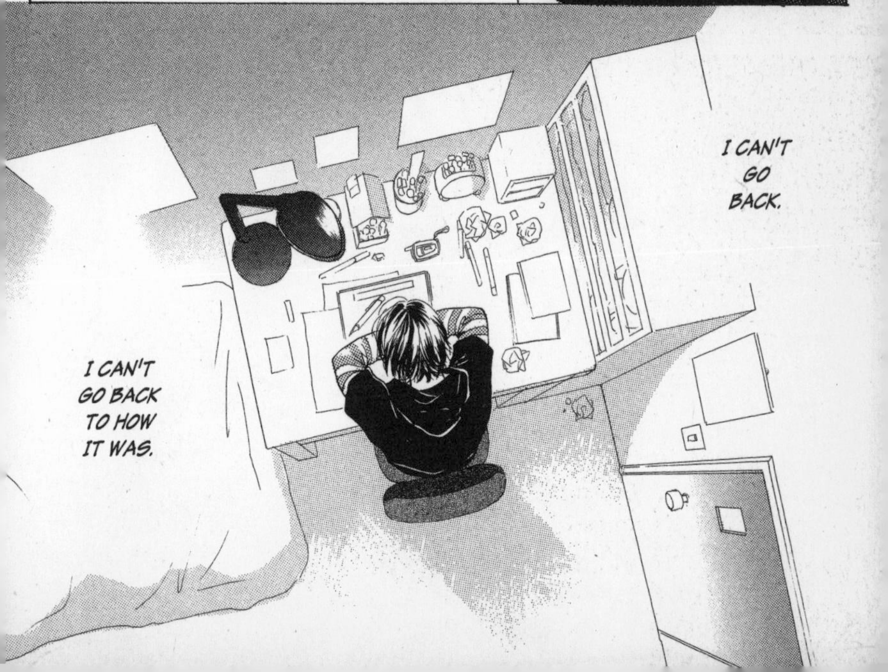
I CAN'T GO BACK.
I CAN'T GO BACK TO HOW IT WAS.

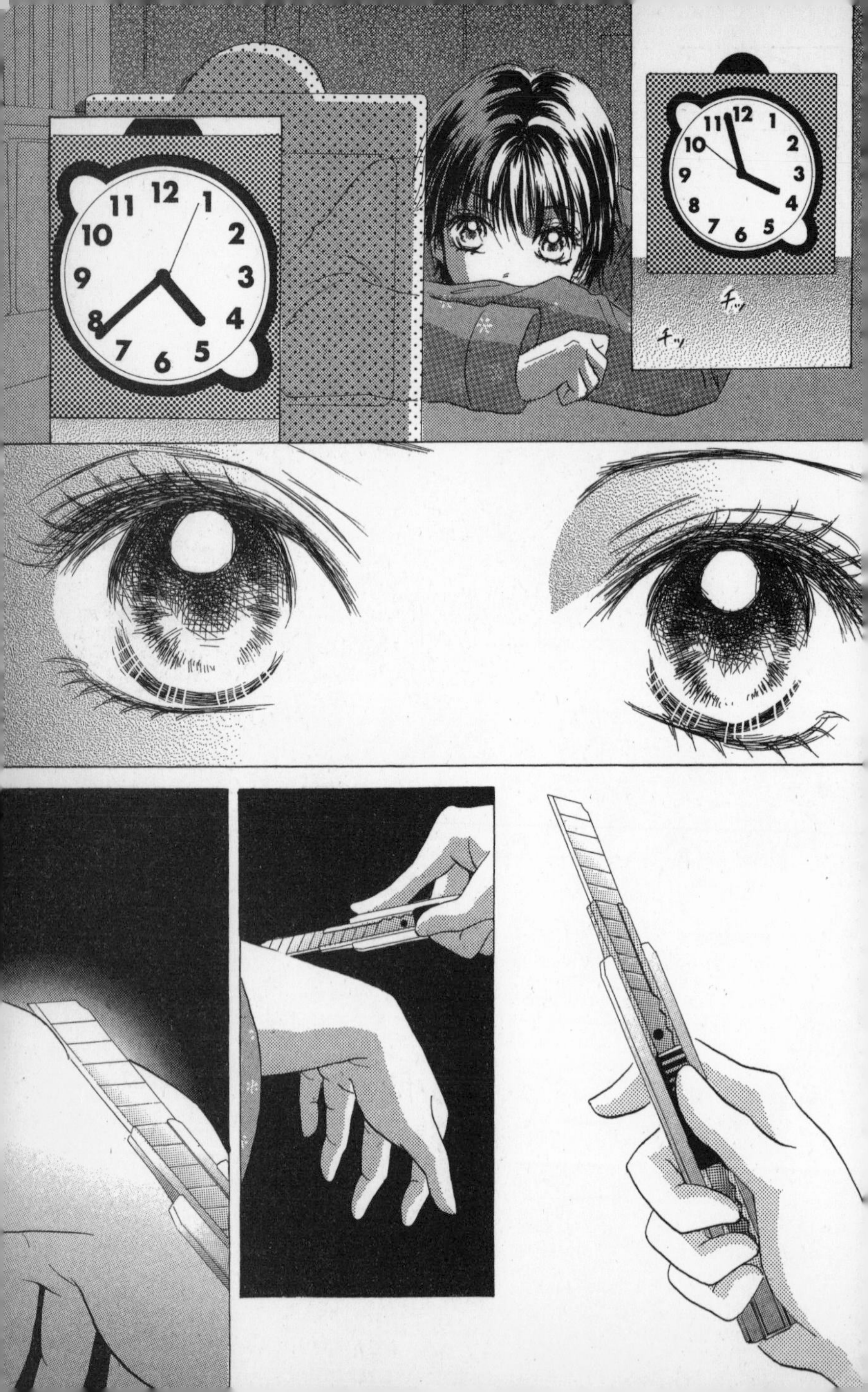
チッ
チッ

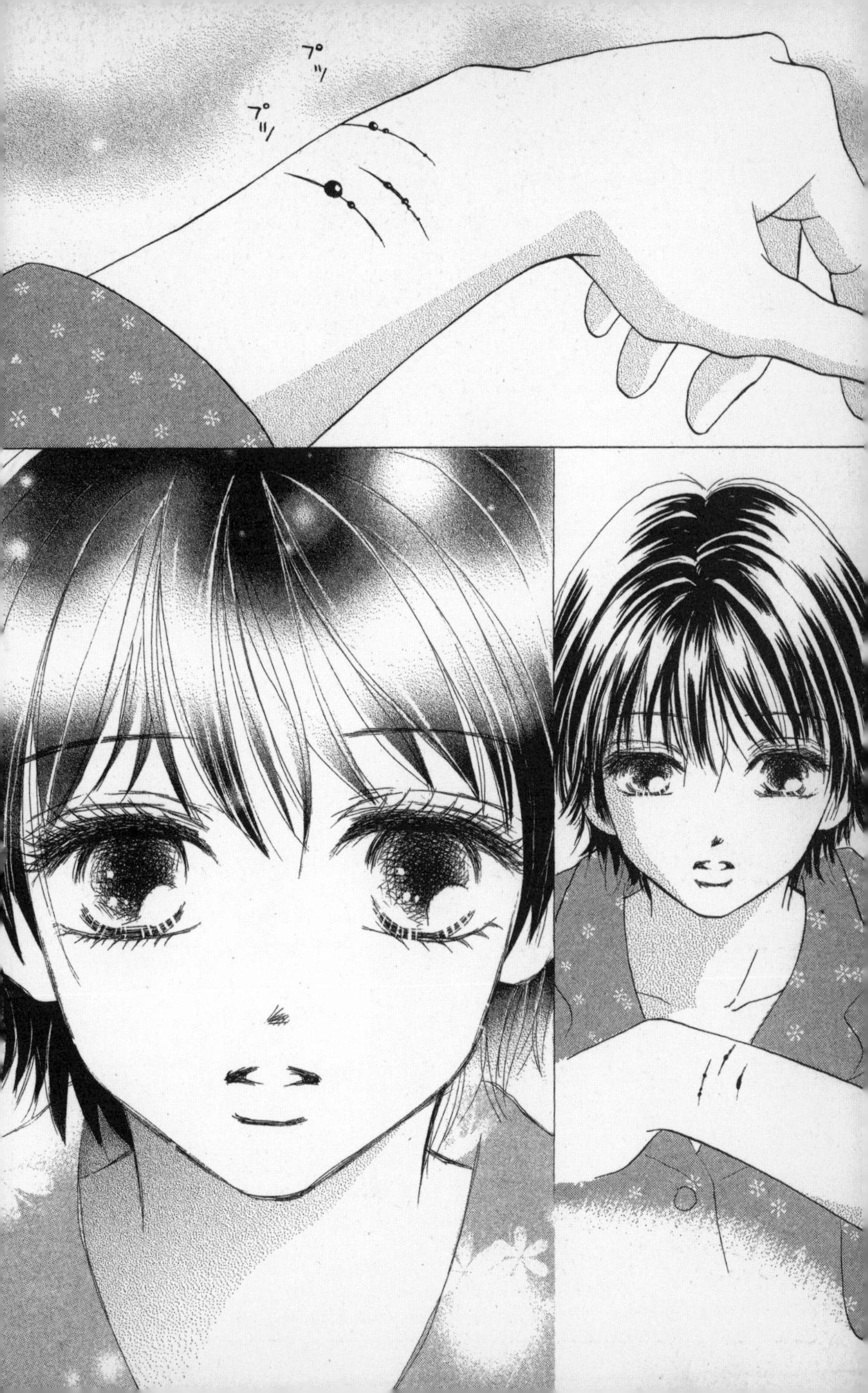
プツ
プツ

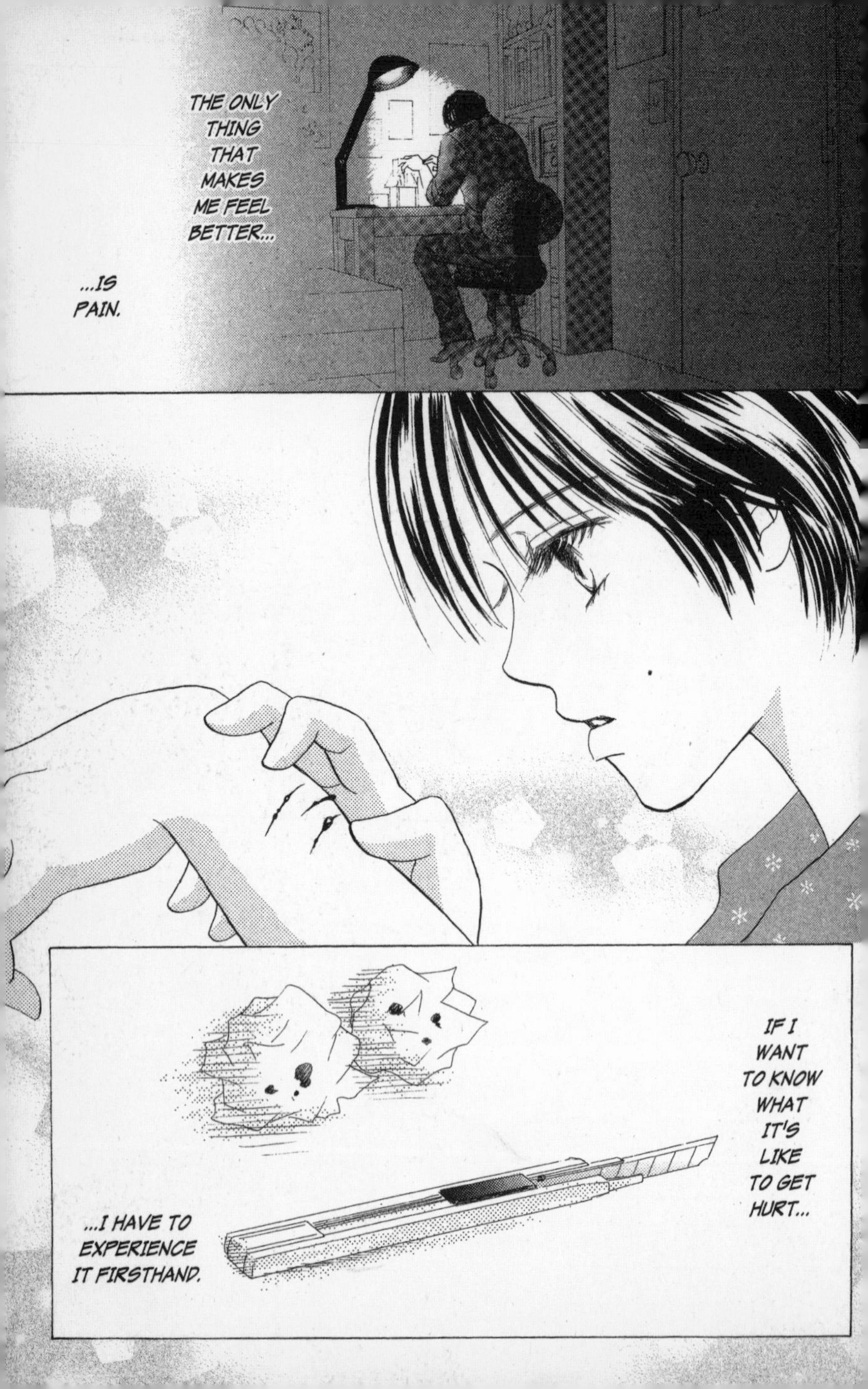
THE ONLY THING THAT MAKES ME FEEL BETTER...
...IS PAIN.
IF I WANT TO KNOW WHAT IT'S LIKE TO GET HURT...
...I HAVE TO EXPERIENCE IT FIRSTHAND.

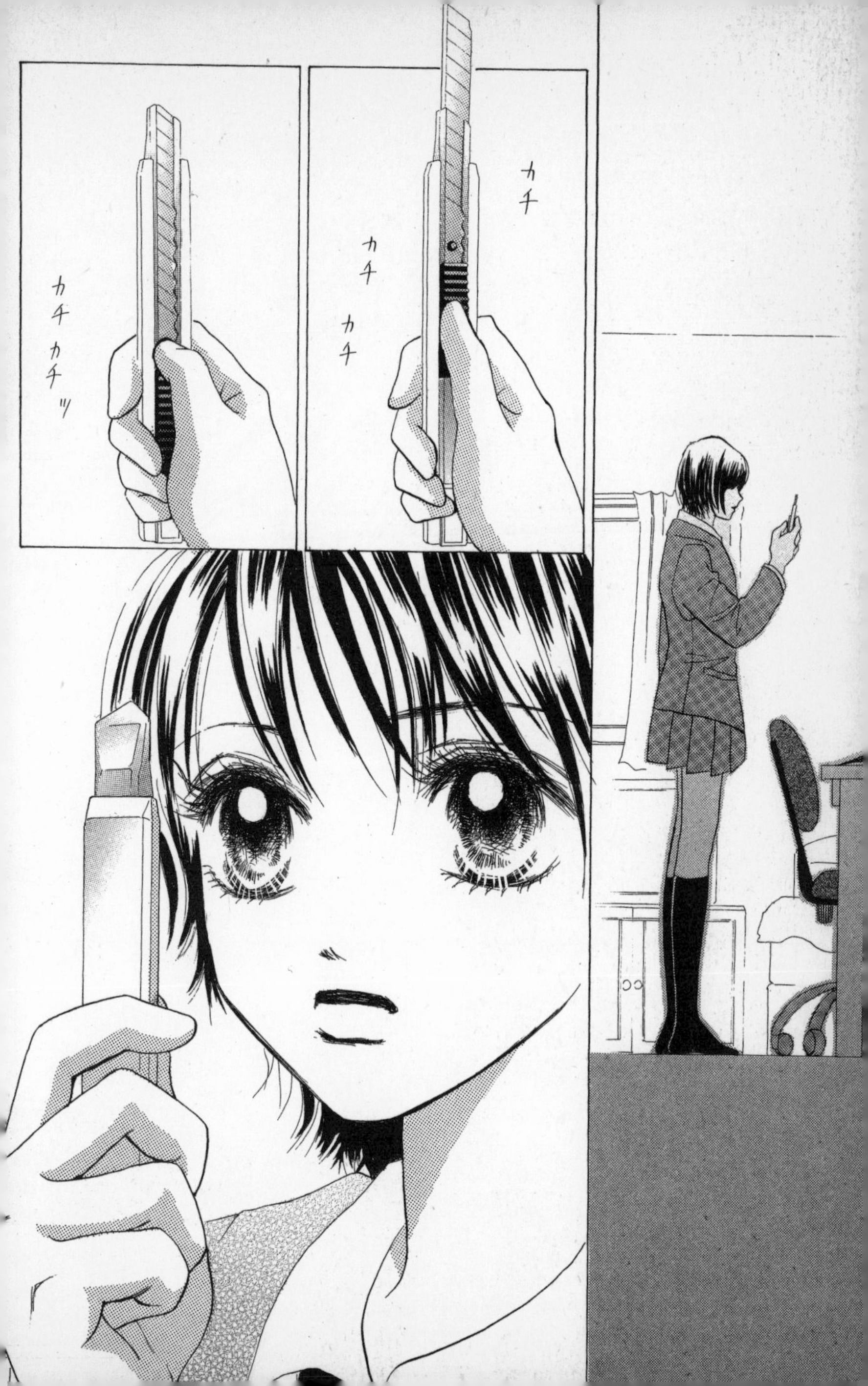
カチ
カチ
カチ
カチカチッ

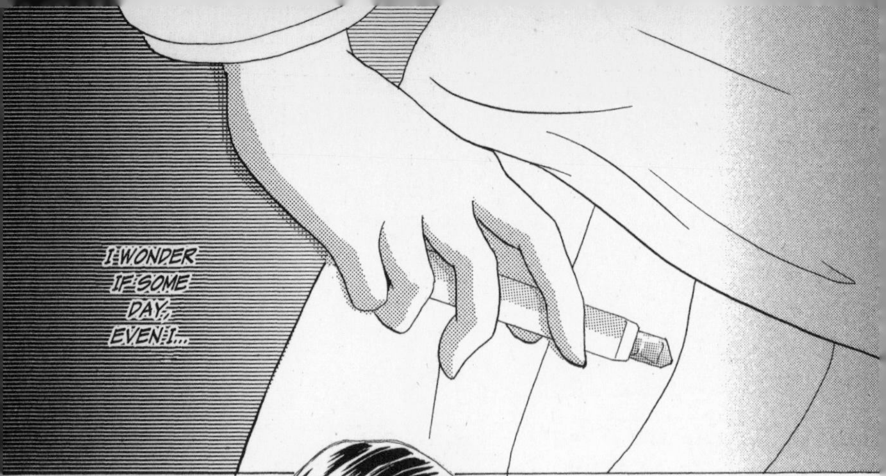
I WONDER IF SOME DAY, EVEN I...
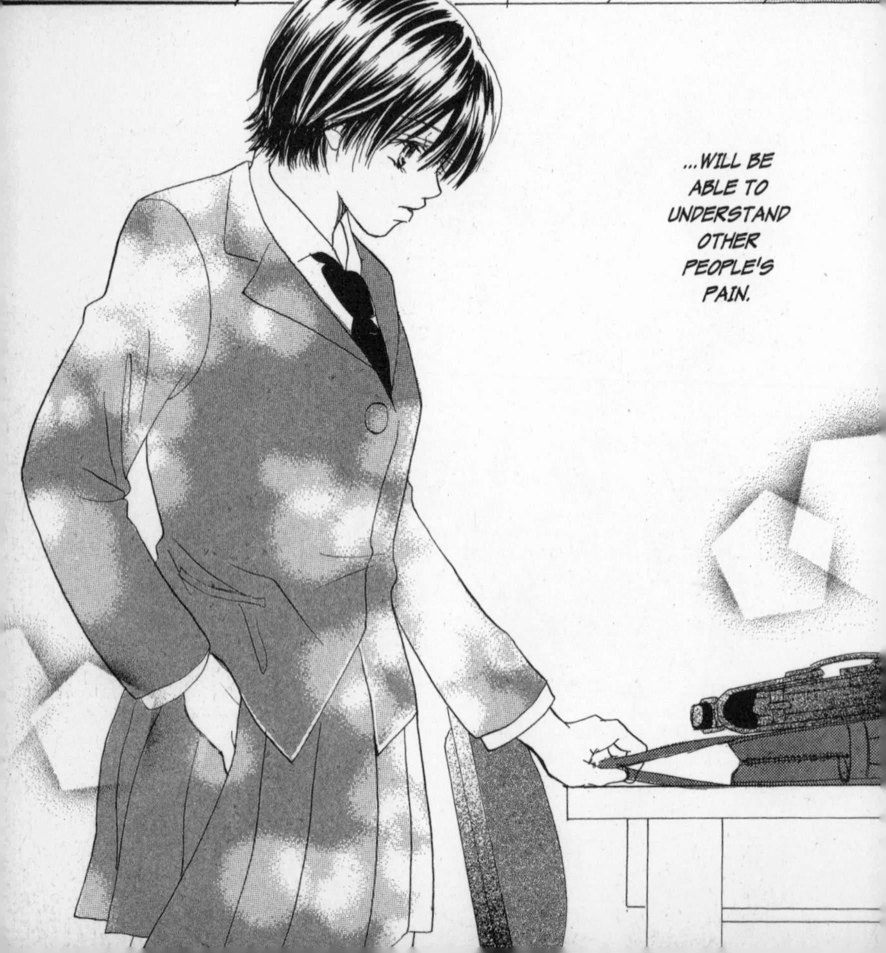
...WILL BE ABLE TO UNDERSTAND OTHER PEOPLE'S PAIN.

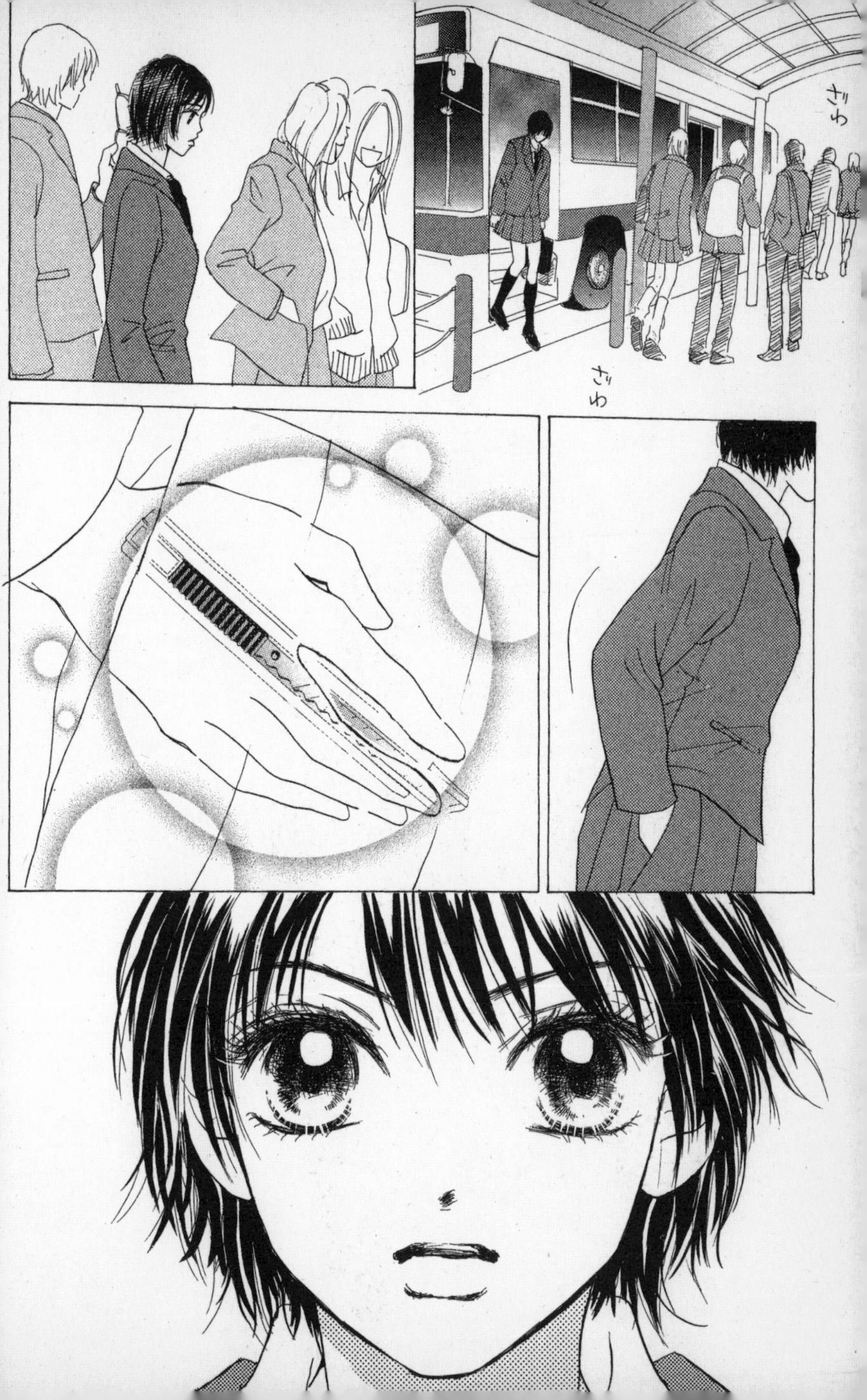
ざわ
ざわ

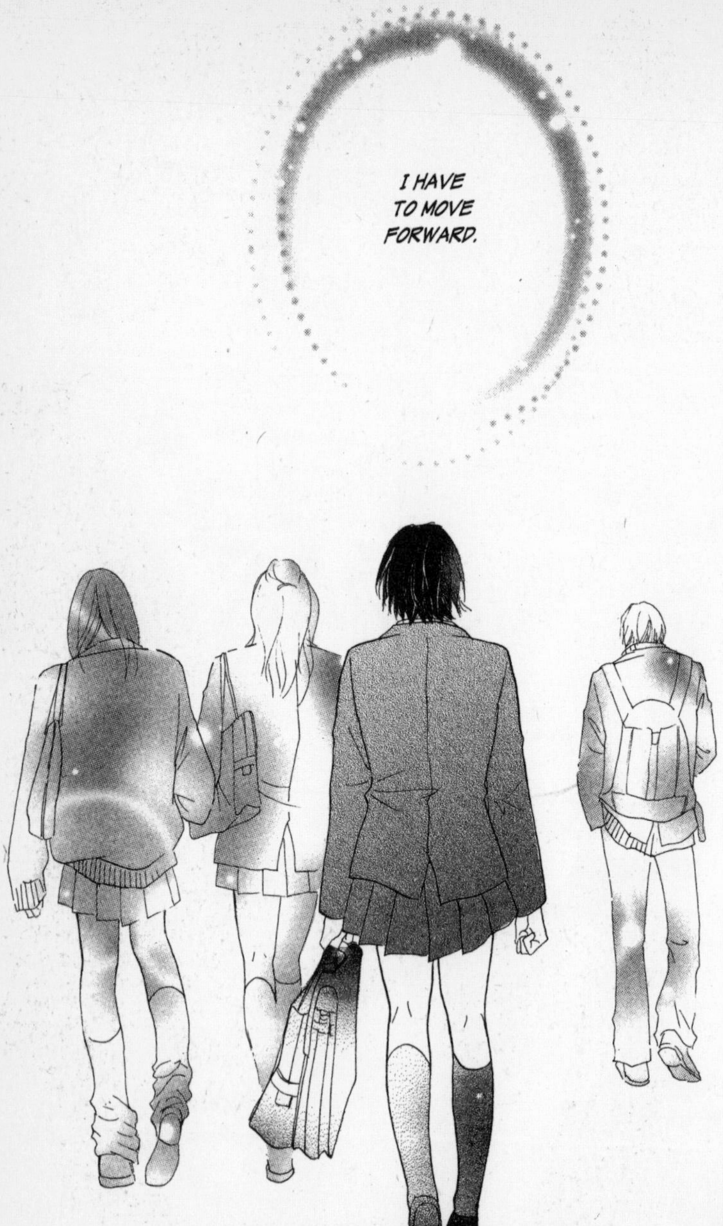
I HAVE
TO MOVE
FORWARD.

ライフ *Life*

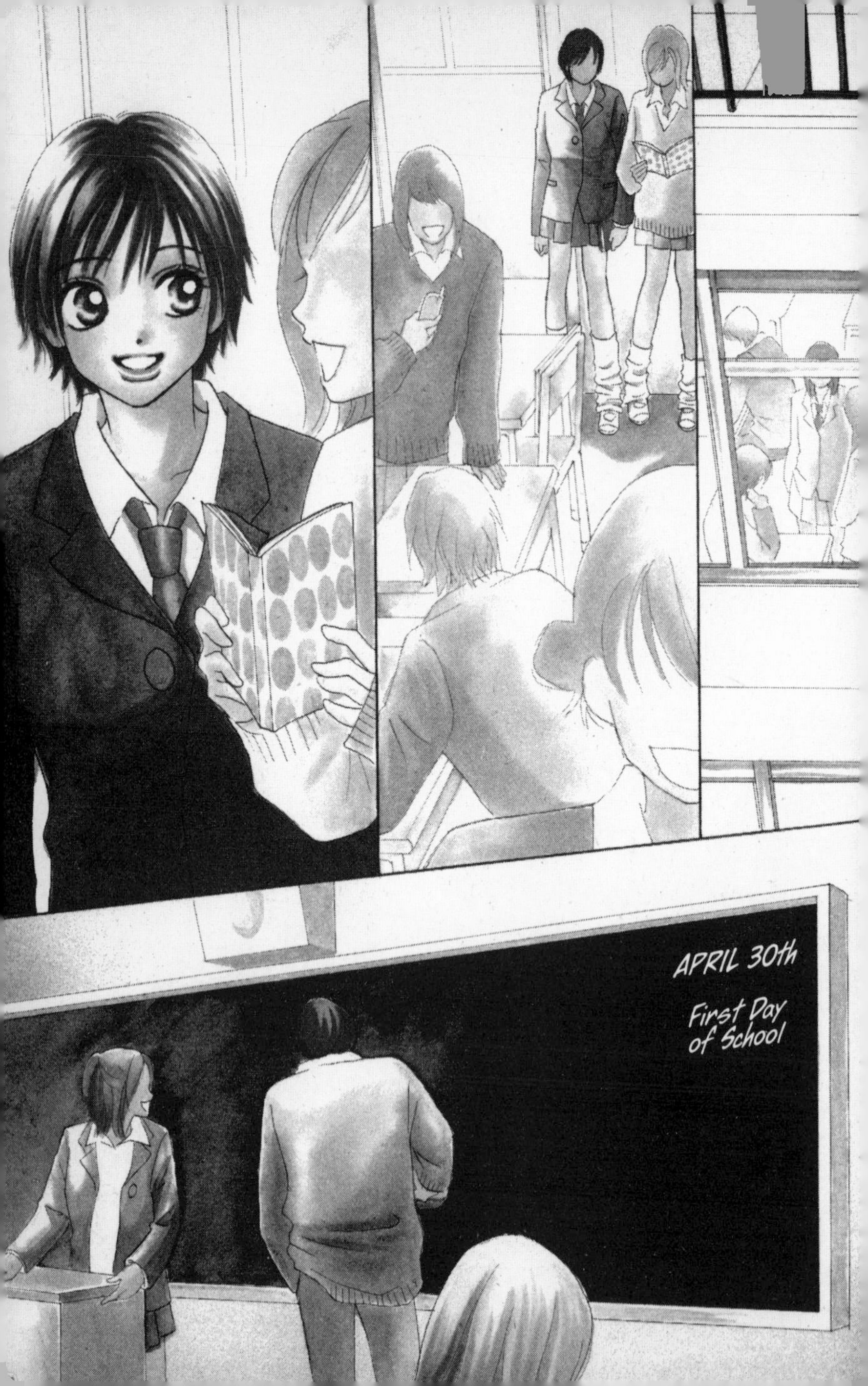
APRIL 30th
First Day of School

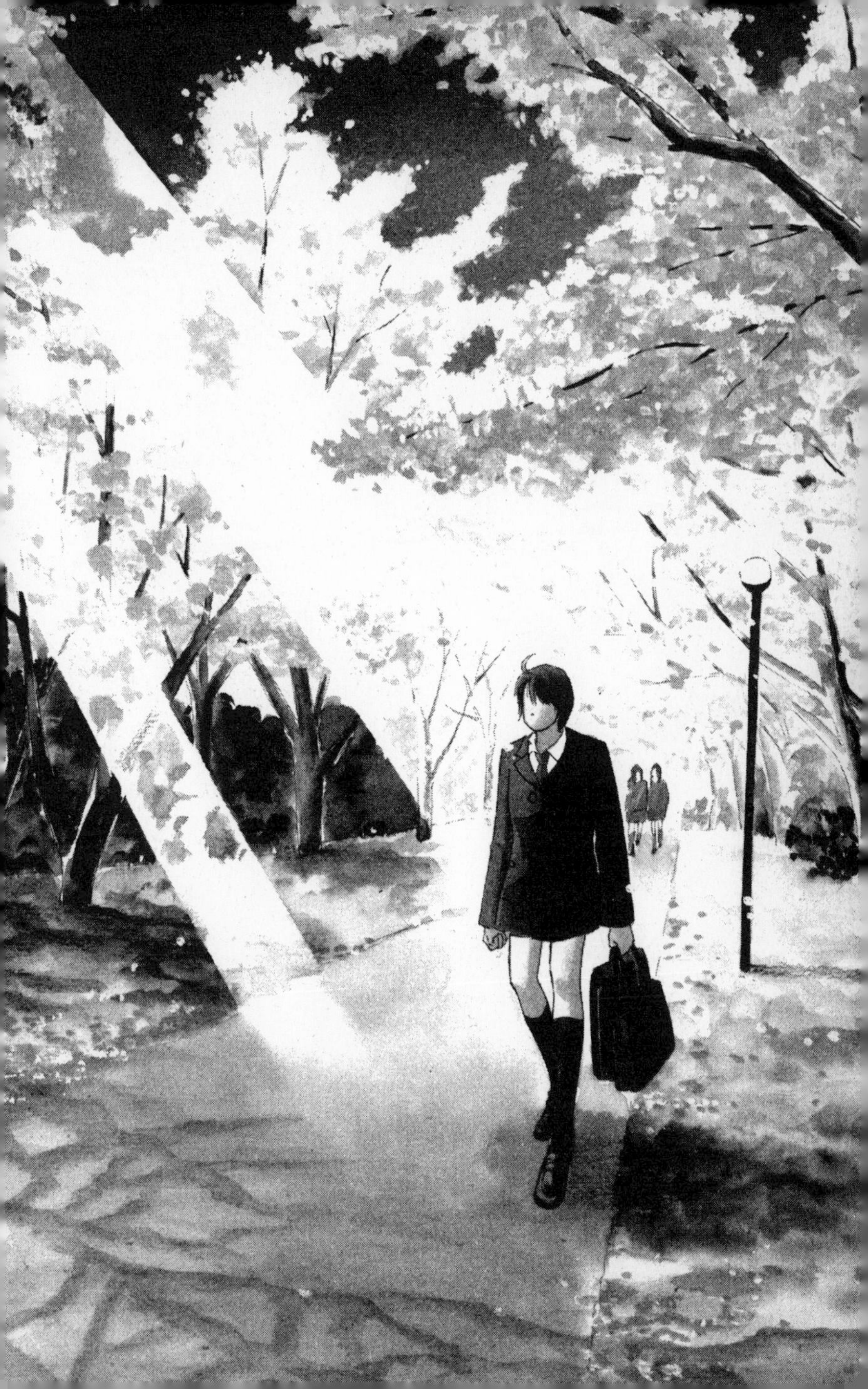

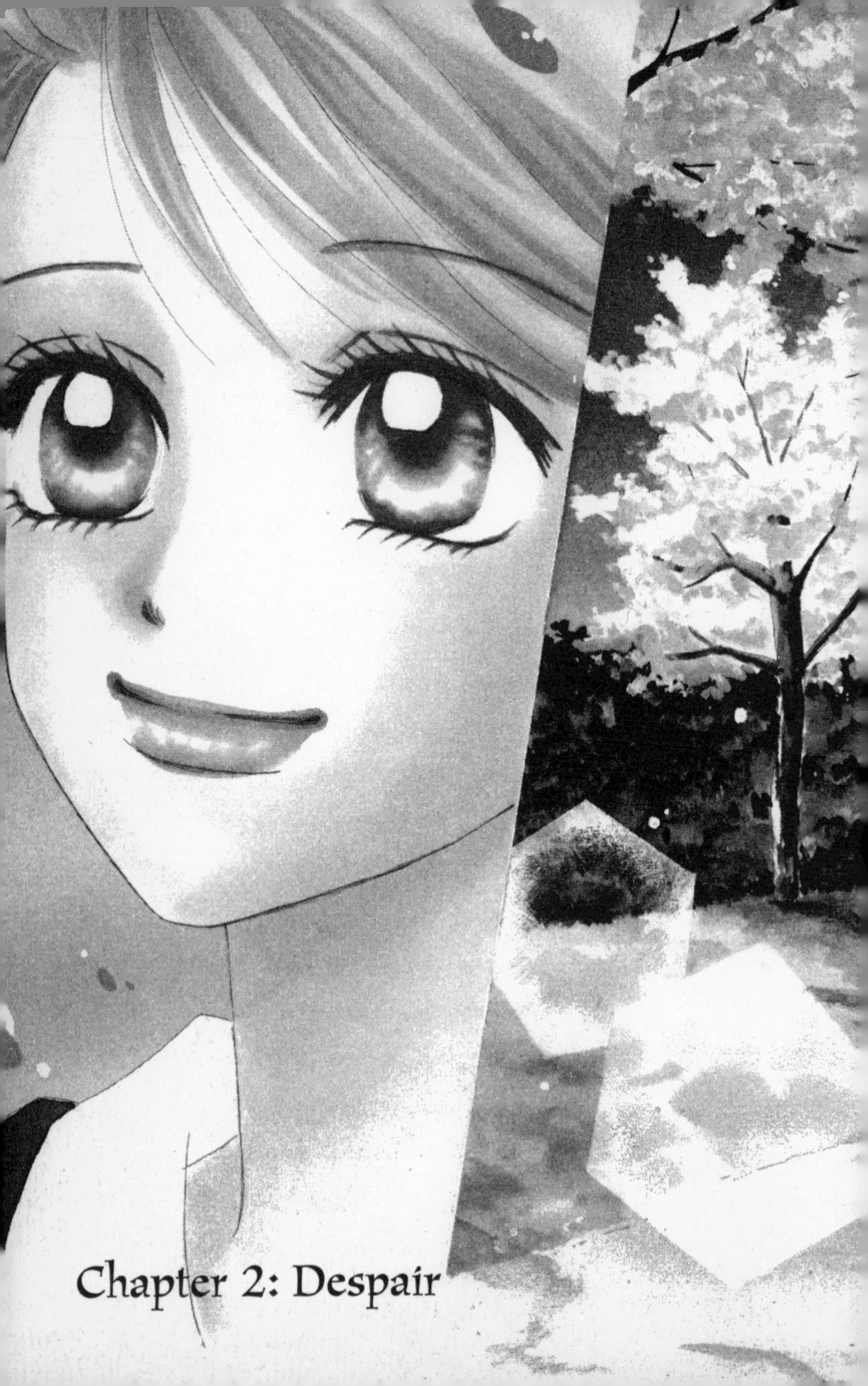
Chapter 2: Despair

ライフ
Life

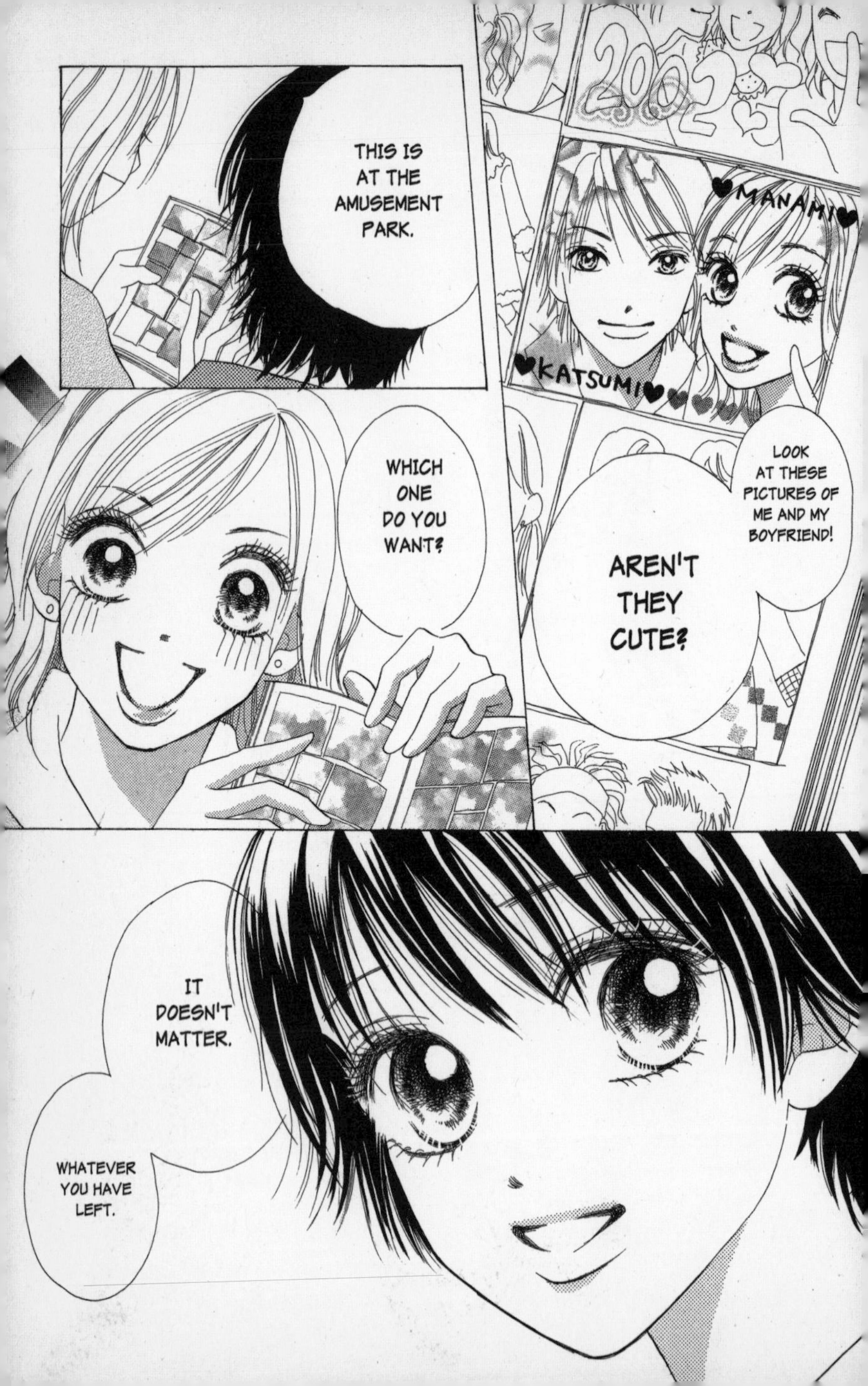
2002
MANAMI
KATSUMI
LOOK AT THESE PICTURES OF ME AND MY BOYFRIEND!
AREN'T THEY CUTE?
THIS IS AT THE AMUSEMENT PARK.
WHICH ONE DO YOU WANT?
IT DOESN'T MATTER.
WHATEVER YOU HAVE LEFT.

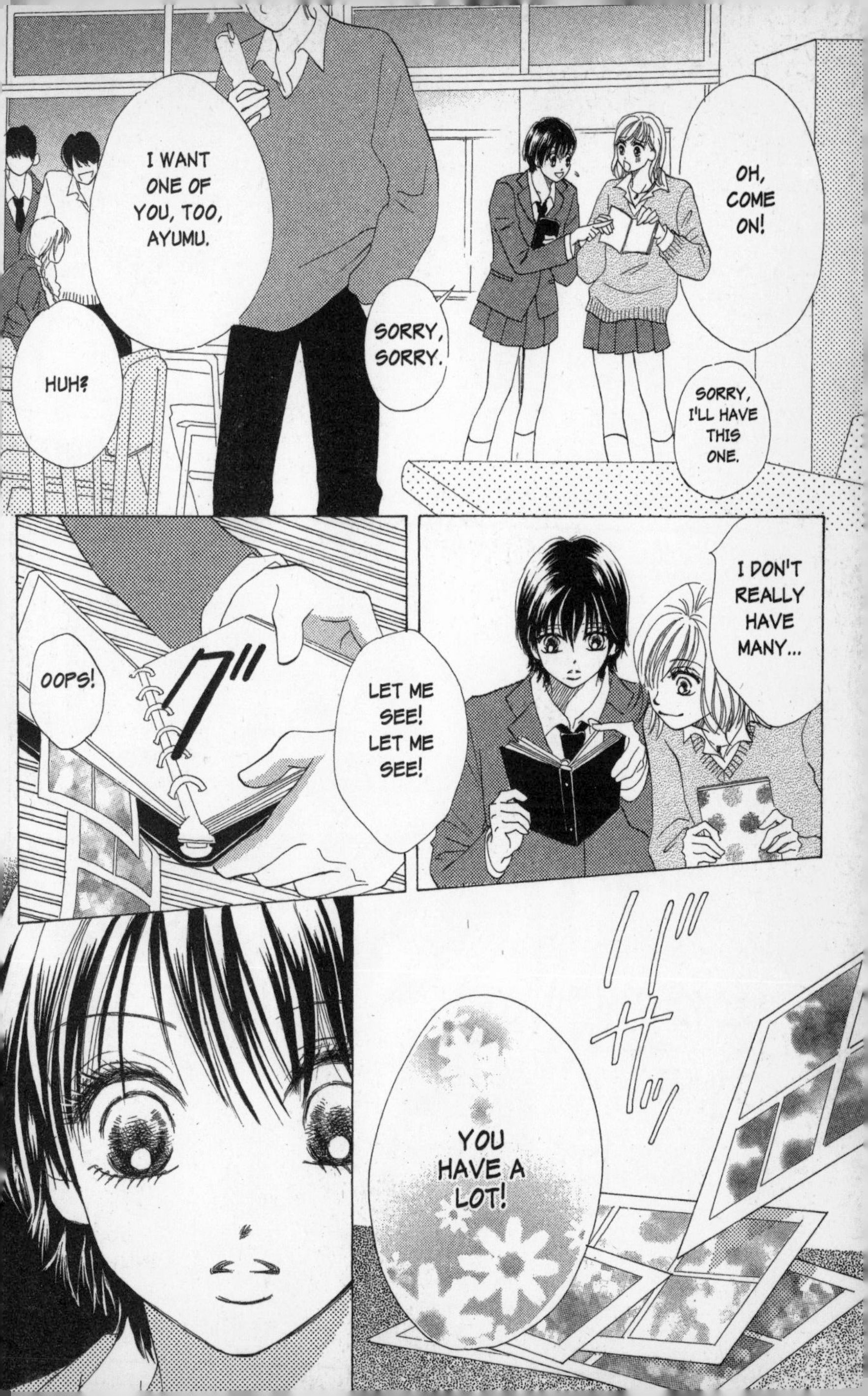
OH, COME ON!
SORRY, SORRY.
SORRY, I'LL HAVE THIS ONE.
I WANT ONE OF YOU, TOO, AYUMU.
HUH?
I DON'T REALLY HAVE MANY...
LET ME SEE! LET ME SEE!
OOPS!
YOU HAVE A LOT!

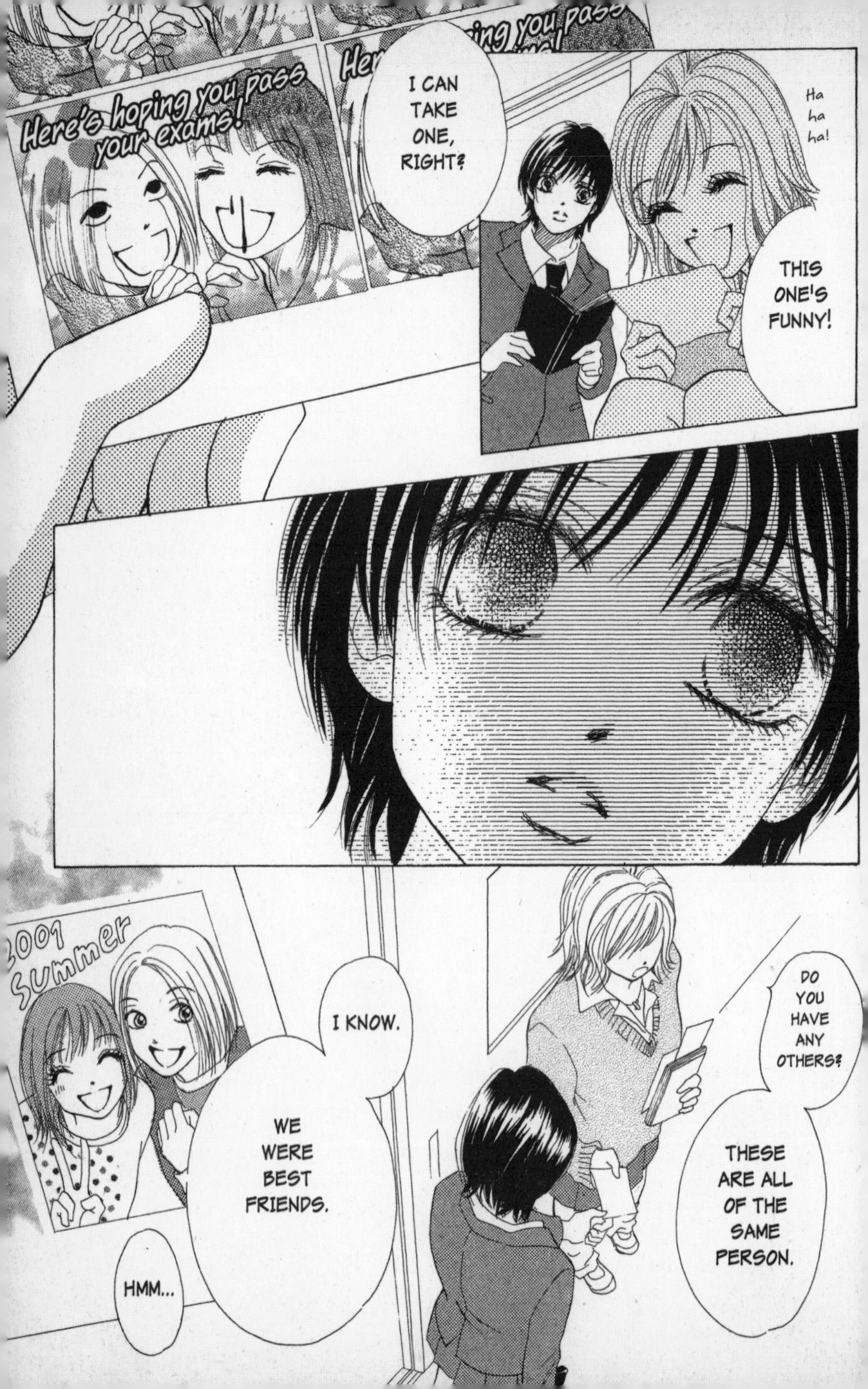
Ha ha ha!
THIS ONE'S FUNNY!
I CAN TAKE ONE, RIGHT?
Here's hoping you pass your exams!
DO YOU HAVE ANY OTHERS?
THESE ARE ALL OF THE SAME PERSON.
I KNOW.
WE WERE BEST FRIENDS.
HMM...
2001 Summer

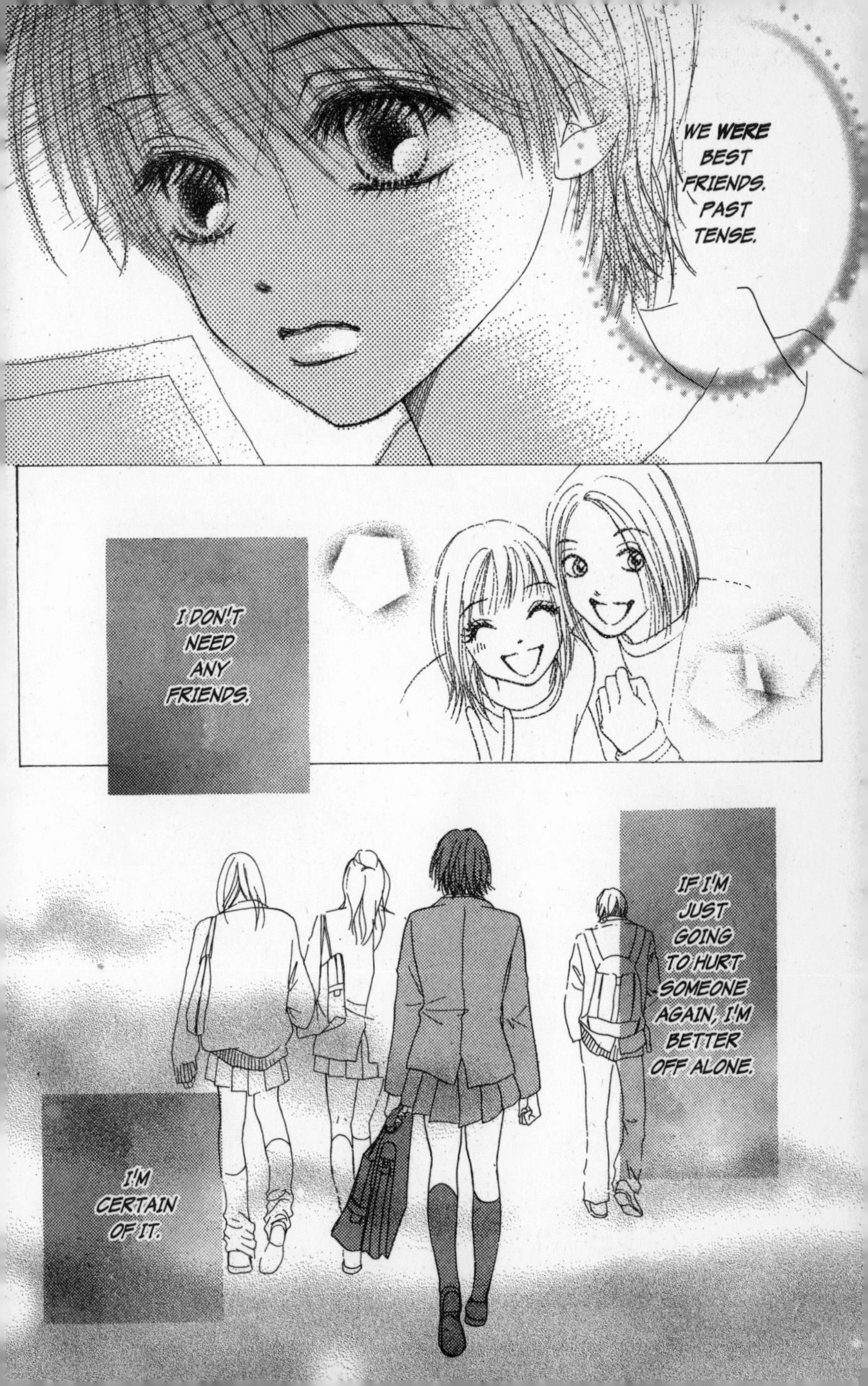
WE WERE BEST FRIENDS. PAST TENSE.
I DON'T NEED ANY FRIENDS.
IF I'M JUST GOING TO HURT SOMEONE AGAIN, I'M BETTER OFF ALONE.
I'M CERTAIN OF IT.

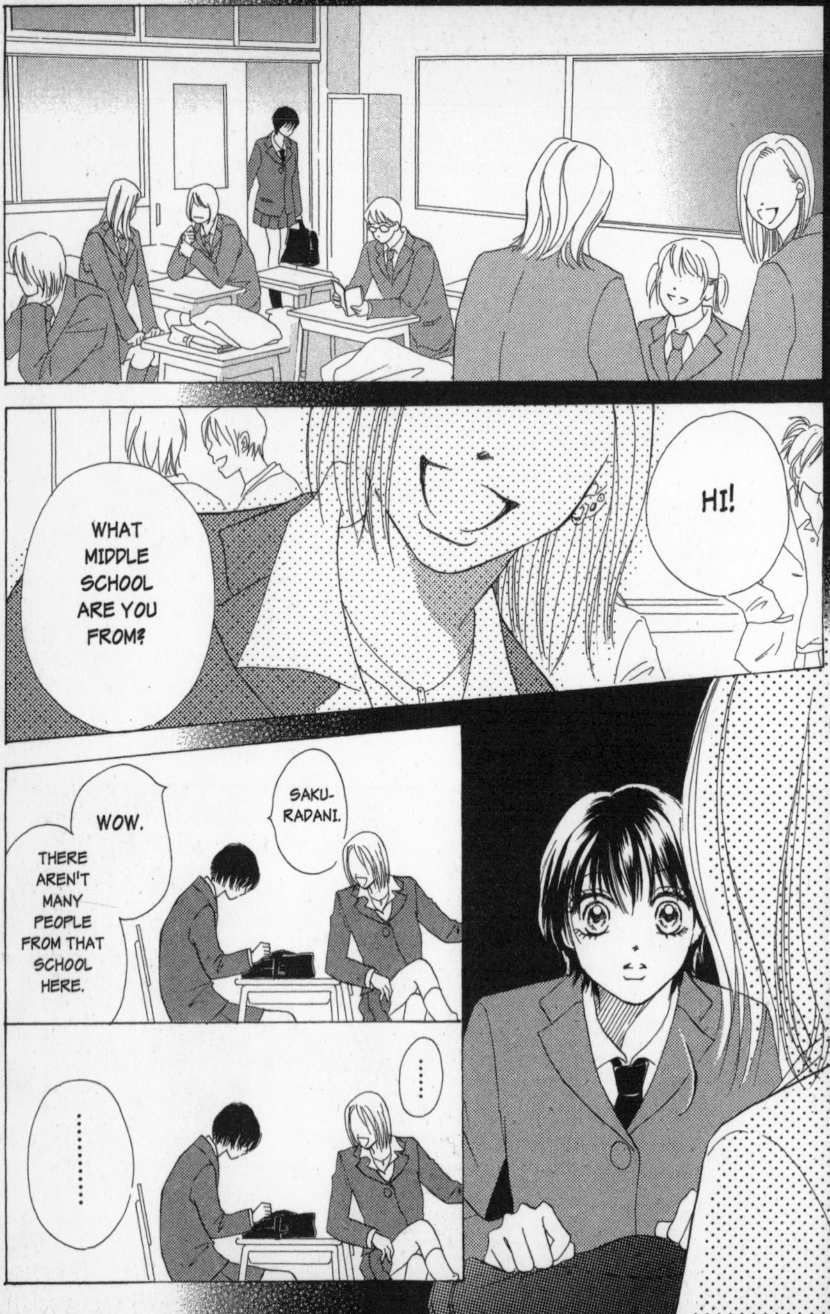
HI!
WHAT MIDDLE SCHOOL ARE YOU FROM?
SAKU-RADANI.
WOW.
THERE AREN'T MANY PEOPLE FROM THAT SCHOOL HERE.
......
....

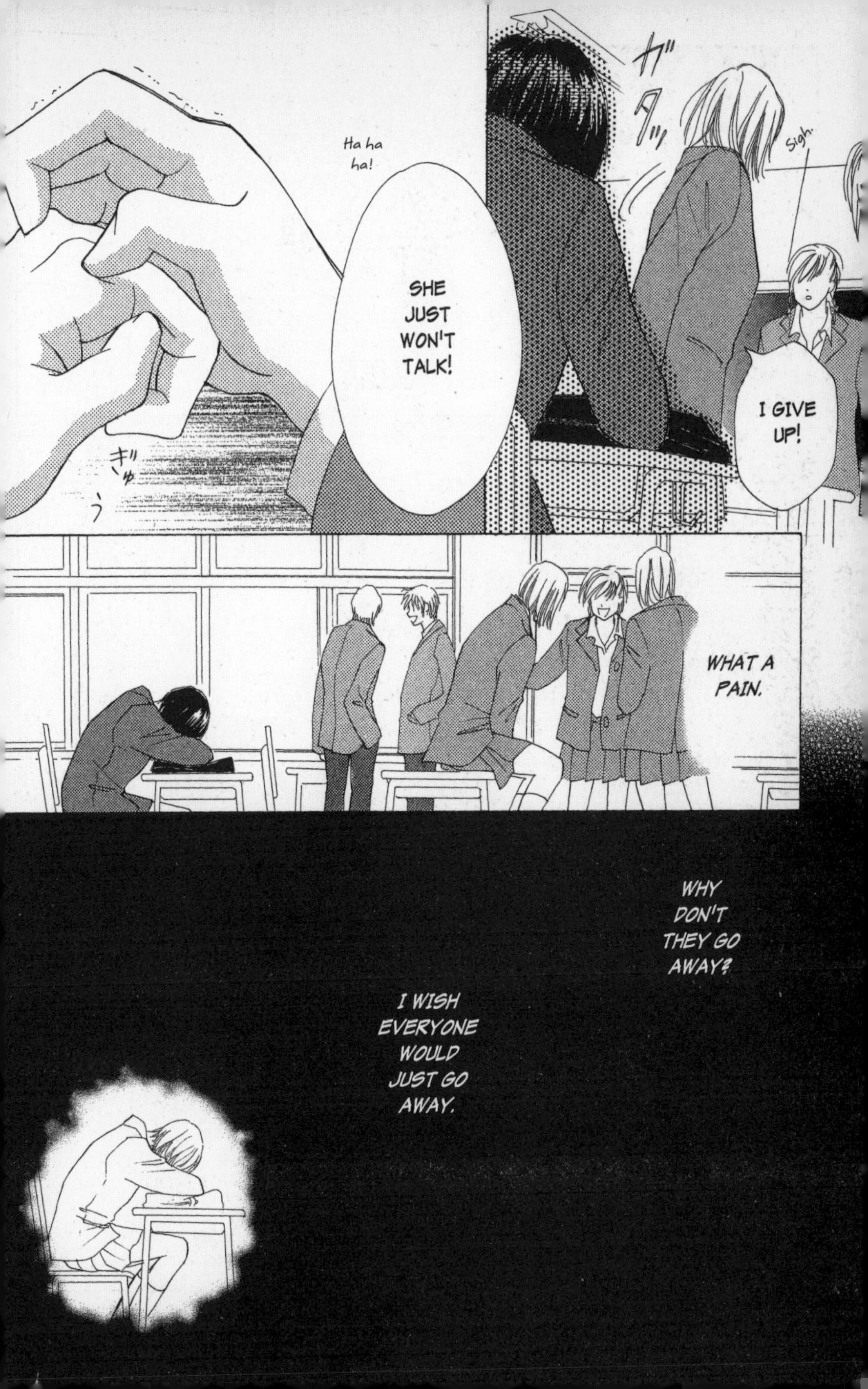
ガタッ
Sigh.
I GIVE UP!
Ha ha ha!
SHE JUST WON'T TALK!
ぎゅう
WHAT A PAIN.
WHY DON'T THEY GO AWAY?
I WISH EVERYONE WOULD JUST GO AWAY.

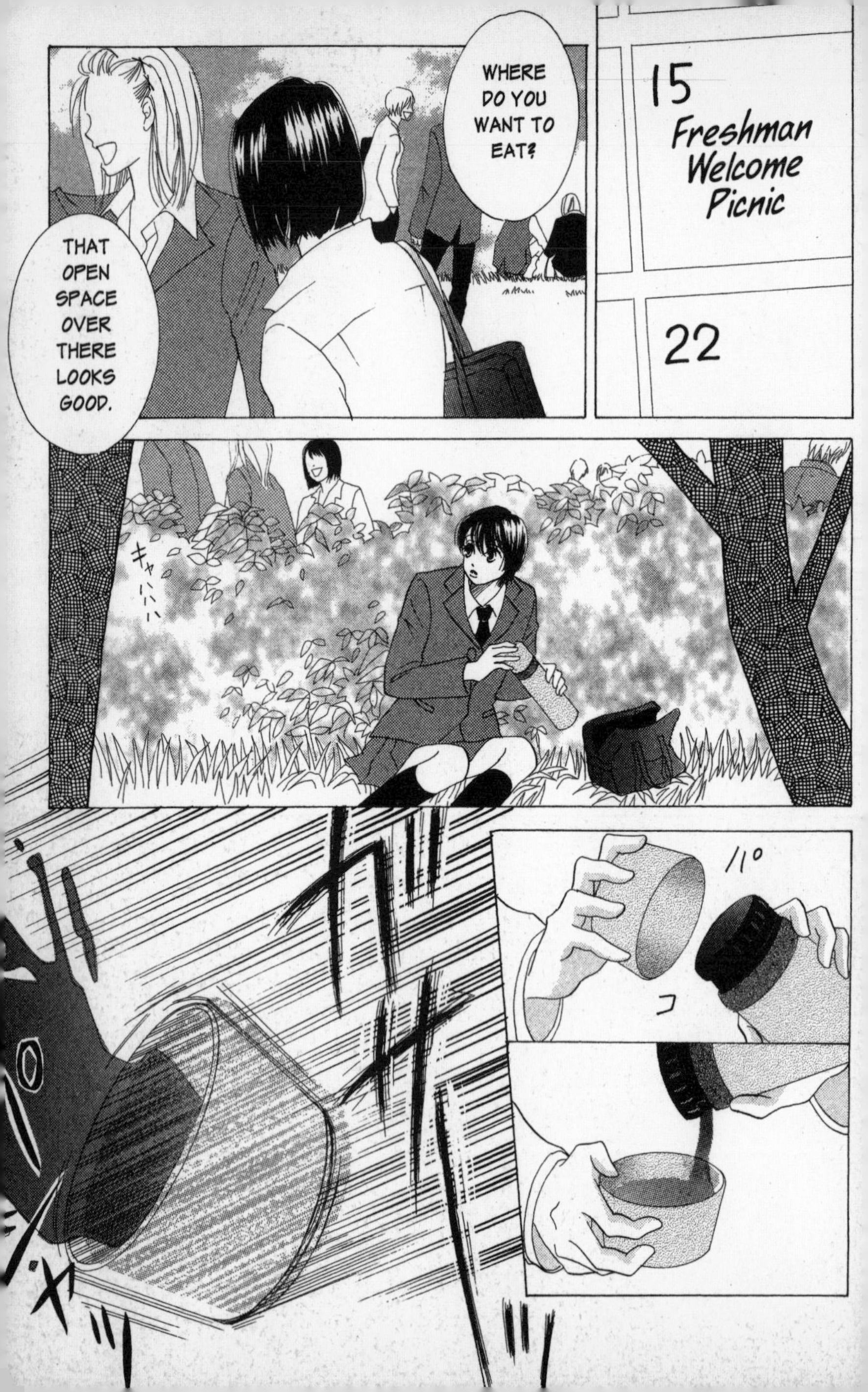
15
Freshman Welcome Picnic
22
WHERE DO YOU WANT TO EAT?
THAT OPEN SPACE OVER THERE LOOKS GOOD.

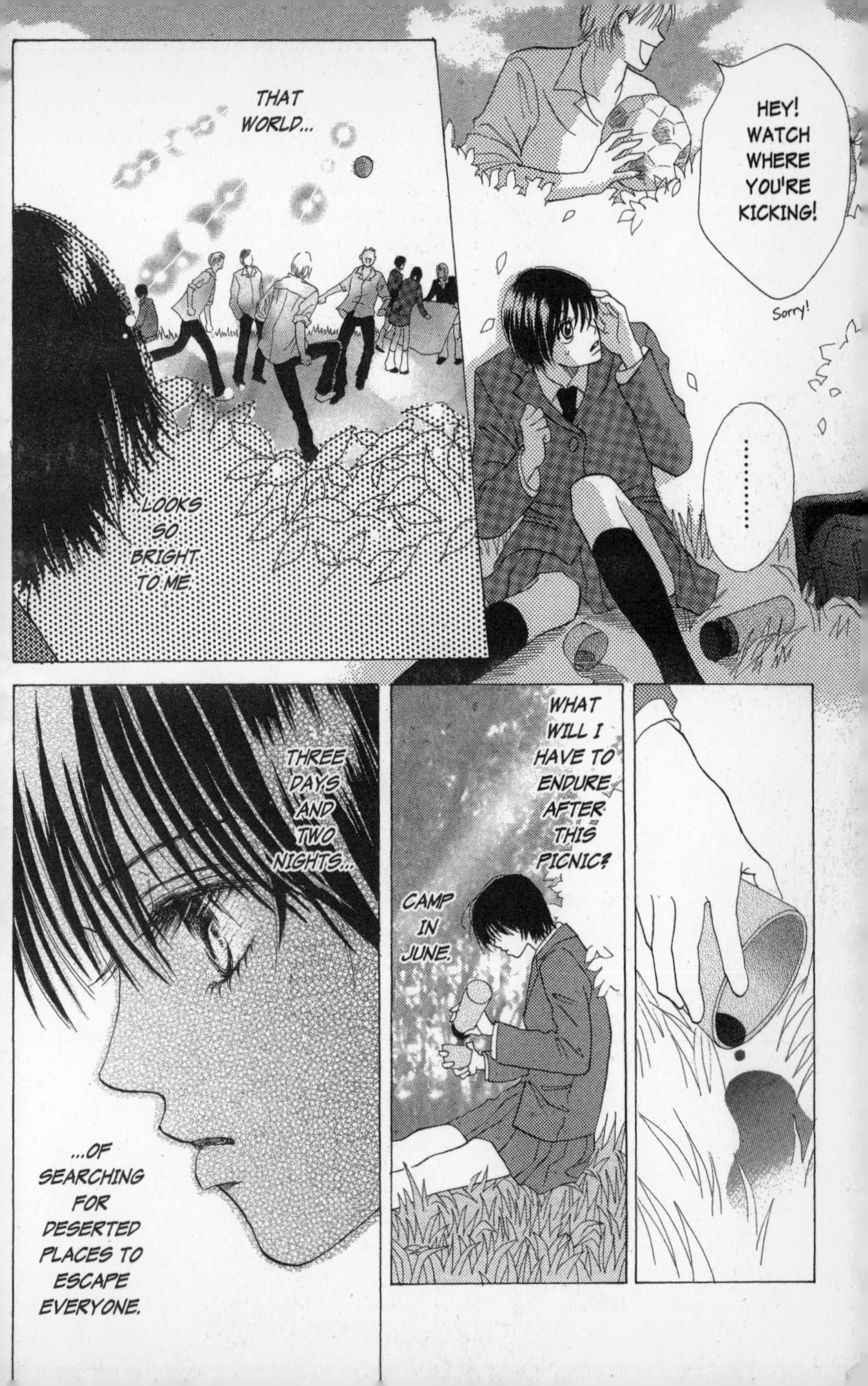
HEY! WATCH WHERE YOU'RE KICKING!
Sorry!
......
THAT WORLD...
...LOOKS SO BRIGHT TO ME.
WHAT WILL I HAVE TO ENDURE AFTER THIS PICNIC?
CAMP IN JUNE.
THREE DAYS AND TWO NIGHTS...
...OF SEARCHING FOR DESERTED PLACES TO ESCAPE EVERYONE.

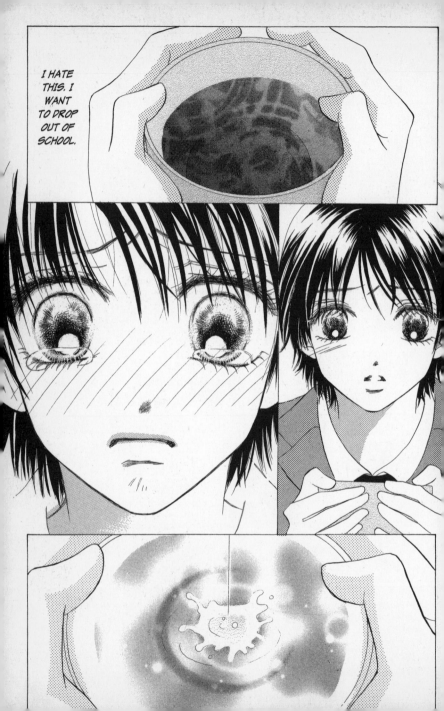

I HATE THIS. I WANT TO DROP OUT OF SCHOOL.

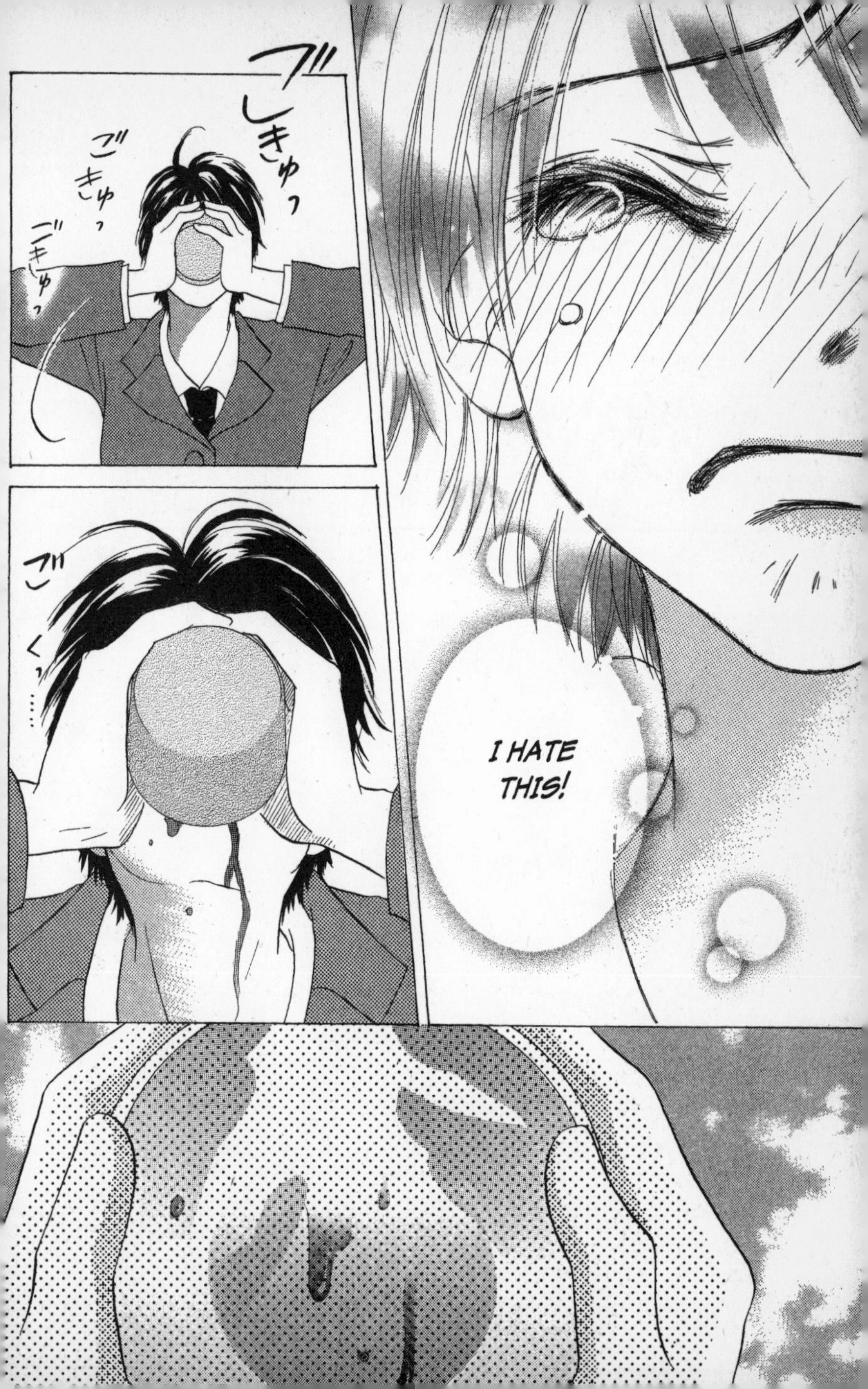
I HATE THIS!
ブ
しきゅっ
ごきゅっ
ゴキュっ
ごくっ……

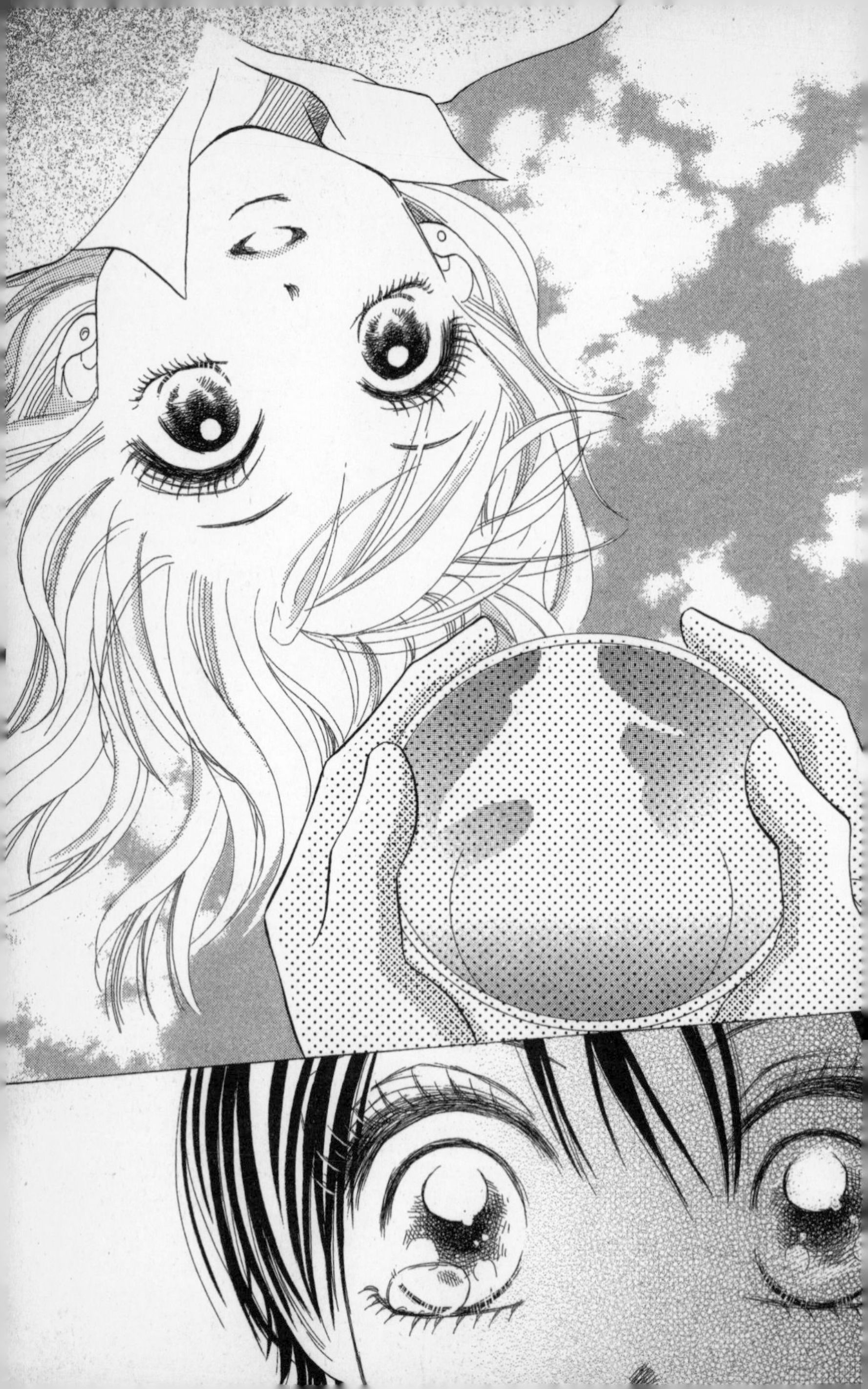

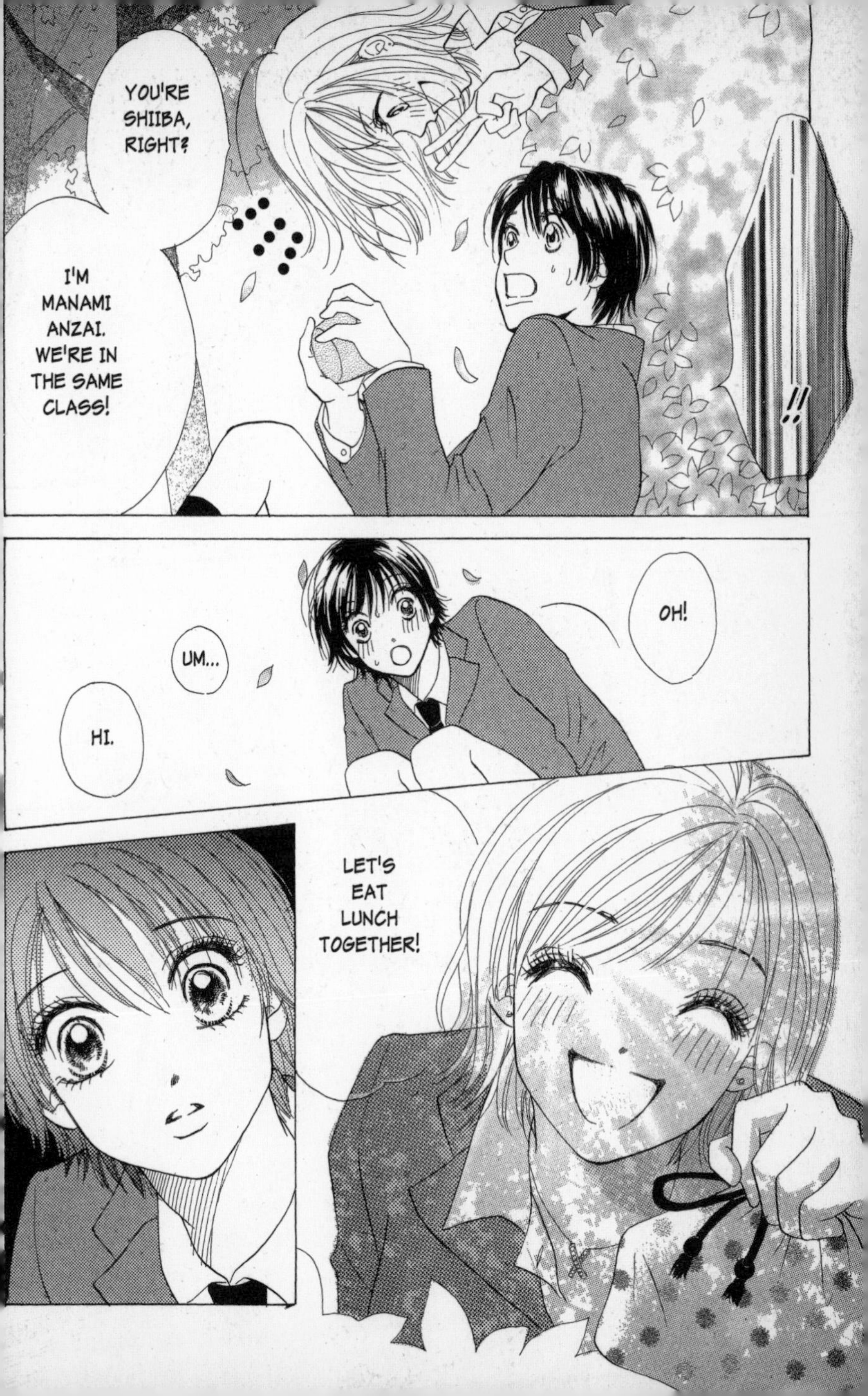
!!
YOU'RE SHIIBA, RIGHT?
I'M MANAMI ANZAI. WE'RE IN THE SAME CLASS!
OH!
UM...
HI.
LET'S EAT LUNCH TOGETHER!

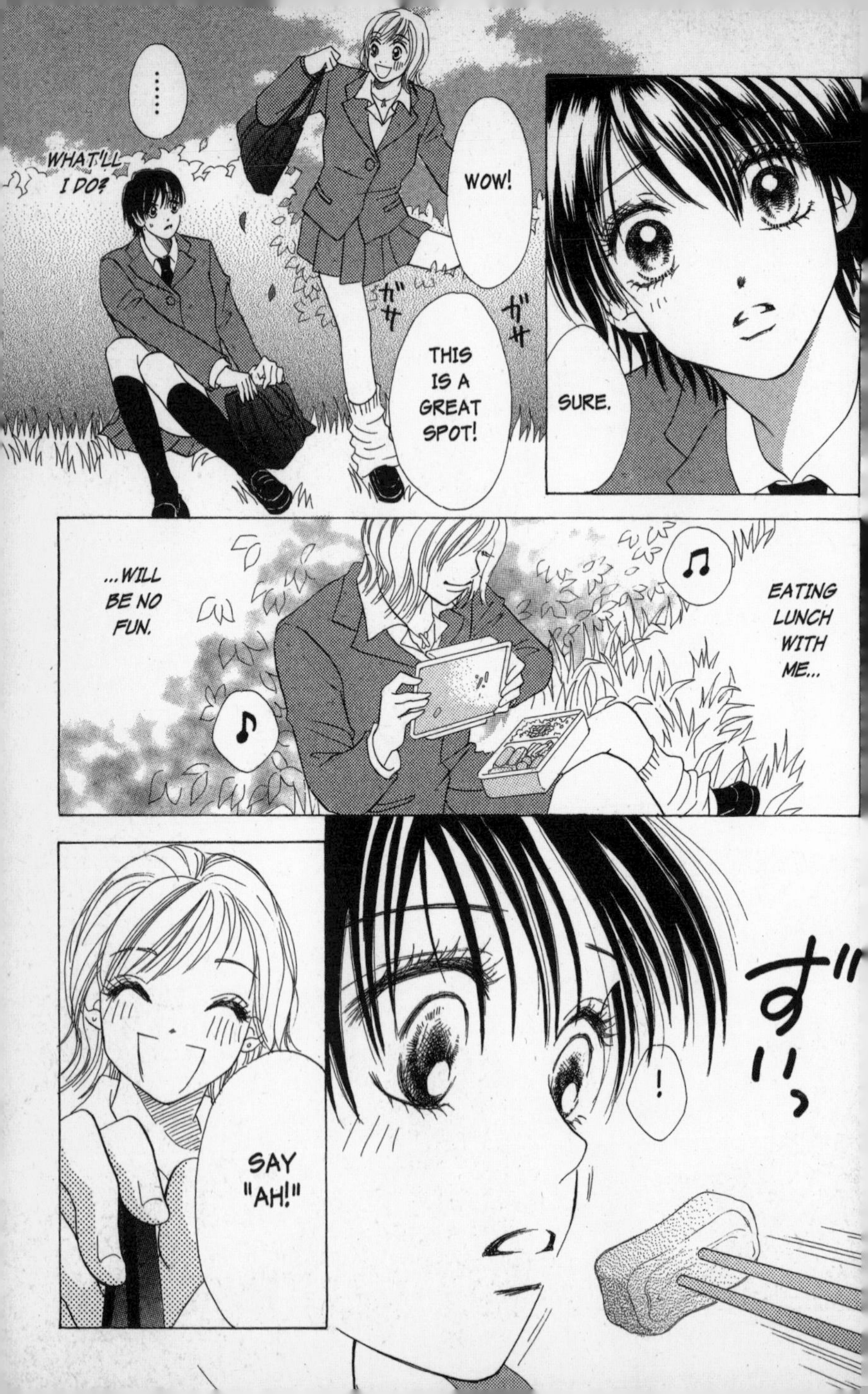
SURE.
WOW!
......
THIS IS A GREAT SPOT!
ガサ
ガサ
WHAT'LL I DO?
EATING LUNCH WITH ME...
♫
♪
...WILL BE NO FUN.
ずいっ
!
SAY "AH!"

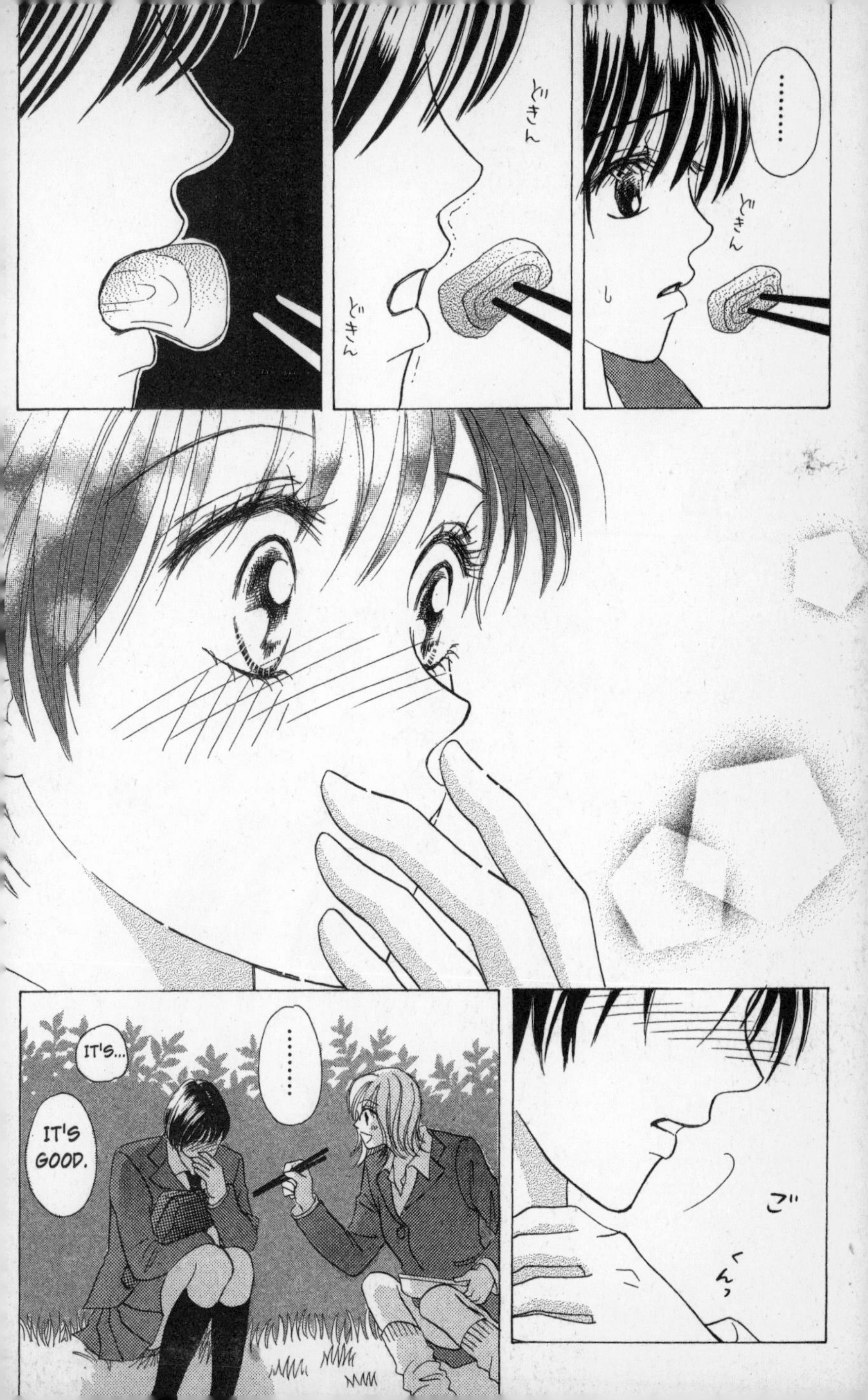
....
どきん
どきん
どきん
ごくんっ
....
IT'S...
IT'S GOOD.

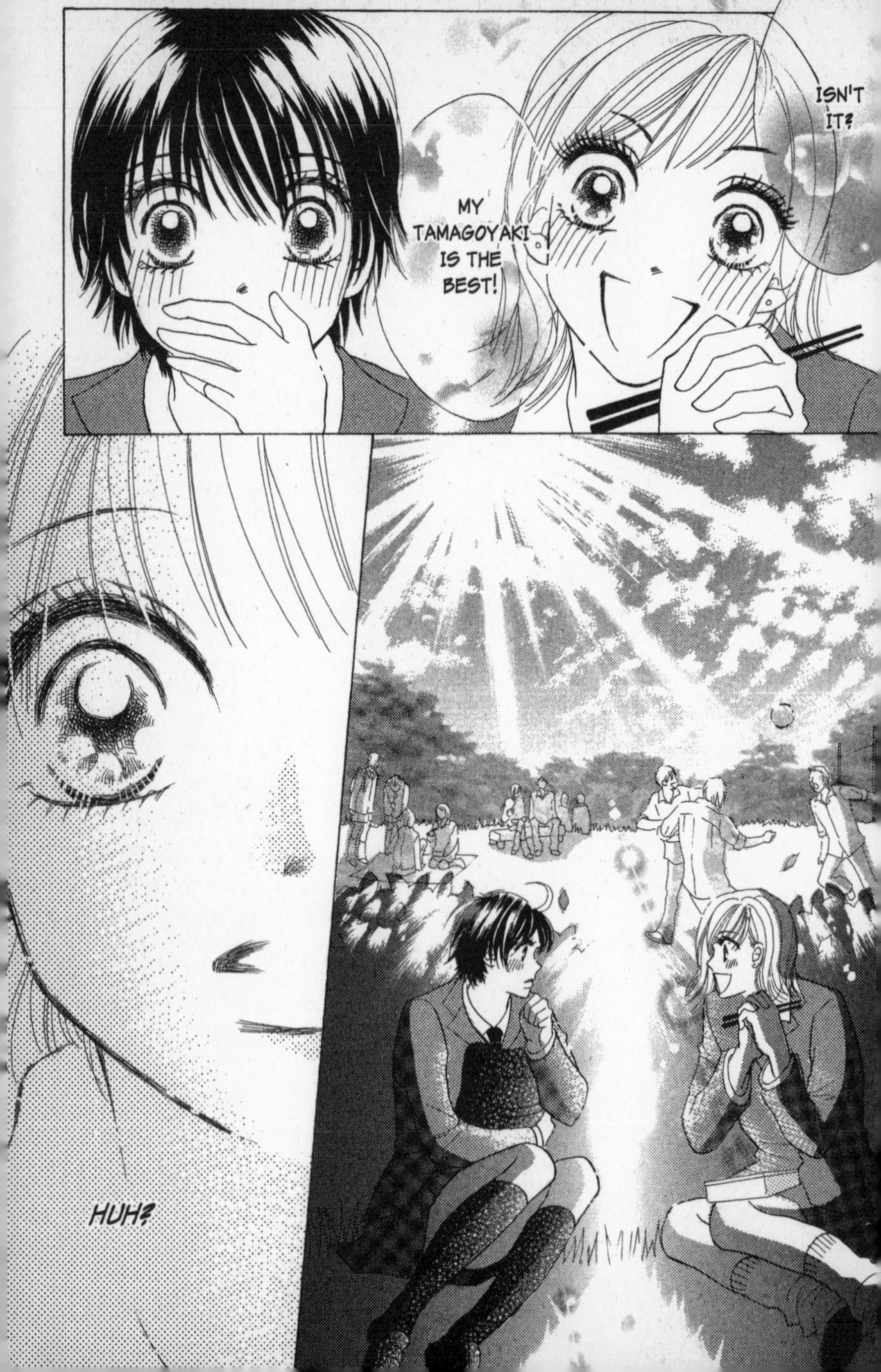
MY TAMAGOYAKI IS THE BEST!
ISN'T IT?
HUH?

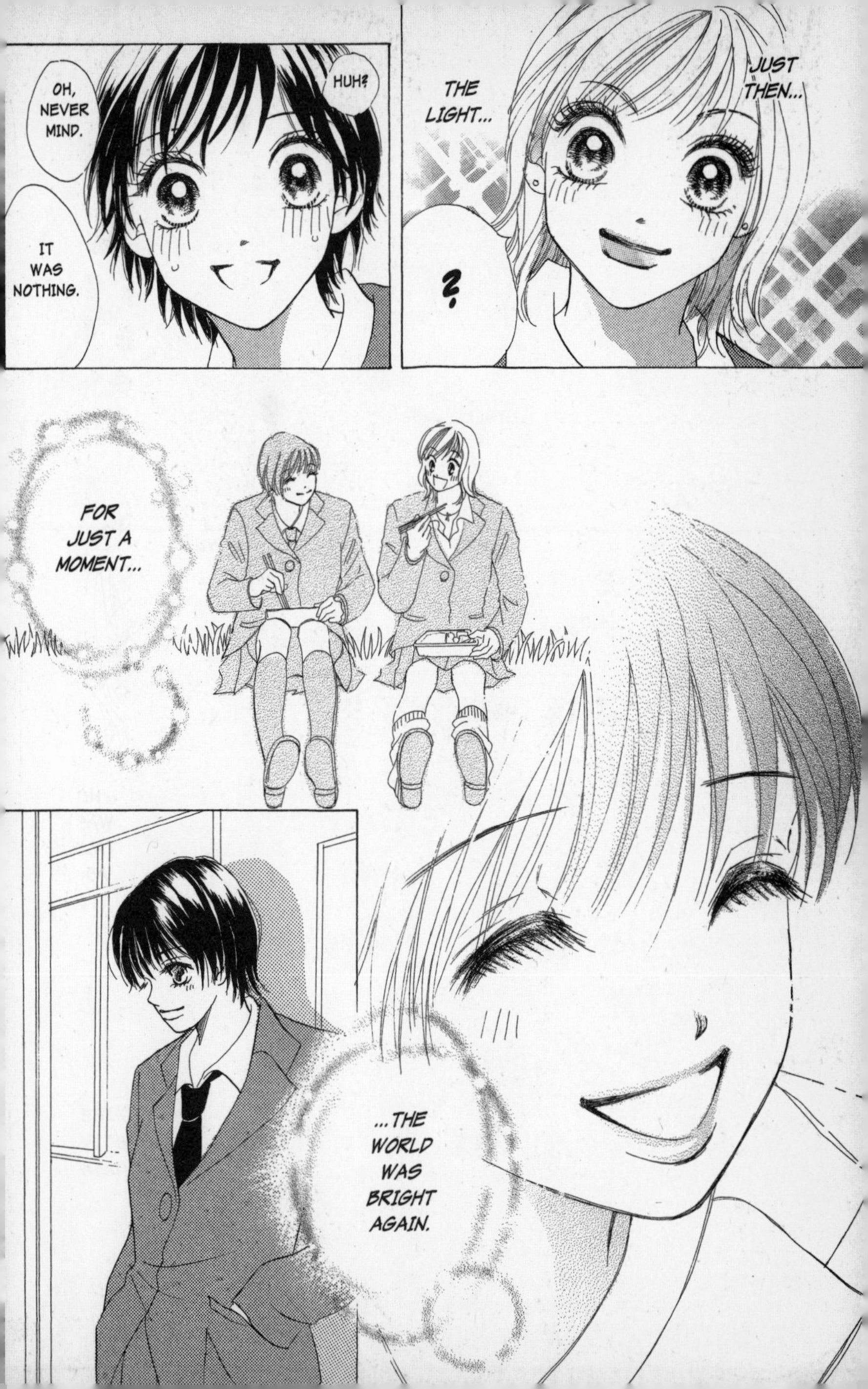
JUST THEN...
THE LIGHT...
?
HUH?
OH, NEVER MIND.
IT WAS NOTHING.
FOR JUST A MOMENT...
...THE WORLD WAS BRIGHT AGAIN.

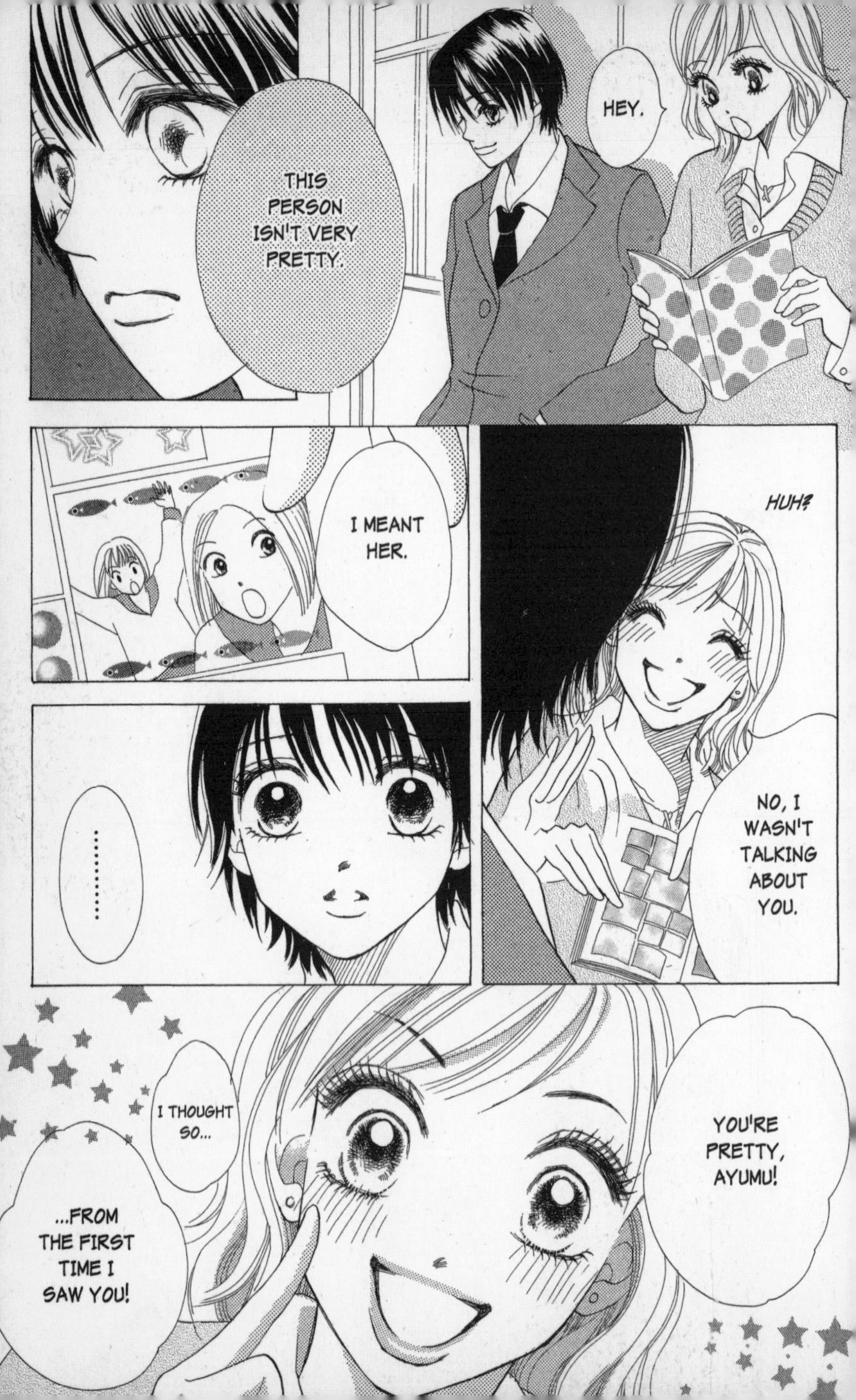
HEY.
THIS PERSON ISN'T VERY PRETTY.
HUH?
NO, I WASN'T TALKING ABOUT YOU.
I MEANT HER.
....
YOU'RE PRETTY, AYUMU!
I THOUGHT SO...
...FROM THE FIRST TIME I SAW YOU!

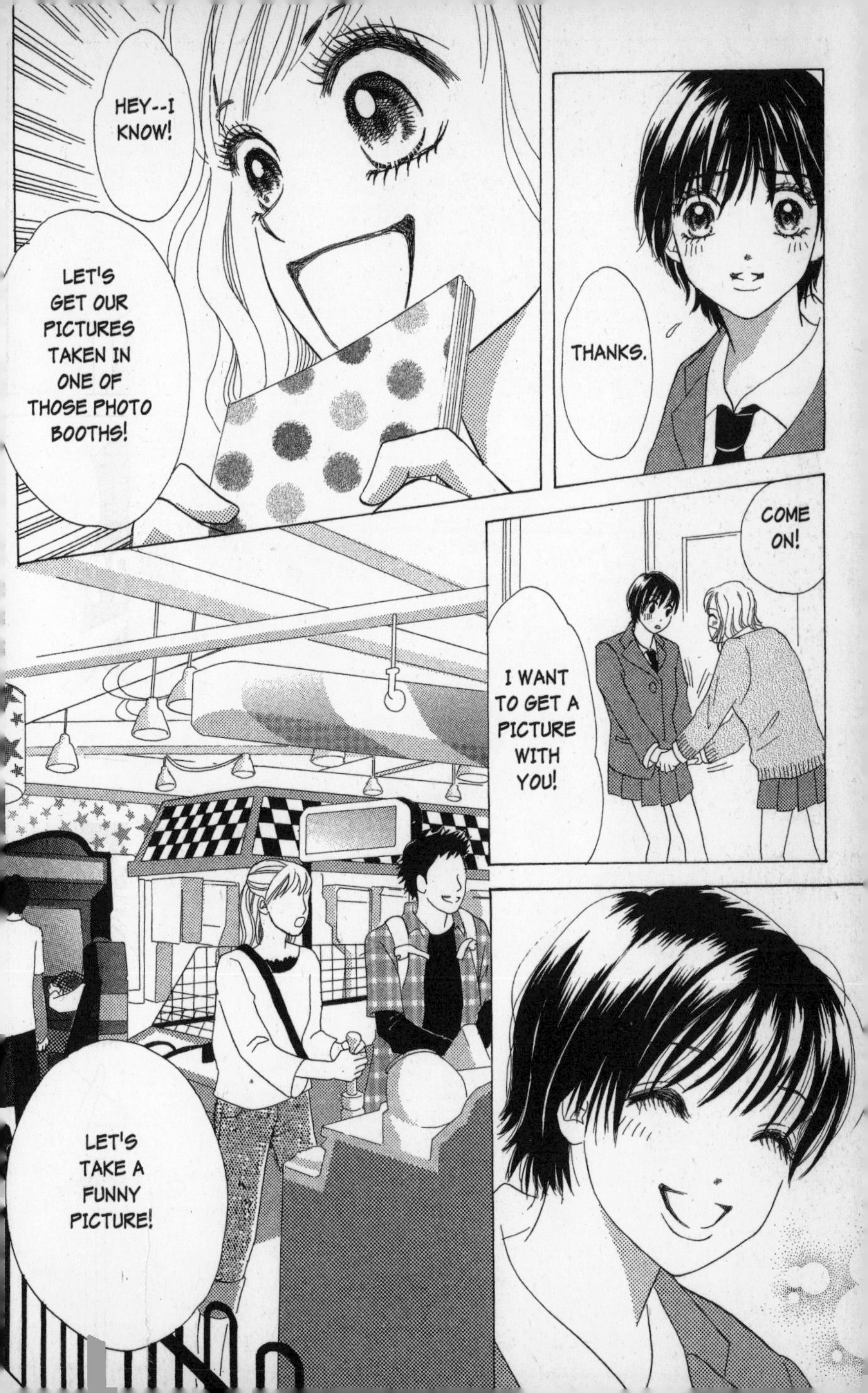
THANKS.
HEY--I KNOW!
LET'S GET OUR PICTURES TAKEN IN ONE OF THOSE PHOTO BOOTHS!
COME ON!
I WANT TO GET A PICTURE WITH YOU!
LET'S TAKE A FUNNY PICTURE!

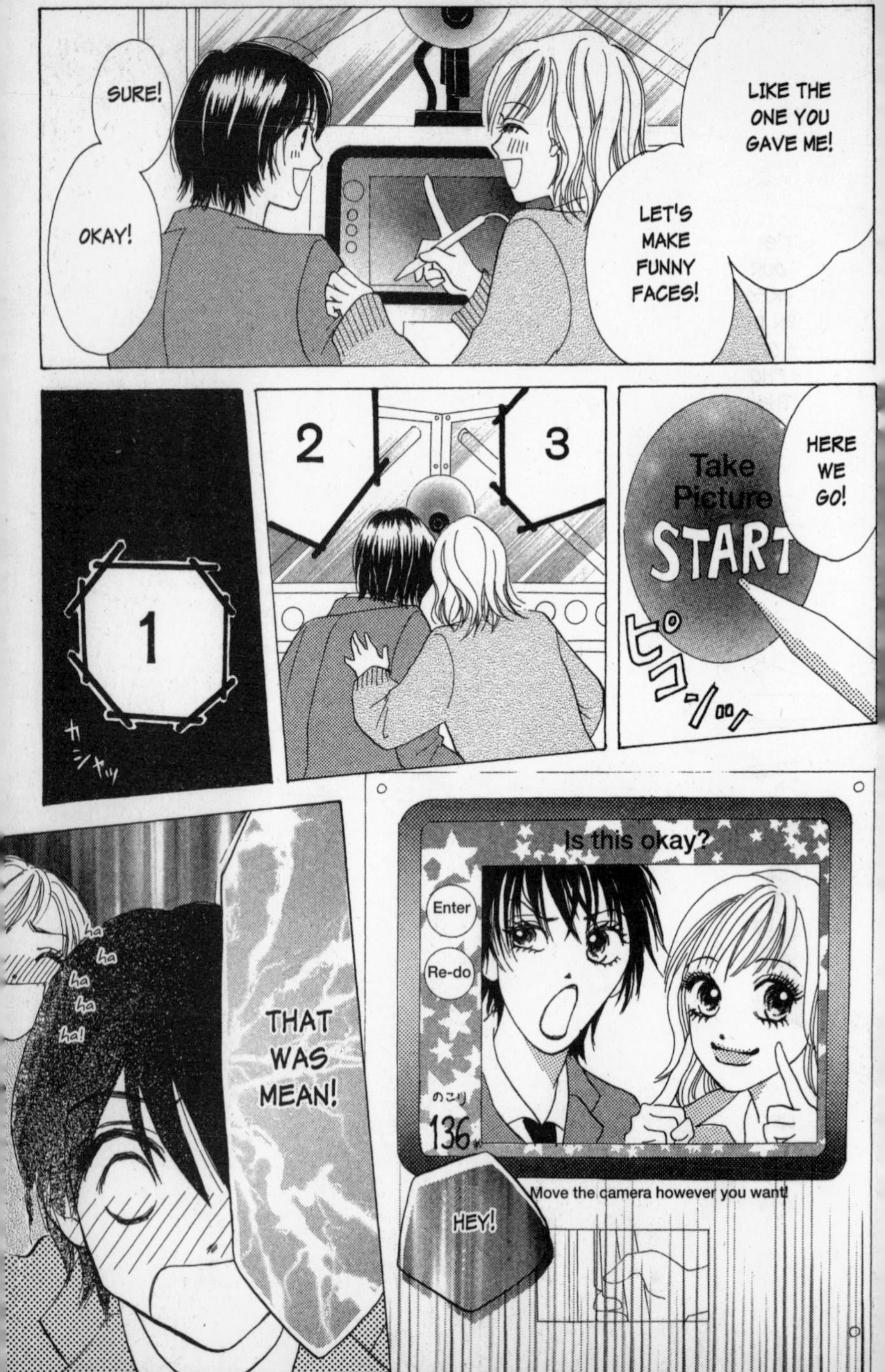
LIKE THE ONE YOU GAVE ME!
LET'S MAKE FUNNY FACES!
SURE!
OKAY!
HERE WE GO!
Take Picture
START
3
2
1
カシャッ
Is this okay?
Enter
Re-do
のこり
136
Move the camera however you want!
HEY!
ha ha ha ha ha!
THAT WAS MEAN!

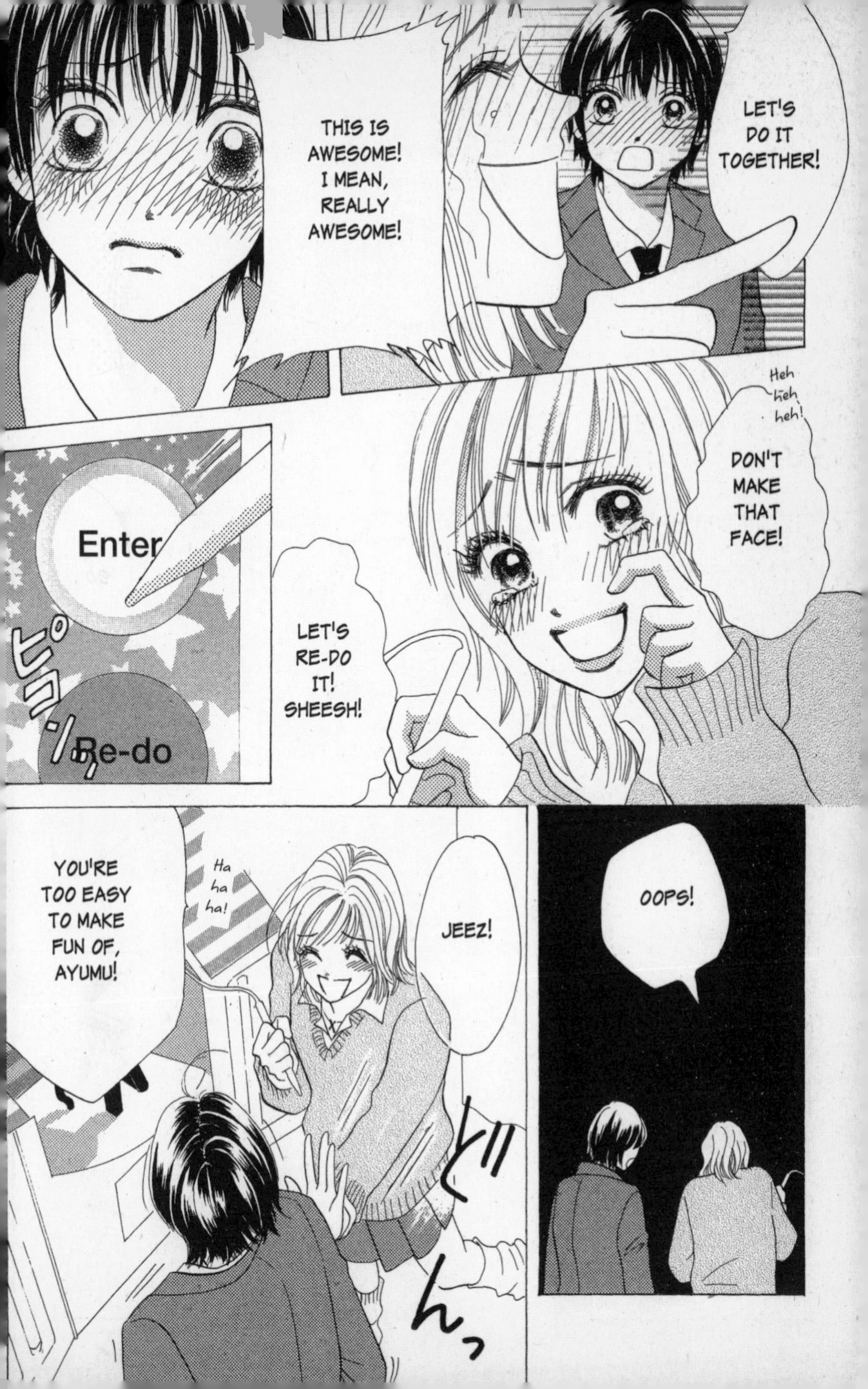
LET'S DO IT TOGETHER!
THIS IS AWESOME! I MEAN, REALLY AWESOME!
Heh heh heh!
DON'T MAKE THAT FACE!
LET'S RE-DO IT! SHEESH!
Enter
Re-do
OOPS!
YOU'RE TOO EASY TO MAKE FUN OF, AYUMU!
Ha ha ha!
JEEZ!

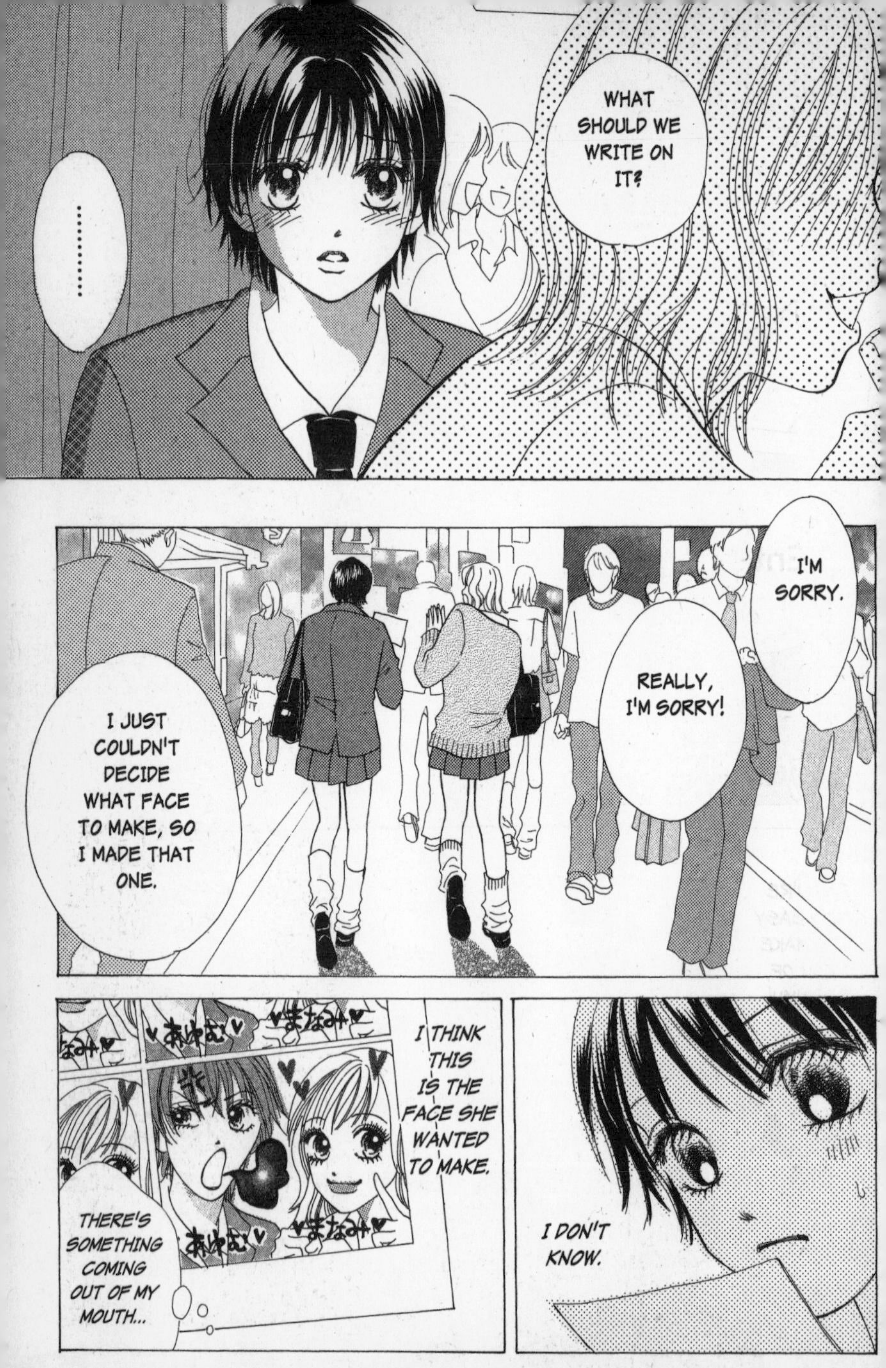
WHAT SHOULD WE WRITE ON IT?
......
I'M SORRY.
REALLY, I'M SORRY!
I JUST COULDN'T DECIDE WHAT FACE TO MAKE, SO I MADE THAT ONE.
I DON'T KNOW.
I THINK THIS IS THE FACE SHE WANTED TO MAKE.
THERE'S SOMETHING COMING OUT OF MY MOUTH...

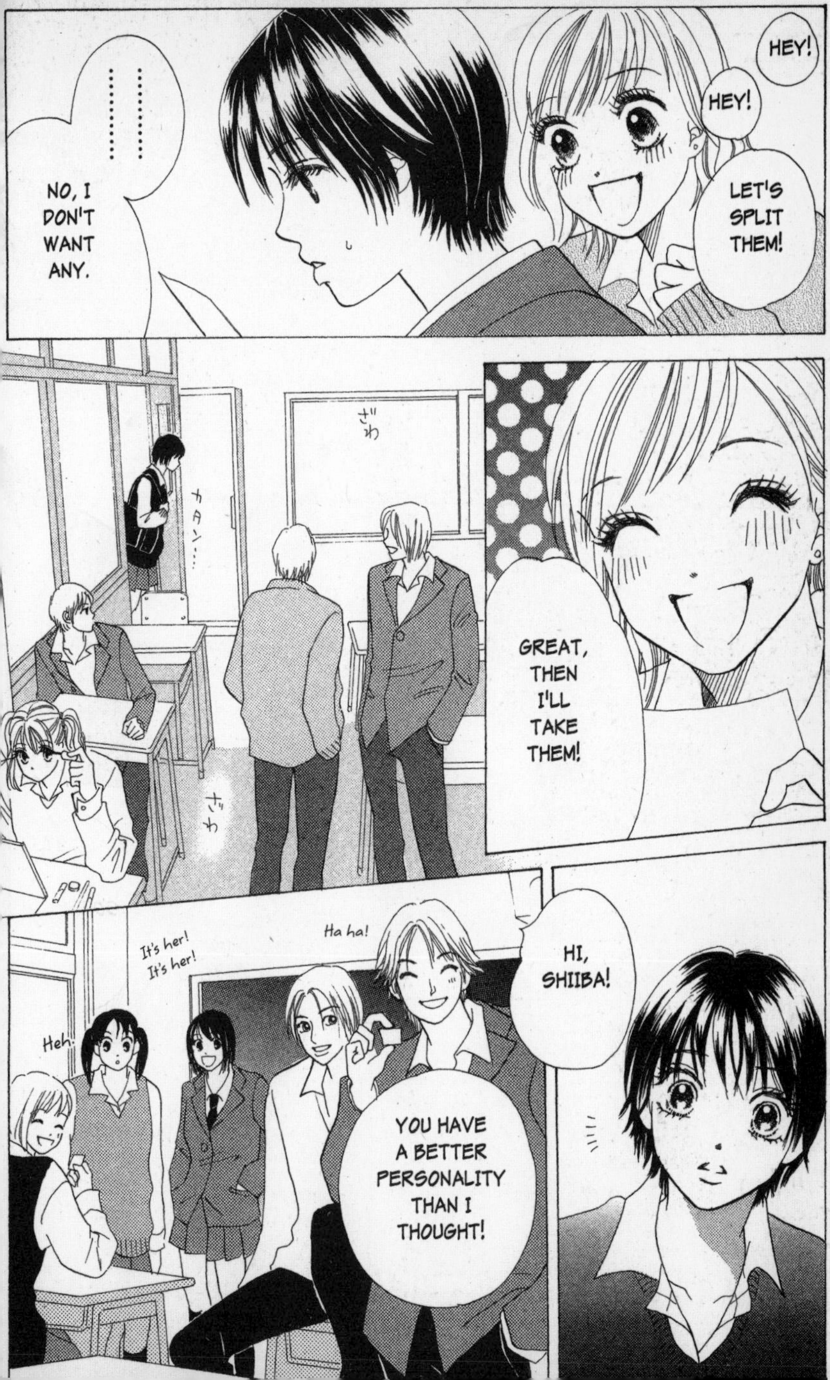
HEY!
HEY!
LET'S SPLIT THEM!
......
NO, I DON'T WANT ANY.
GREAT, THEN I'LL TAKE THEM!
ざわ
カタン…
ざわ
HI, SHIIBA!
Ha ha!
It's her! It's her!
Heh.
YOU HAVE A BETTER PERSONALITY THAN I THOUGHT!

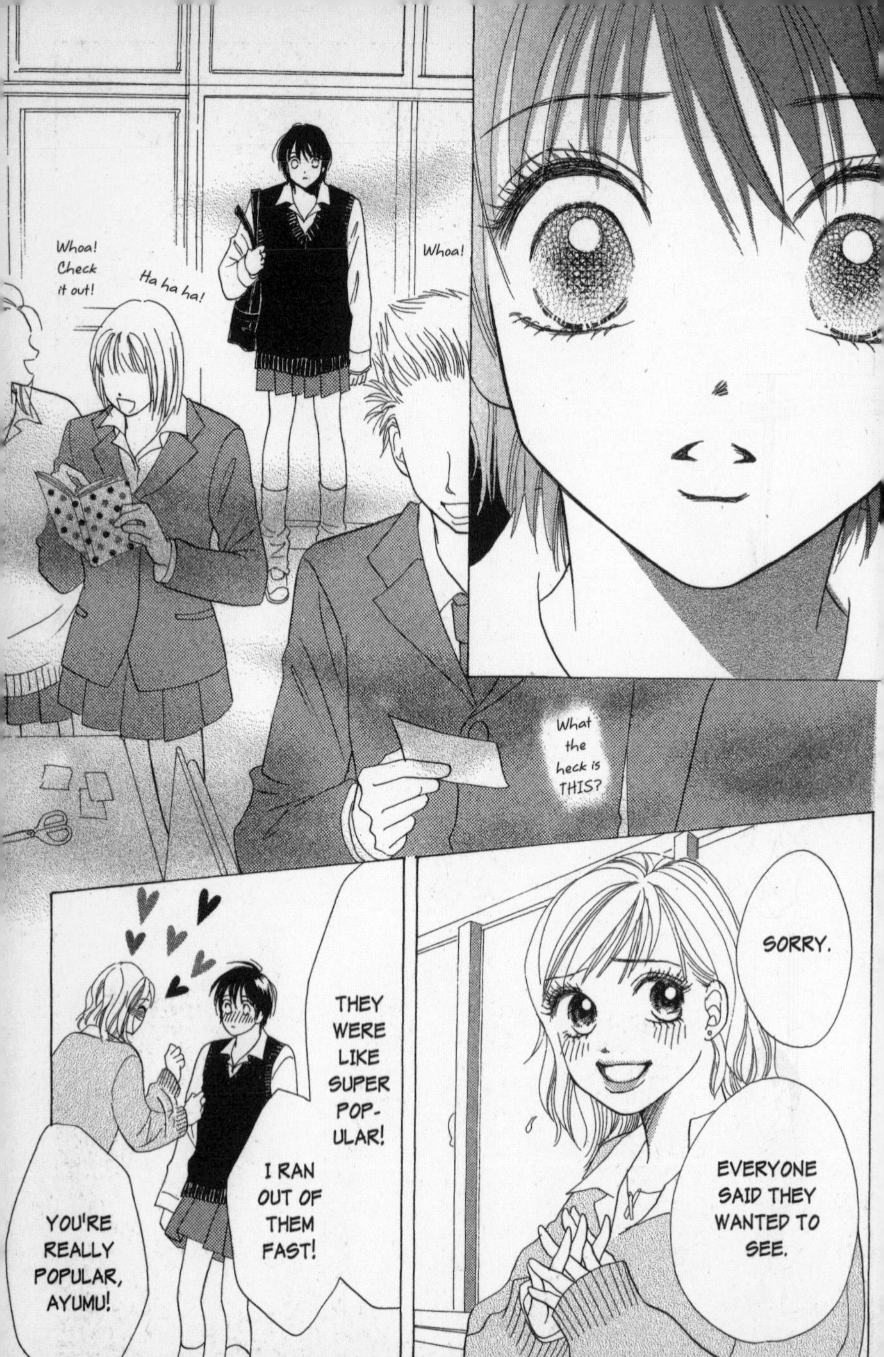
Whoa!
Ha ha ha!
Whoa! Check it out!
What the heck is THIS?
SORRY.
EVERYONE SAID THEY WANTED TO SEE.
THEY WERE LIKE SUPER POP-ULAR!
I RAN OUT OF THEM FAST!
YOU'RE REALLY POPULAR, AYUMU!

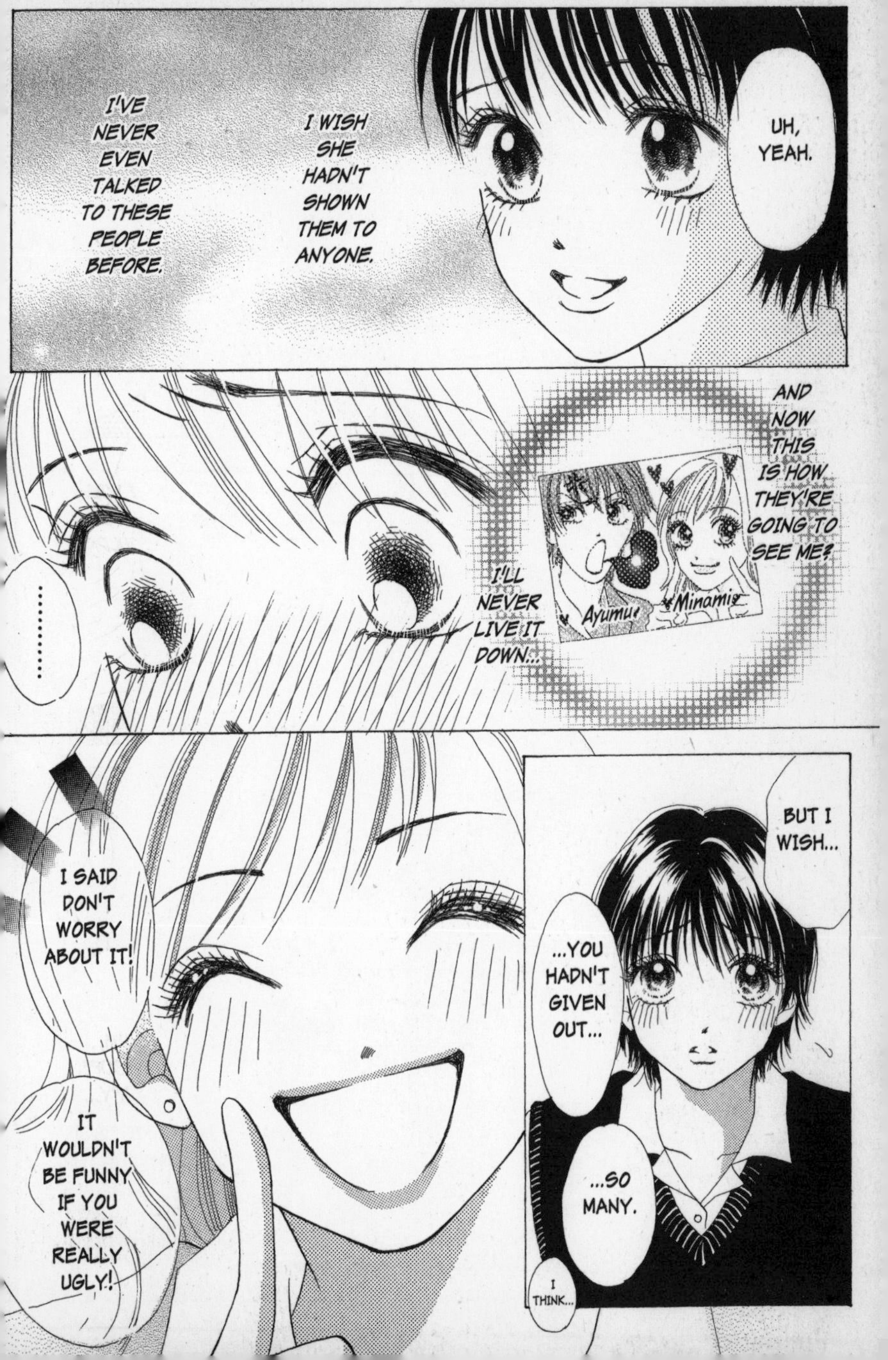

UH, YEAH.
I WISH SHE HADN'T SHOWN THEM TO ANYONE.
I'VE NEVER EVEN TALKED TO THESE PEOPLE BEFORE.
AND NOW THIS IS HOW THEY'RE GOING TO SEE ME?
Ayumu
Minami
I'LL NEVER LIVE IT DOWN...
......
BUT I WISH...
...YOU HADN'T GIVEN OUT...
...SO MANY.
I THINK...
I SAID DON'T WORRY ABOUT IT!
IT WOULDN'T BE FUNNY IF YOU WERE REALLY UGLY!

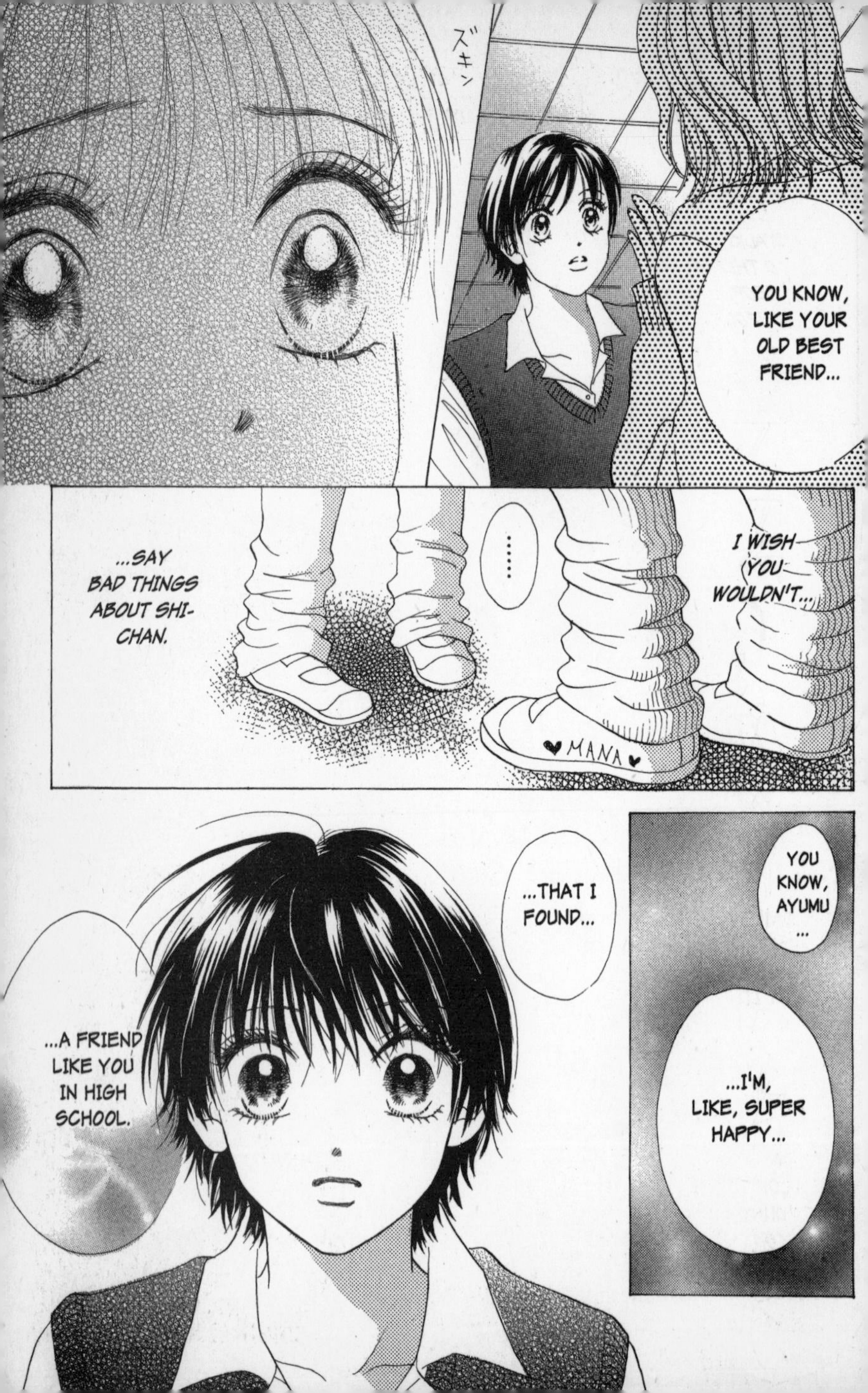
YOU KNOW, LIKE YOUR OLD BEST FRIEND...
ズキン
I WISH YOU WOULDN'T...
......
...SAY BAD THINGS ABOUT SHI-CHAN.
MANA
YOU KNOW, AYUMU ...
...I'M, LIKE, SUPER HAPPY...
...THAT I FOUND...
...A FRIEND LIKE YOU IN HIGH SCHOOL.

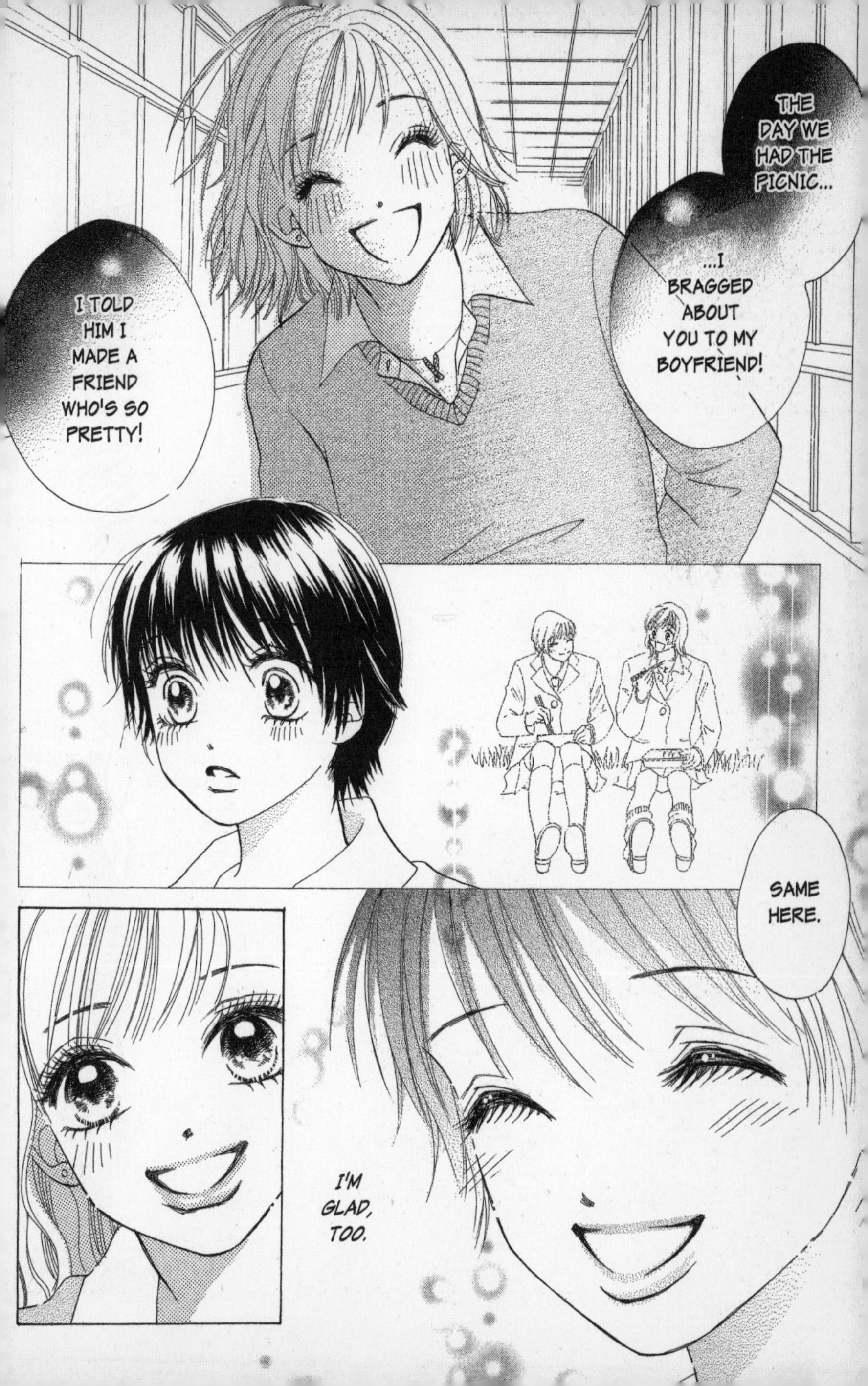
THE DAY WE HAD THE PICNIC...
...I BRAGGED ABOUT YOU TO MY BOYFRIEND!
I TOLD HIM I MADE A FRIEND WHO'S SO PRETTY!
SAME HERE.
I'M GLAD, TOO.

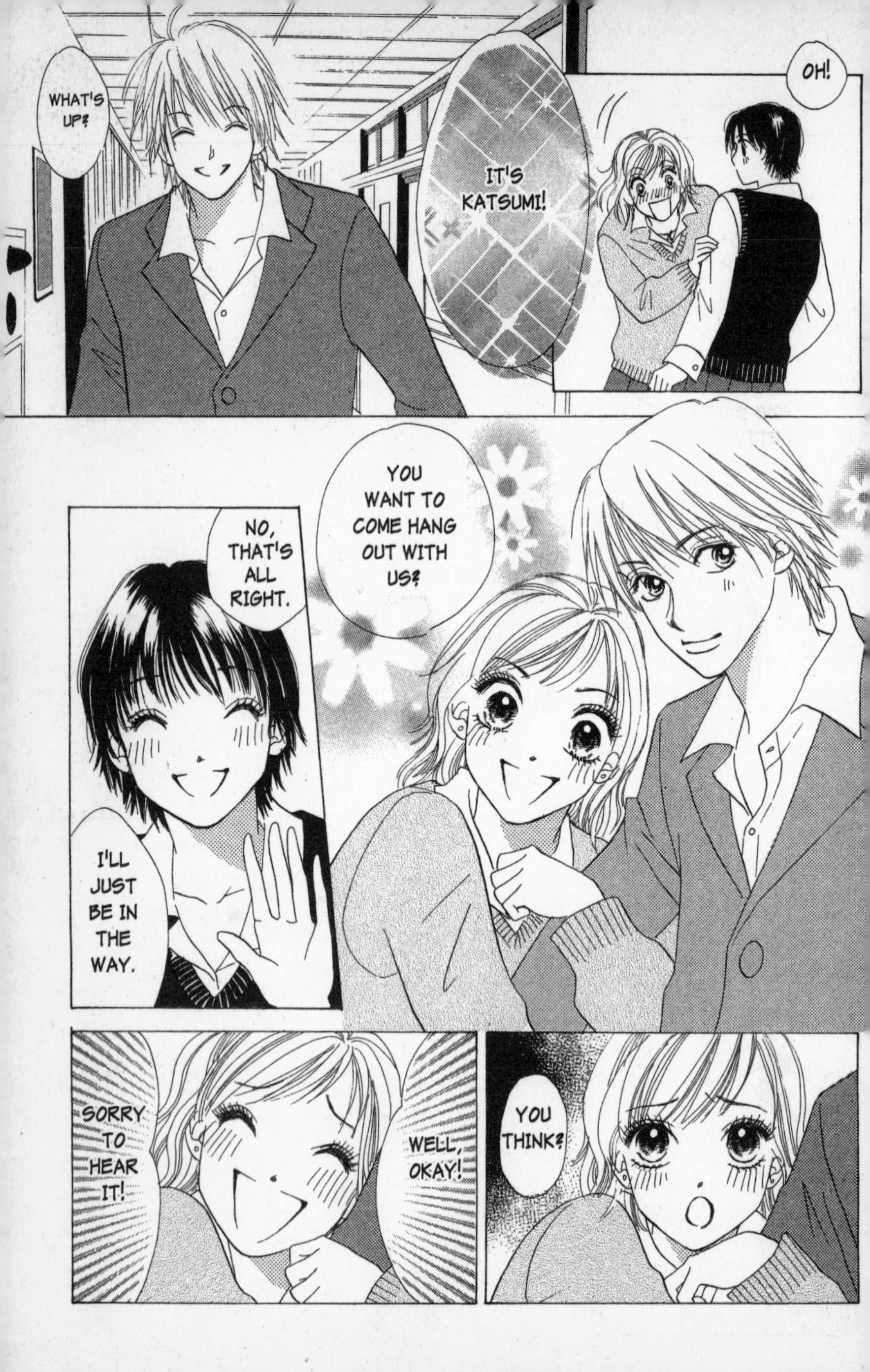
OH!
IT'S KATSUMI!
WHAT'S UP?
YOU WANT TO COME HANG OUT WITH US?
NO, THAT'S ALL RIGHT.
I'LL JUST BE IN THE WAY.
YOU THINK?
WELL, OKAY!
SORRY TO HEAR IT!

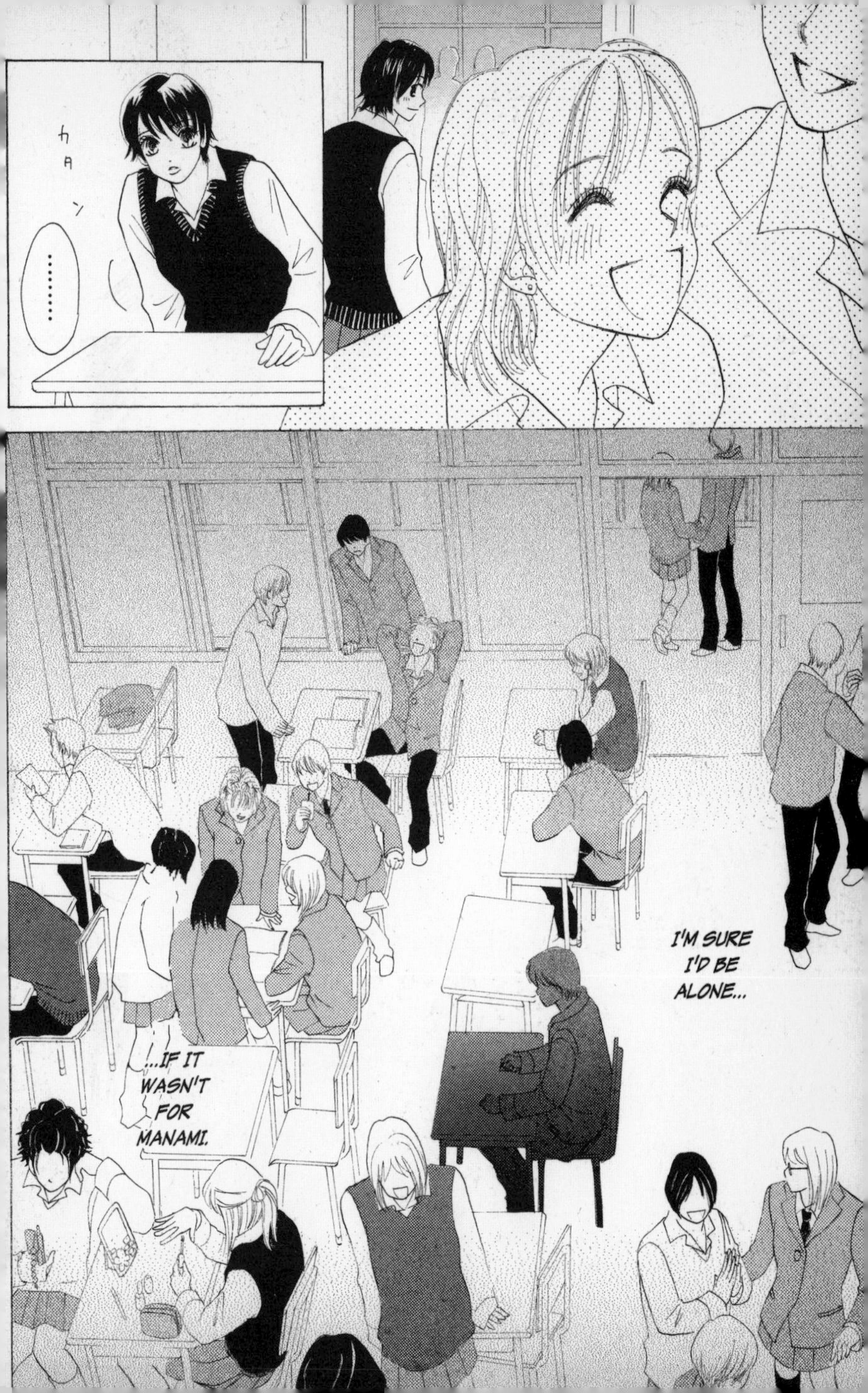
カタン
....
I'M SURE I'D BE ALONE...
...IF IT WASN'T FOR MANAMI.

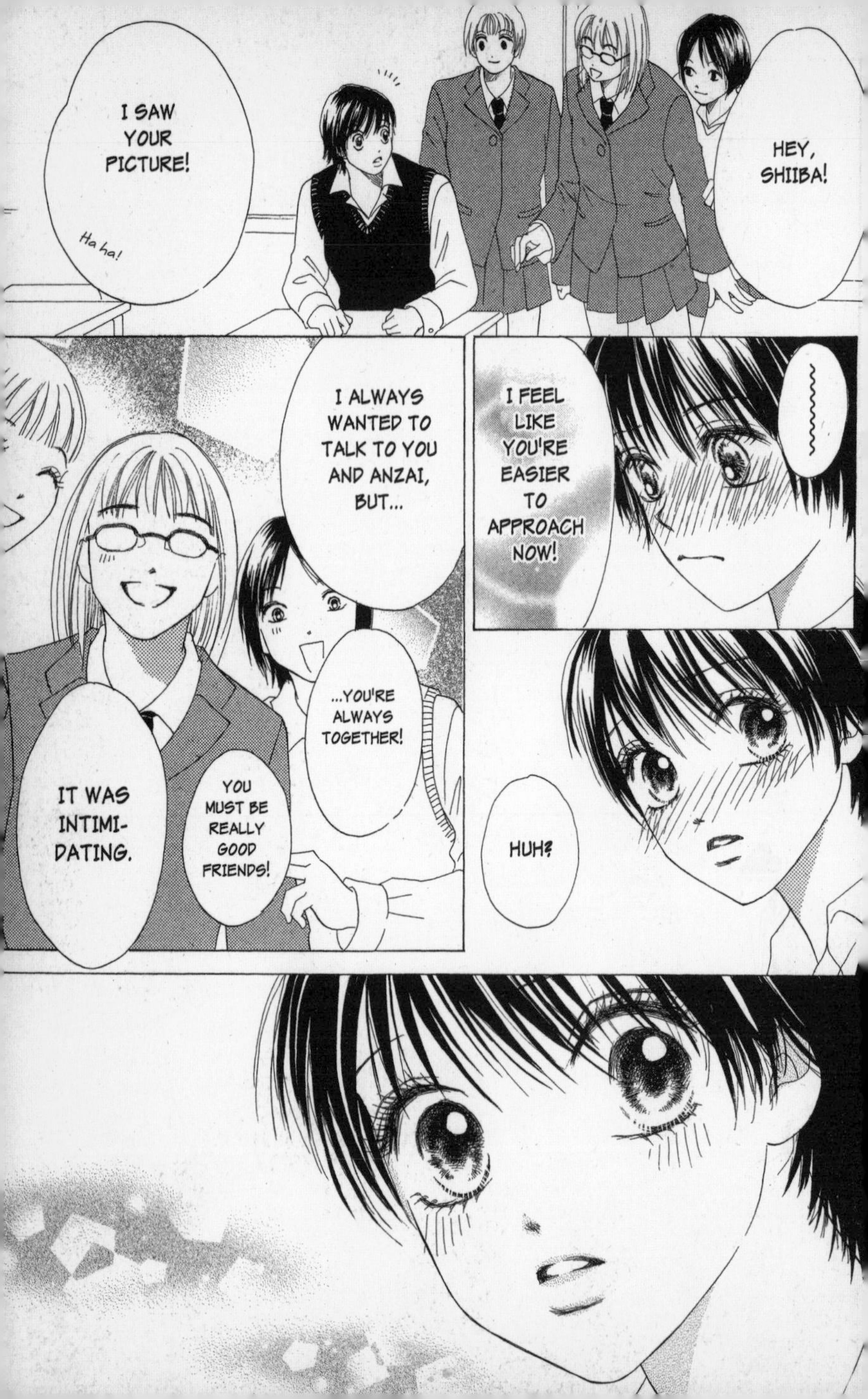
HEY, SHIIBA!
I SAW YOUR PICTURE!
Ha ha!
I FEEL LIKE YOU'RE EASIER TO APPROACH NOW!
HUH?
I ALWAYS WANTED TO TALK TO YOU AND ANZAI, BUT...
...YOU'RE ALWAYS TOGETHER!
YOU MUST BE REALLY GOOD FRIENDS!
IT WAS INTIMI-DATING.

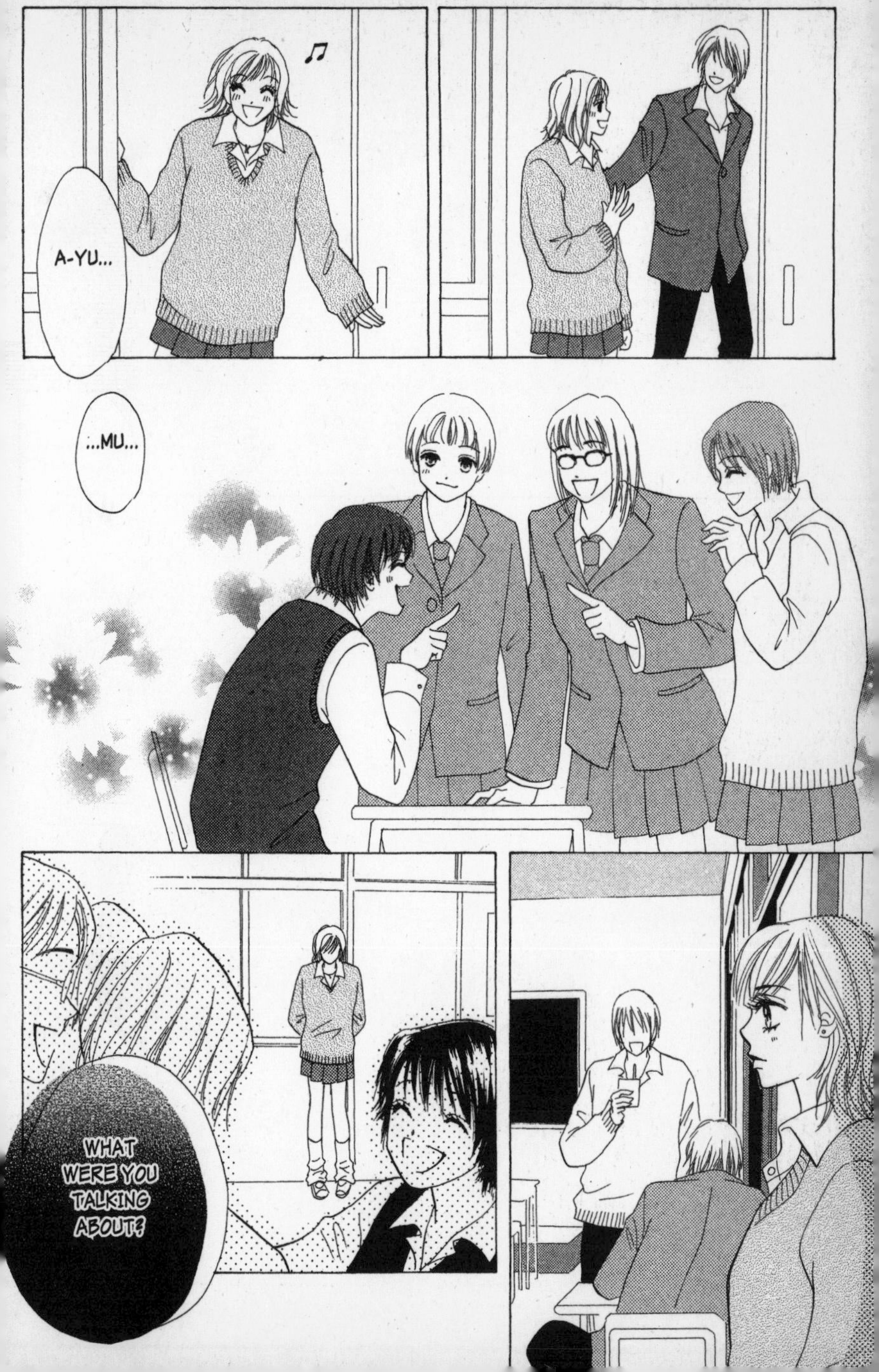
A-YU...
...MU...
WHAT WERE YOU TALKING ABOUT?

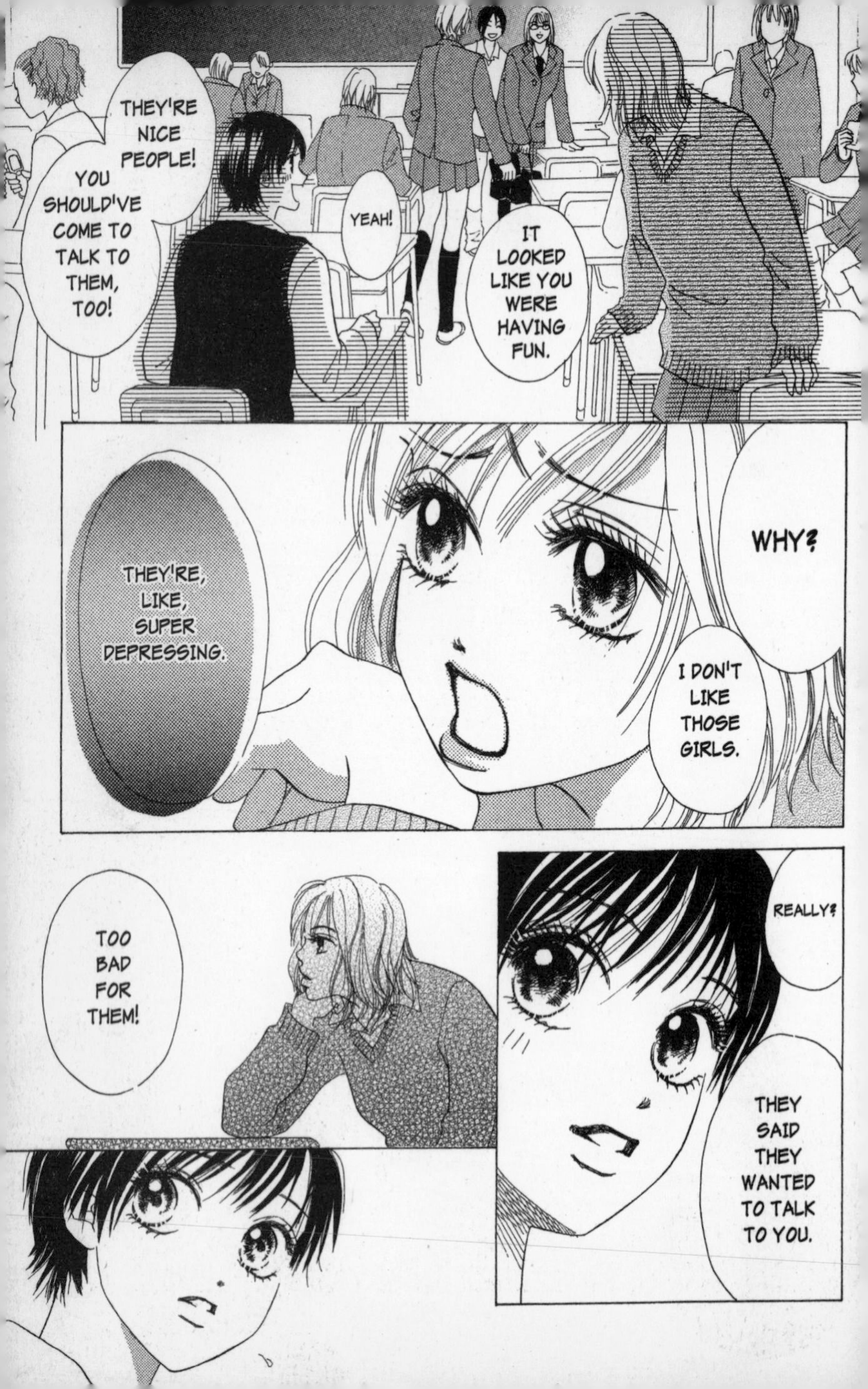
IT LOOKED LIKE YOU WERE HAVING FUN.
YEAH!
THEY'RE NICE PEOPLE!
YOU SHOULD'VE COME TO TALK TO THEM, TOO!
WHY?
I DON'T LIKE THOSE GIRLS.
THEY'RE, LIKE, SUPER DEPRESSING.
REALLY?
THEY SAID THEY WANTED TO TALK TO YOU.
TOO BAD FOR THEM!

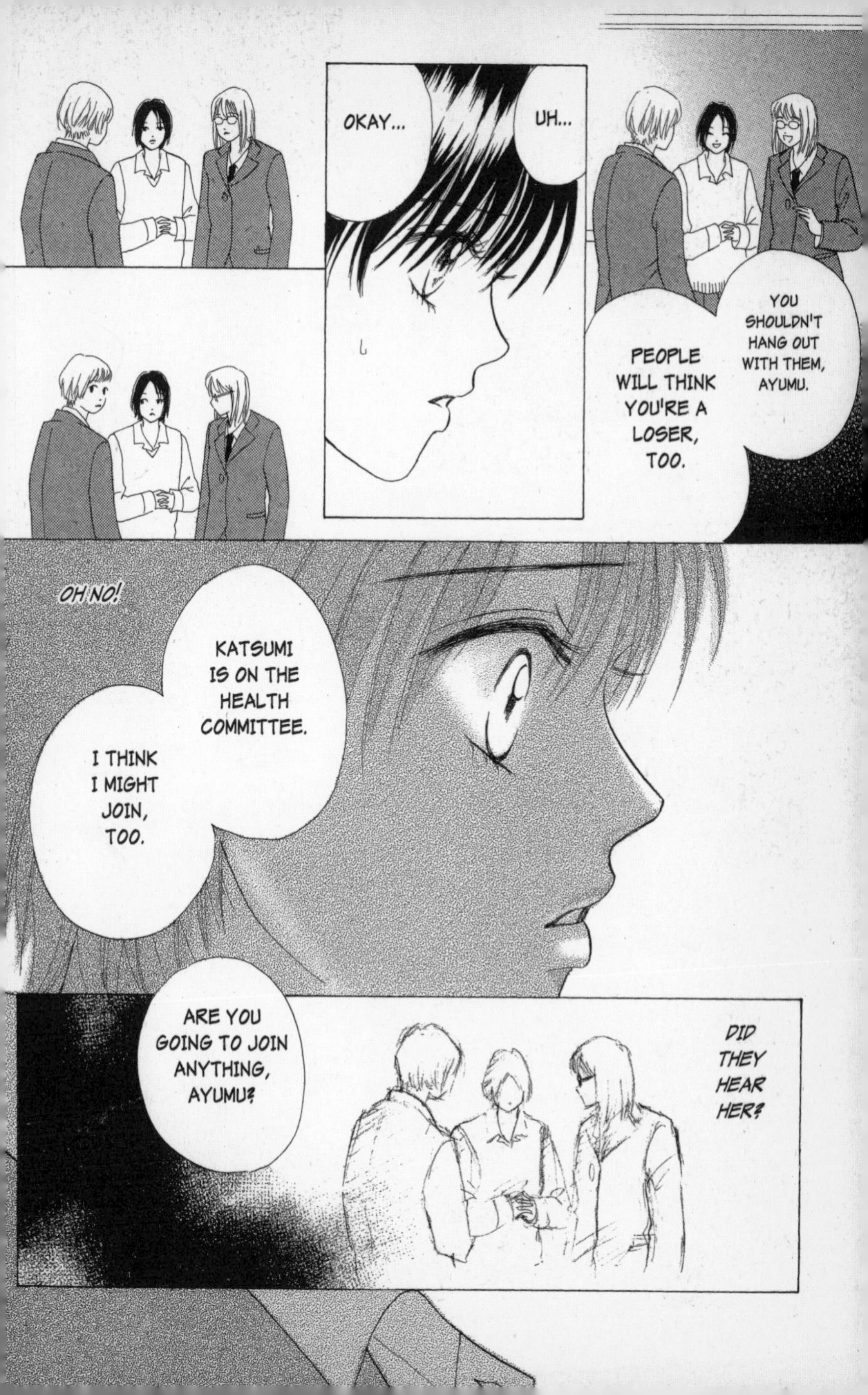
YOU SHOULDN'T HANG OUT WITH THEM, AYUMU.
PEOPLE WILL THINK YOU'RE A LOSER, TOO.
UH...
OKAY...
KATSUMI IS ON THE HEALTH COMMITTEE.
I THINK I MIGHT JOIN, TOO.
OH NO!
DID THEY HEAR HER?
ARE YOU GOING TO JOIN ANYTHING, AYUMU?

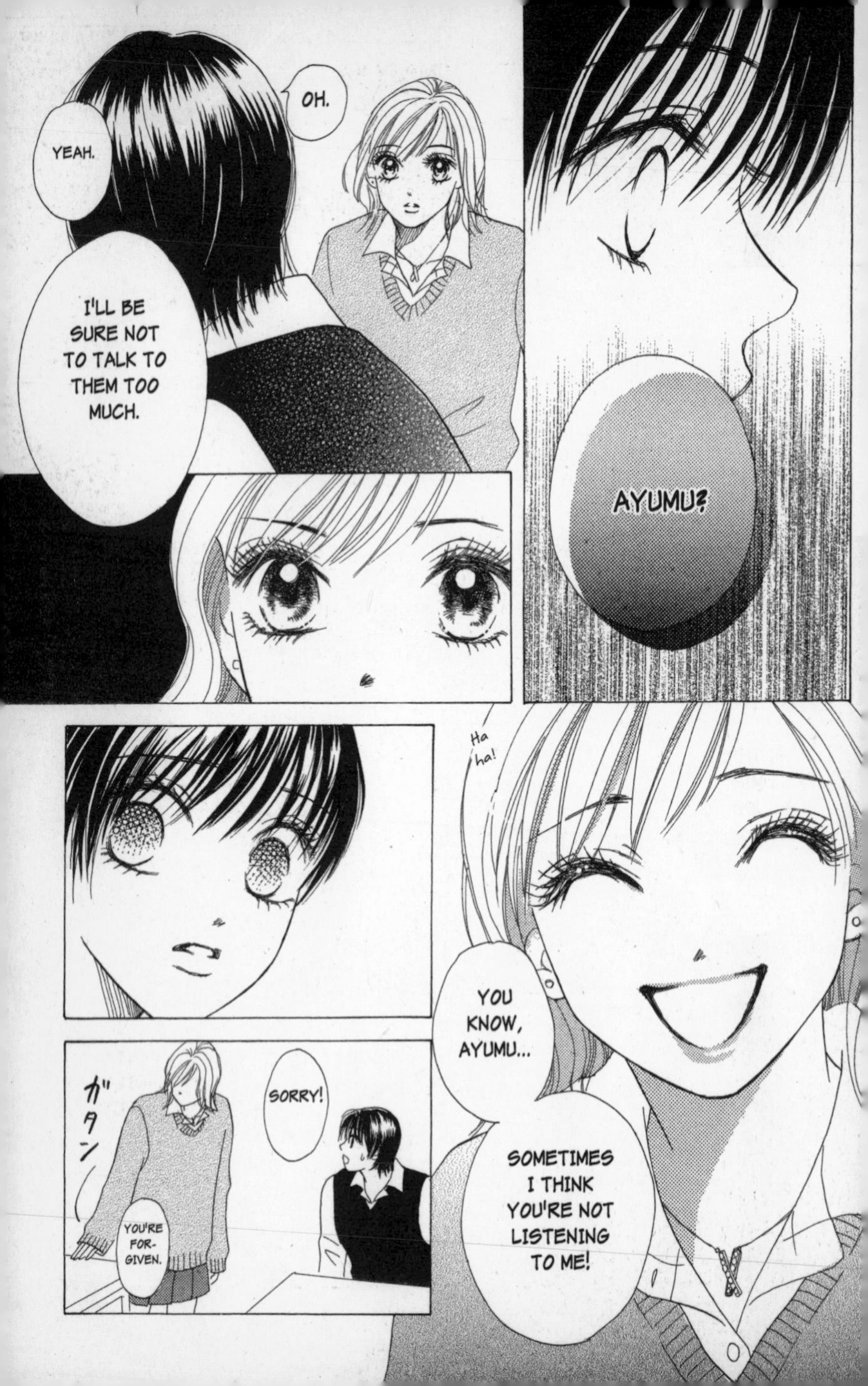
OH.
YEAH.
I'LL BE SURE NOT TO TALK TO THEM TOO MUCH.
AYUMU?
Ha ha!
YOU KNOW, AYUMU...
SOMETIMES I THINK YOU'RE NOT LISTENING TO ME!
SORRY!
ガタン
YOU'RE FOR-GIVEN.

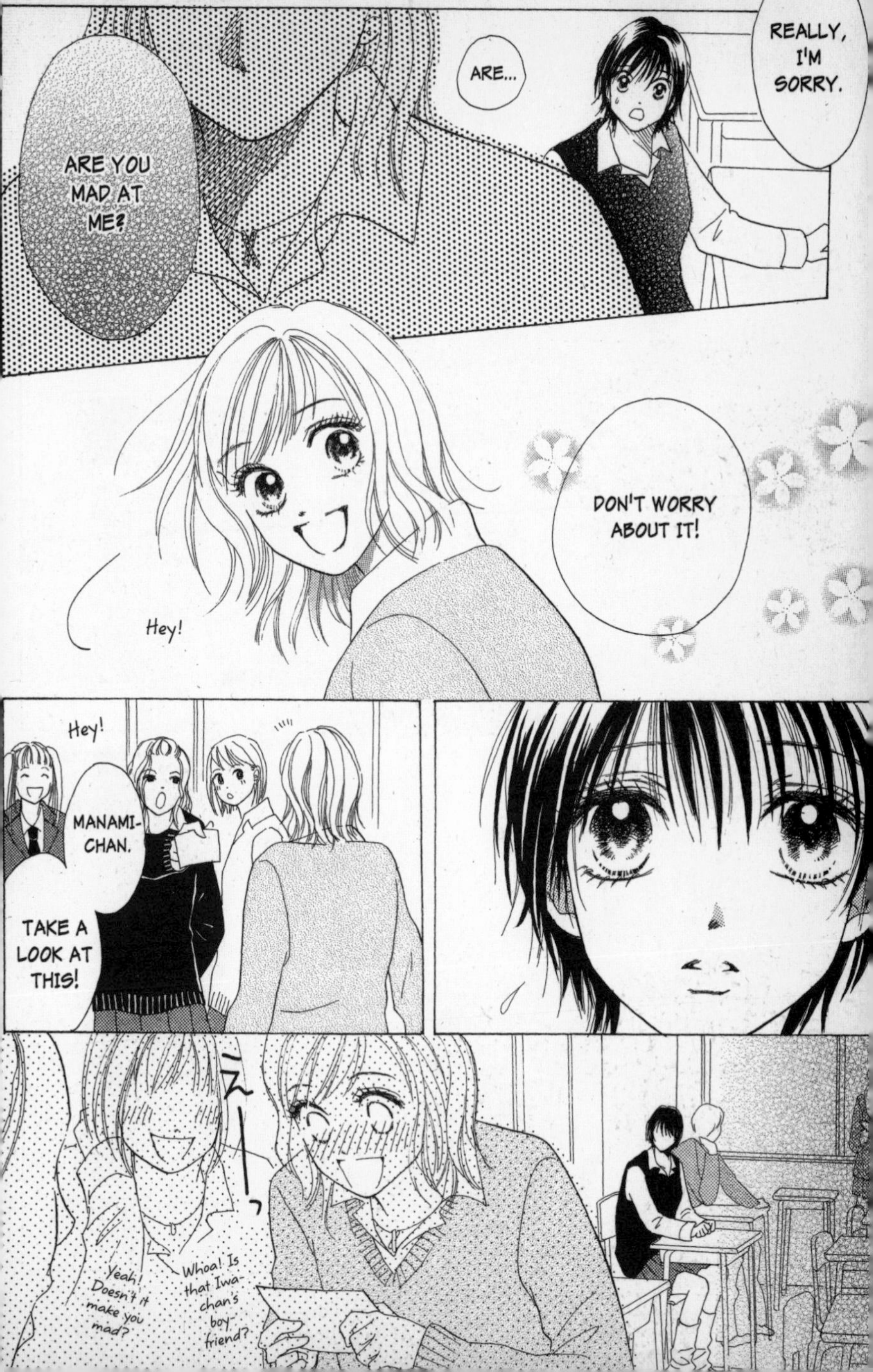
REALLY, I'M SORRY.
ARE...
ARE YOU MAD AT ME?
DON'T WORRY ABOUT IT!
Hey!
Hey!
MANAMI-CHAN.
TAKE A LOOK AT THIS!
Whoa! Is that Iwa-chan's boy-friend?
Yeah! Doesn't it make you mad?

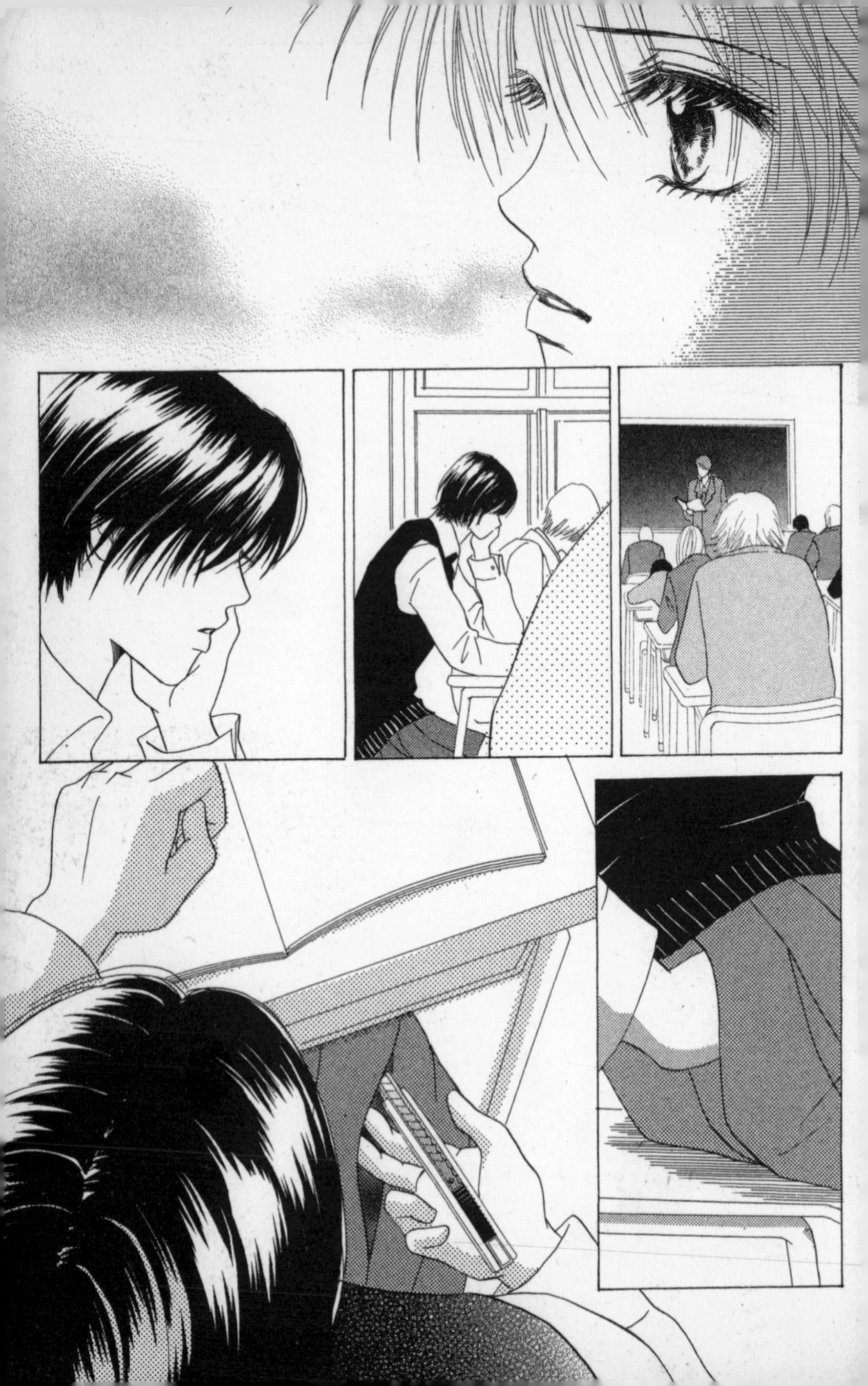

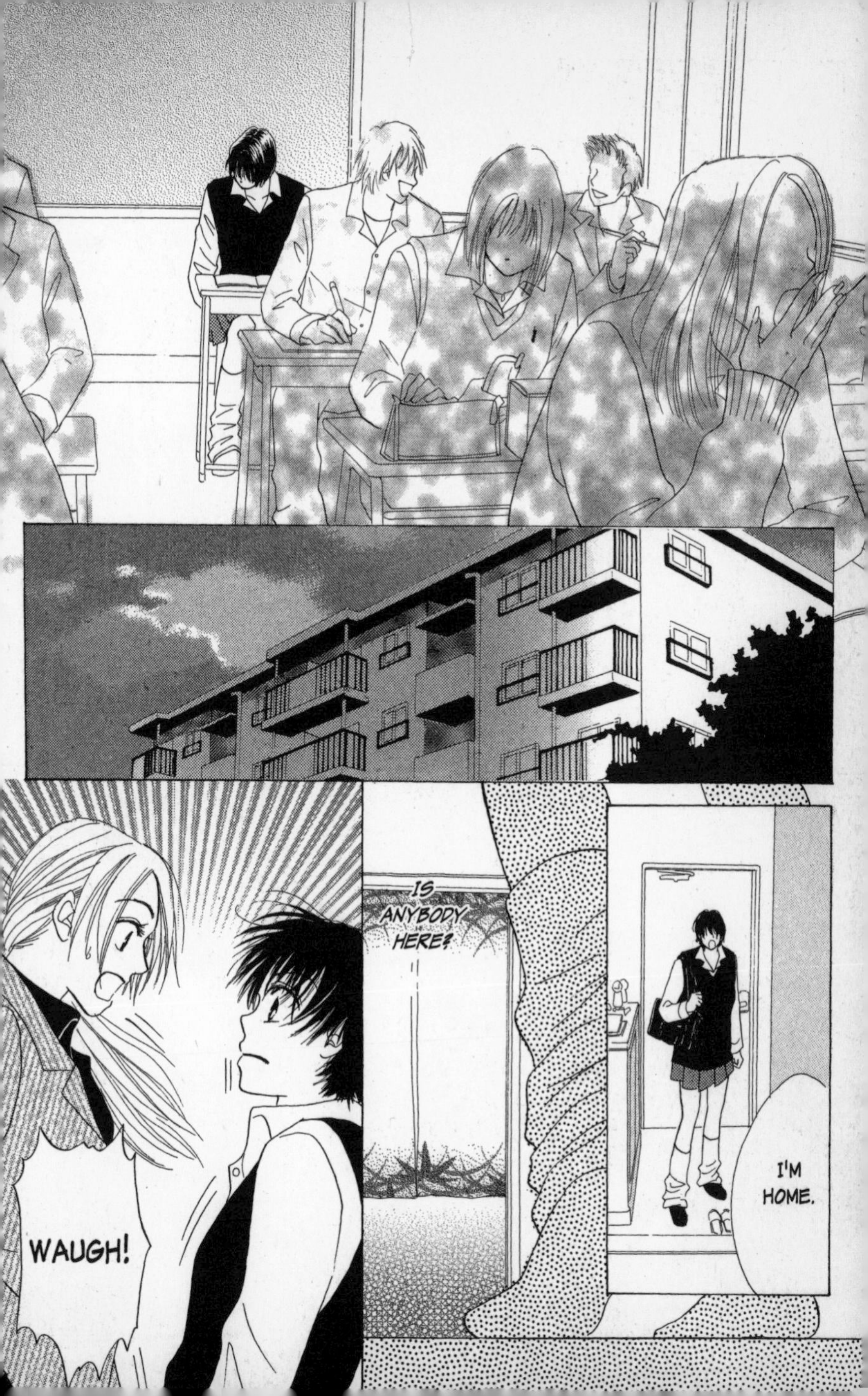
I'M HOME.
IS ANYBODY HERE?
WAUGH!

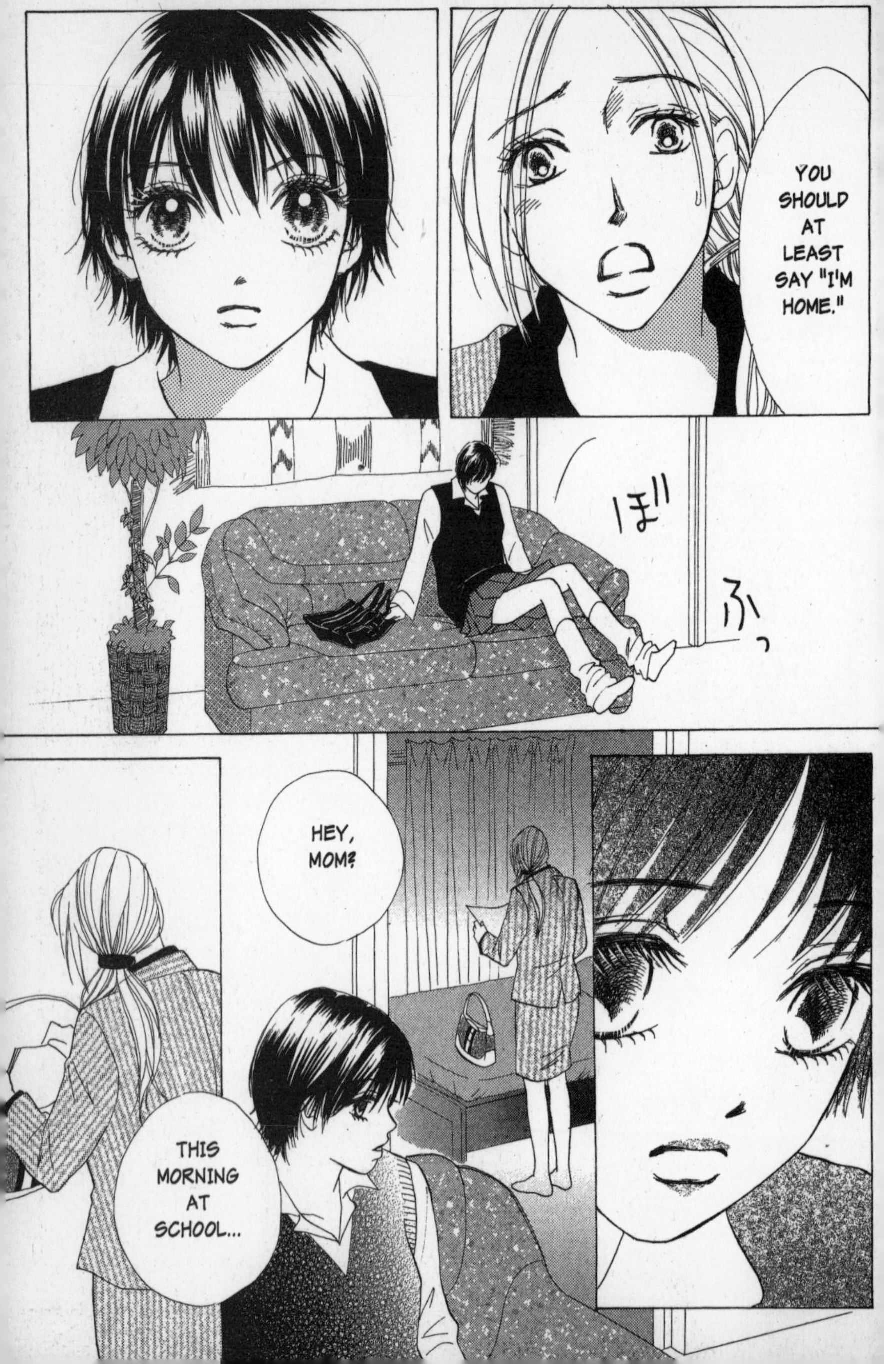
YOU SHOULD AT LEAST SAY "I'M HOME."
ぼ
ふっ
HEY, MOM?
THIS MORNING AT SCHOOL...

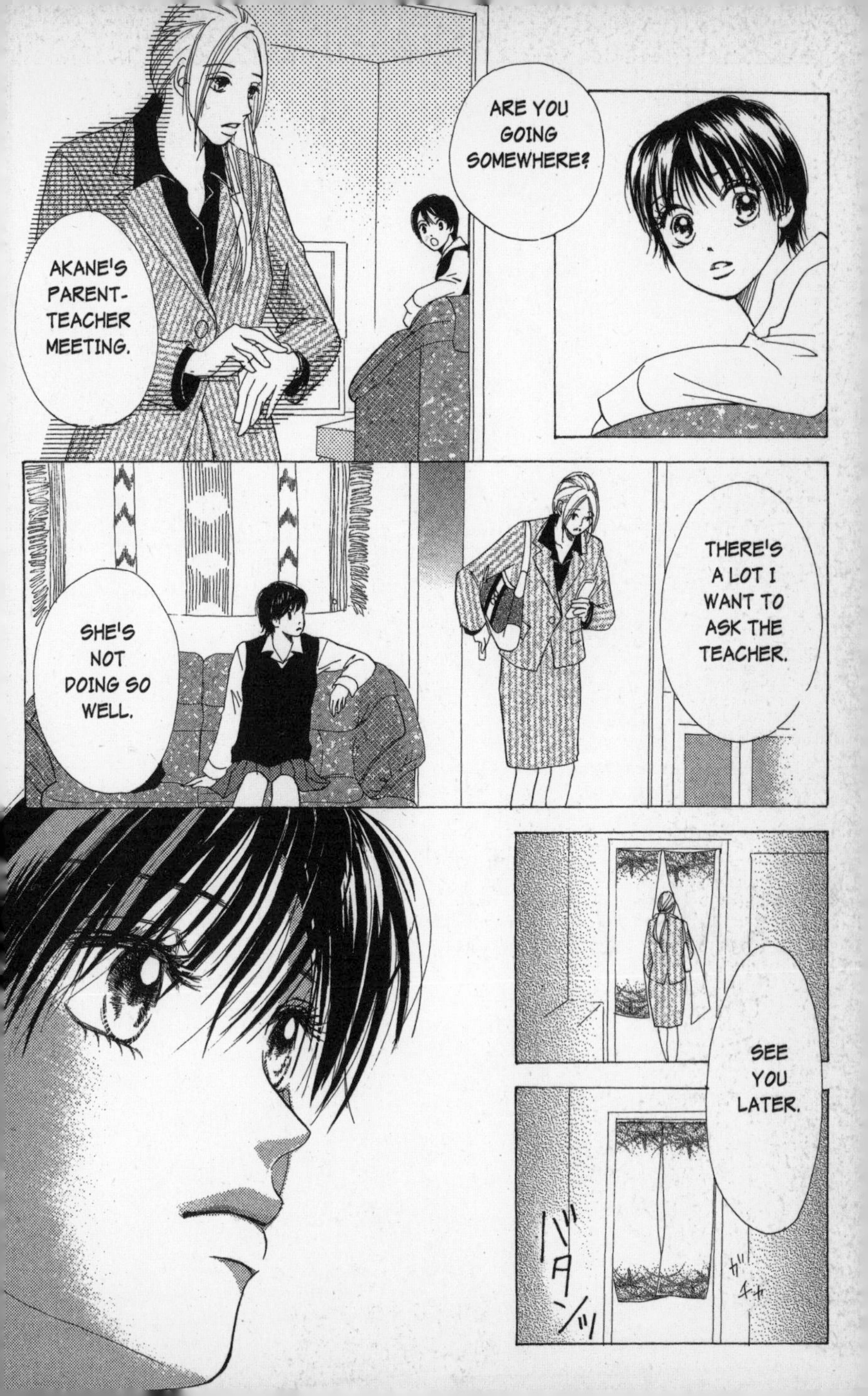
ARE YOU GOING SOMEWHERE?
AKANE'S PARENT-TEACHER MEETING.
THERE'S A LOT I WANT TO ASK THE TEACHER.
SHE'S NOT DOING SO WELL.
SEE YOU LATER.
ガチャ
バタンッ

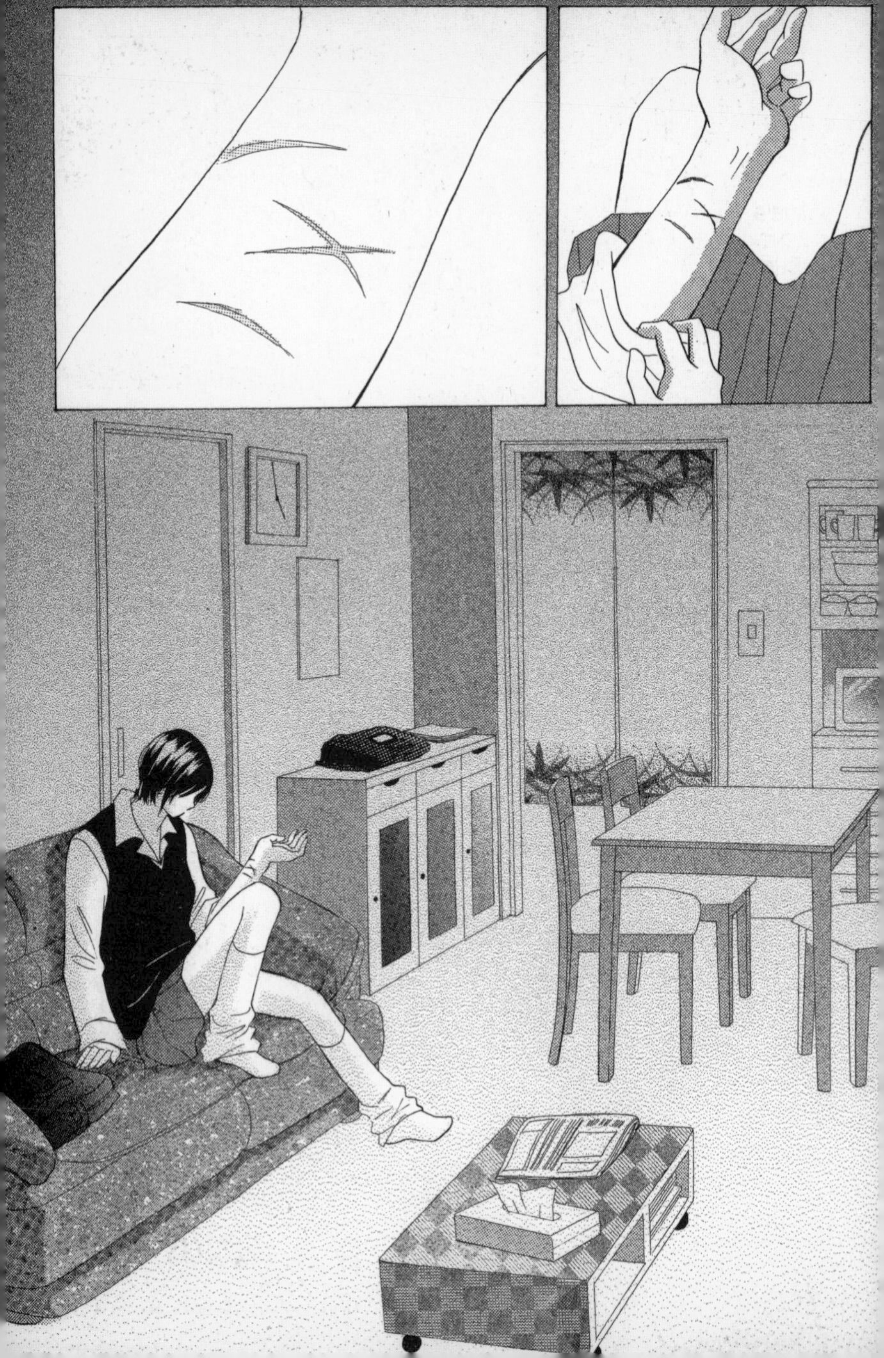

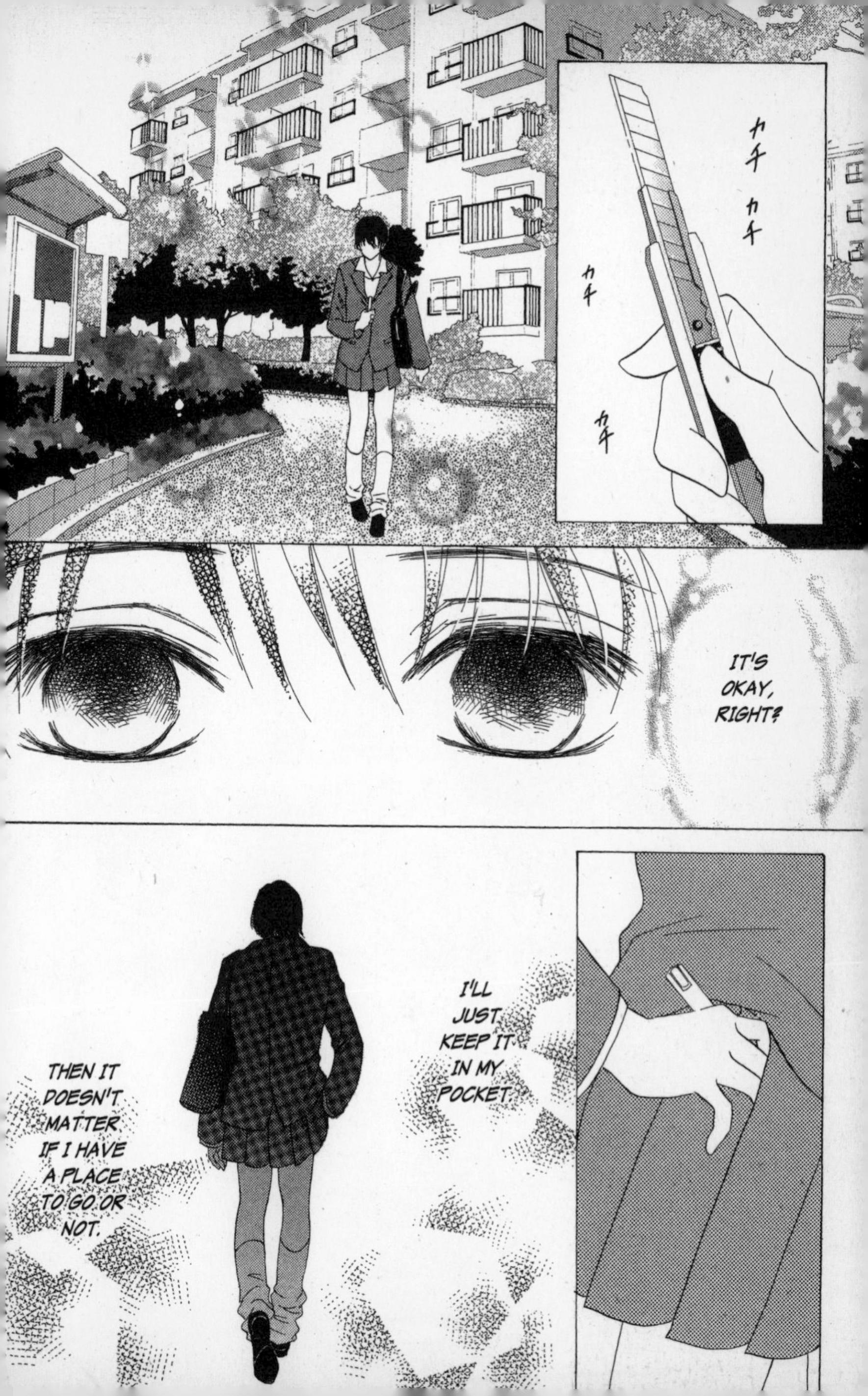
カチ
カチ
カチ
カチ
IT'S OKAY, RIGHT?
I'LL JUST KEEP IT IN MY POCKET.
THEN IT DOESN'T MATTER IF I HAVE A PLACE TO GO OR NOT.

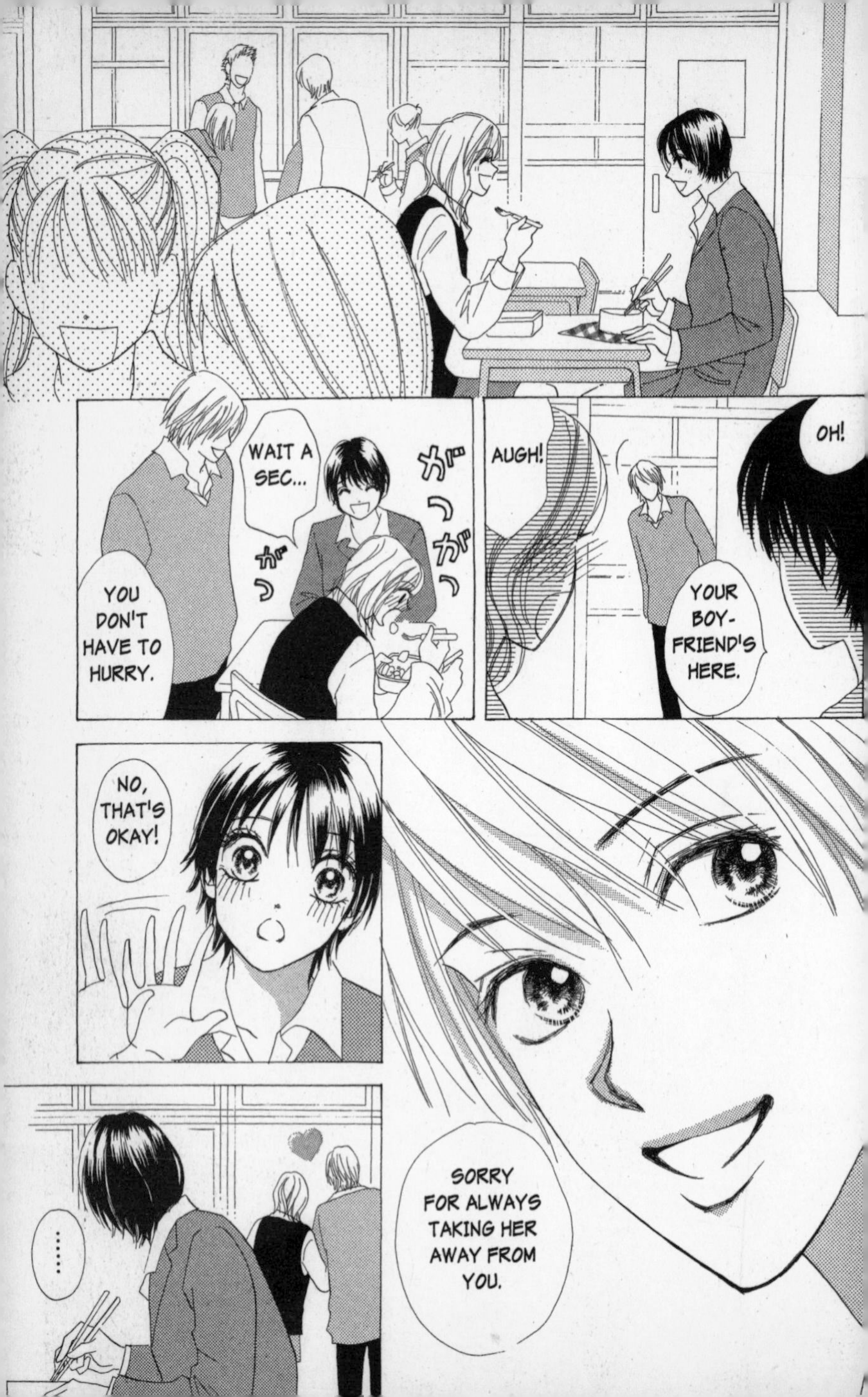
OH!
YOUR BOY-FRIEND'S HERE.
AUGH!
WAIT A SEC...
ガッガッ
ガッ
YOU DON'T HAVE TO HURRY.
SORRY FOR ALWAYS TAKING HER AWAY FROM YOU.
NO, THAT'S OKAY!
......

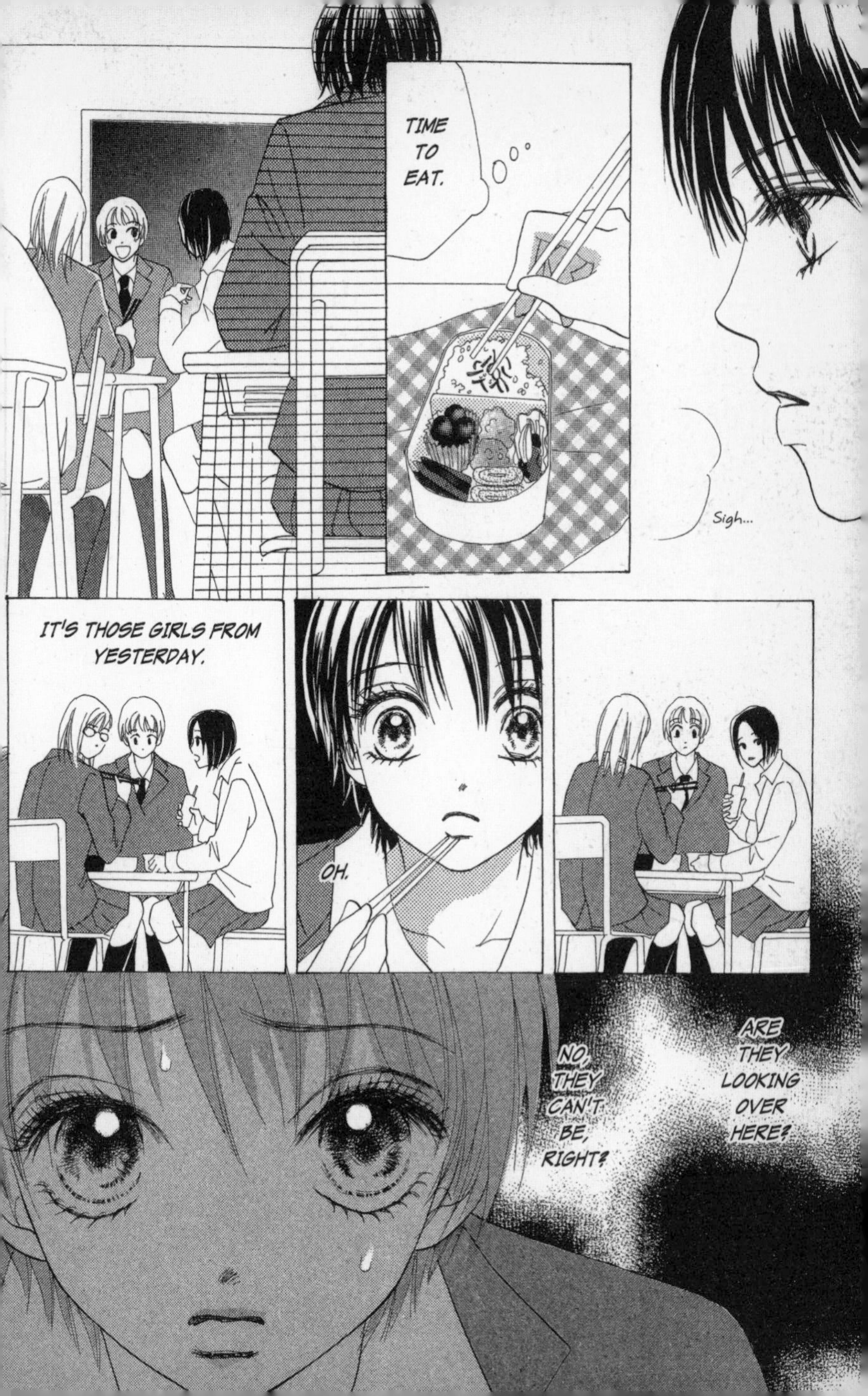
Sigh...
TIME TO EAT.
OH.
IT'S THOSE GIRLS FROM YESTERDAY.
ARE THEY LOOKING OVER HERE?
NO, THEY CAN'T BE, RIGHT?

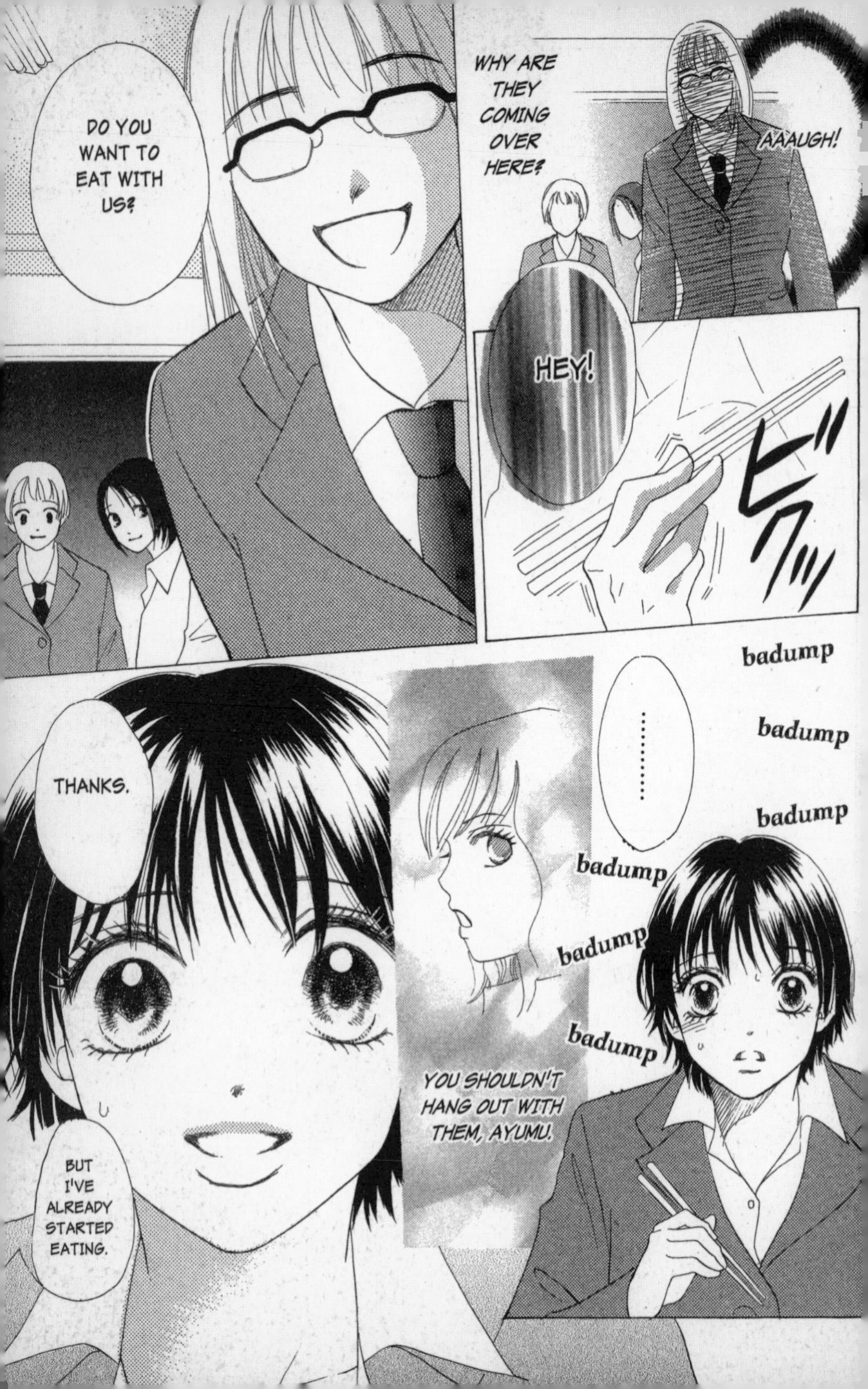
WHY ARE THEY COMING OVER HERE?
AAAUGH!
HEY!
DO YOU WANT TO EAT WITH US?
badump
badump
badump
......
badump
badump
badump
YOU SHOULDN'T HANG OUT WITH THEM, AYUMU.
THANKS.
BUT I'VE ALREADY STARTED EATING.

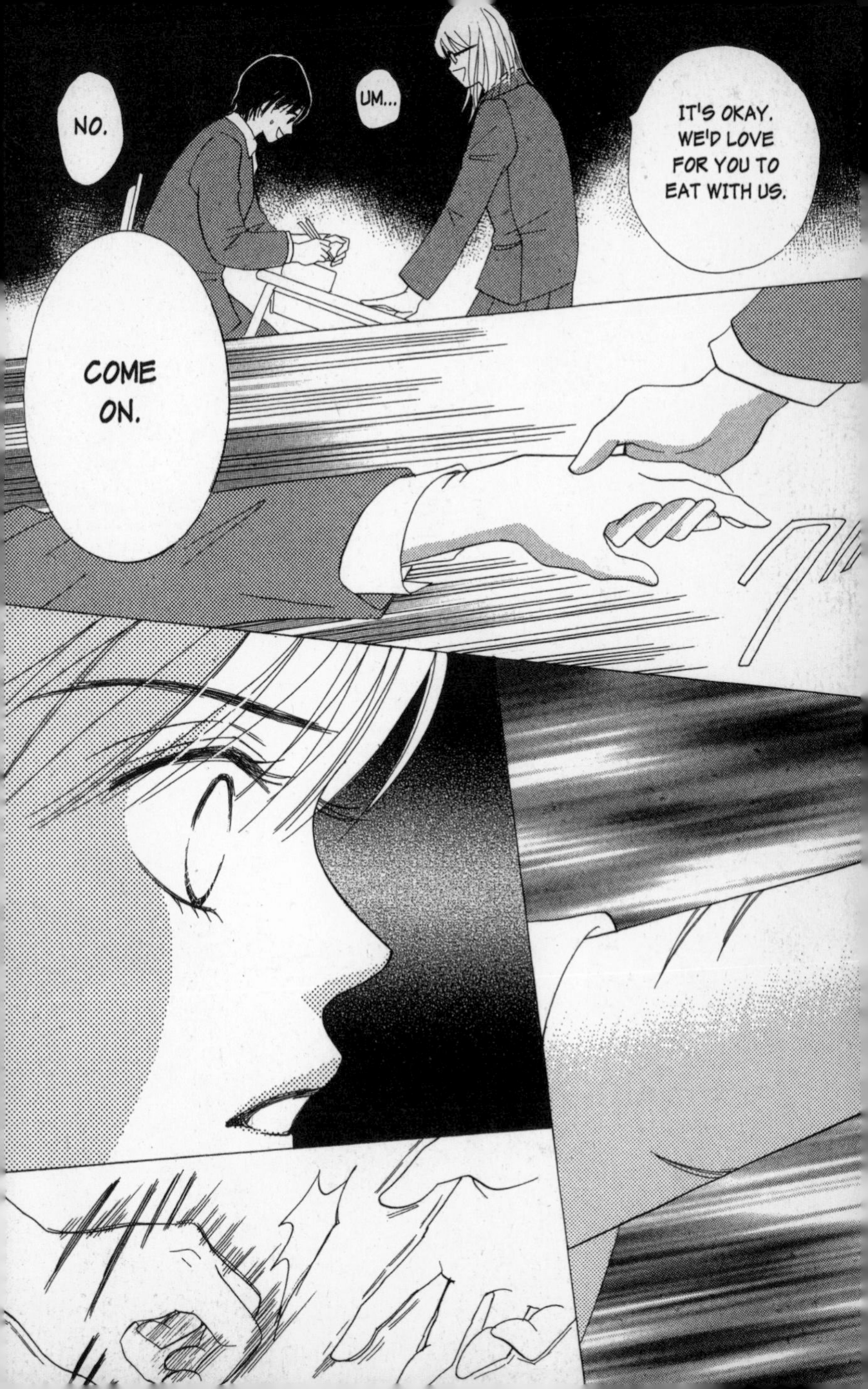
IT'S OKAY. WE'D LOVE FOR YOU TO EAT WITH US.
UM...
NO.
COME ON.

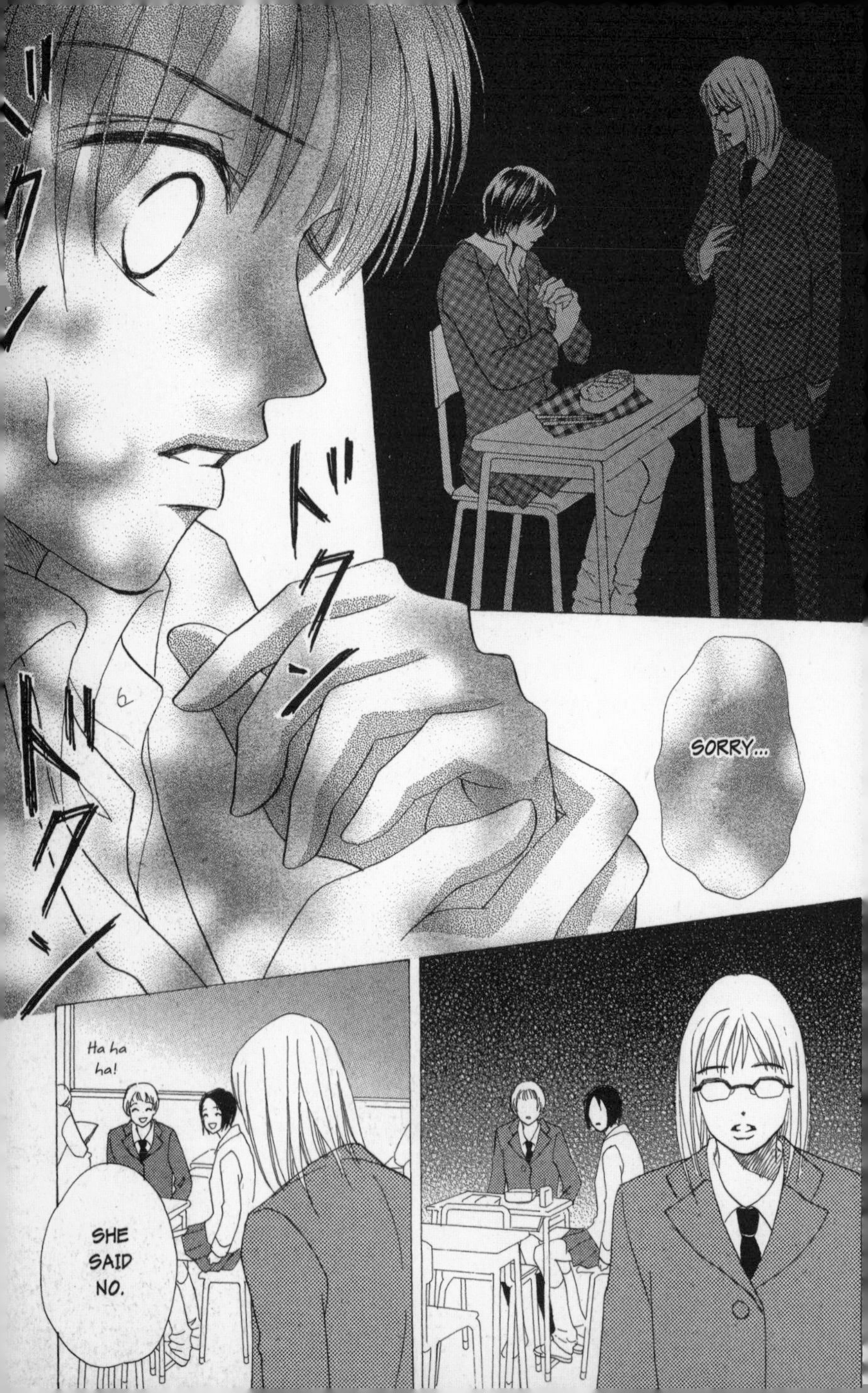

ドクン
ドクン
ドクン
SORRY...
Ha ha ha!
SHE SAID NO.

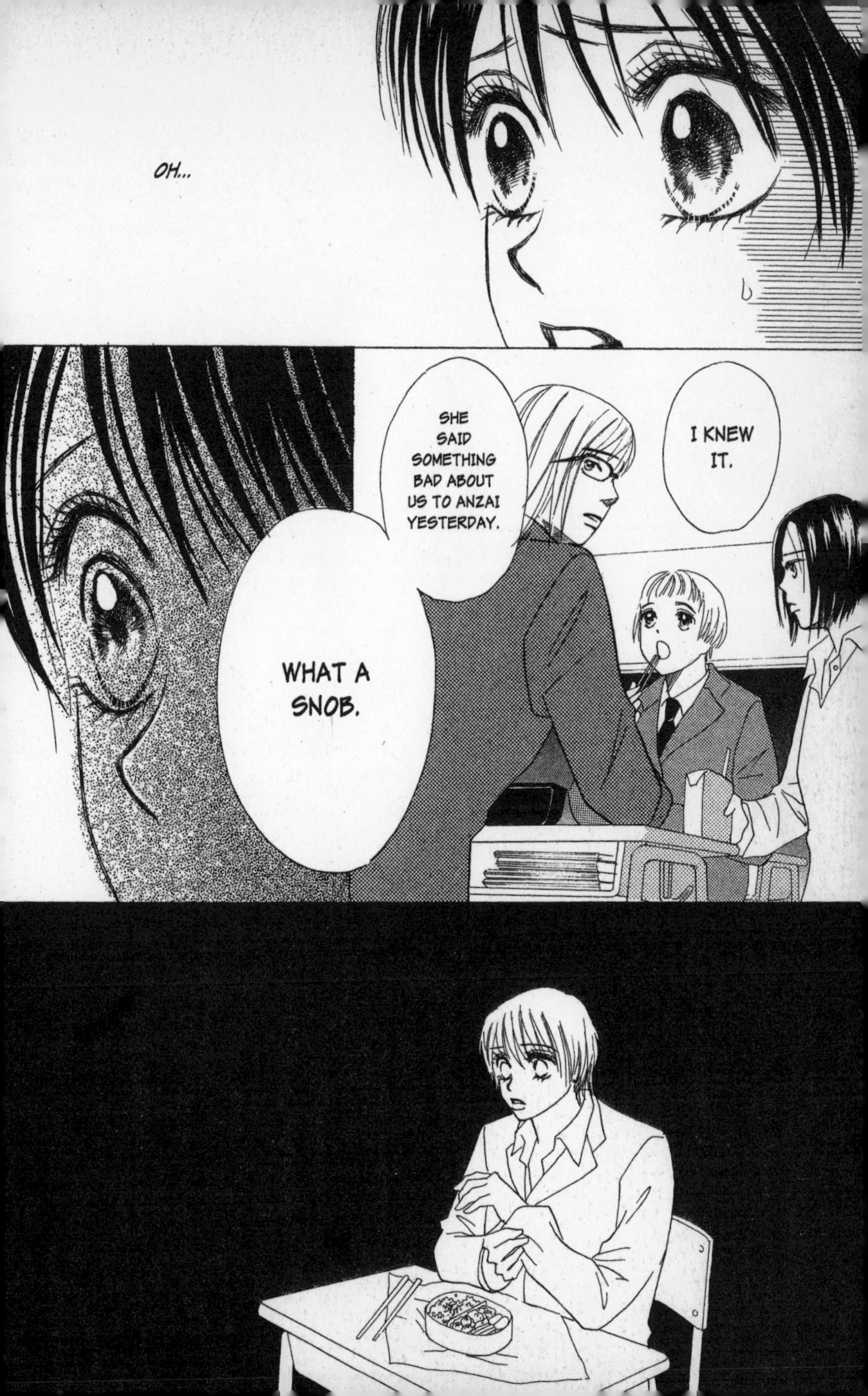
OH...
I KNEW IT.
SHE SAID SOMETHING BAD ABOUT US TO ANZAI YESTERDAY.
WHAT A SNOB.

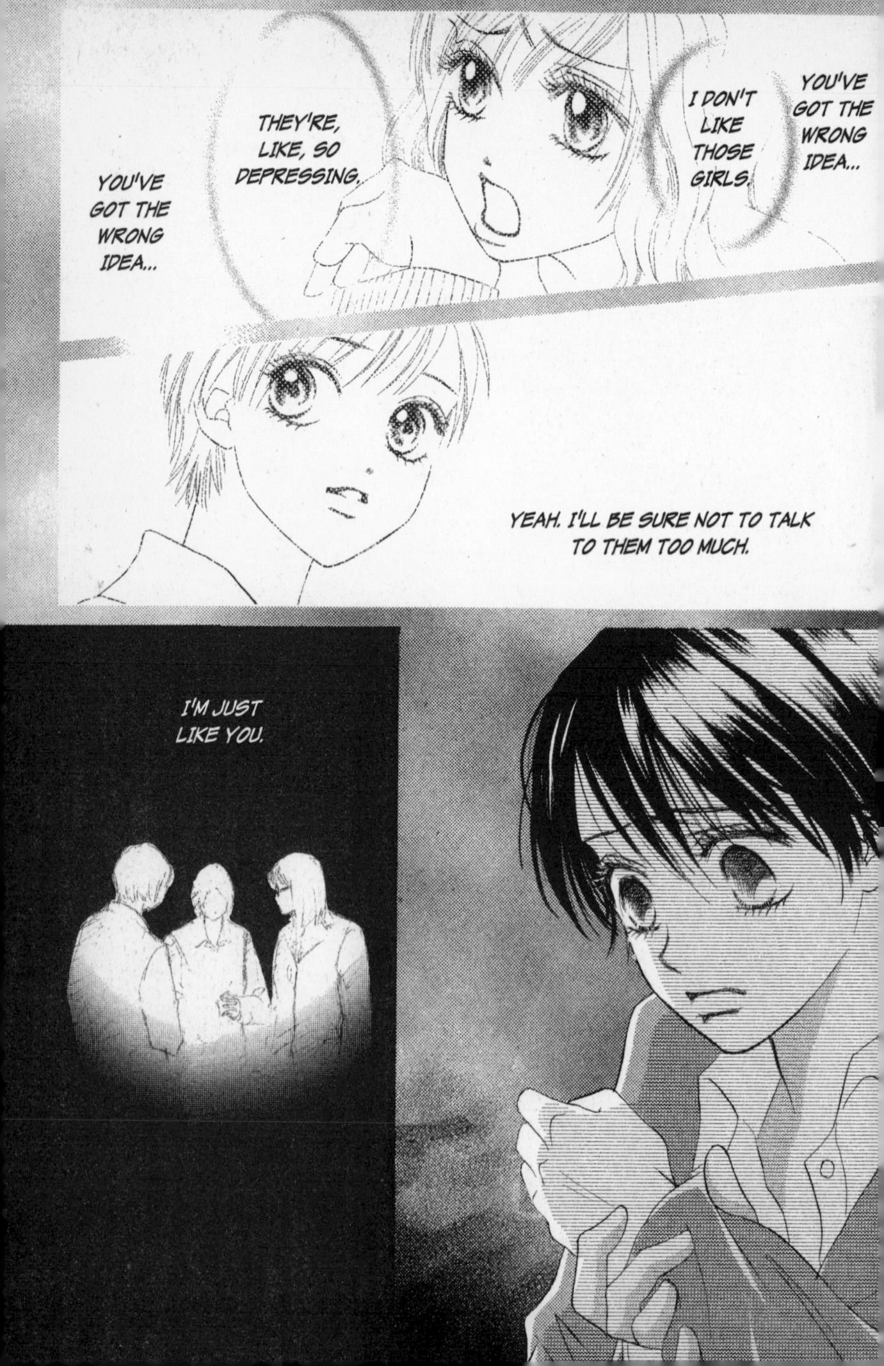
YOU'VE GOT THE WRONG IDEA...
I DON'T LIKE THOSE GIRLS.
THEY'RE, LIKE, SO DEPRESSING.
YOU'VE GOT THE WRONG IDEA...
YEAH. I'LL BE SURE NOT TO TALK TO THEM TOO MUCH.
I'M JUST LIKE YOU.

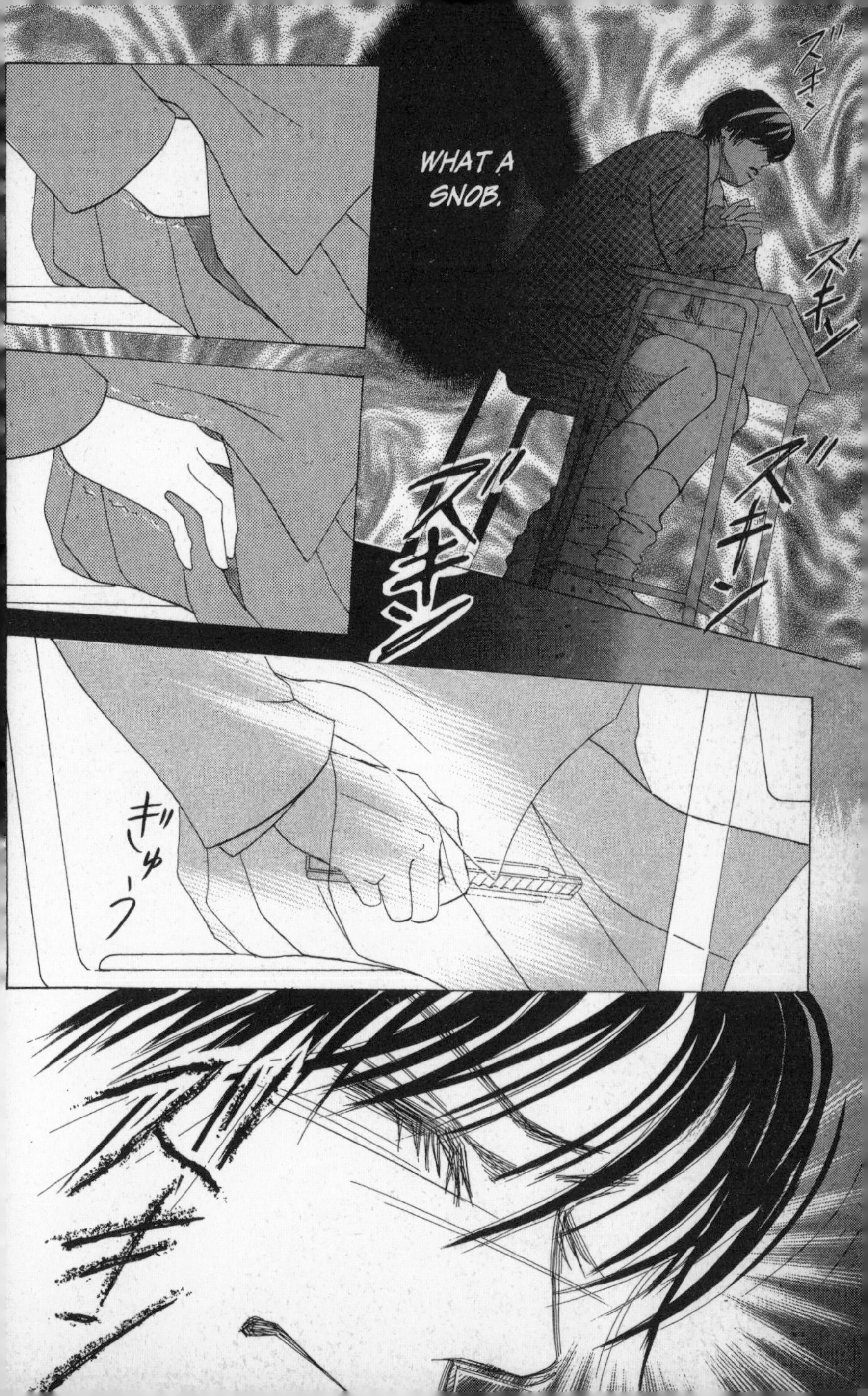
ズキン
ズキン
WHAT A SNOB.
ズキン
ズキン
ぎゅーっ
ズキン

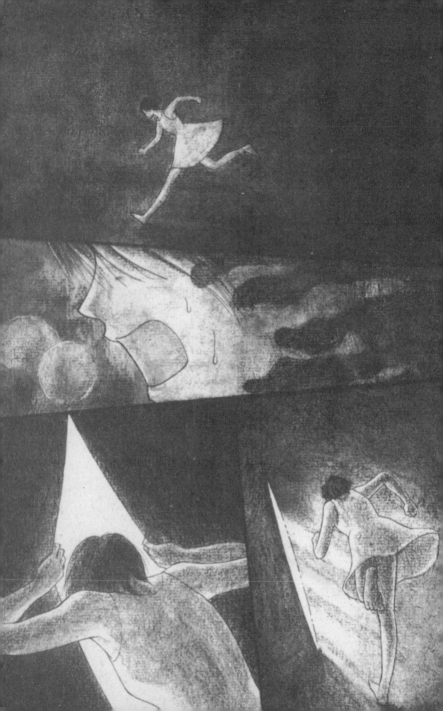

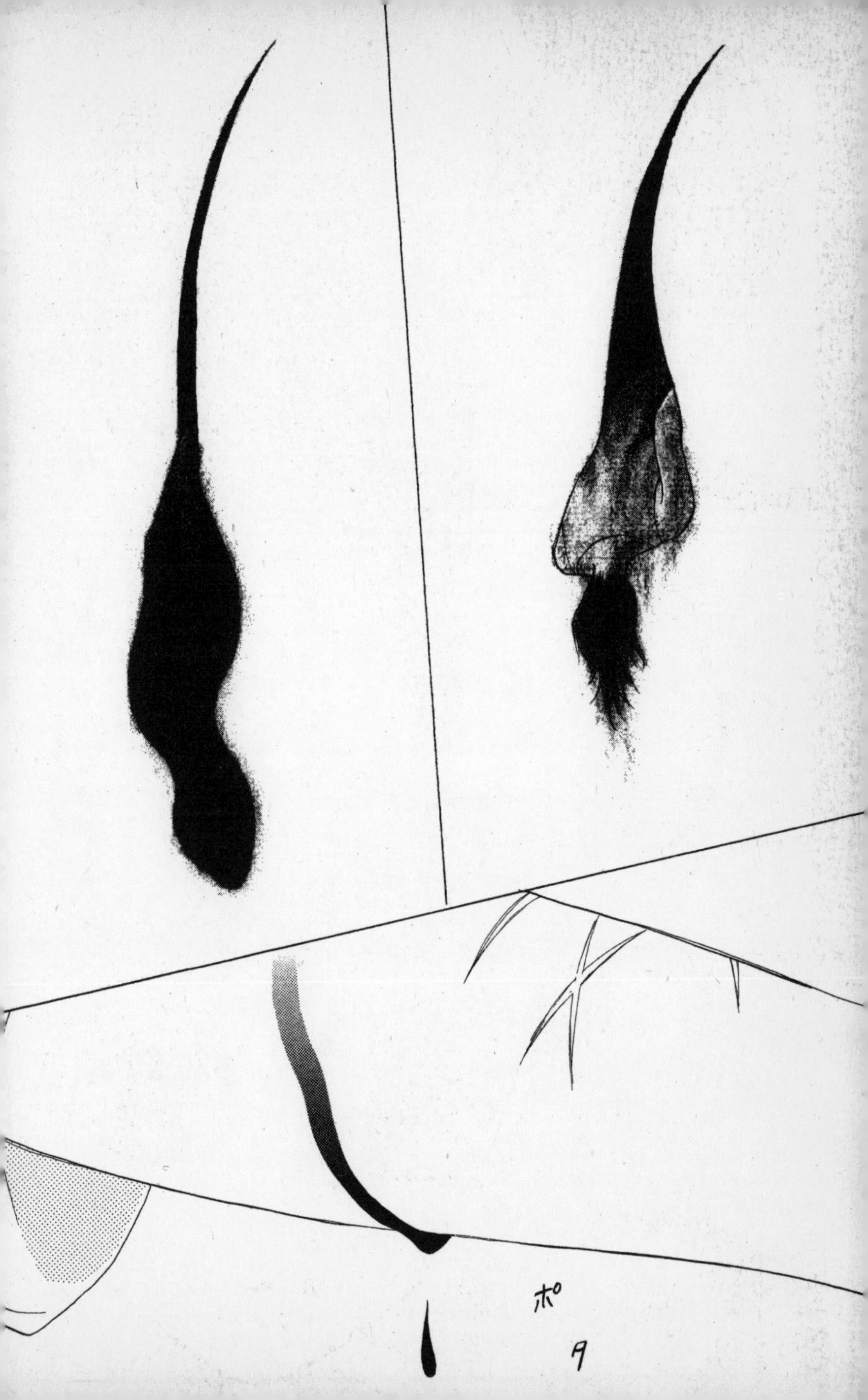
ポタ

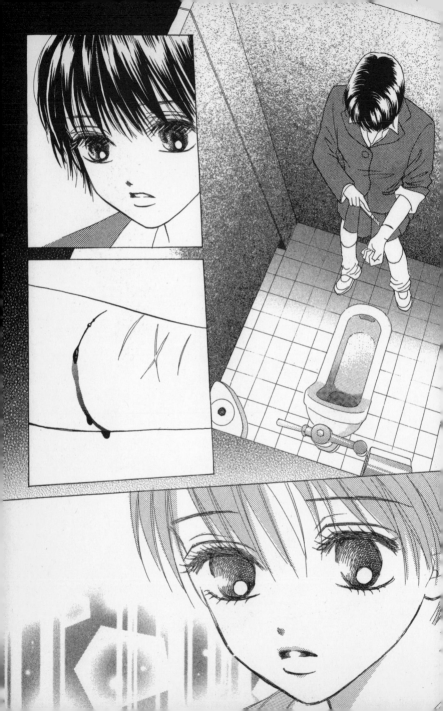

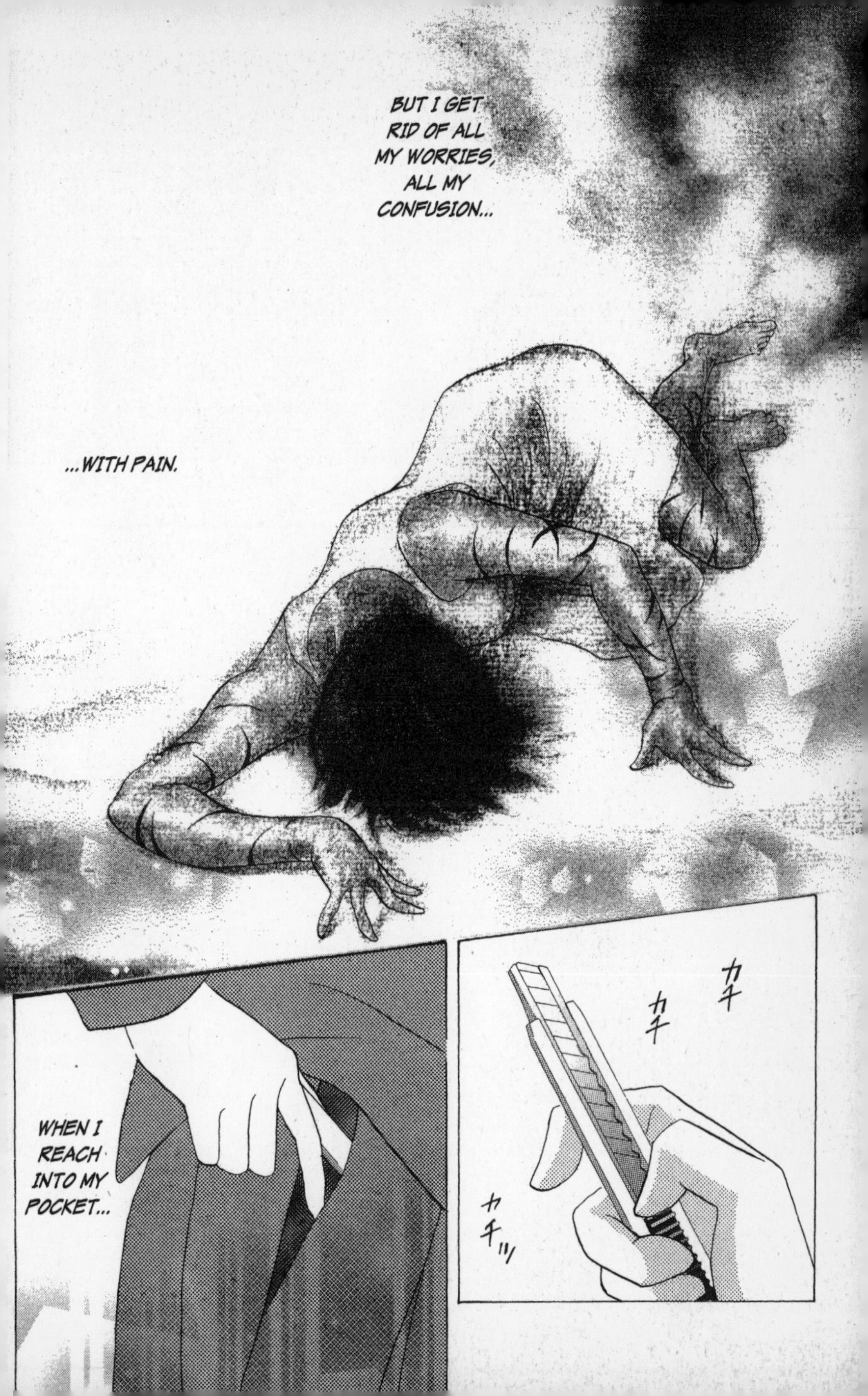
BUT I GET RID OF ALL MY WORRIES, ALL MY CONFUSION...
...WITH PAIN.
カチ
カチ
カチッ
WHEN I REACH INTO MY POCKET...

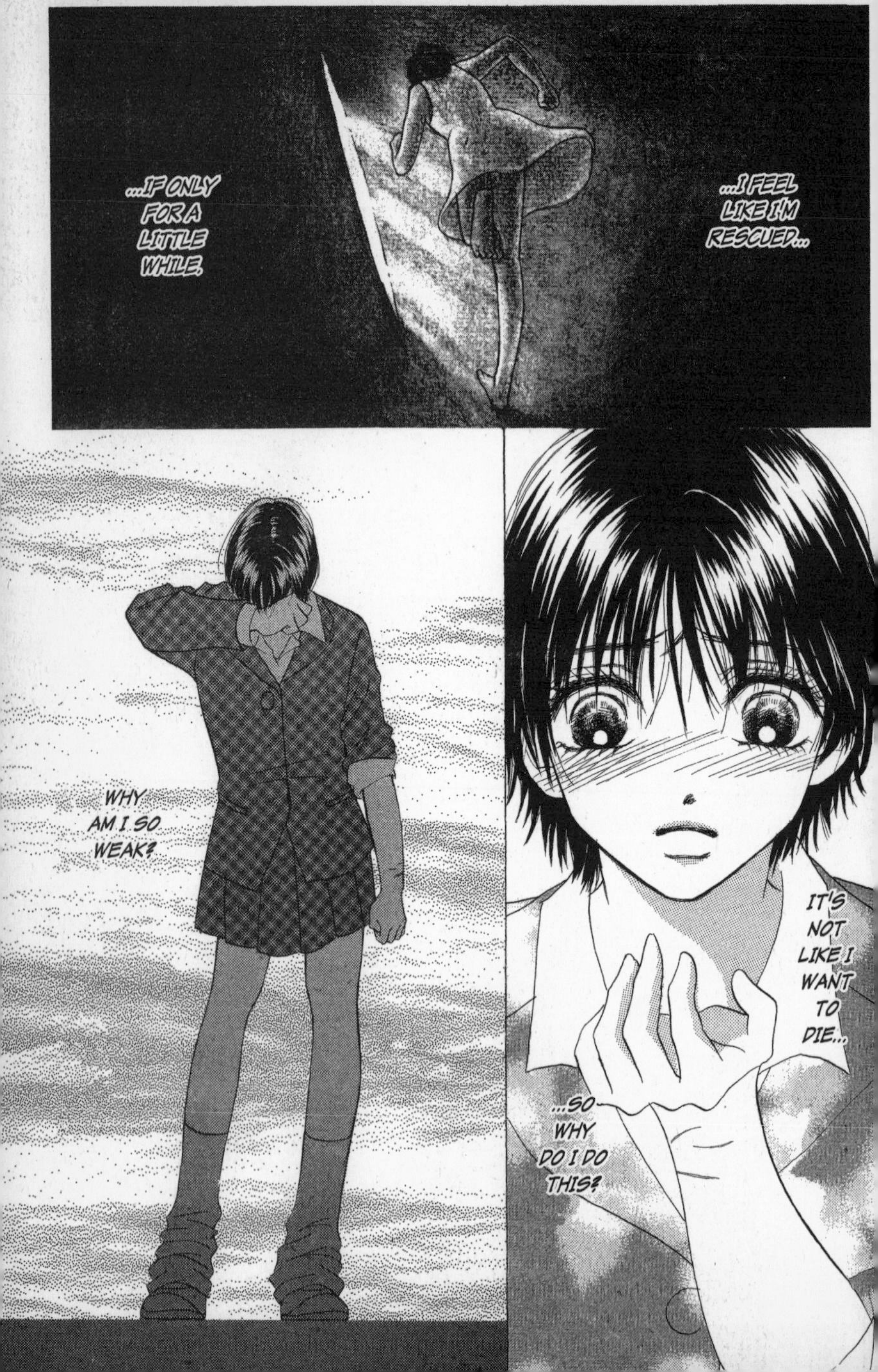
...I FEEL LIKE I'M RESCUED...
...IF ONLY FOR A LITTLE WHILE.
IT'S NOT LIKE I WANT TO DIE...
...SO WHY DO I DO THIS?
WHY AM I SO WEAK?

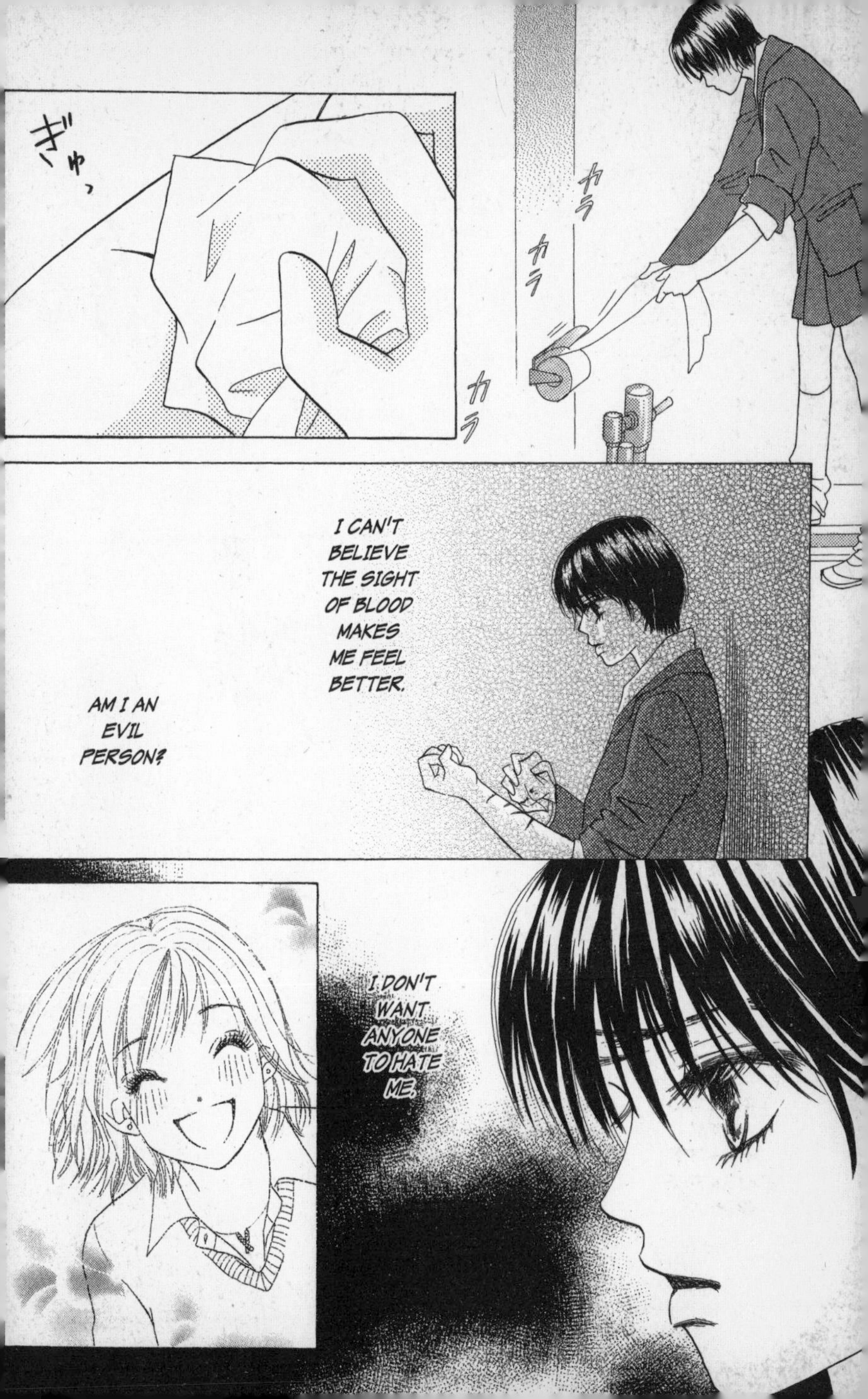
カラ
カラ
カラ
ぎゅっ
I CAN'T BELIEVE THE SIGHT OF BLOOD MAKES ME FEEL BETTER.
AM I AN EVIL PERSON?
I DON'T WANT ANYONE TO HATE ME.

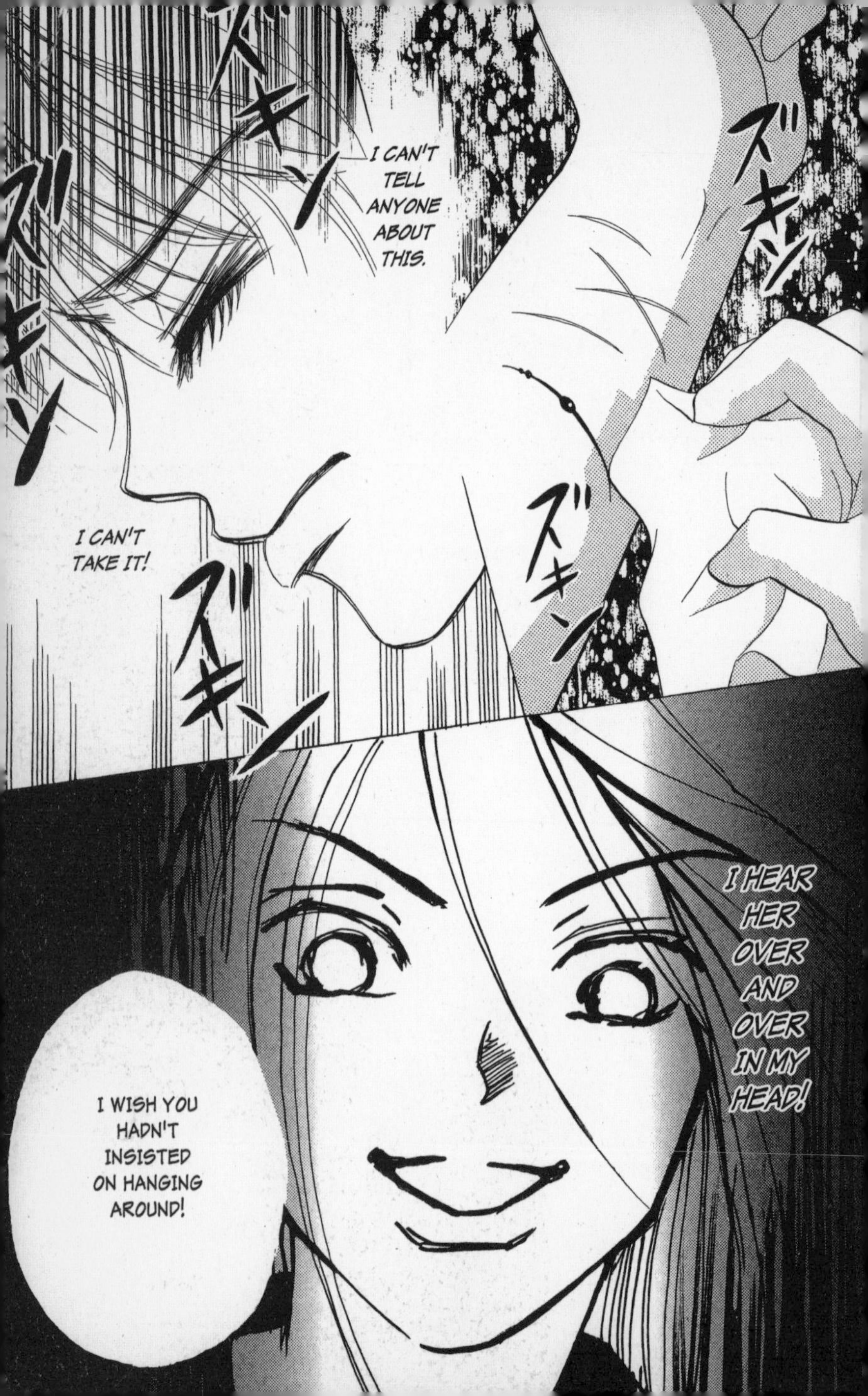
I CAN'T TELL ANYONE ABOUT THIS.
I CAN'T TAKE IT!
I HEAR HER OVER AND OVER IN MY HEAD!
I WISH YOU HADN'T INSISTED ON HANGING AROUND!

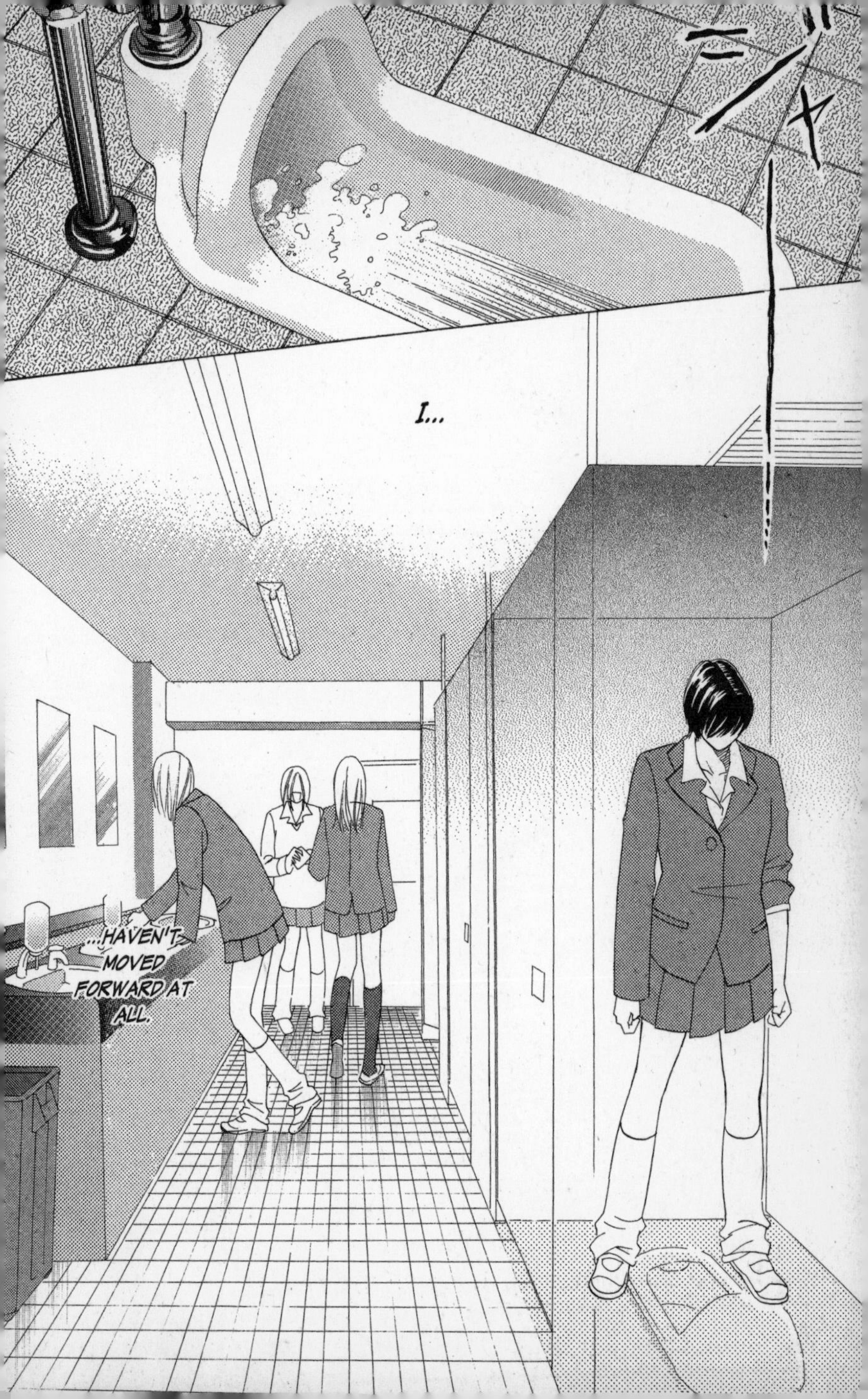
I...
...HAVEN'T MOVED FORWARD AT ALL.

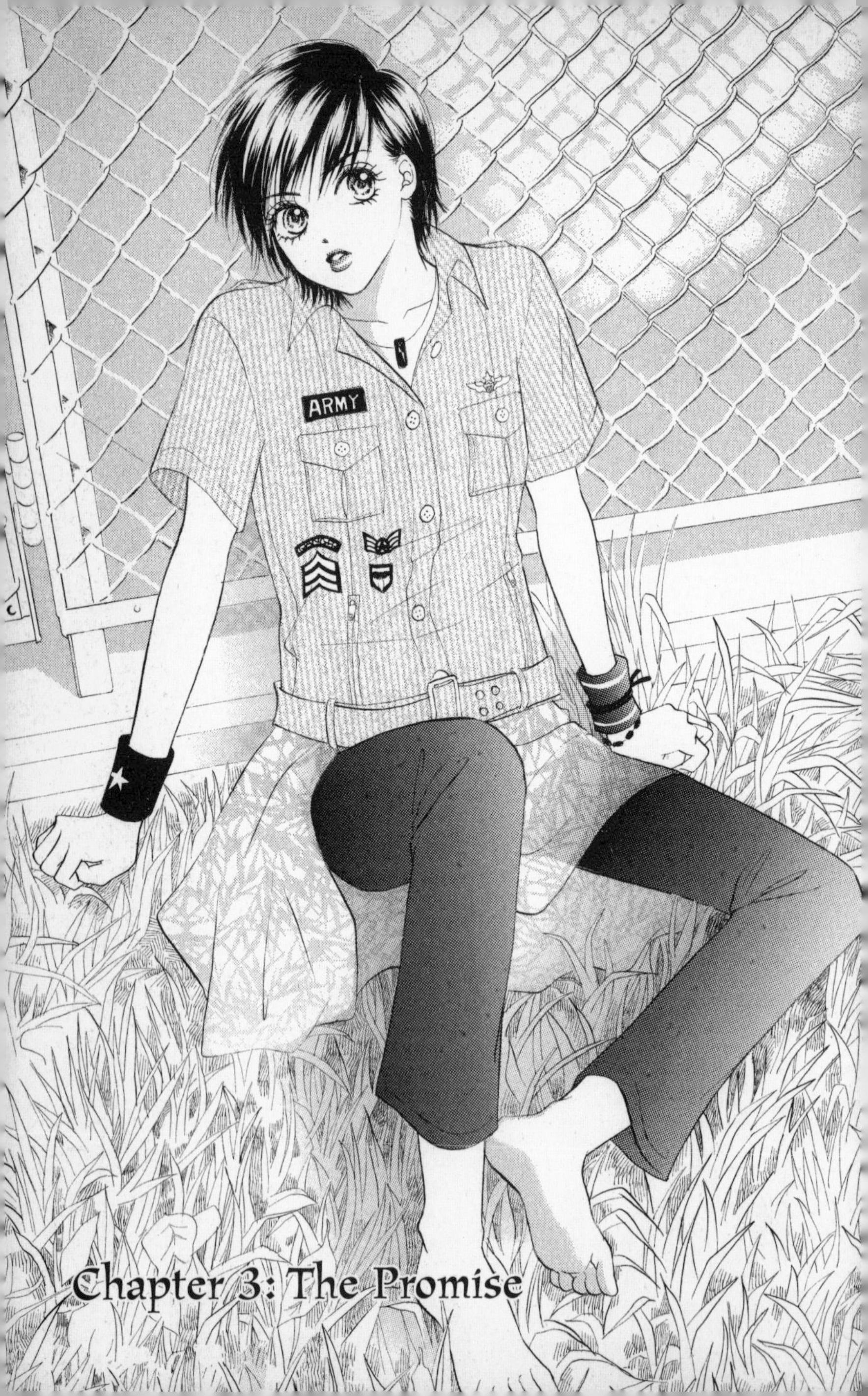
ARMY

Chapter 3: The Promise

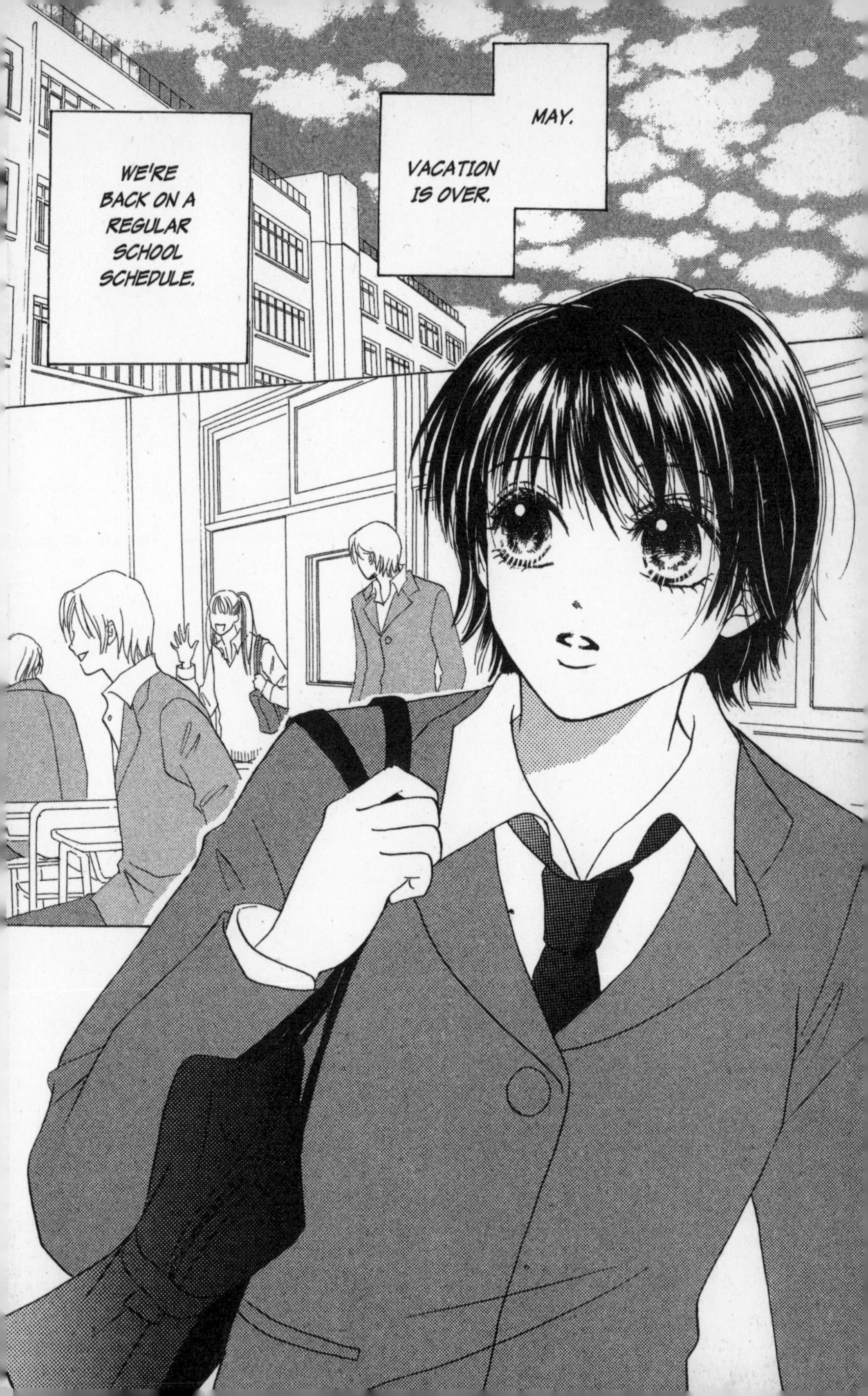
MAY.
VACATION IS OVER.
WE'RE BACK ON A REGULAR SCHOOL SCHEDULE.

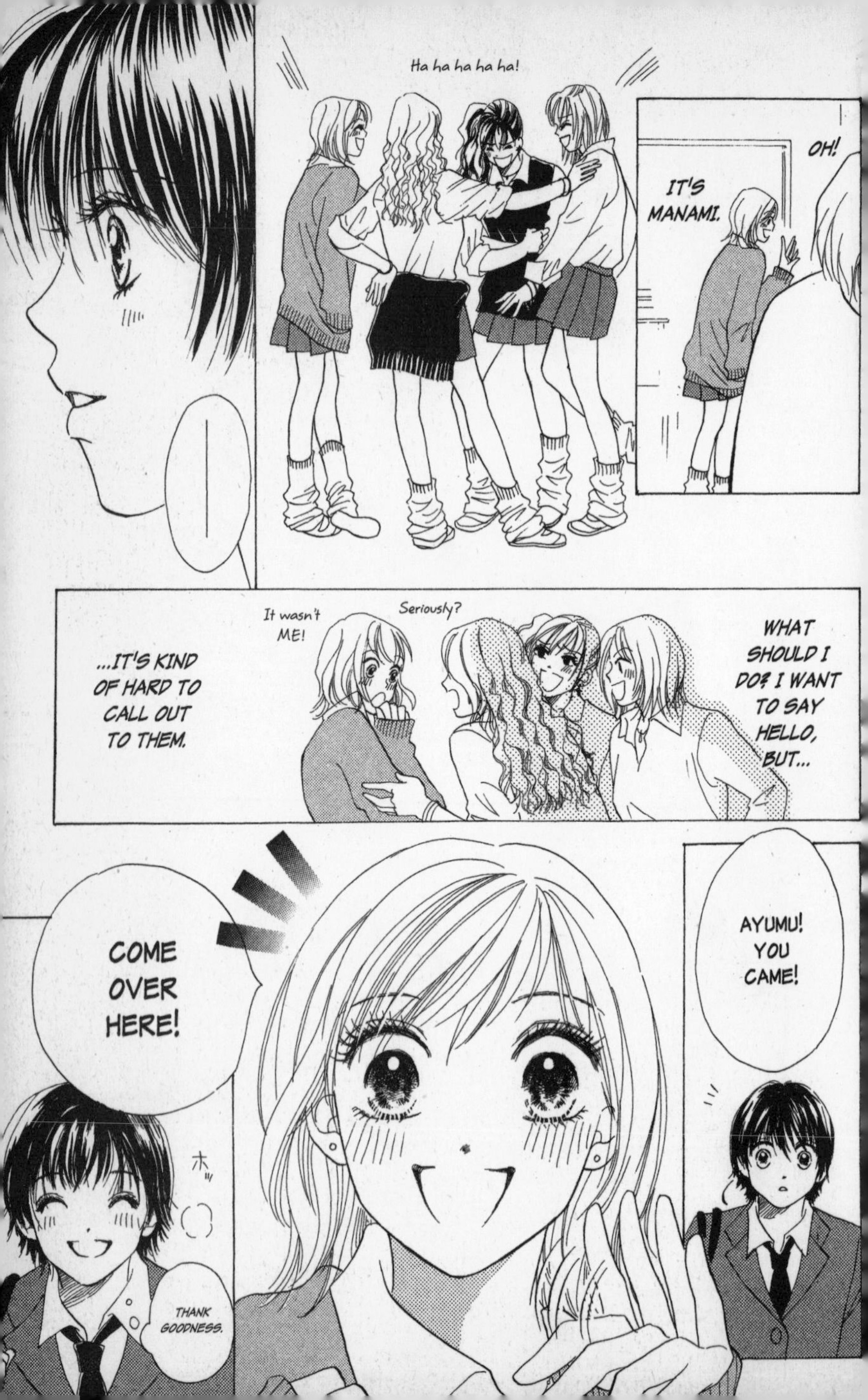
OH!
IT'S MANAMI.
Ha ha ha ha ha!
WHAT SHOULD I DO? I WANT TO SAY HELLO, BUT...
Seriously?
It wasn't ME!
...IT'S KIND OF HARD TO CALL OUT TO THEM.
AYUMU! YOU CAME!
COME OVER HERE!
ホッ
THANK GOODNESS.

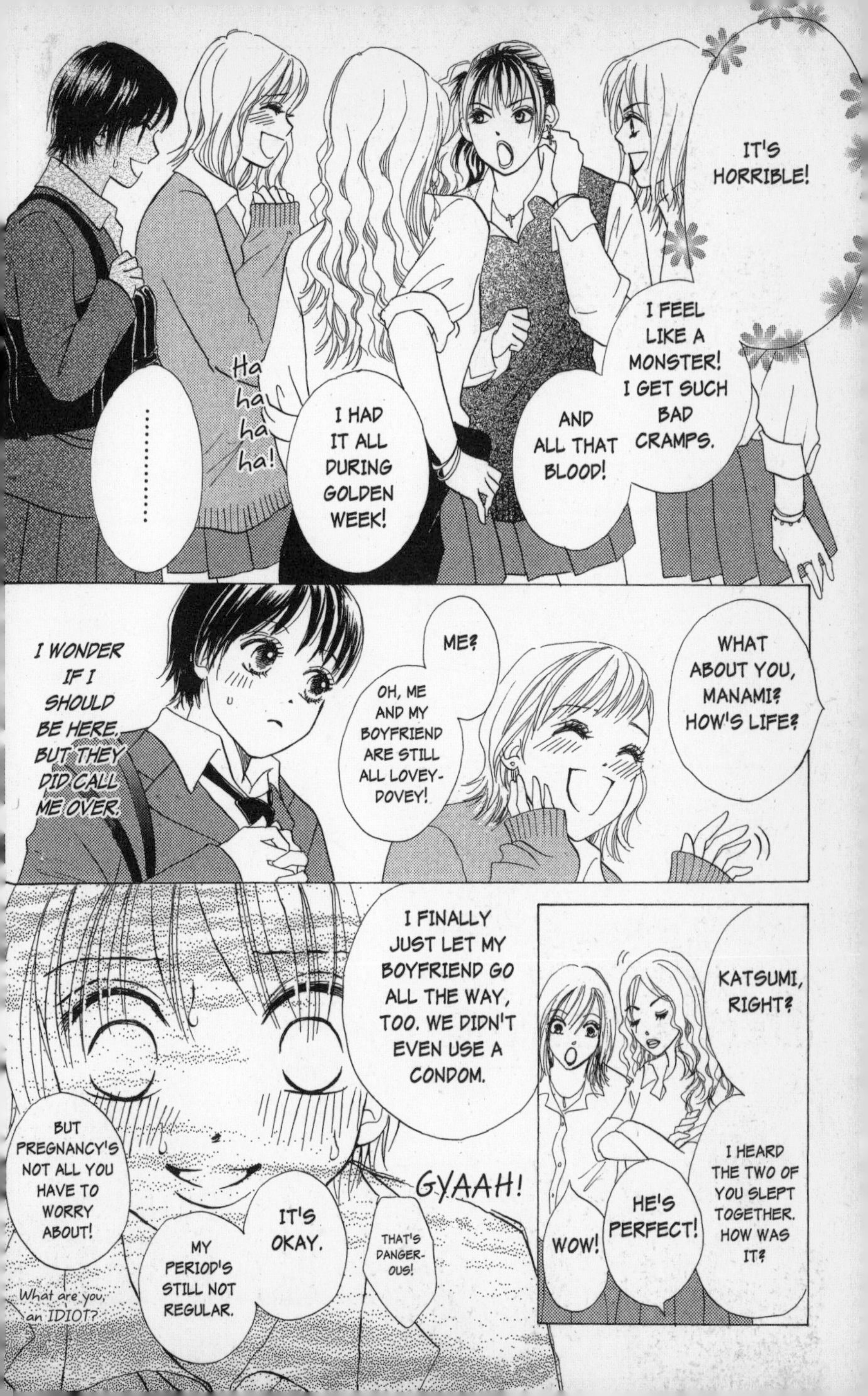
IT'S HORRIBLE!
I FEEL LIKE A MONSTER! I GET SUCH BAD CRAMPS.
AND ALL THAT BLOOD!
I HAD IT ALL DURING GOLDEN WEEK!
Ha ha ha ha!
......
WHAT ABOUT YOU, MANAMI? HOW'S LIFE?
ME?
OH, ME AND MY BOYFRIEND ARE STILL ALL LOVEY-DOVEY!
I WONDER IF I SHOULD BE HERE, BUT THEY DID CALL ME OVER.
KATSUMI, RIGHT?
I HEARD THE TWO OF YOU SLEPT TOGETHER. HOW WAS IT?
HE'S PERFECT!
WOW!
I FINALLY JUST LET MY BOYFRIEND GO ALL THE WAY, TOO. WE DIDN'T EVEN USE A CONDOM.
GYAAH!
THAT'S DANGER-OUS!
IT'S OKAY.
MY PERIOD'S STILL NOT REGULAR.
BUT PREGNANCY'S NOT ALL YOU HAVE TO WORRY ABOUT!
What are you, an IDIOT?

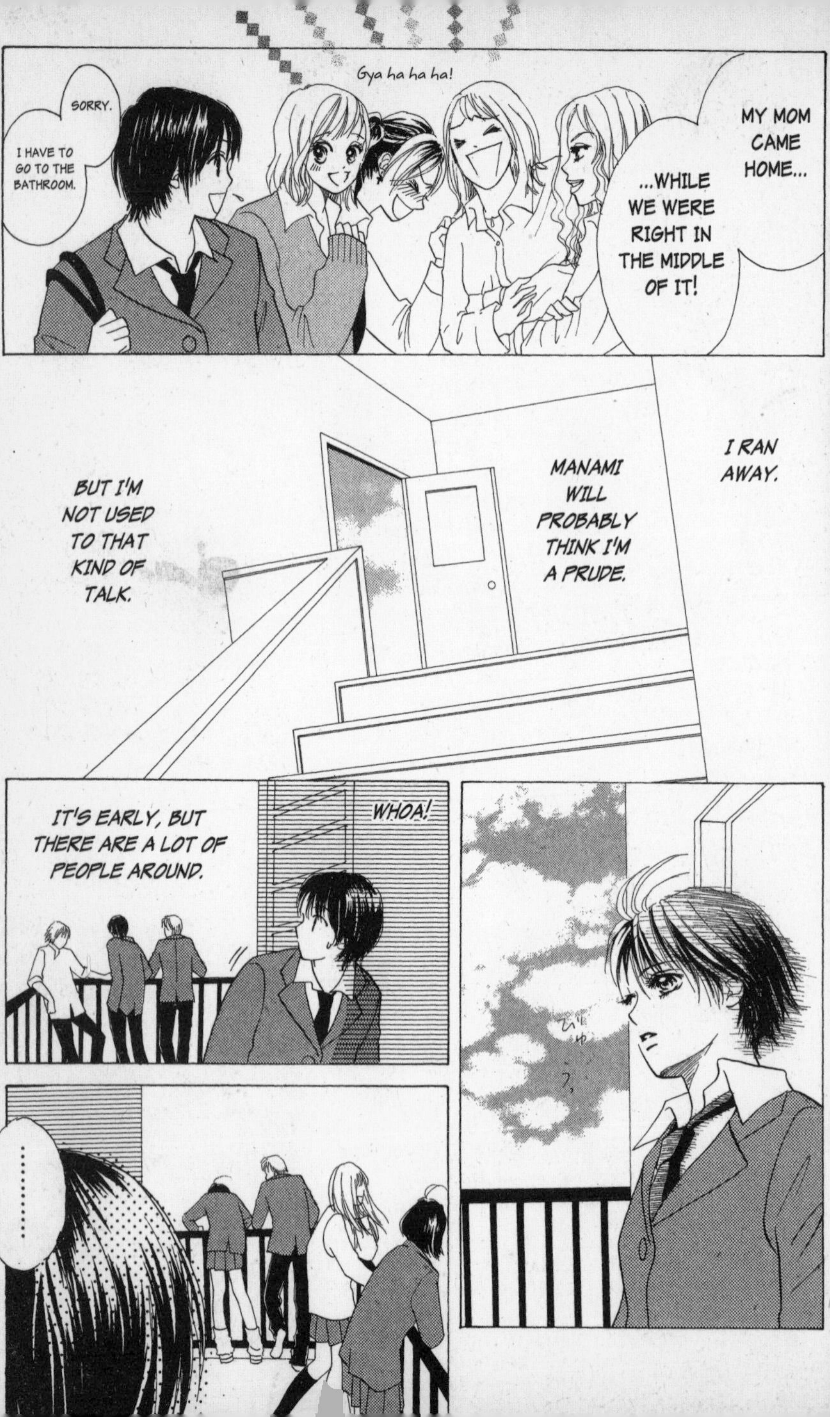
MY MOM CAME HOME...
...WHILE WE WERE RIGHT IN THE MIDDLE OF IT!
Gya ha ha ha!
SORRY.
I HAVE TO GO TO THE BATHROOM.
I RAN AWAY.
MANAMI WILL PROBABLY THINK I'M A PRUDE.
BUT I'M NOT USED TO THAT KIND OF TALK.
IT'S EARLY, BUT THERE ARE A LOT OF PEOPLE AROUND.
WHOA!
......

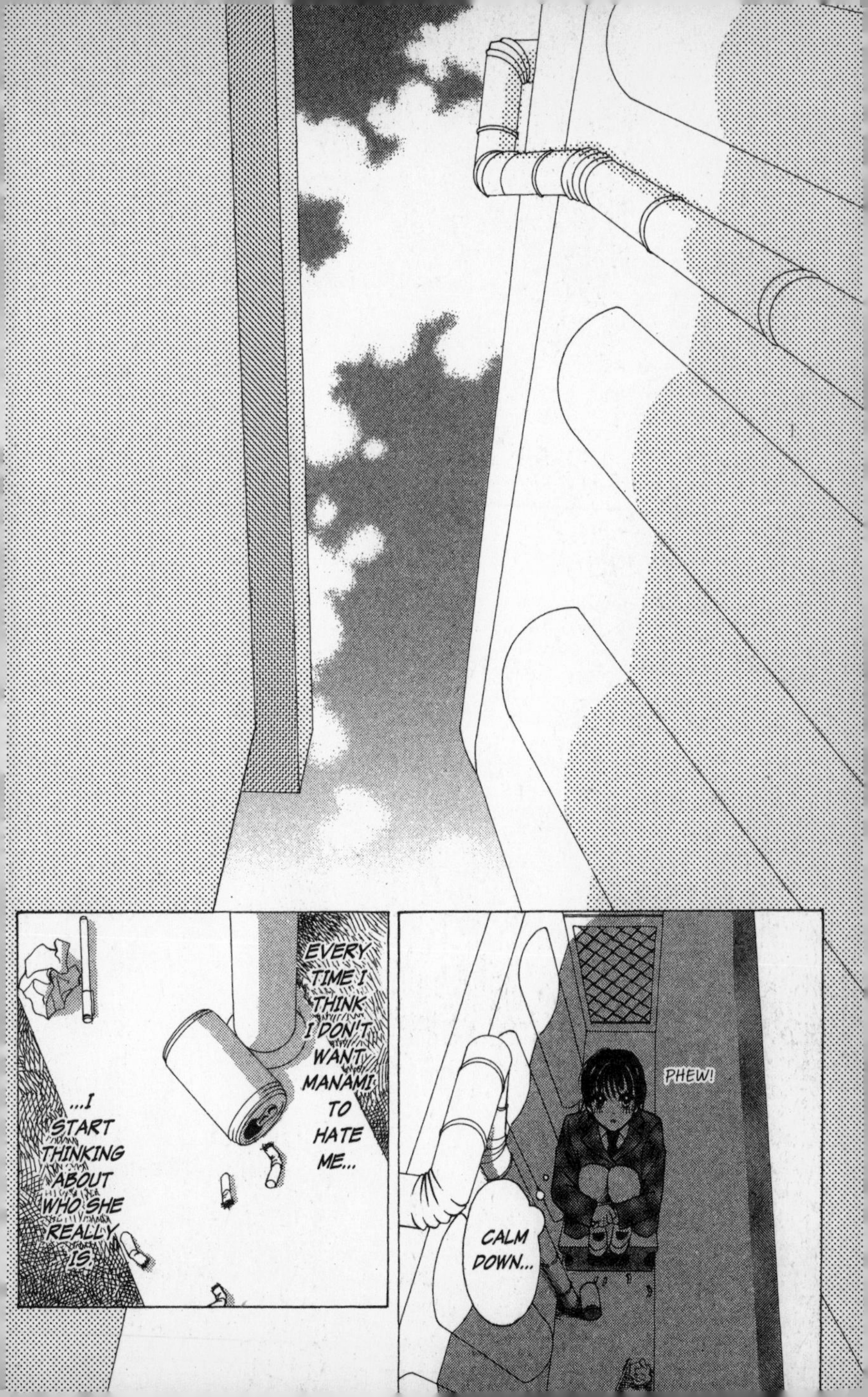
PHEW!
CALM DOWN...
EVERY TIME I THINK I DON'T WANT MANAMI TO HATE ME...
...I START THINKING ABOUT WHO SHE REALLY IS.

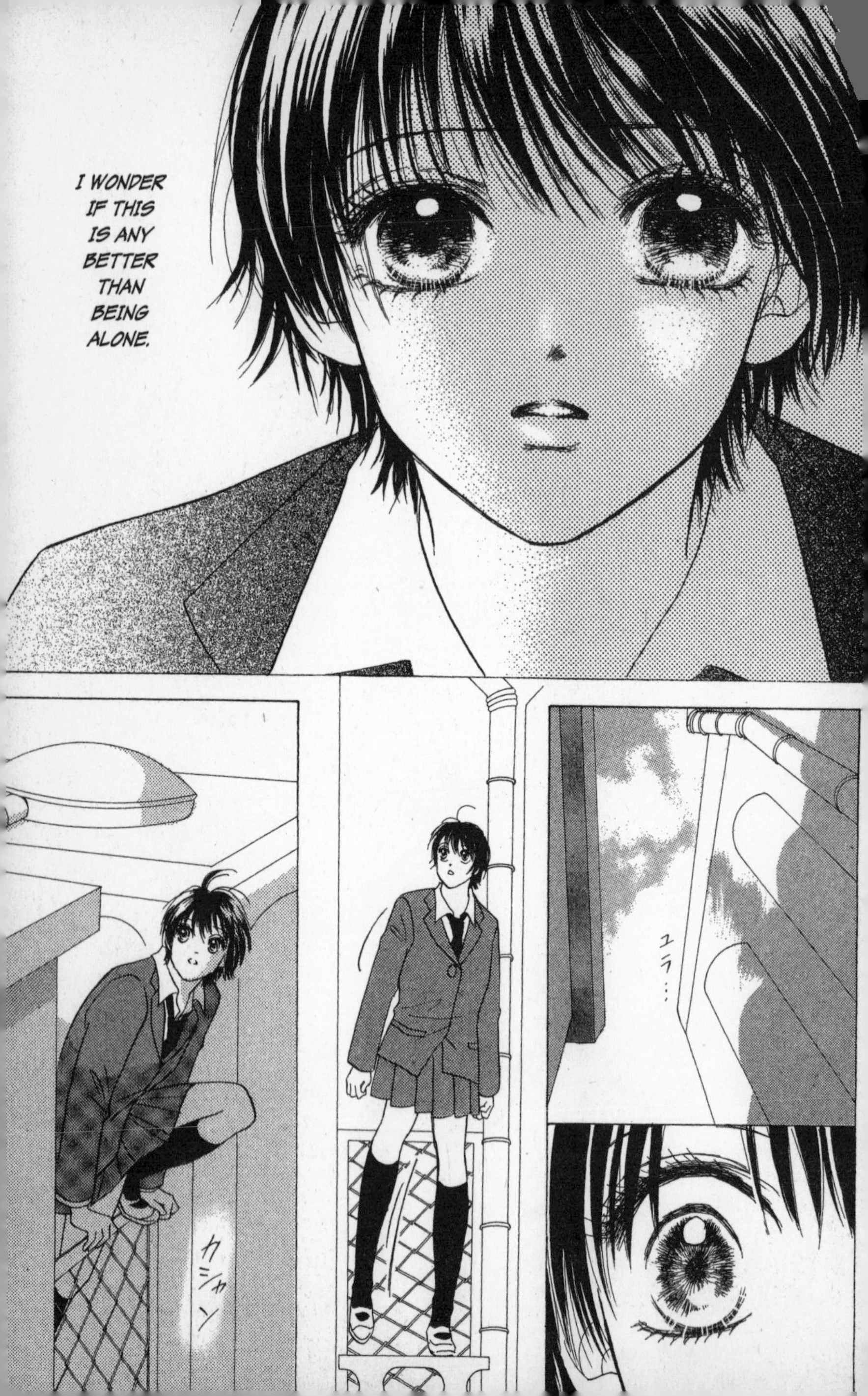
I WONDER IF THIS IS ANY BETTER THAN BEING ALONE.
ユラ…
カシャン

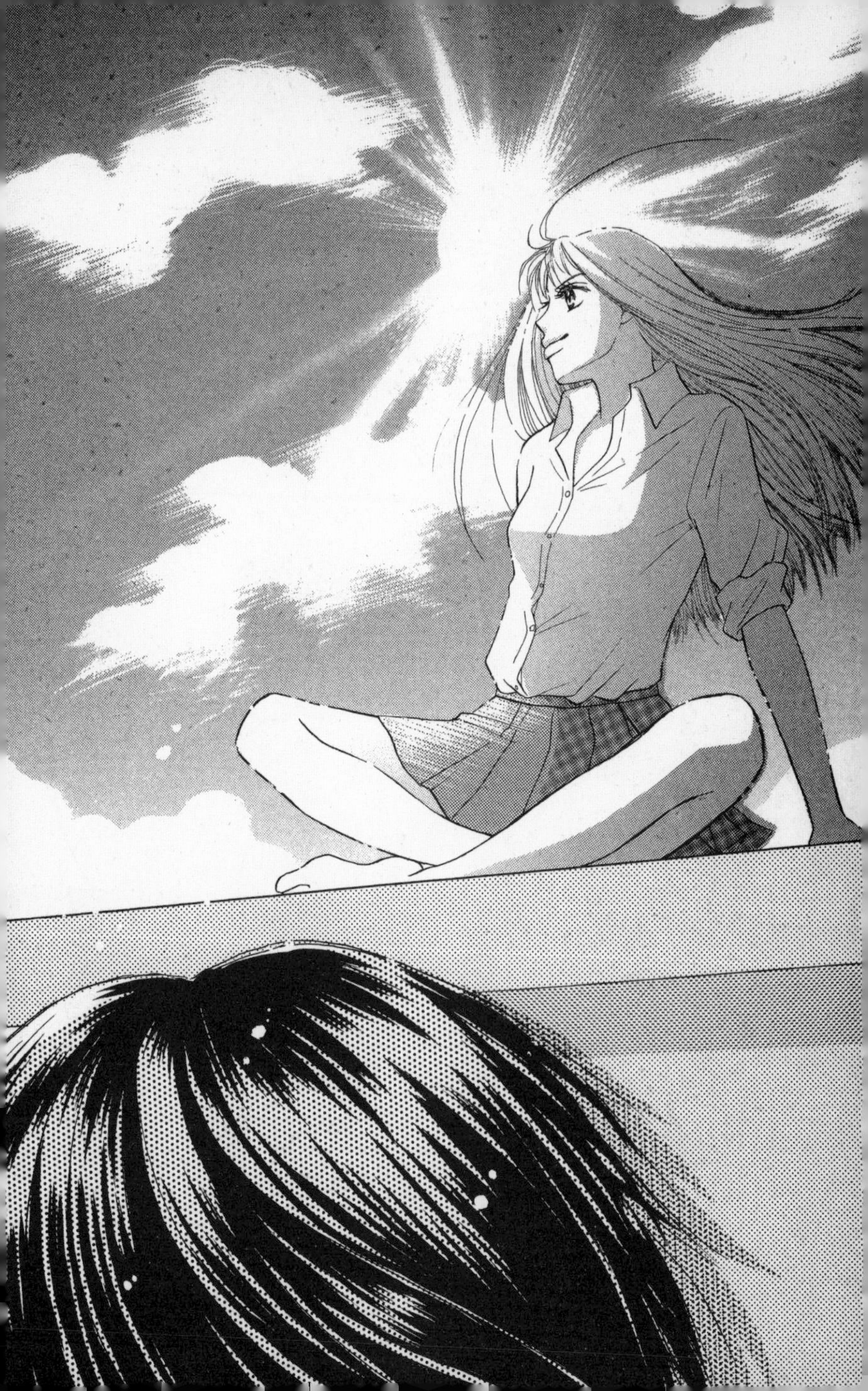

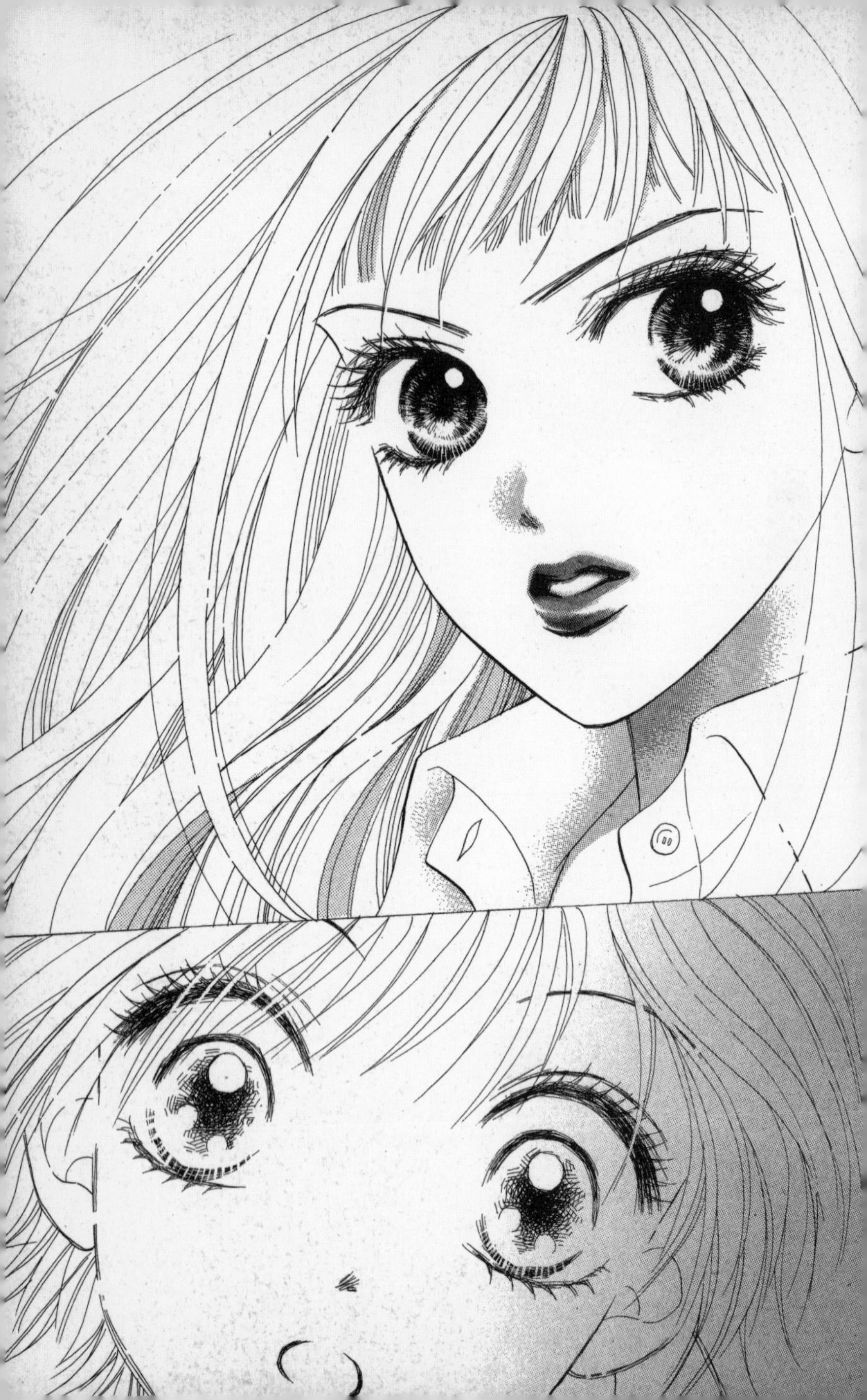

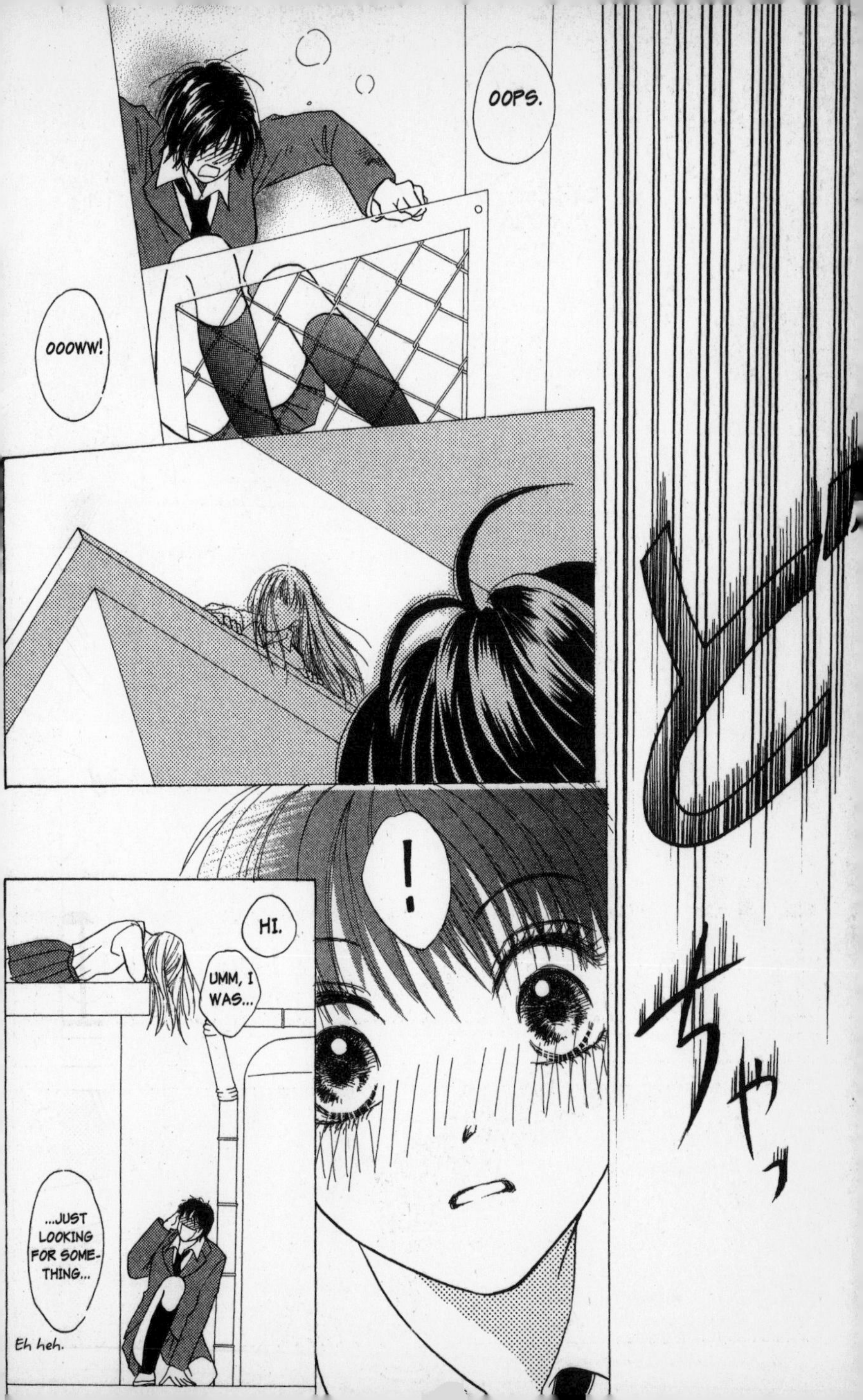
OOPS.
OOOWW!
どちゃっ
!
HI.
UMM, I WAS...
...JUST LOOKING FOR SOME-THING...
Eh heh.

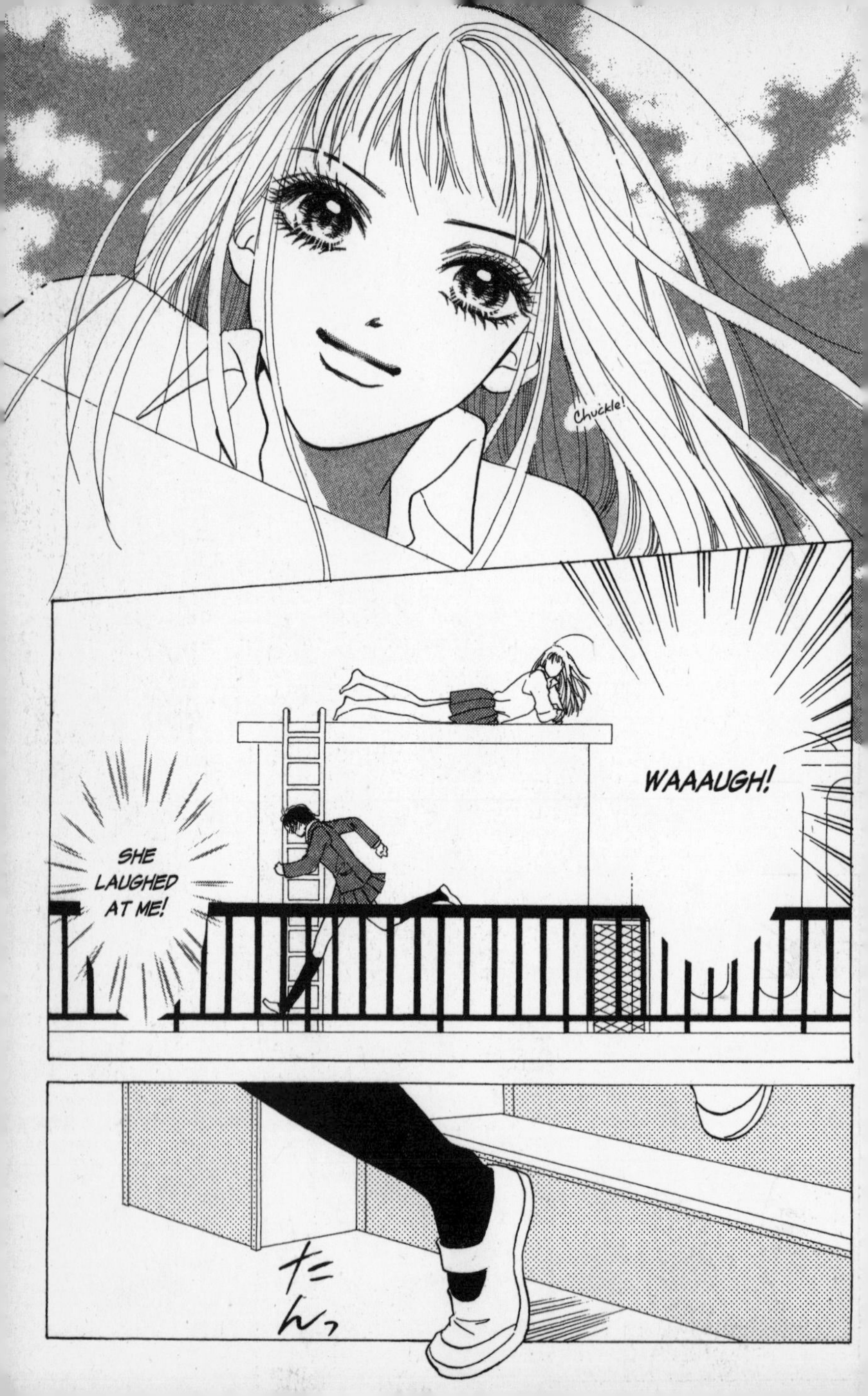
Chuckle!
WAAAUGH!
SHE LAUGHED AT ME!
たんっ

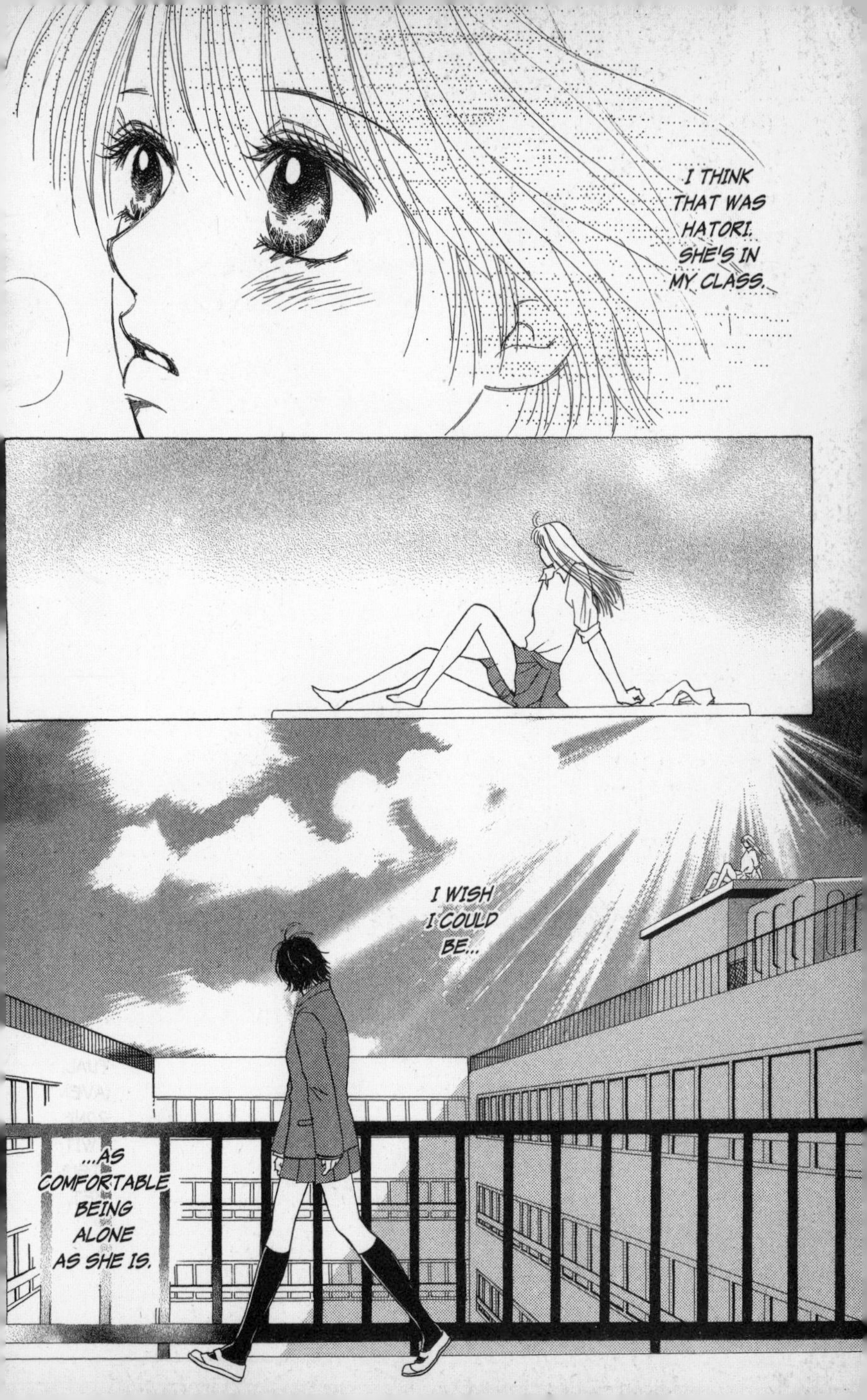
I THINK THAT WAS HATORI. SHE'S IN MY CLASS.
I WISH I COULD BE...
...AS COMFORTABLE BEING ALONE AS SHE IS.

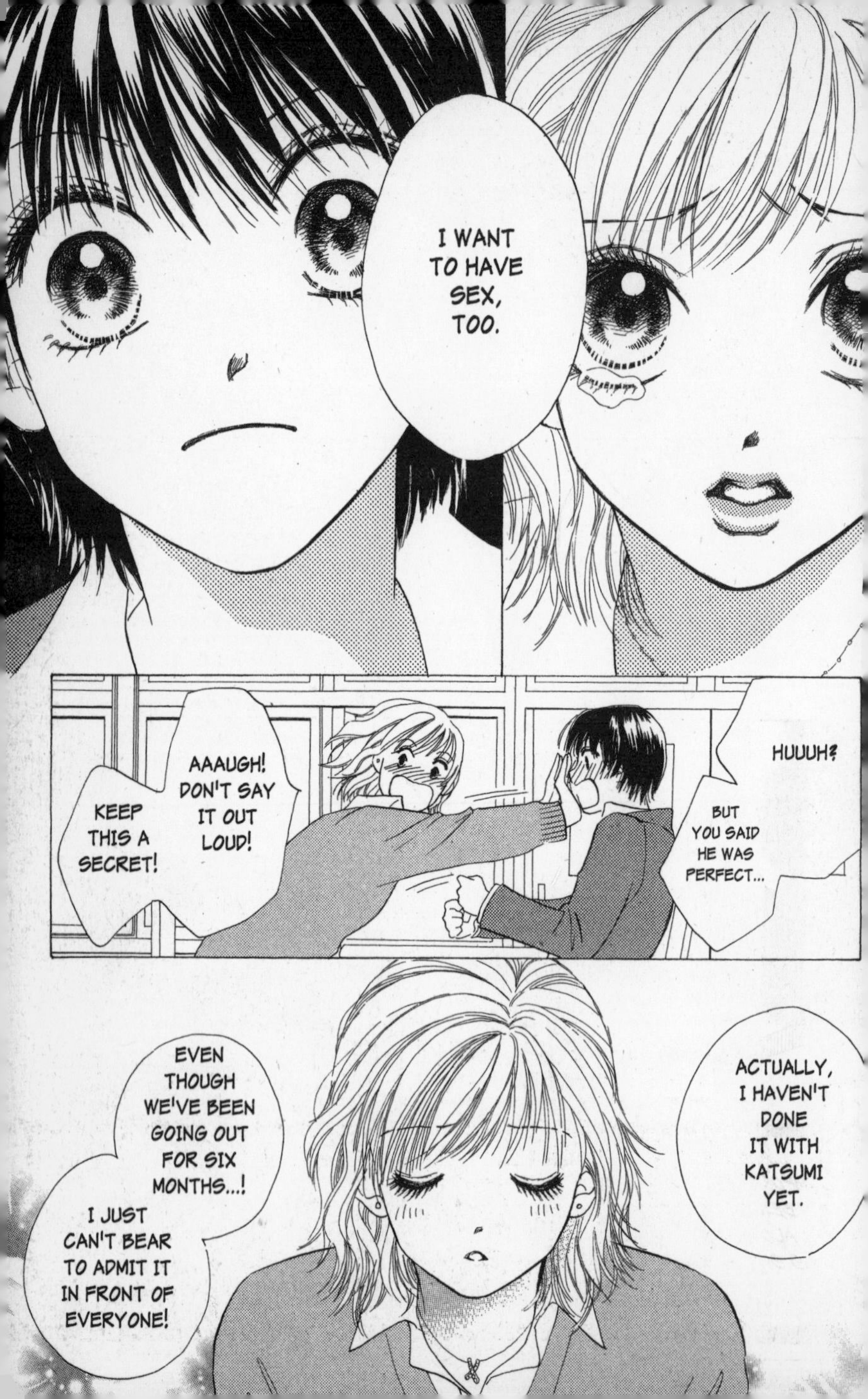

I WANT TO HAVE SEX, TOO.
HUUUH?
BUT YOU SAID HE WAS PERFECT...
AAAUGH! DON'T SAY IT OUT LOUD!
KEEP THIS A SECRET!
ACTUALLY, I HAVEN'T DONE IT WITH KATSUMI YET.
EVEN THOUGH WE'VE BEEN GOING OUT FOR SIX MONTHS...!
I JUST CAN'T BEAR TO ADMIT IT IN FRONT OF EVERYONE!

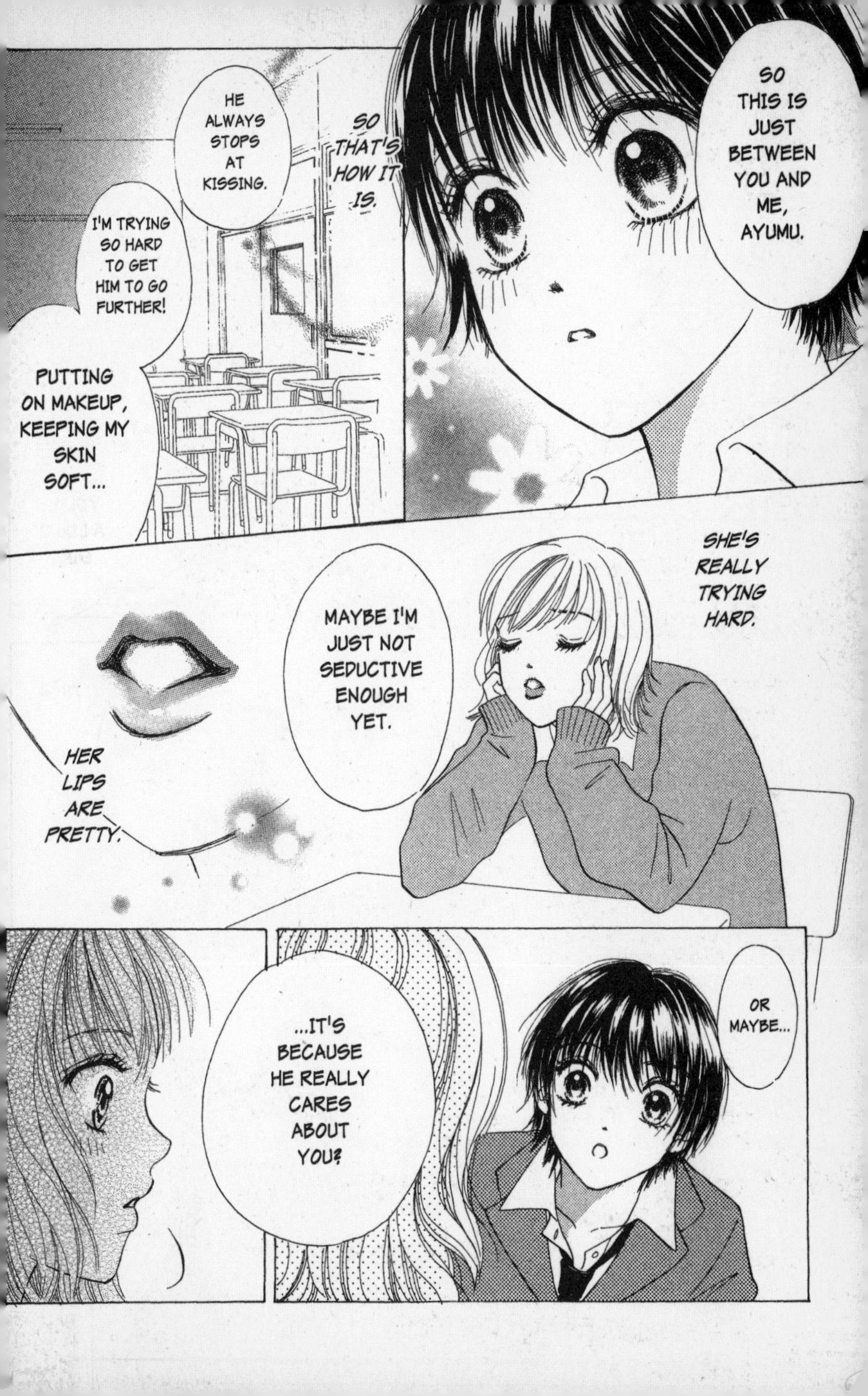
SO THIS IS JUST BETWEEN YOU AND ME, AYUMU.
SO THAT'S HOW IT IS.
HE ALWAYS STOPS AT KISSING.
I'M TRYING SO HARD TO GET HIM TO GO FURTHER!
PUTTING ON MAKEUP, KEEPING MY SKIN SOFT...
SHE'S REALLY TRYING HARD.
MAYBE I'M JUST NOT SEDUCTIVE ENOUGH YET.
HER LIPS ARE PRETTY.
OR MAYBE...
...IT'S BECAUSE HE REALLY CARES ABOUT YOU?

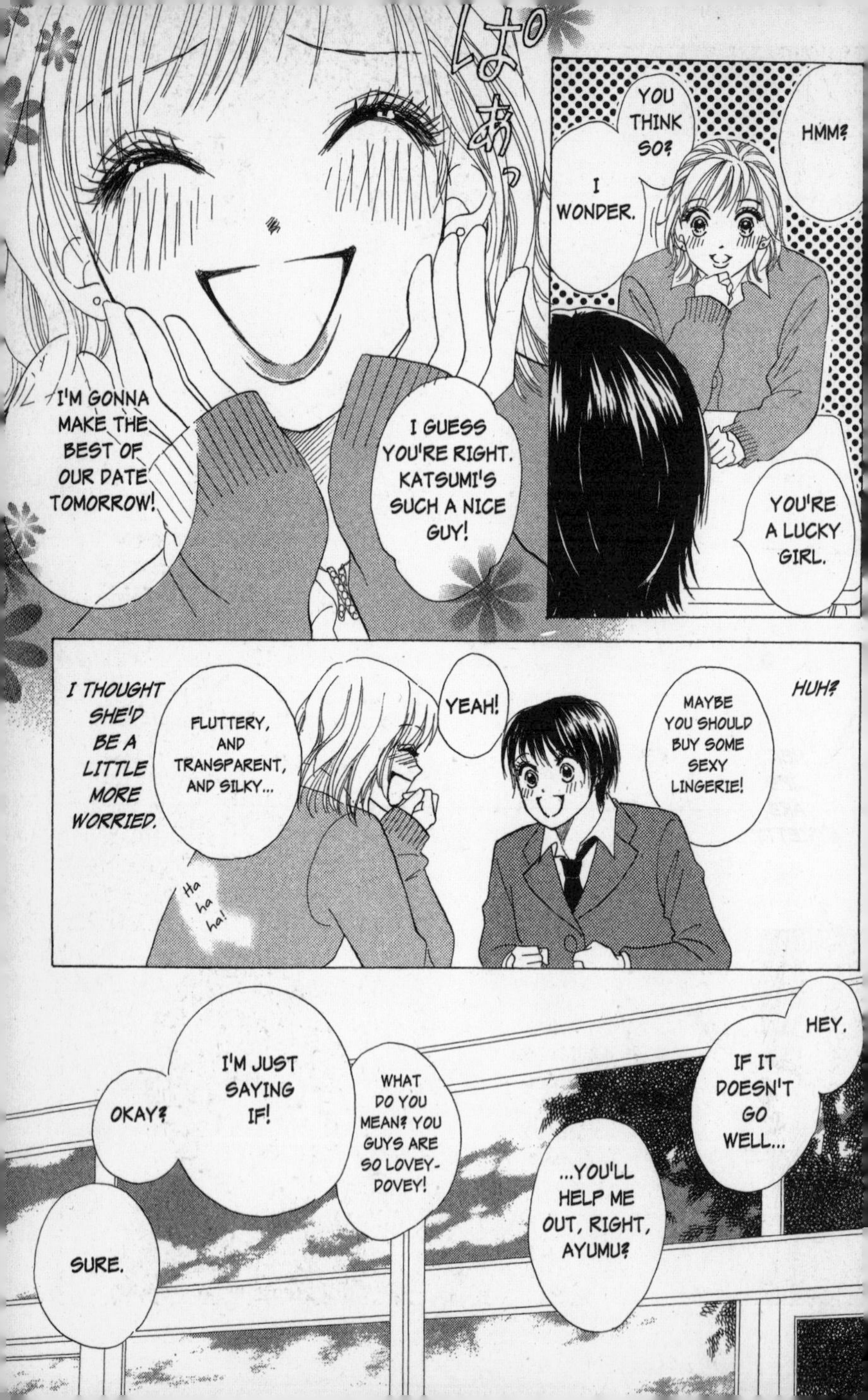
HMM?
YOU THINK SO?
I WONDER.
YOU'RE A LUCKY GIRL.
ぱあっ
I GUESS YOU'RE RIGHT. KATSUMI'S SUCH A NICE GUY!
I'M GONNA MAKE THE BEST OF OUR DATE TOMORROW!
HUH?
MAYBE YOU SHOULD BUY SOME SEXY LINGERIE!
YEAH!
FLUTTERY, AND TRANSPARENT, AND SILKY...
I THOUGHT SHE'D BE A LITTLE MORE WORRIED.
Ha ha ha!
HEY.
IF IT DOESN'T GO WELL...
...YOU'LL HELP ME OUT, RIGHT, AYUMU?
WHAT DO YOU MEAN? YOU GUYS ARE SO LOVEY-DOVEY!
I'M JUST SAYING IF!
OKAY?
SURE.

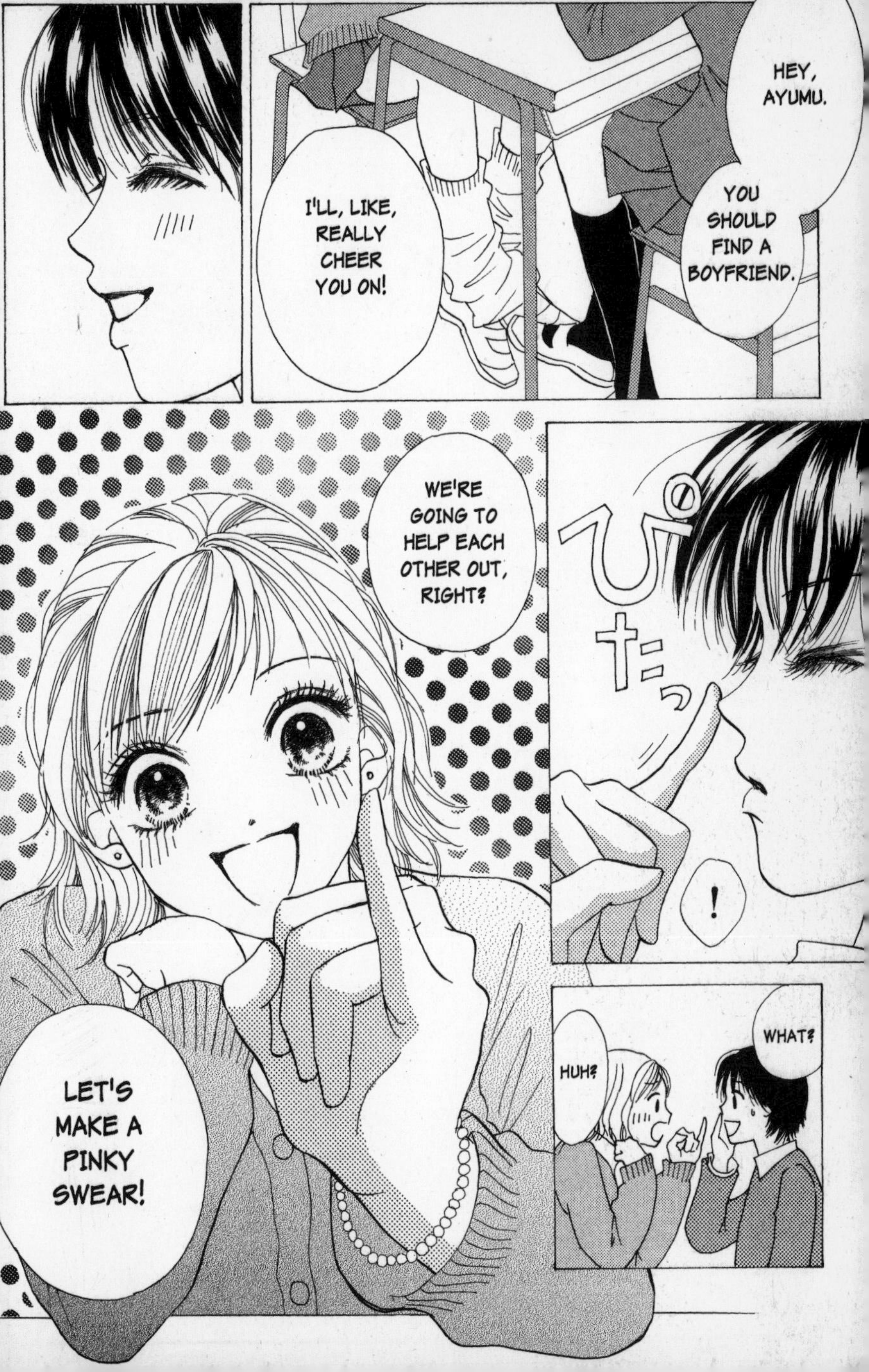
HEY, AYUMU.
YOU SHOULD FIND A BOYFRIEND.
I'LL, LIKE, REALLY CHEER YOU ON!
ぴたっ
!
WHAT?
HUH?
WE'RE GOING TO HELP EACH OTHER OUT, RIGHT?
LET'S MAKE A PINKY SWEAR!

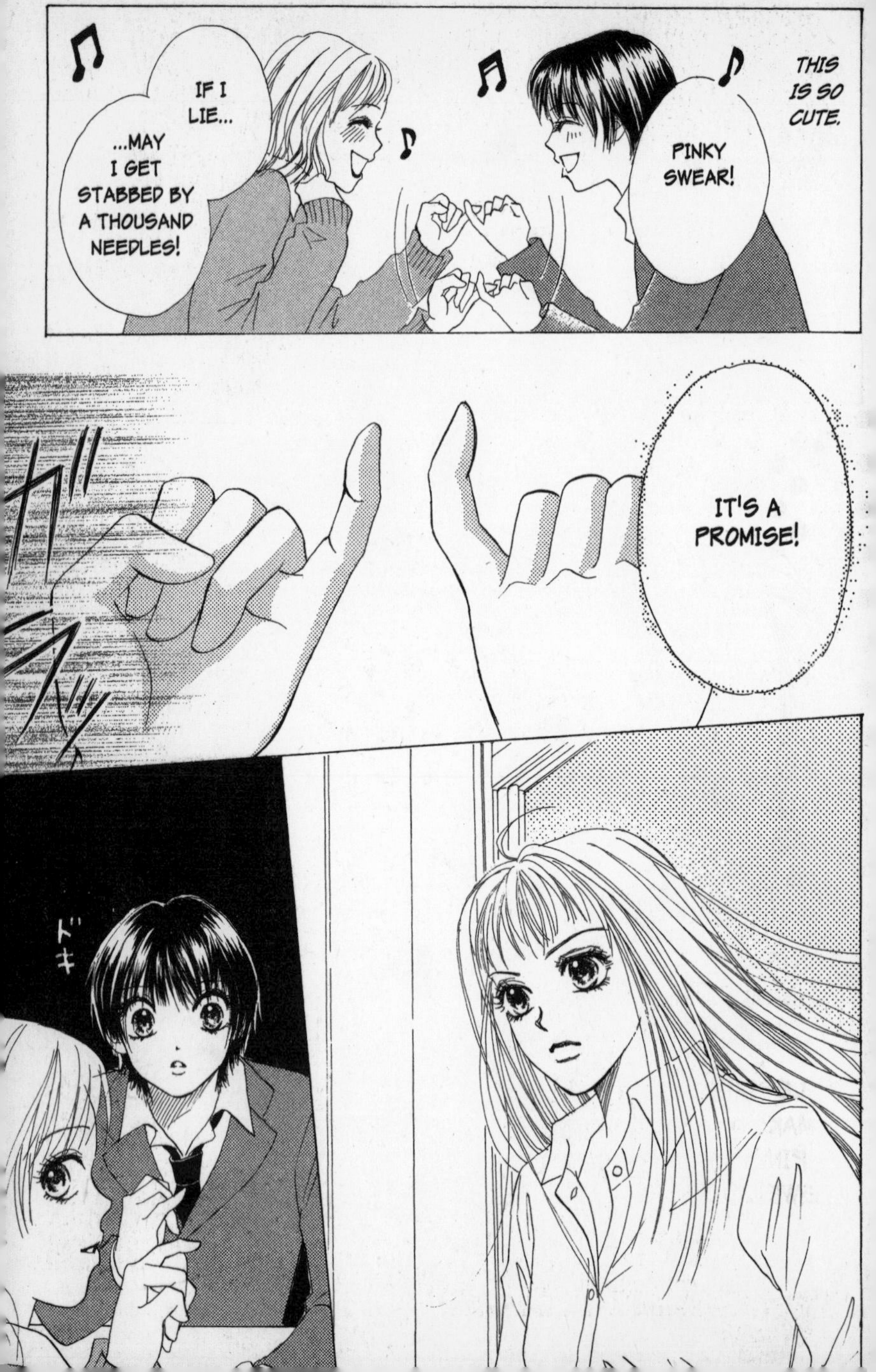
THIS IS SO CUTE.
PINKY SWEAR!
IF I LIE...
...MAY I GET STABBED BY A THOUSAND NEEDLES!
IT'S A PROMISE!
ドキ

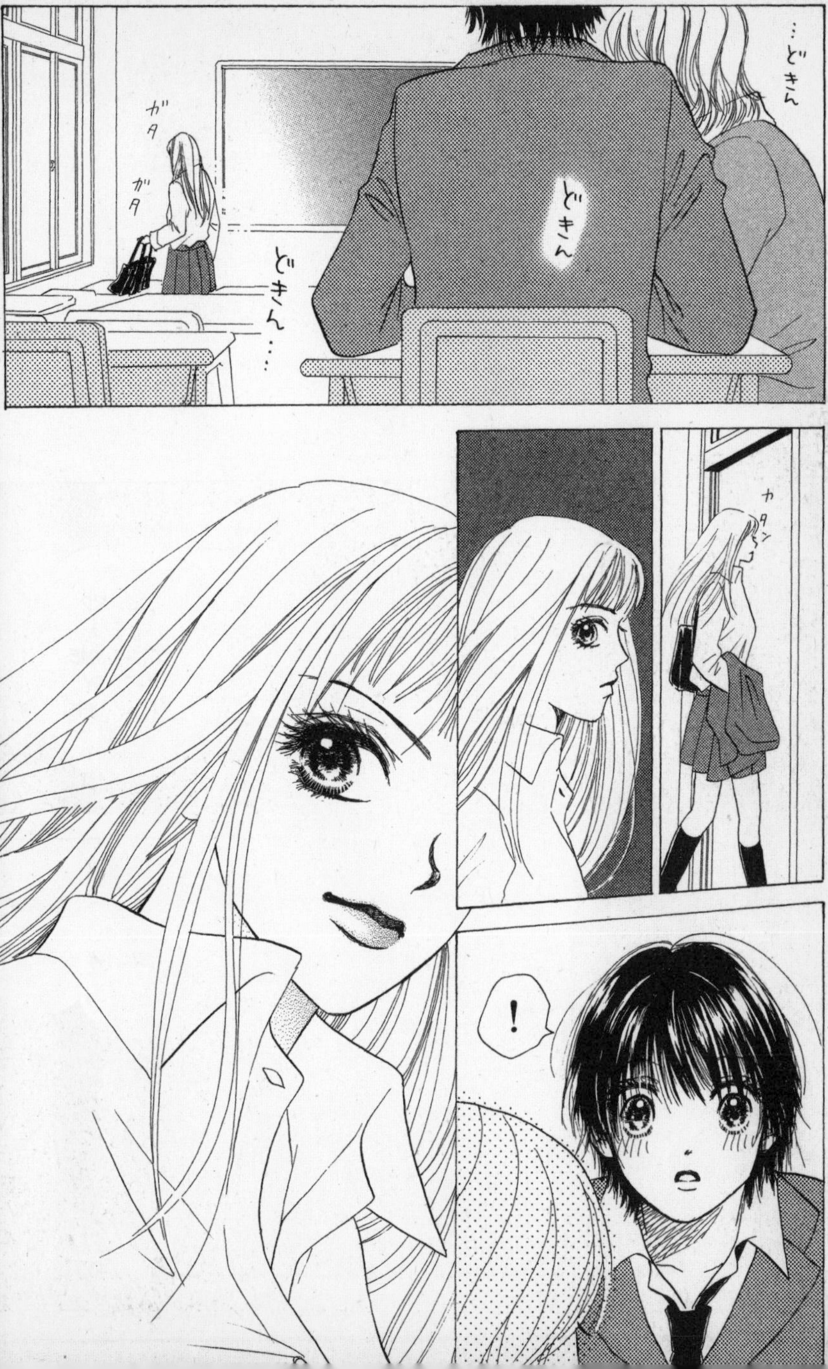
…どきん
どきん
ガタ
ガタ
どきん…
カタン
!

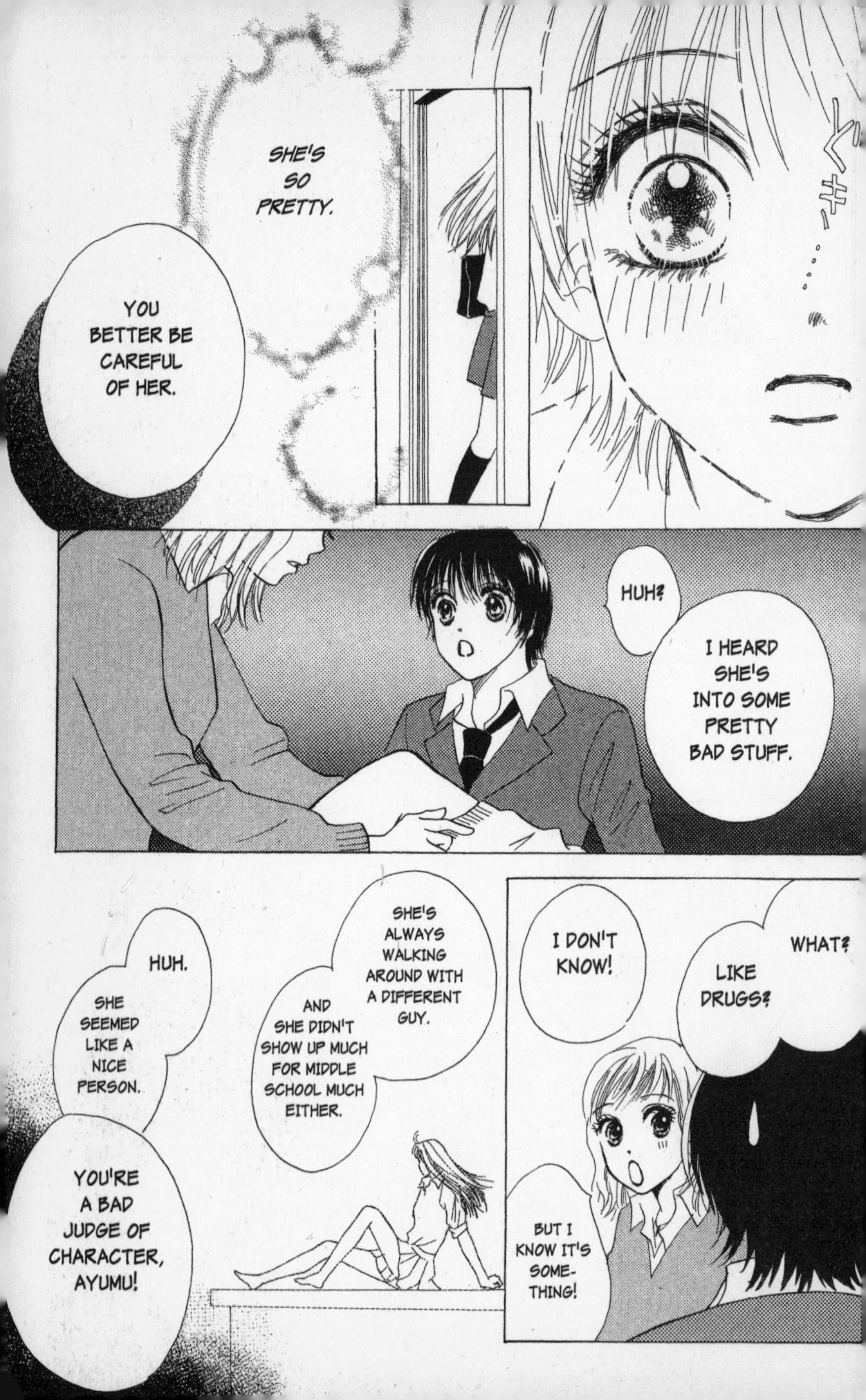
どき
SHE'S SO PRETTY.
YOU BETTER BE CAREFUL OF HER.
HUH?
I HEARD SHE'S INTO SOME PRETTY BAD STUFF.
WHAT?
LIKE DRUGS?
I DON'T KNOW!
BUT I KNOW IT'S SOME-THING!
SHE'S ALWAYS WALKING AROUND WITH A DIFFERENT GUY.
AND SHE DIDN'T SHOW UP MUCH FOR MIDDLE SCHOOL MUCH EITHER.
HUH.
SHE SEEMED LIKE A NICE PERSON.
YOU'RE A BAD JUDGE OF CHARACTER, AYUMU!

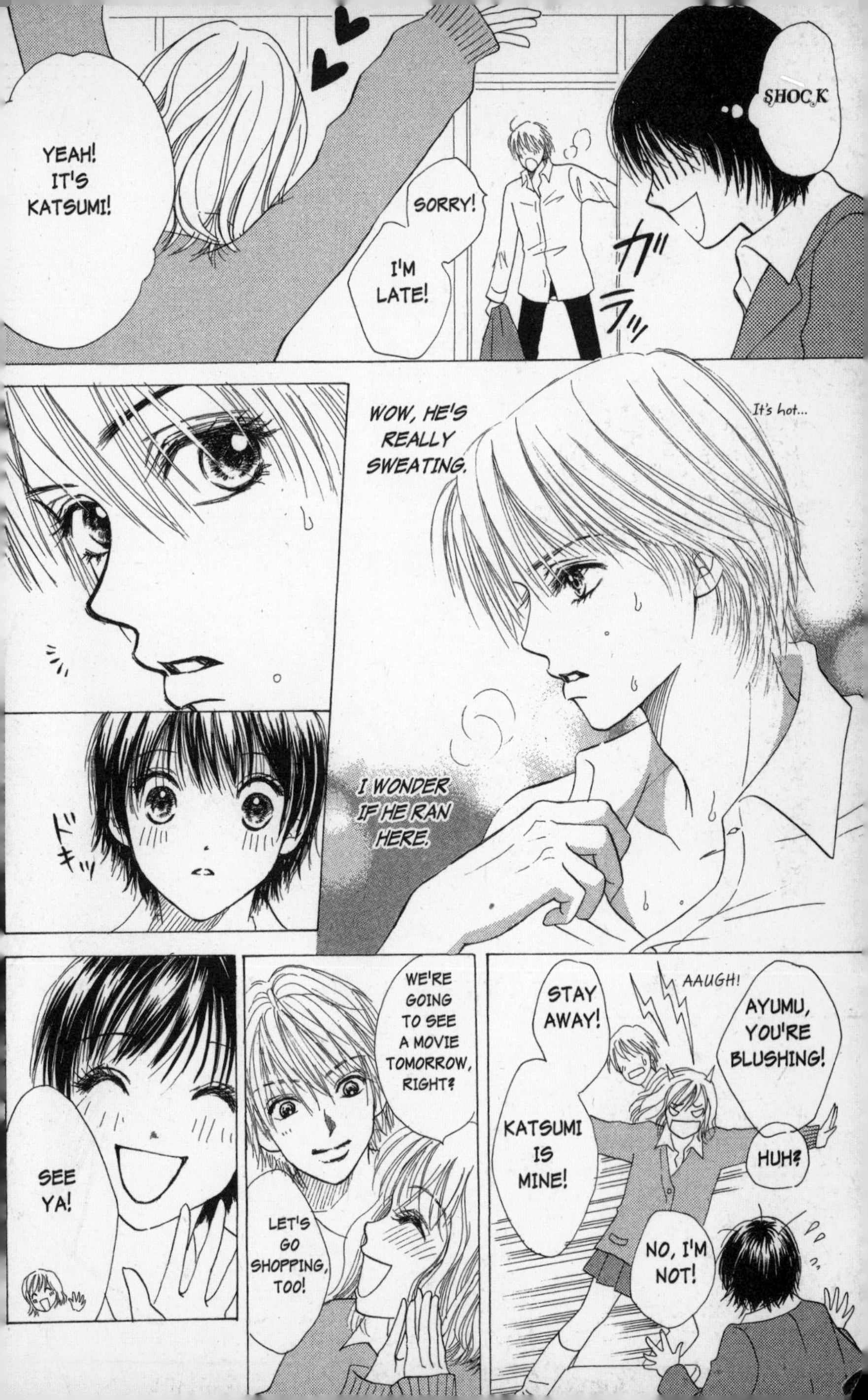
SHOCK
ガラッ
SORRY!
I'M LATE!
YEAH! IT'S KATSUMI!
It's hot...
WOW, HE'S REALLY SWEATING.
I WONDER IF HE RAN HERE.
ドキッ
AYUMU, YOU'RE BLUSHING!
AAUGH!
STAY AWAY!
HUH?
KATSUMI IS MINE!
NO, I'M NOT!
WE'RE GOING TO SEE A MOVIE TOMORROW, RIGHT?
LET'S GO SHOPPING, TOO!
SEE YA!

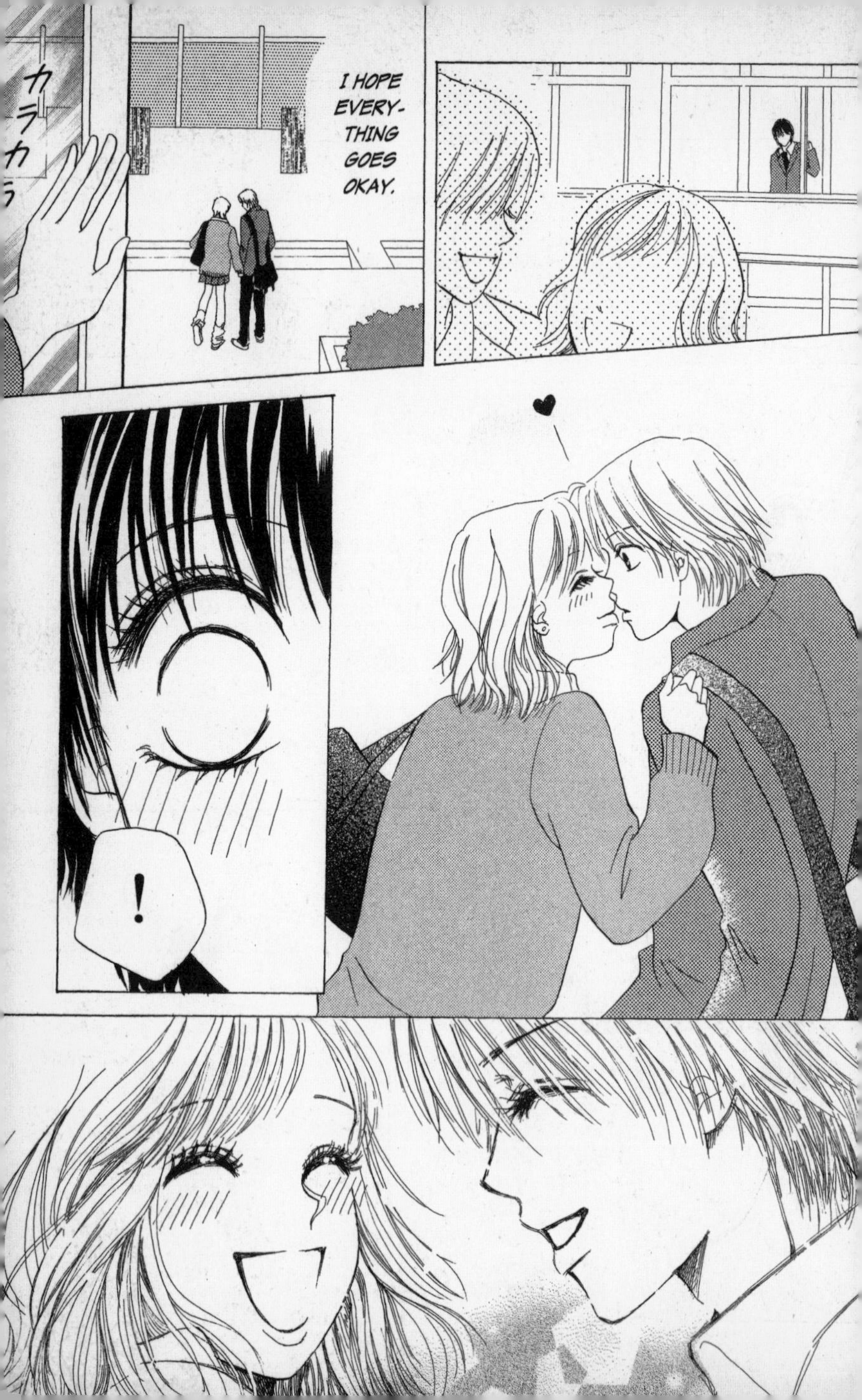
I HOPE EVERY-THING GOES OKAY.
カラカラ
!

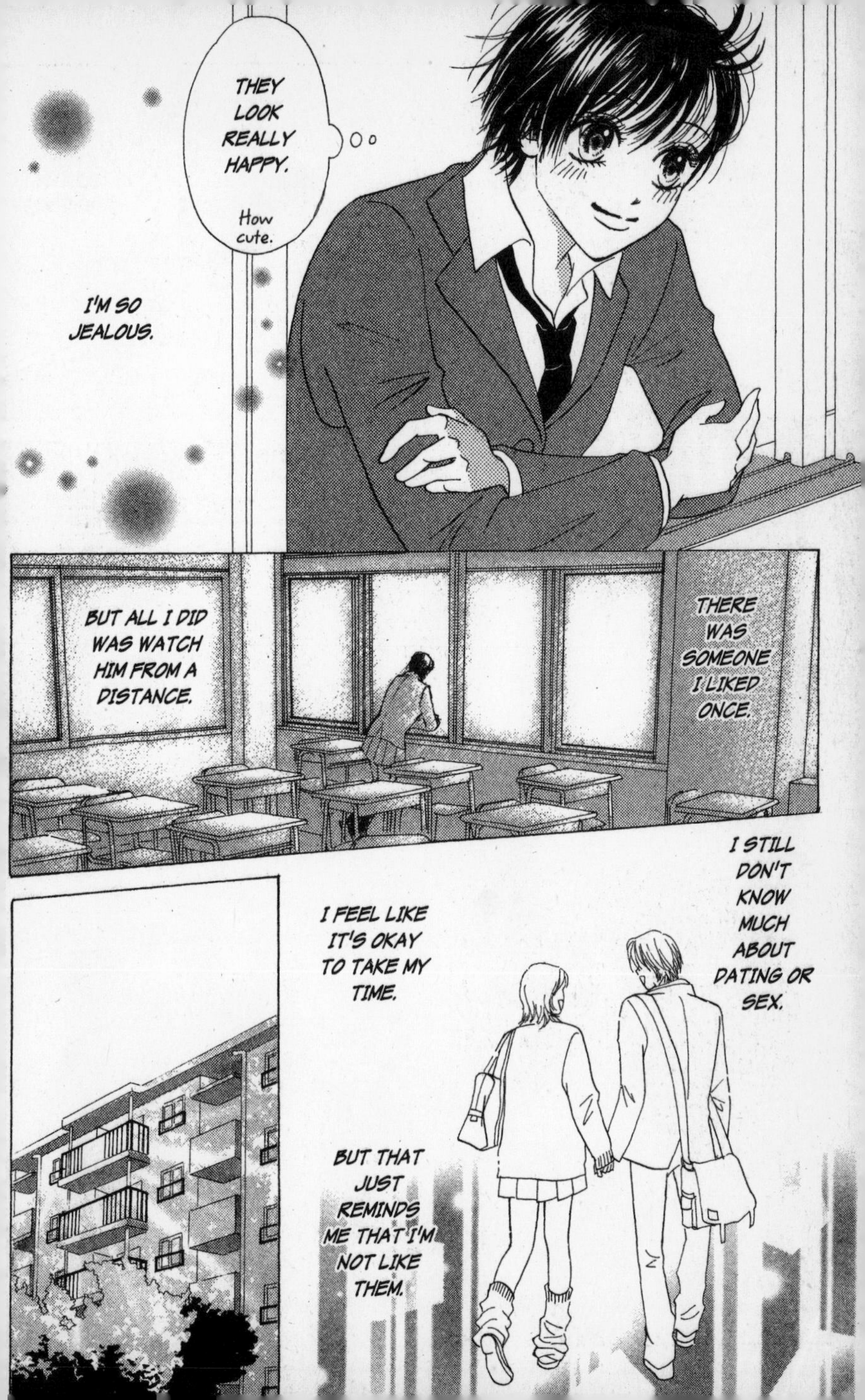
THEY LOOK REALLY HAPPY.
How cute.
I'M SO JEALOUS.
THERE WAS SOMEONE I LIKED ONCE.
BUT ALL I DID WAS WATCH HIM FROM A DISTANCE.
I STILL DON'T KNOW MUCH ABOUT DATING OR SEX.
I FEEL LIKE IT'S OKAY TO TAKE MY TIME.
BUT THAT JUST REMINDS ME THAT I'M NOT LIKE THEM.

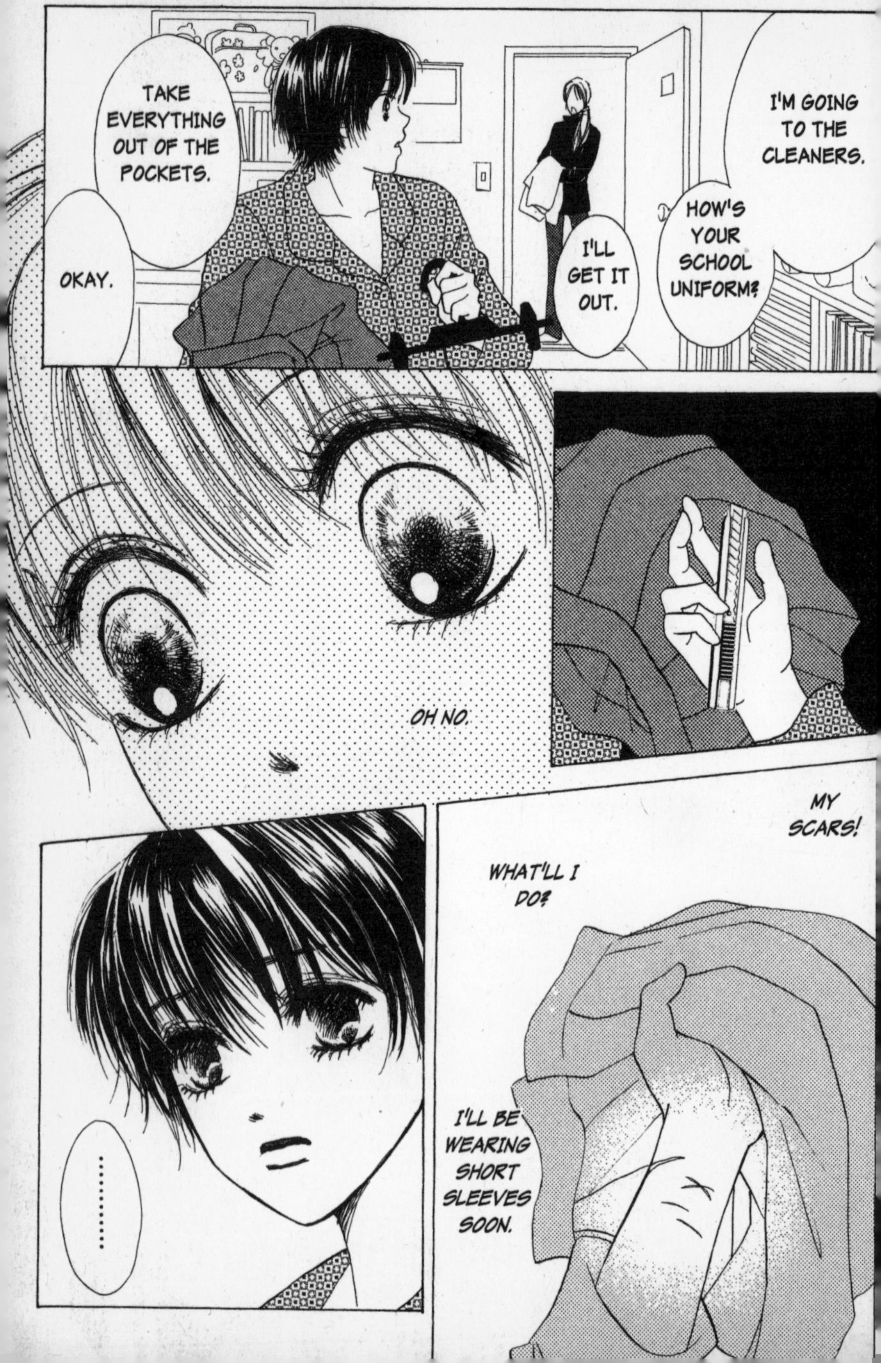
I'M GOING TO THE CLEANERS.
HOW'S YOUR SCHOOL UNIFORM?
I'LL GET IT OUT.
TAKE EVERYTHING OUT OF THE POCKETS.
OKAY.
OH NO.
MY SCARS!
WHAT'LL I DO?
I'LL BE WEARING SHORT SLEEVES SOON.
......

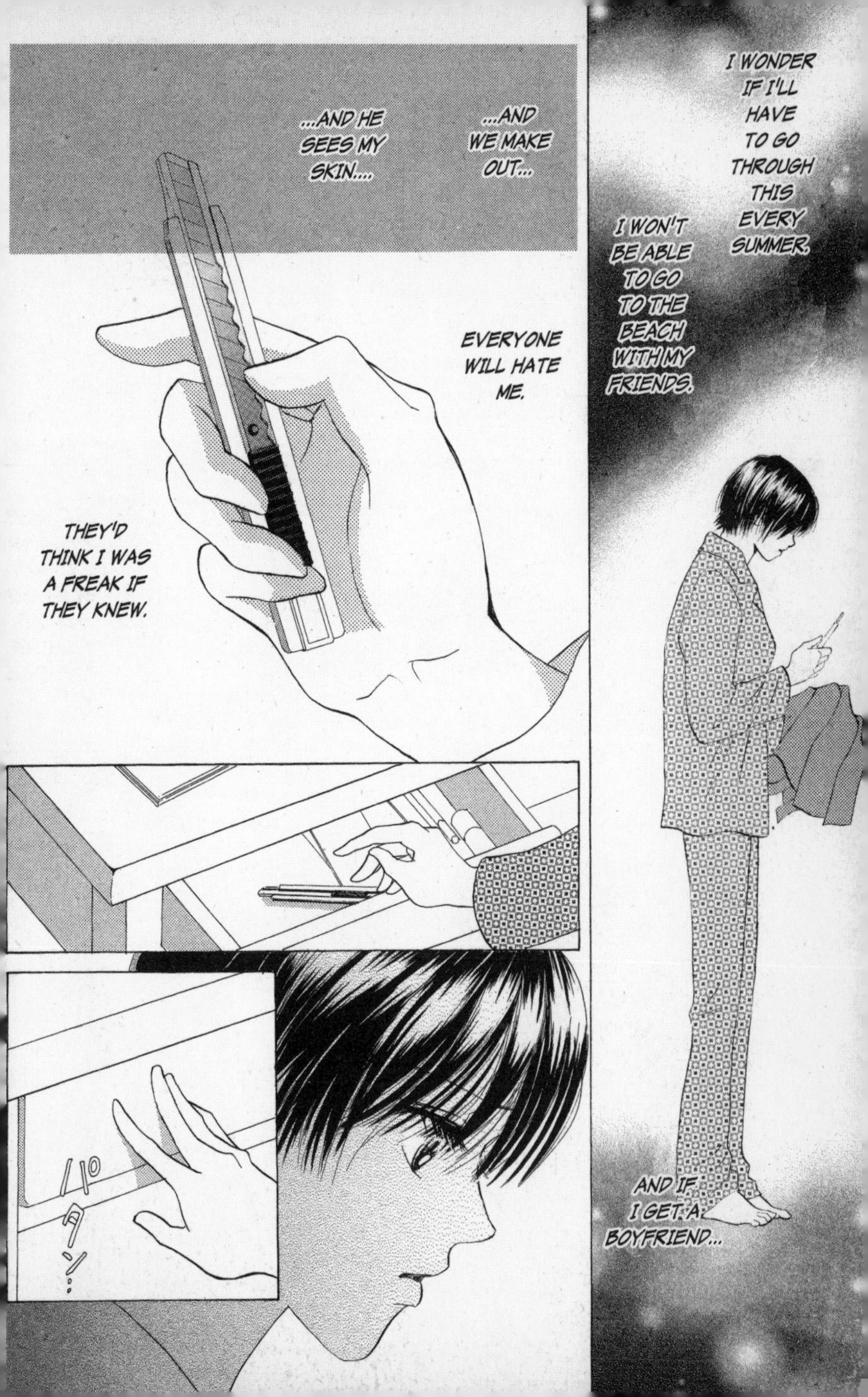
I WONDER IF I'LL HAVE TO GO THROUGH THIS EVERY SUMMER.
I WON'T BE ABLE TO GO TO THE BEACH WITH MY FRIENDS.
AND IF I GET A BOYFRIEND...
...AND WE MAKE OUT...
...AND HE SEES MY SKIN....
EVERYONE WILL HATE ME.
THEY'D THINK I WAS A FREAK IF THEY KNEW.
パタン…

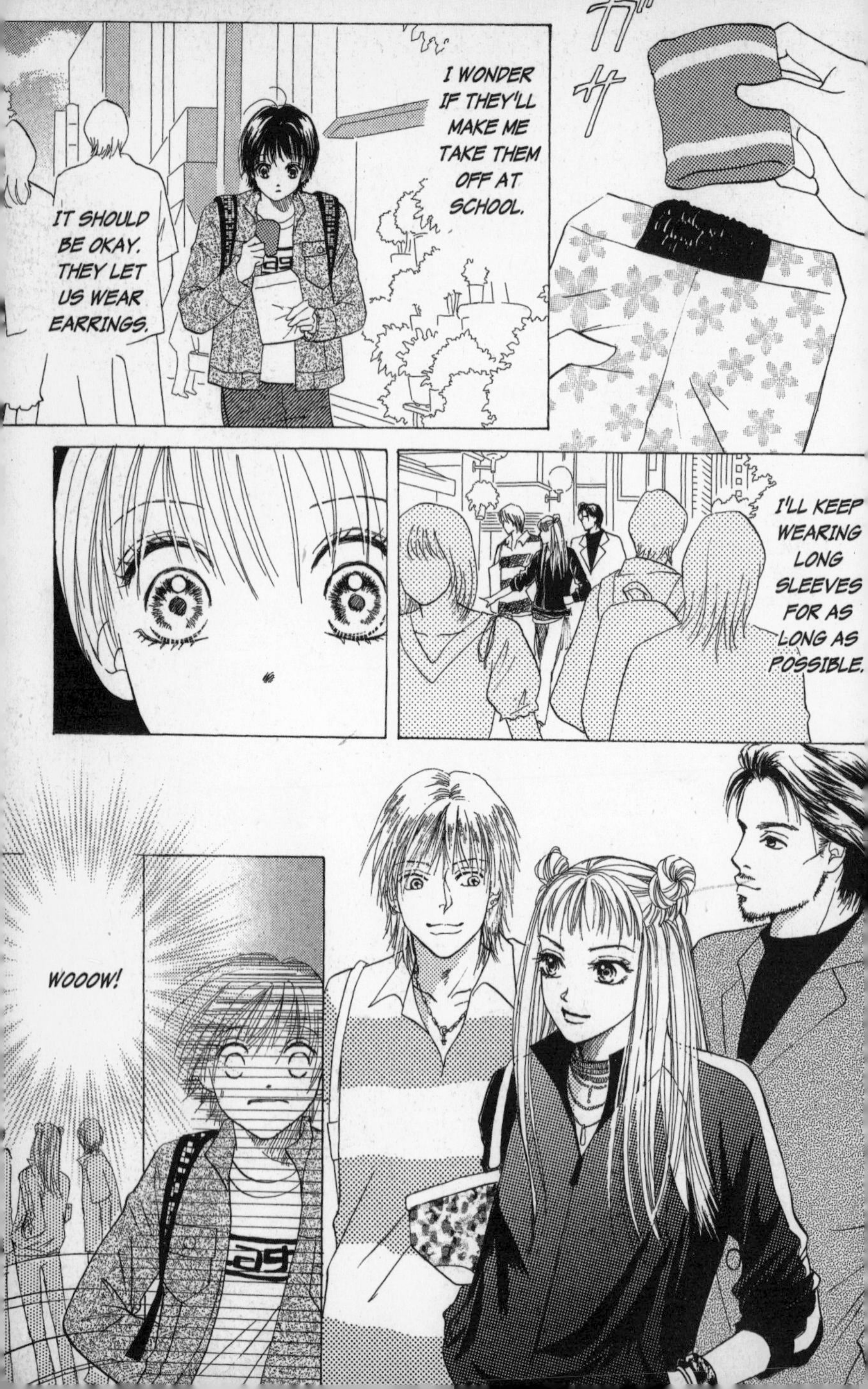
ガザ
I WONDER IF THEY'LL MAKE ME TAKE THEM OFF AT SCHOOL.
IT SHOULD BE OKAY. THEY LET US WEAR EARRINGS.
I'LL KEEP WEARING LONG SLEEVES FOR AS LONG AS POSSIBLE.
WOOOW!

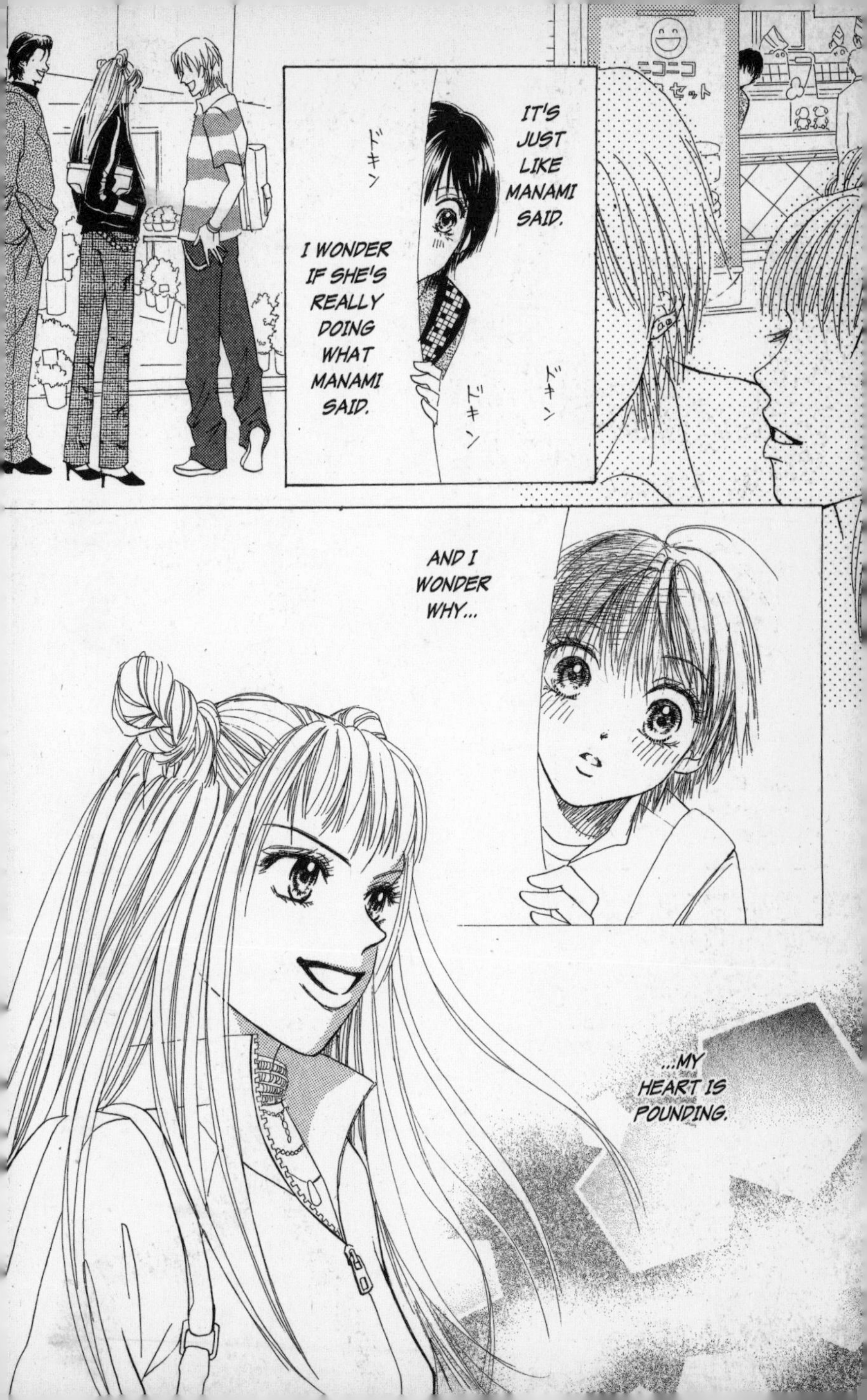
IT'S JUST LIKE MANAMI SAID.
ドキン
ドキン
ドキン
I WONDER IF SHE'S REALLY DOING WHAT MANAMI SAID.
AND I WONDER WHY...
...MY HEART IS POUNDING.

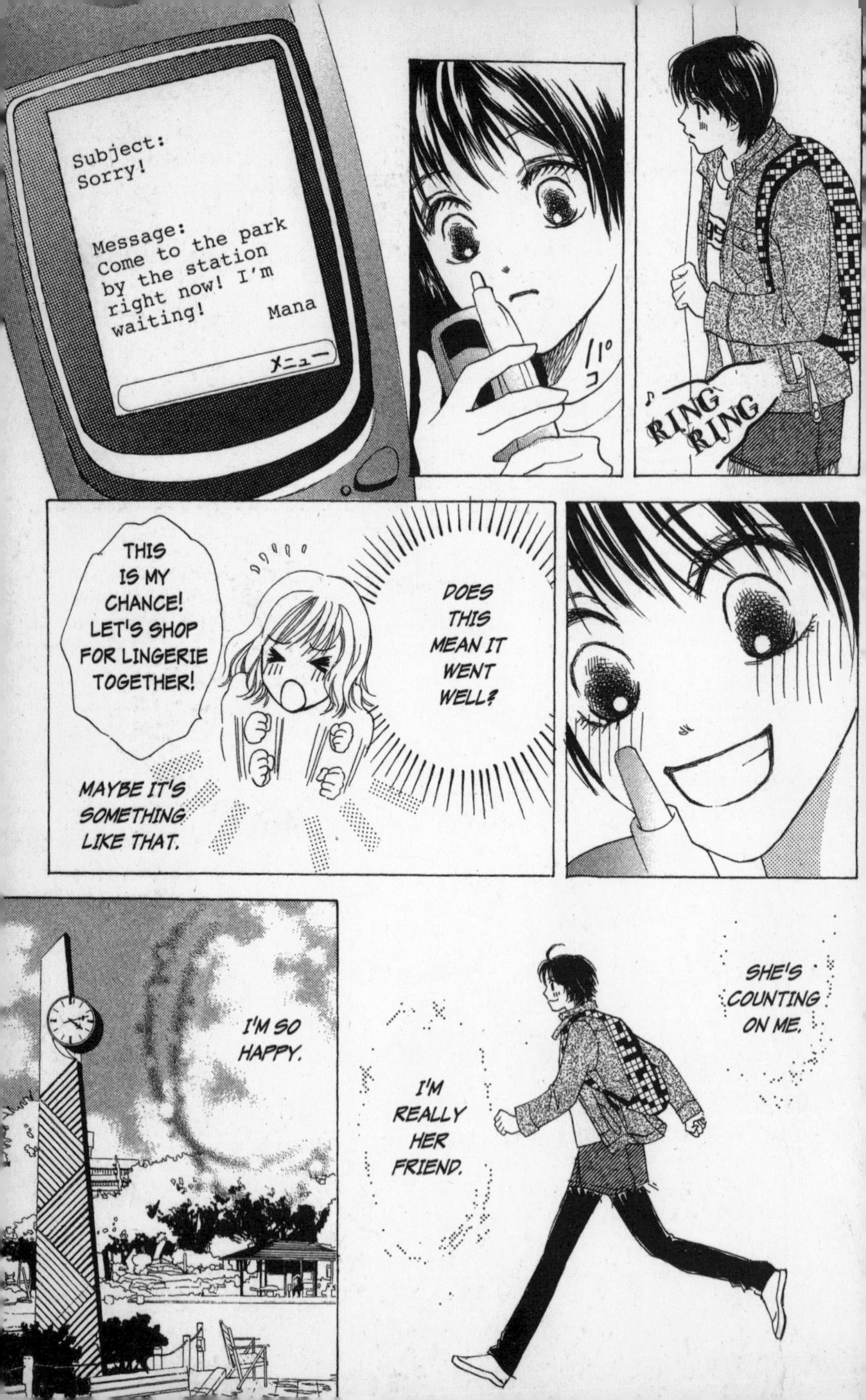
RING RING
パコ
Subject: Sorry!
Message: Come to the park by the station right now! I'm waiting! Mana
メニュー
DOES THIS MEAN IT WENT WELL?
THIS IS MY CHANCE! LET'S SHOP FOR LINGERIE TOGETHER!
MAYBE IT'S SOMETHING LIKE THAT.
SHE'S COUNTING ON ME.
I'M REALLY HER FRIEND.
I'M SO HAPPY.

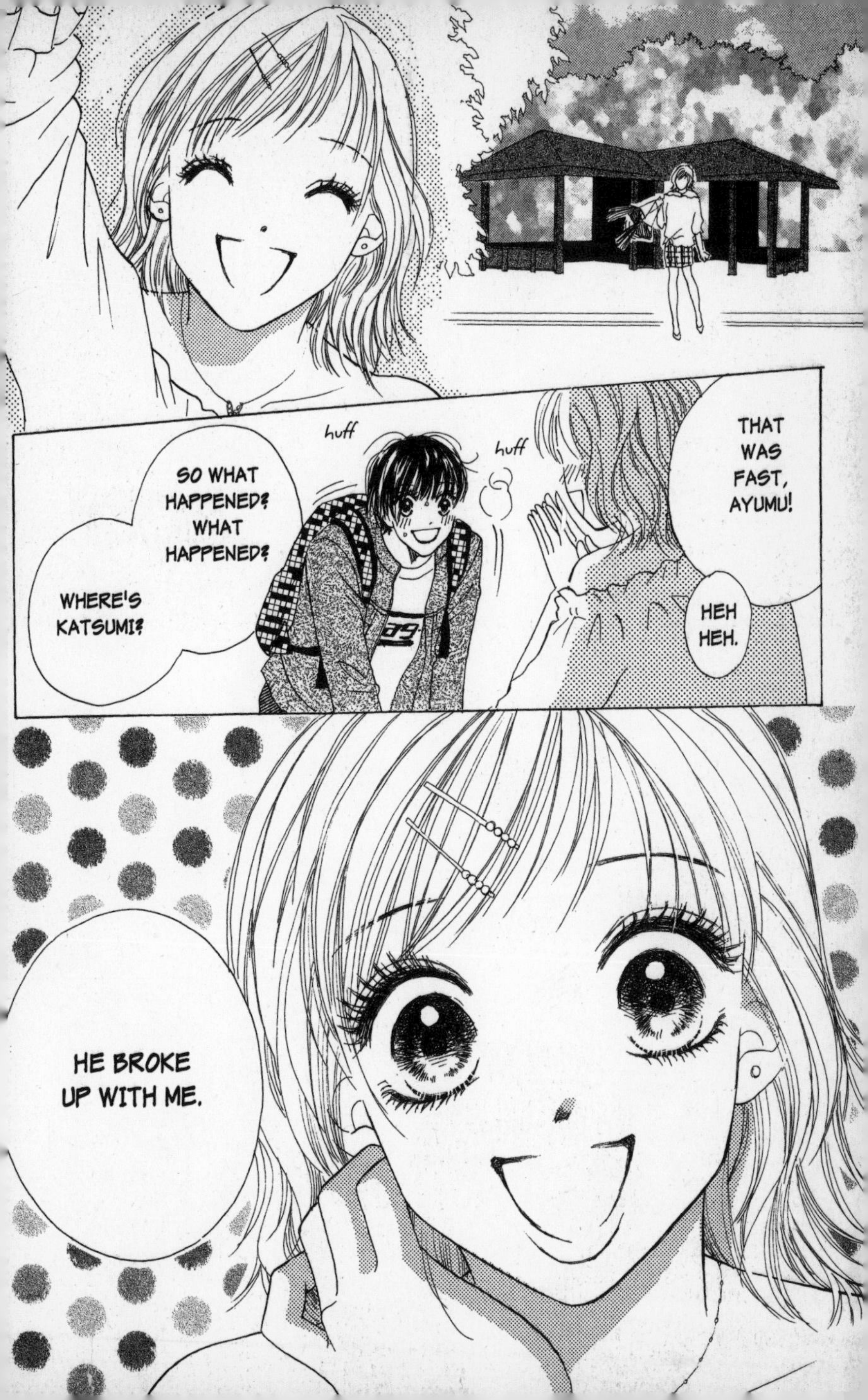
THAT WAS FAST, AYUMU!
HEH HEH.
huff
huff
SO WHAT HAPPENED? WHAT HAPPENED?
WHERE'S KATSUMI?
HE BROKE UP WITH ME.

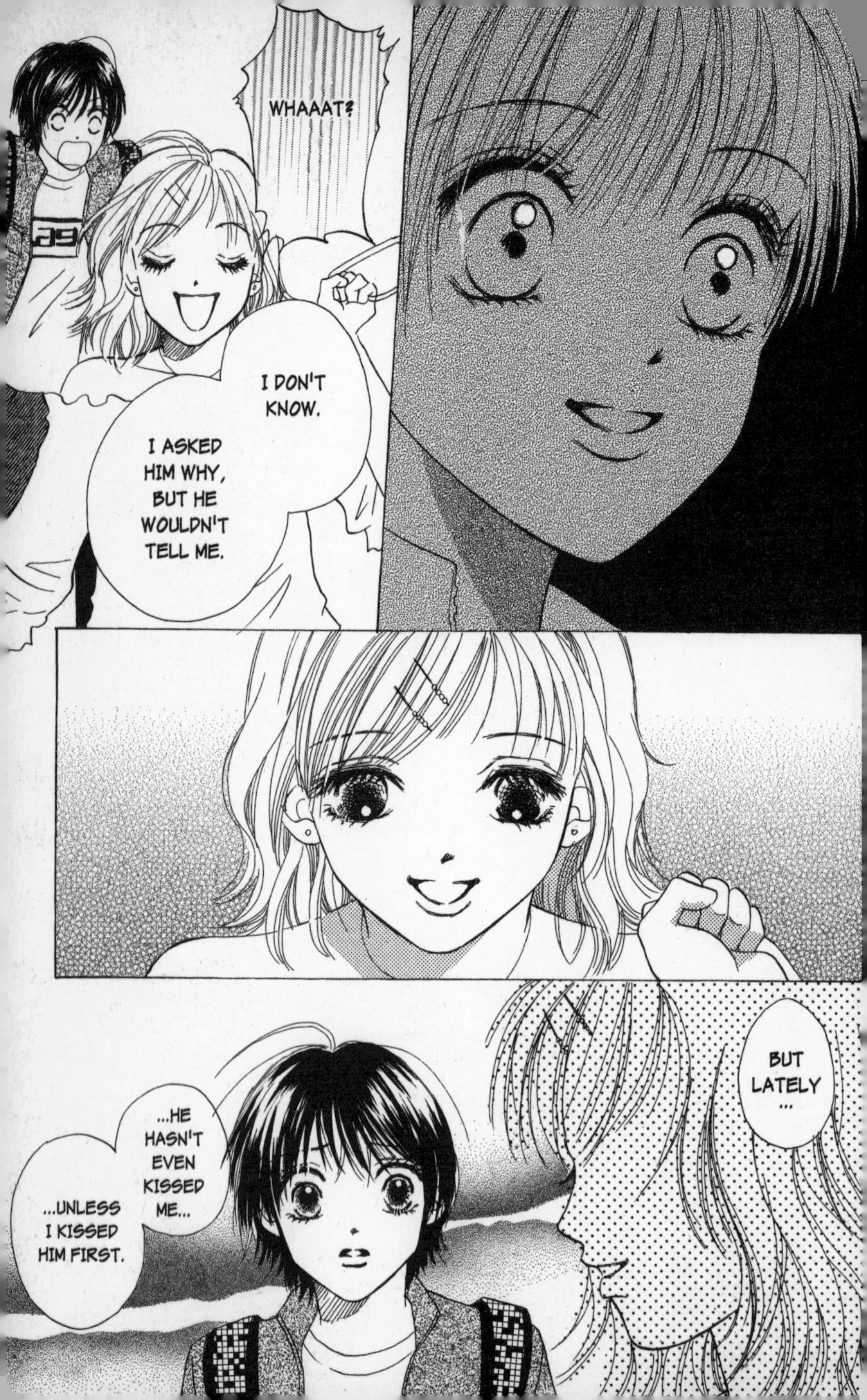
WHAAAT?
I DON'T KNOW.
I ASKED HIM WHY, BUT HE WOULDN'T TELL ME.
BUT LATELY ...
...HE HASN'T EVEN KISSED ME...
...UNLESS I KISSED HIM FIRST.

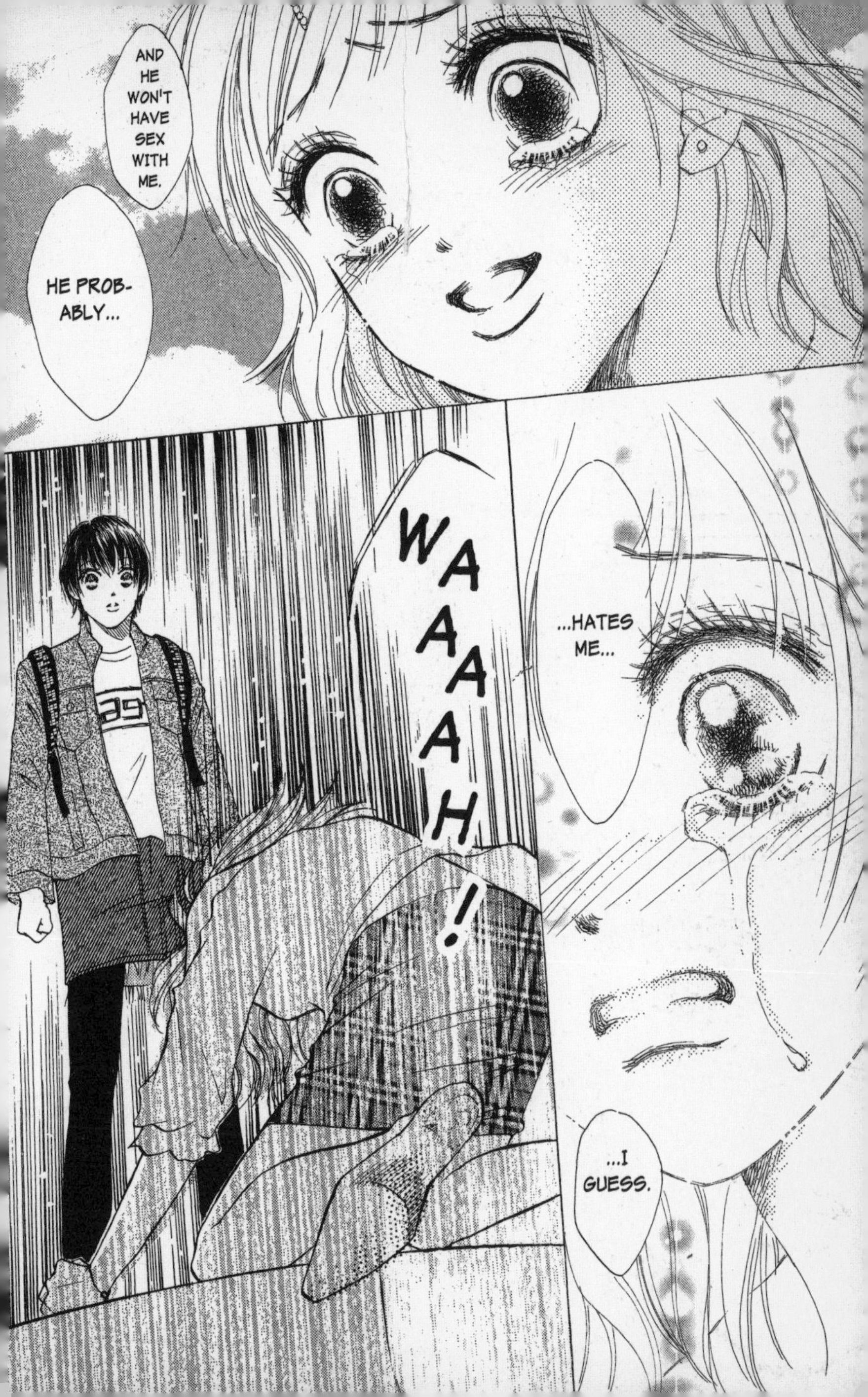
AND HE WON'T HAVE SEX WITH ME.
HE PROB-ABLY...
...HATES ME...
...I GUESS.
WAAAAH!

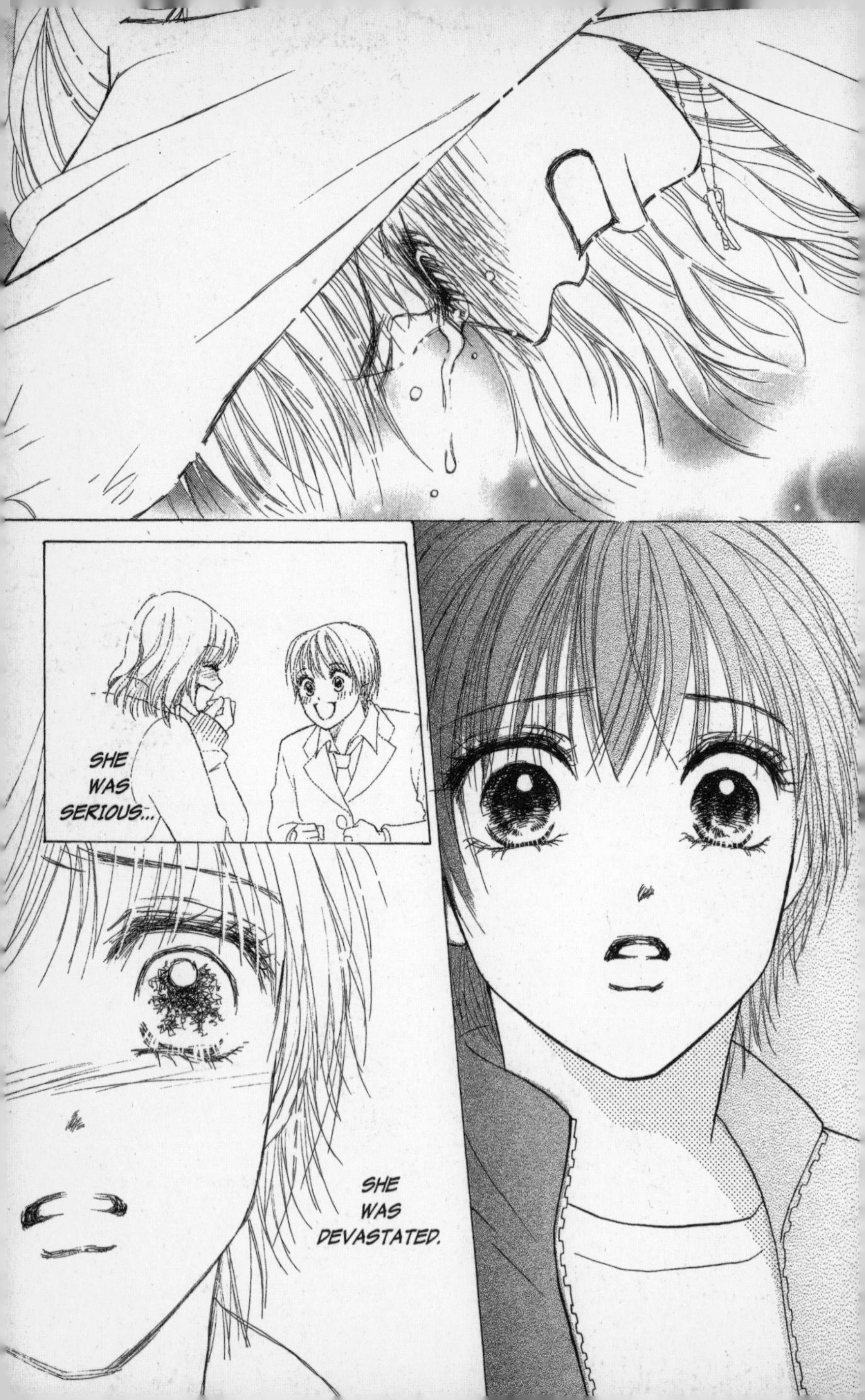
SHE WAS SERIOUS...
SHE WAS DEVASTATED.

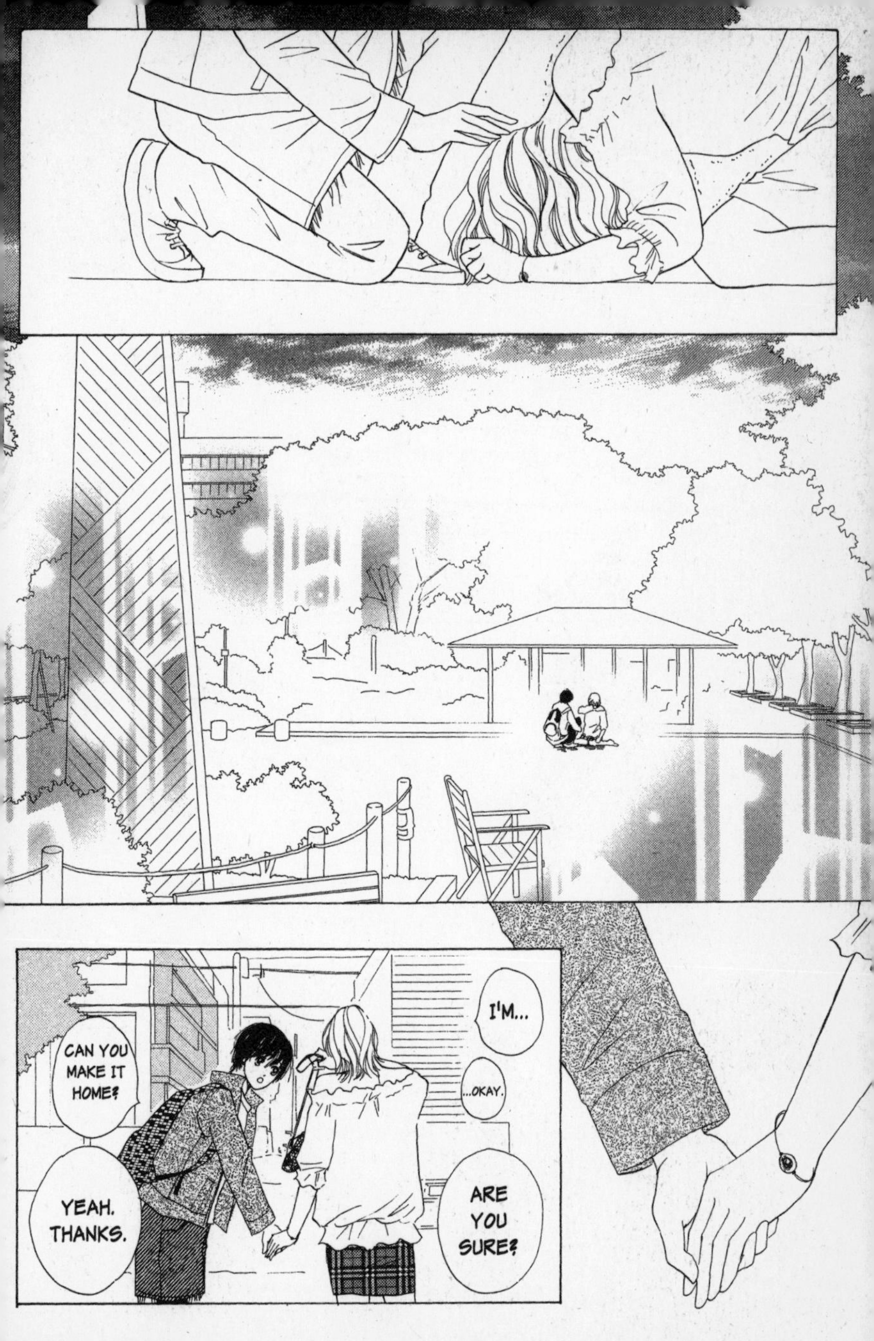
CAN YOU MAKE IT HOME?
I'M...
...OKAY.
ARE YOU SURE?
YEAH. THANKS.

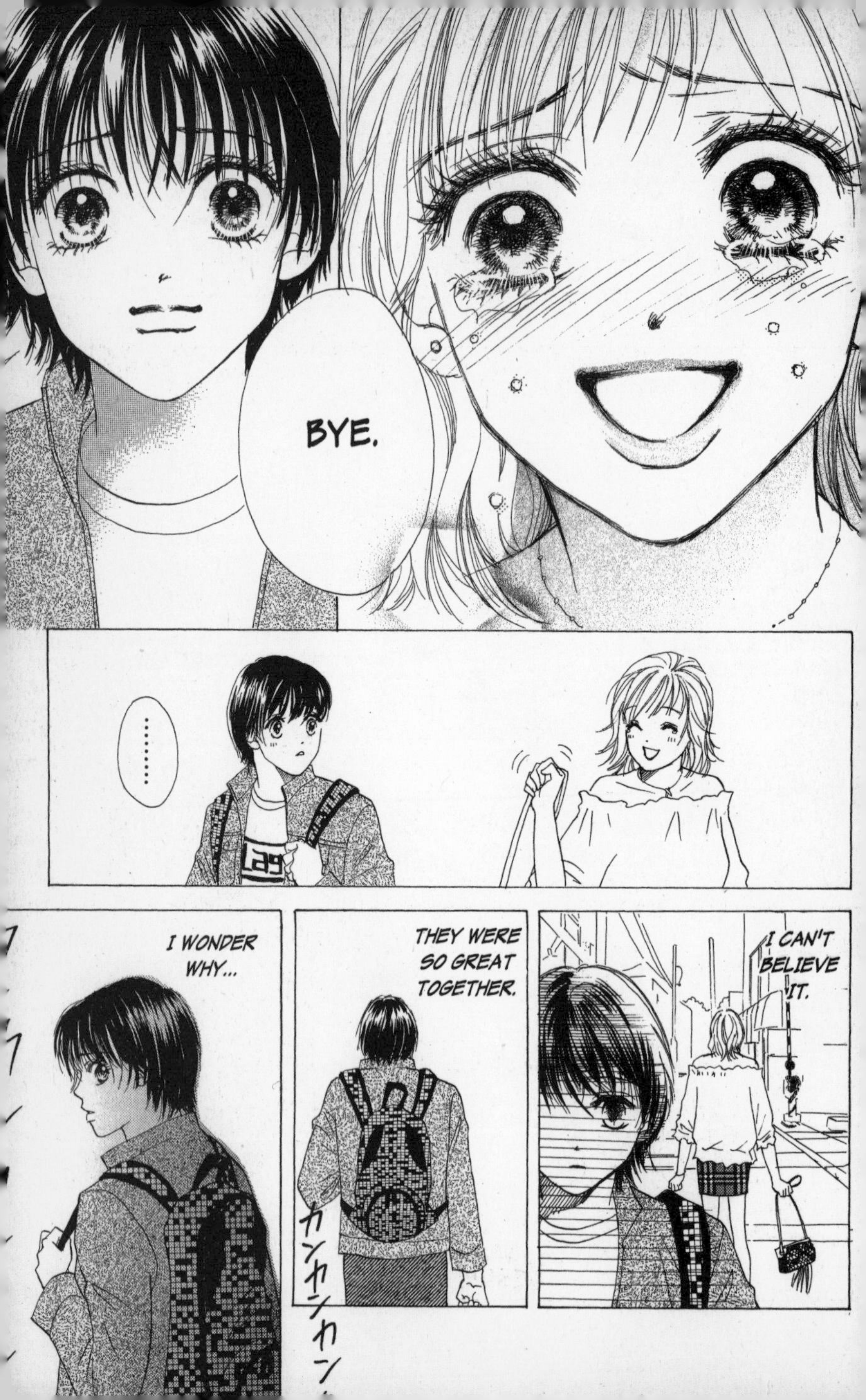
BYE.
....
I CAN'T BELIEVE IT.
THEY WERE SO GREAT TOGETHER.
カンカンカンカン
I WONDER WHY...

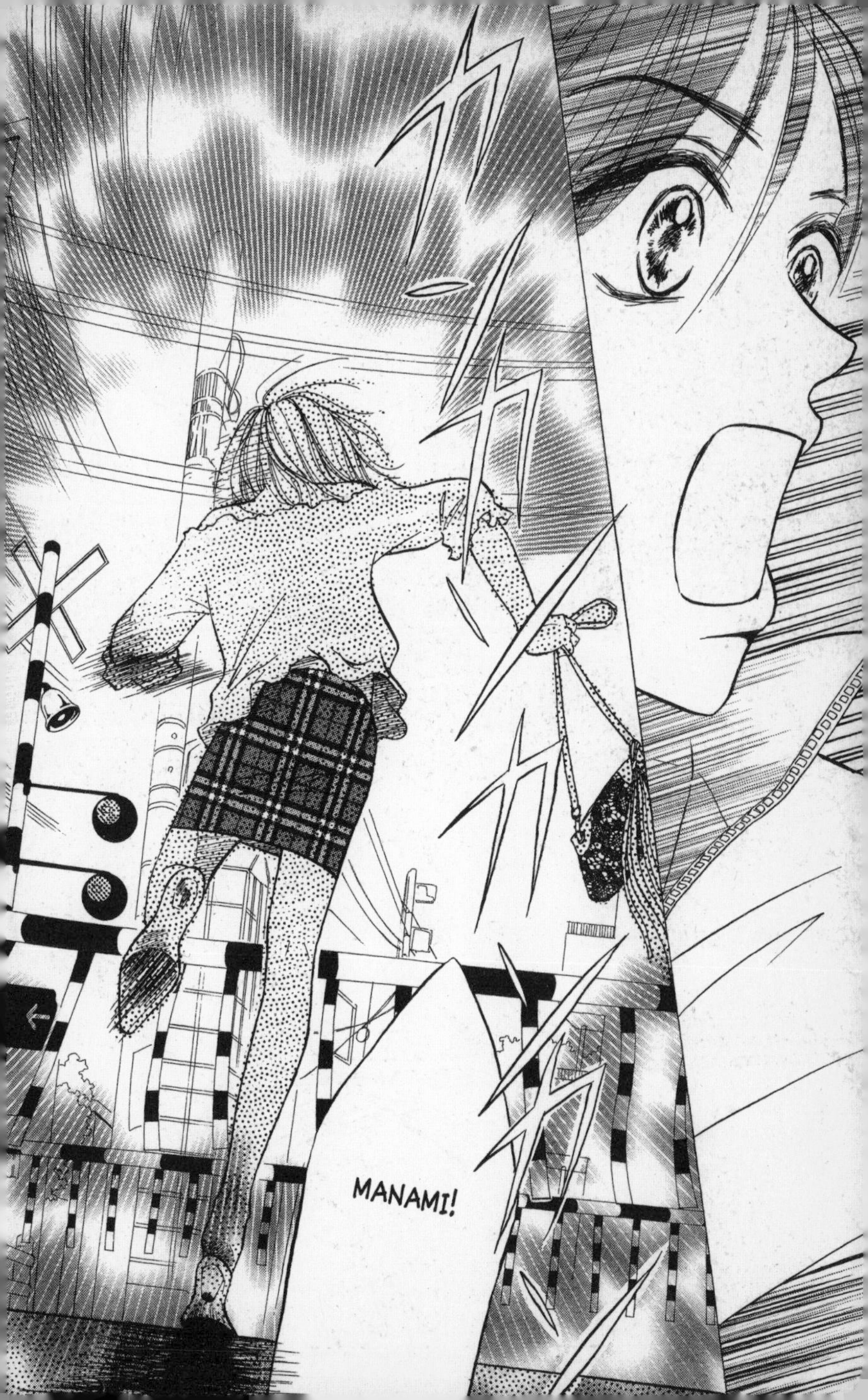
MANAMI!

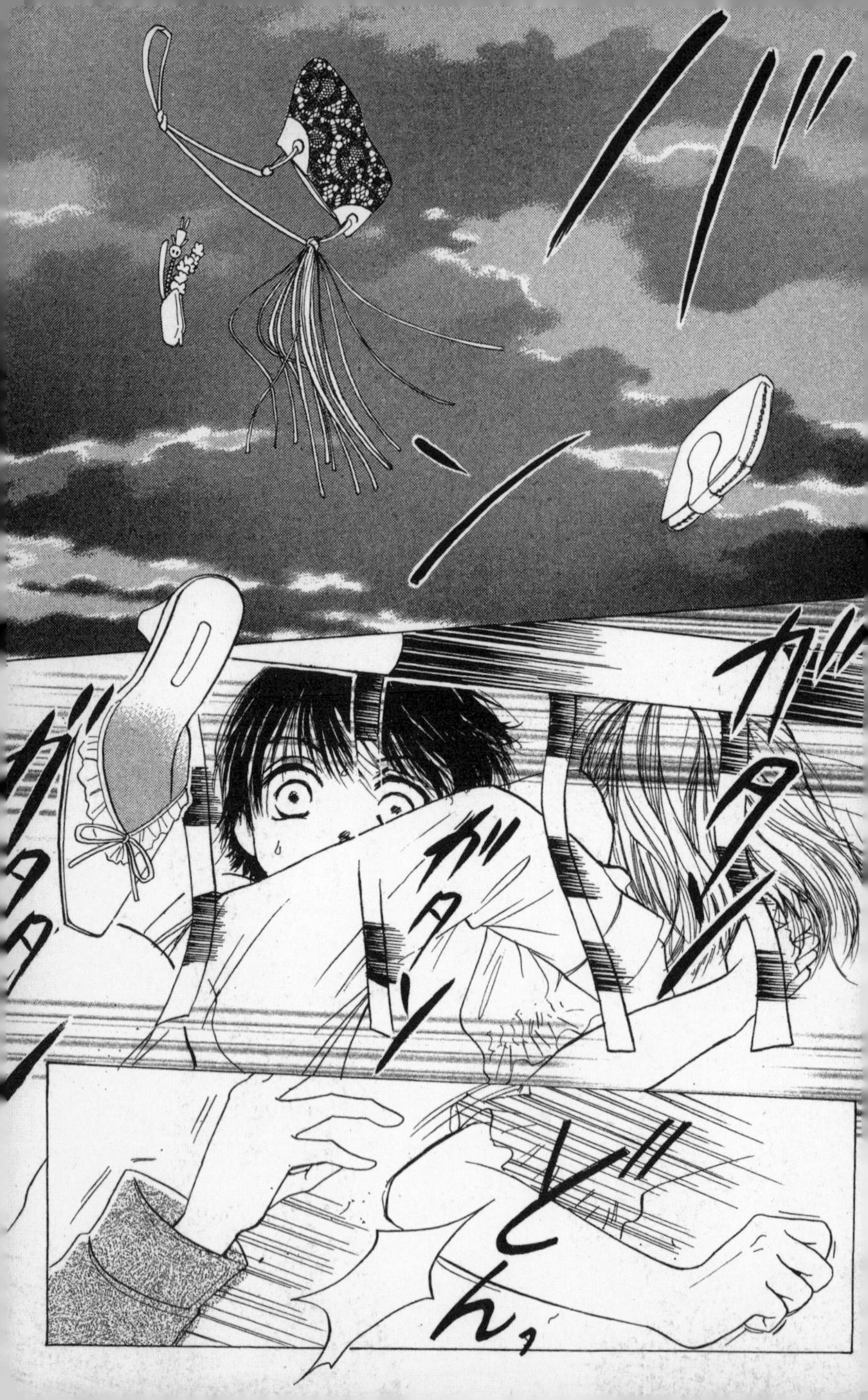
バン
ガタン
ガタン
ガタタン
どん

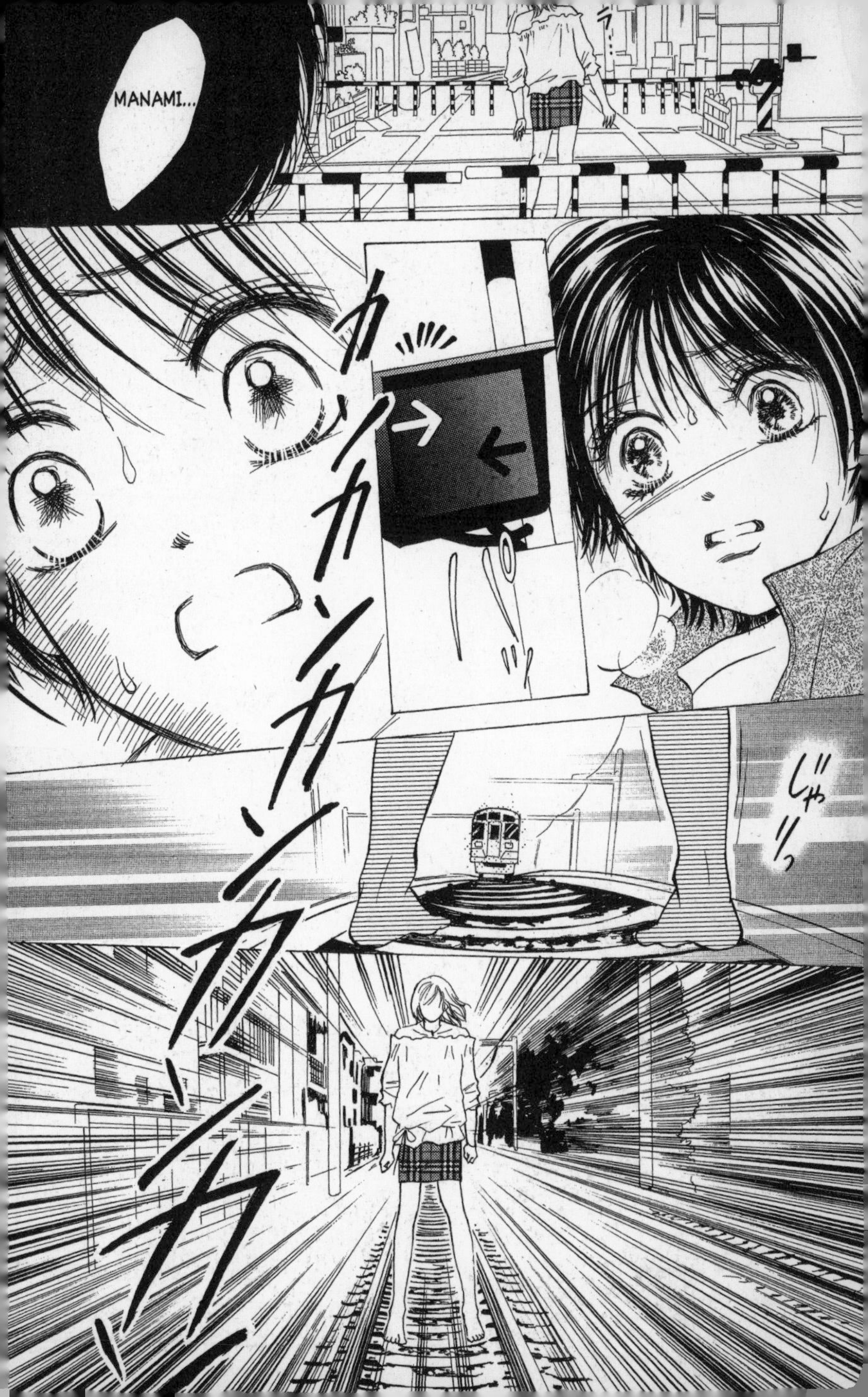
ラ…
MANAMI...
カンカンカンカンカンカ
じゃりっ

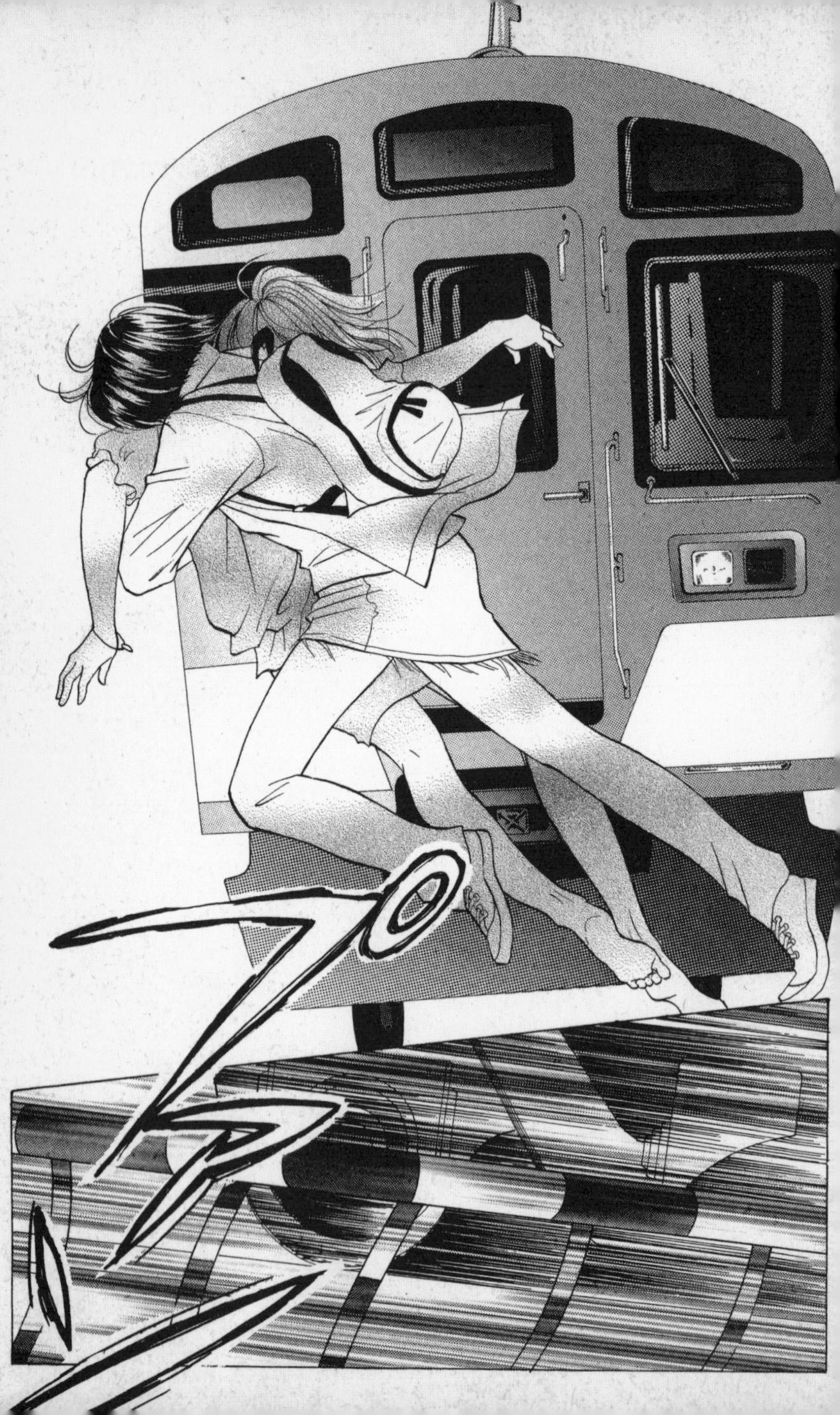

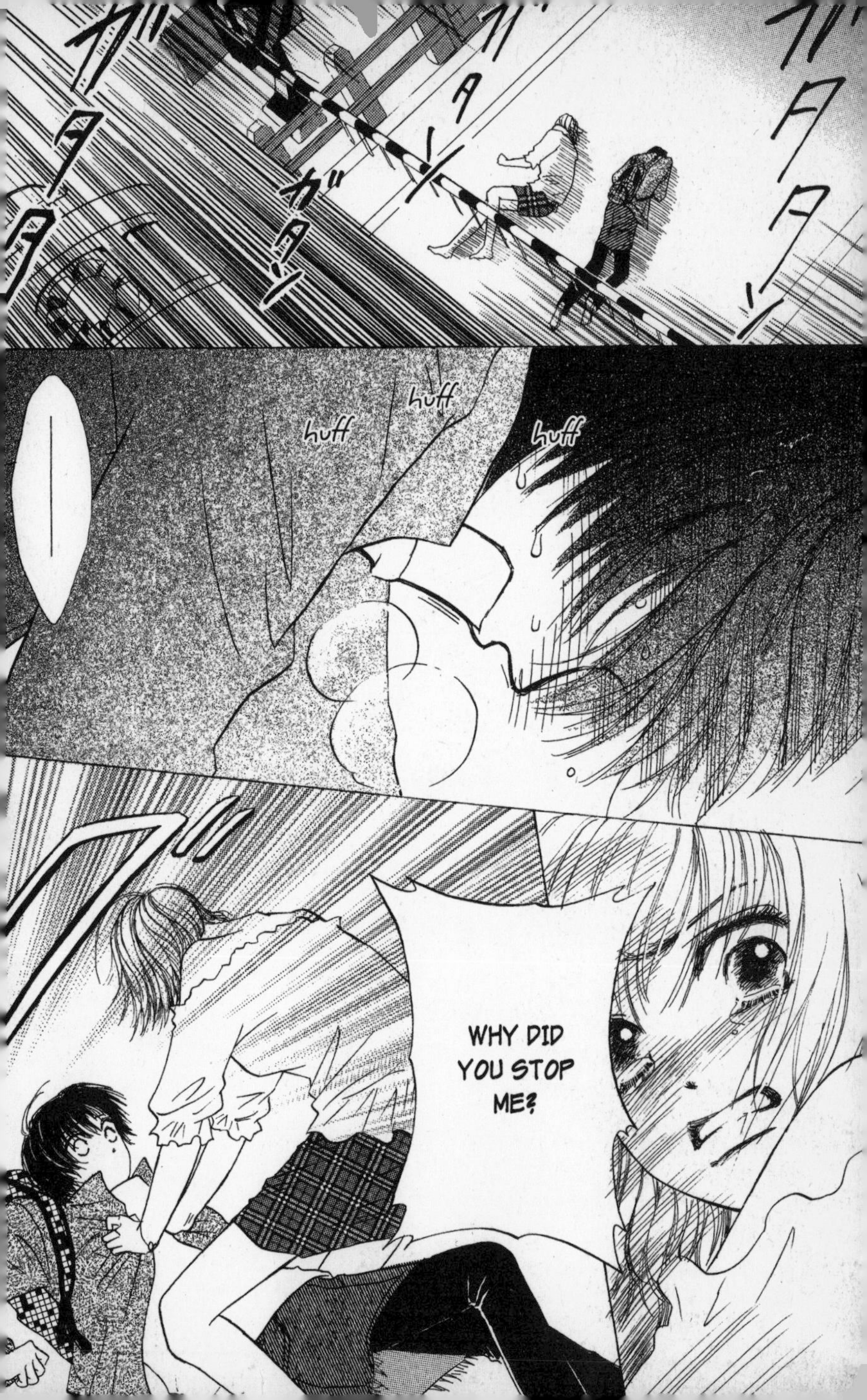

バタン
ガタン
ガタン
バタ
huff
huff
huff
WHY DID YOU STOP ME?

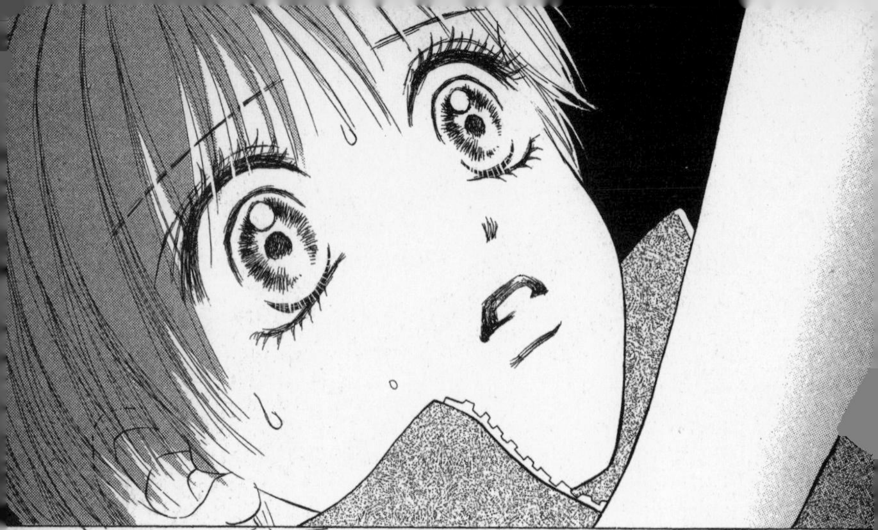
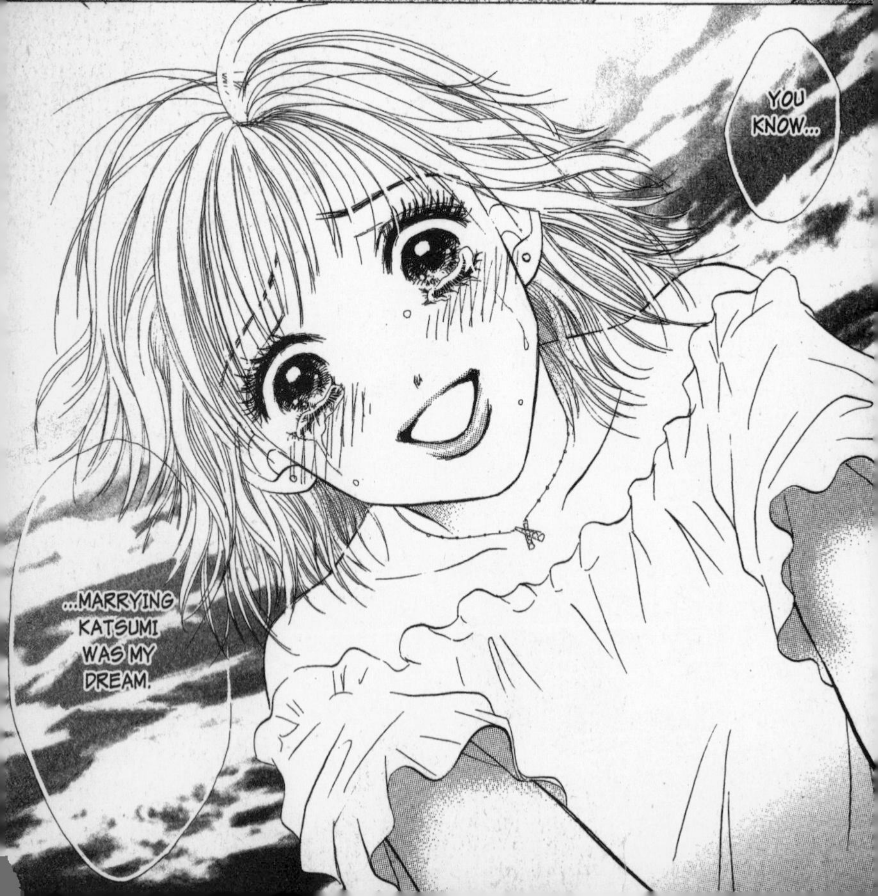
YOU KNOW...
...MARRYING KATSUMI WAS MY DREAM.

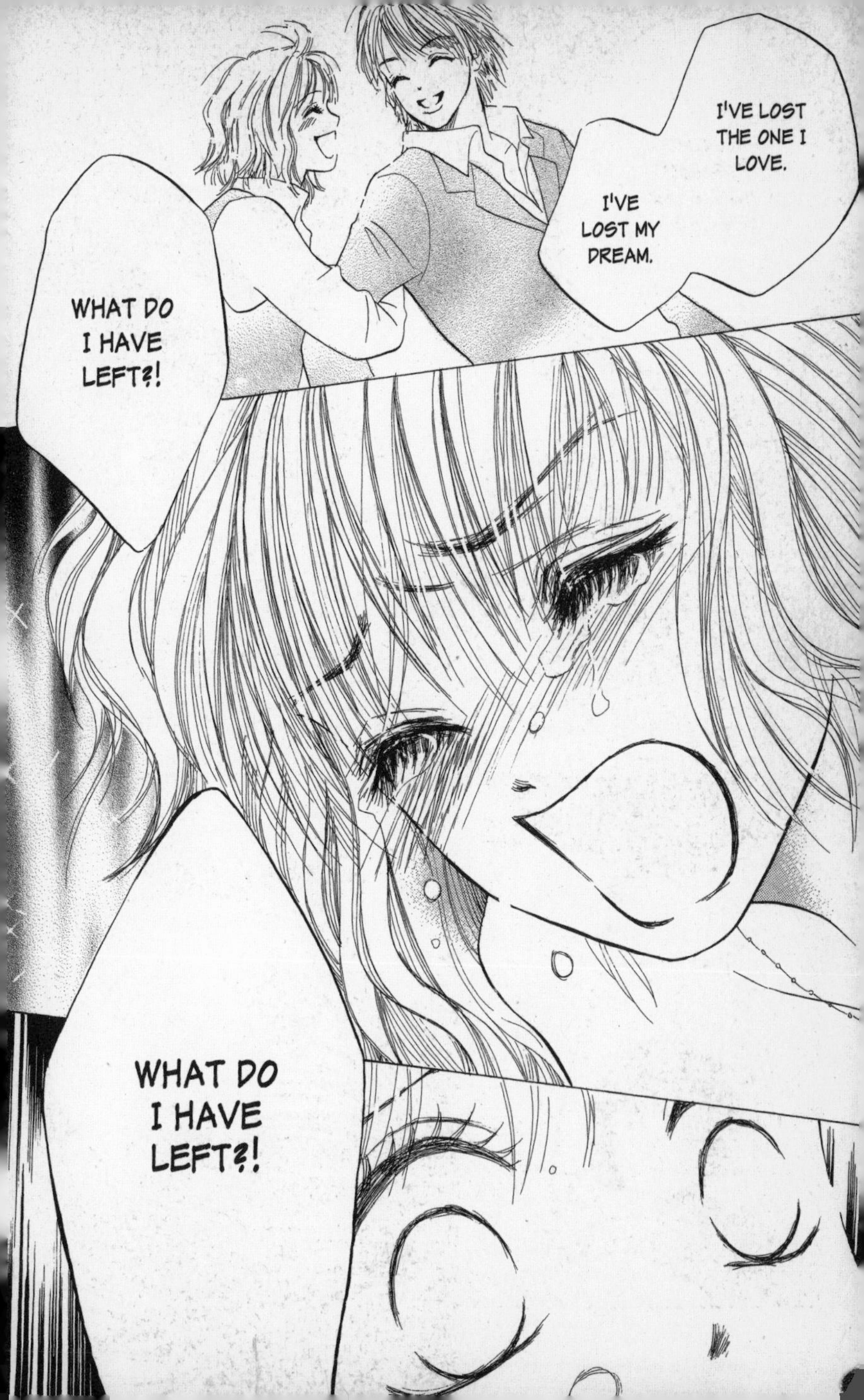
I'VE LOST THE ONE I LOVE.
I'VE LOST MY DREAM.
WHAT DO I HAVE LEFT?!
WHAT DO I HAVE LEFT?!

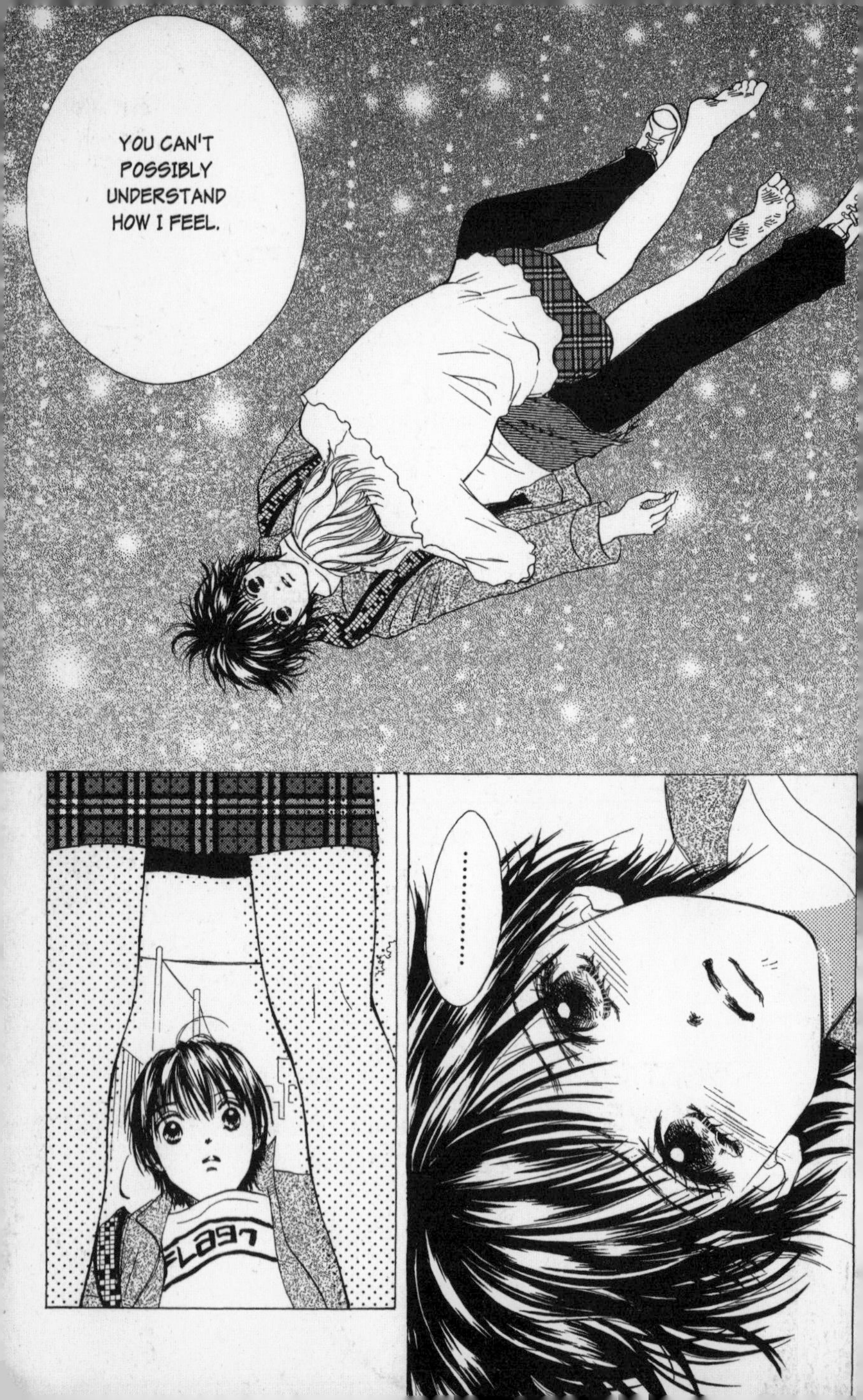
YOU CAN'T POSSIBLY UNDERSTAND HOW I FEEL.
......

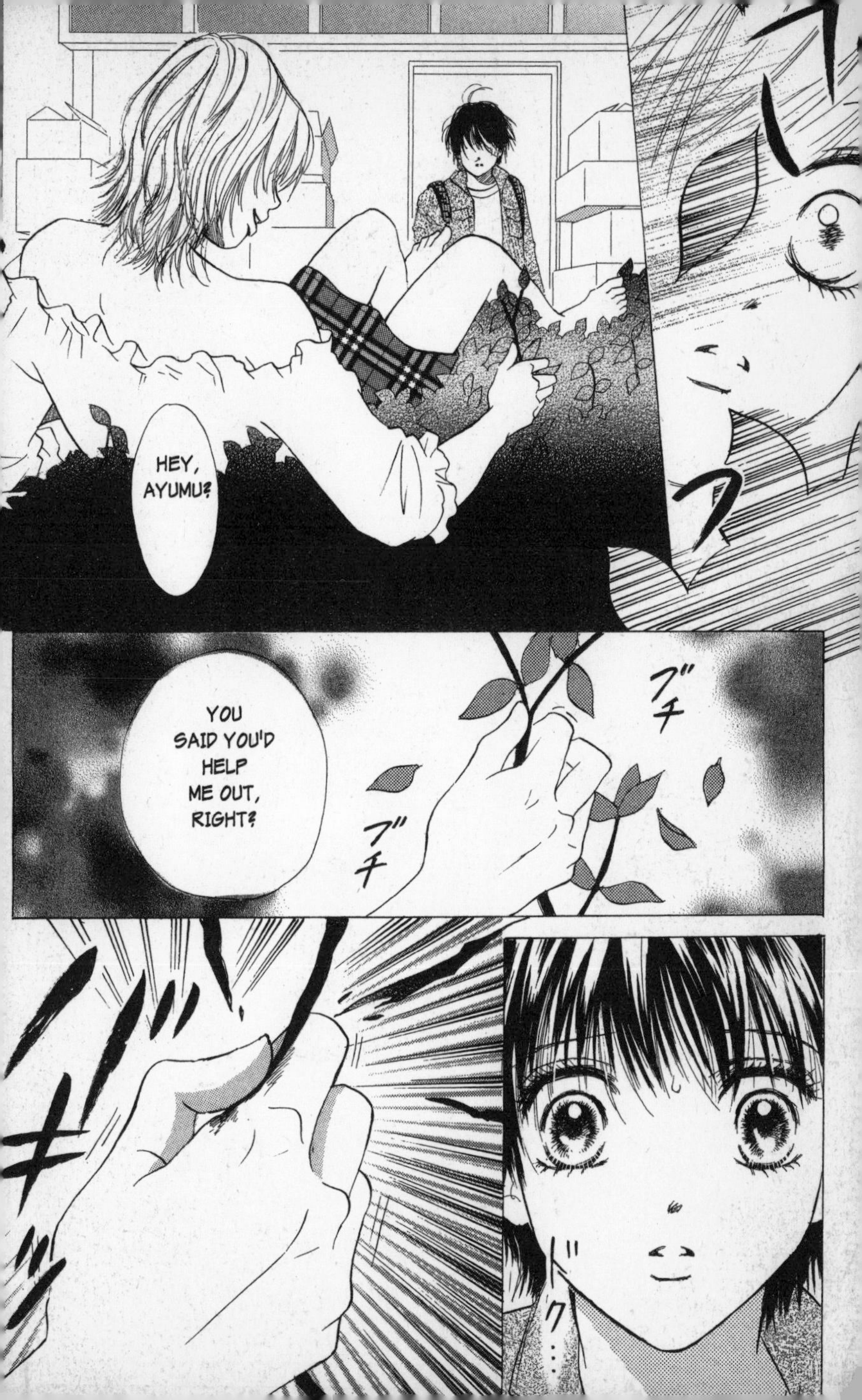
HEY, AYUMU?
YOU SAID YOU'D HELP ME OUT, RIGHT?

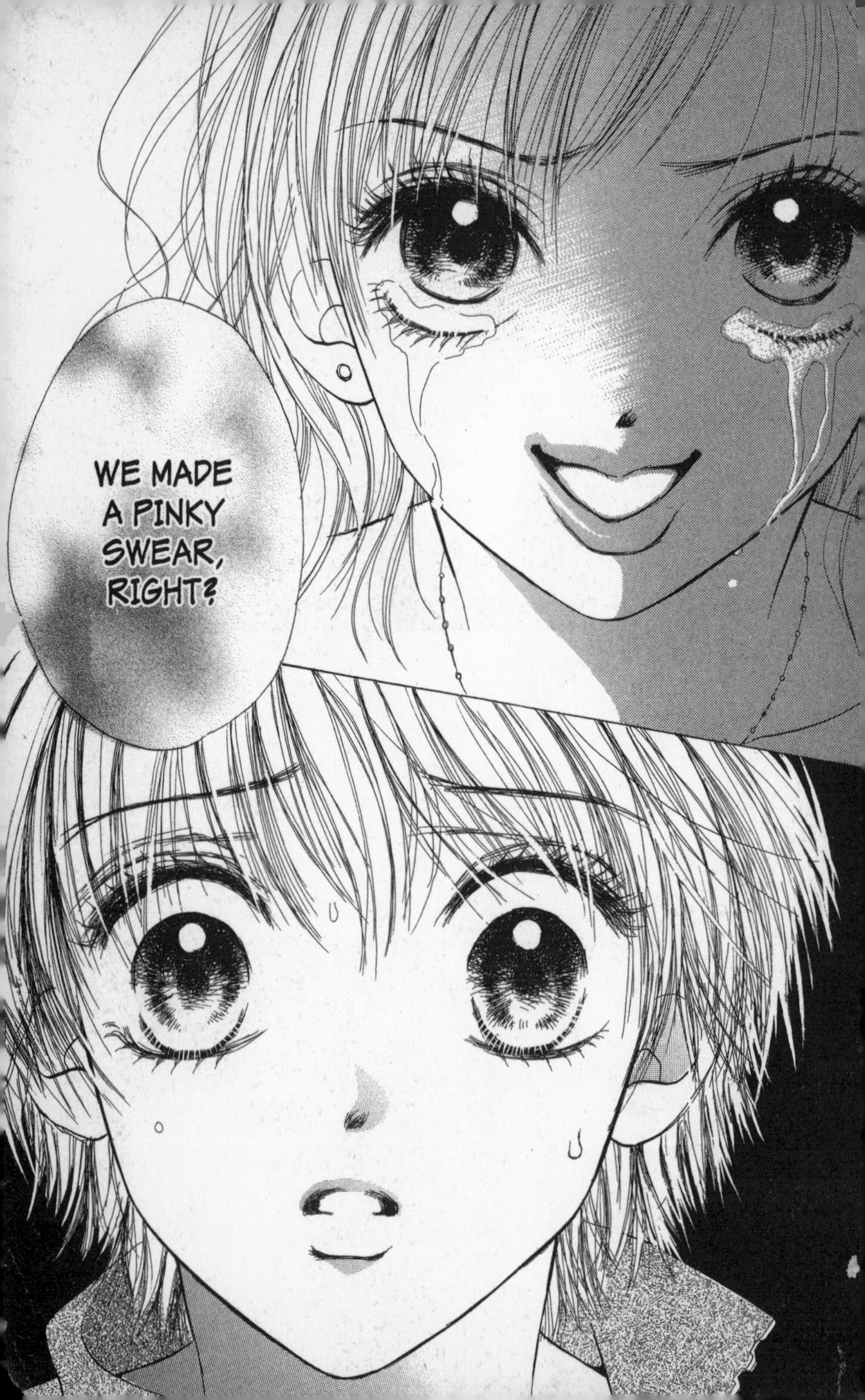
WE MADE A PINKY SWEAR, RIGHT?

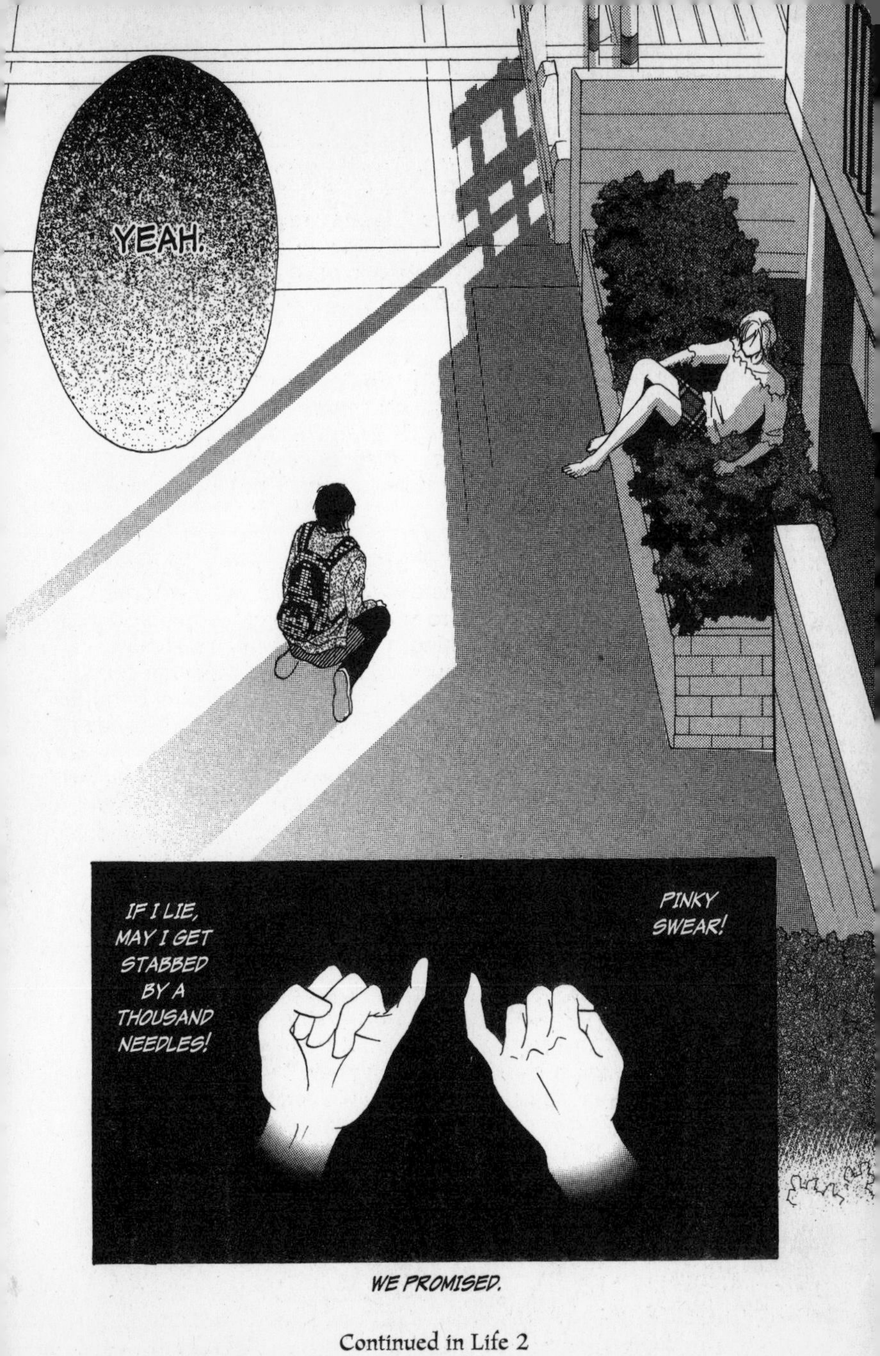
YEAH.
PINKY SWEAR!
IF I LIE, MAY I GET STABBED BY A THOUSAND NEEDLES!
WE PROMISED.

Continued in Life 2

Epilogue

LIFE portrays the experience of Ayumu, who is faced with the pressures of teenage life, and is struggling with emotions that sometimes feel too strong for her to handle. She discovers that hurting herself makes her feel better—temporarily, anyway. Ayumu's behavior is known as cutting, or more generally, self-injury, and is different from Manami's suicidal behavior. (For information on suicide prevention, visit www.dbsalliance.org/info/suicide.html or call the following toll-free suicide hotline: 1-800-273-TALK.)

Self-injury is when a person deliberately harms his or her body. The most common form is cutting (usually on the wrists, upper arms, or other areas that can be hidden), but other forms include burning, scratching, skin-picking, hair-pulling, hitting, bone-breaking, or not letting a wound heal. About 1% of North Americans self-injure, the vast majority of them being female.

Rather than feeling intense pain when cutting, most self-injurers feel relieved and soothed by the act; it is a way of coping with emotions that feel unbearable or impossible to talk about. Some people who feel numb self-injure to feel something, which helps them feel more alive. It can also be a way of communicating to others that they need help. Self-injurers are not trying to kill themselves, nor are they crazy or weak—they simply do not know of other healthier ways to feel better.

More people are learning about self-injury—it may even seem like a fad in some circles—and some people may be tempted to try it. But self-injury is a serious problem; it can lead to infection, the need for medical attention, or even unintentional suicide. Self-injury is not an effective way of coping; it provides only temporary relief and those who self-injure often end up feeling controlled by the need to do it.

People who self-injure need our help. If you know someone who cuts, talk to her in a nonjudgmental, supportive way, since she likely feels shame about it. Let her know that she can be helped by admitting her problem to someone she trusts, like a school nurse, parent, or teacher. This trusted adult can assist her in receiving help from a mental health professional. Only then can she sort out painful feelings and learn new, healthy ways of coping.

For more information on self-injury, visit:
kidshealth.org/teen/your_mind/feeling_sad/cutting.html

Susan M. Axtell, Psy.D.
Licensed Clinical Psychologist

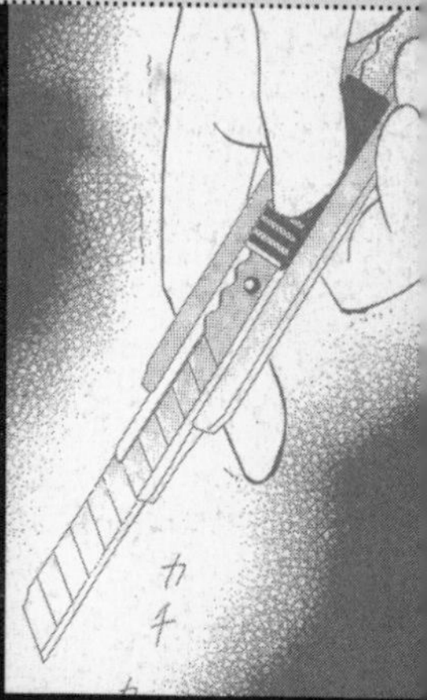

Ayumu struggles with her studies, and the all-important high school entrance exams are approaching. Fortunately, she has help from her best bud Shii-chan, who is at the top of the class. But when the test results come back, the friends are surprised: Ayumu surpasses Shii-chan's scores and gets into the school of her choice—without Shii-chan! Losing her friend is so painful for Ayumu that she starts cutting herself to ease her sorrow. Finally, Ayumu seeks comfort in a new friend, Manami. But will Manami prove to be the friend that Ayumu truly needs? Or will Ayumu continue down a dark path?

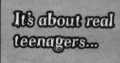

It's about real teenagers...

It's about real high school...

It's about real life.

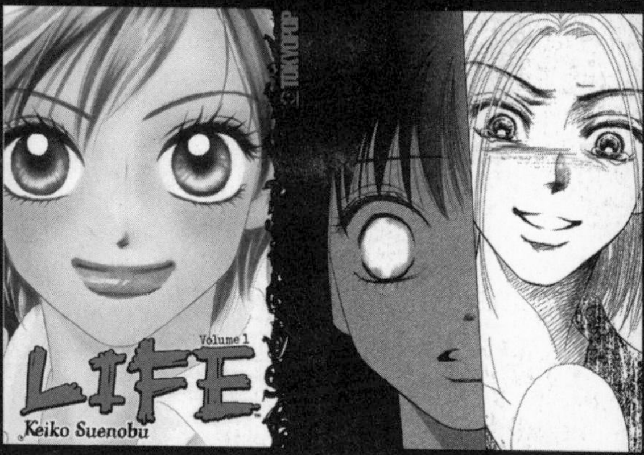
TOKYOPOP
Volume 1
LIFE
Keiko Suenobu

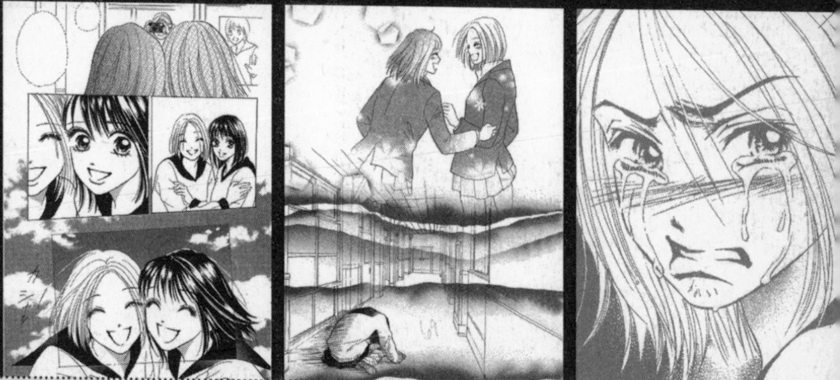

WWW.TOKYOPOP.COM/LIFE

LIFE
BY KEIKO SUENOBU

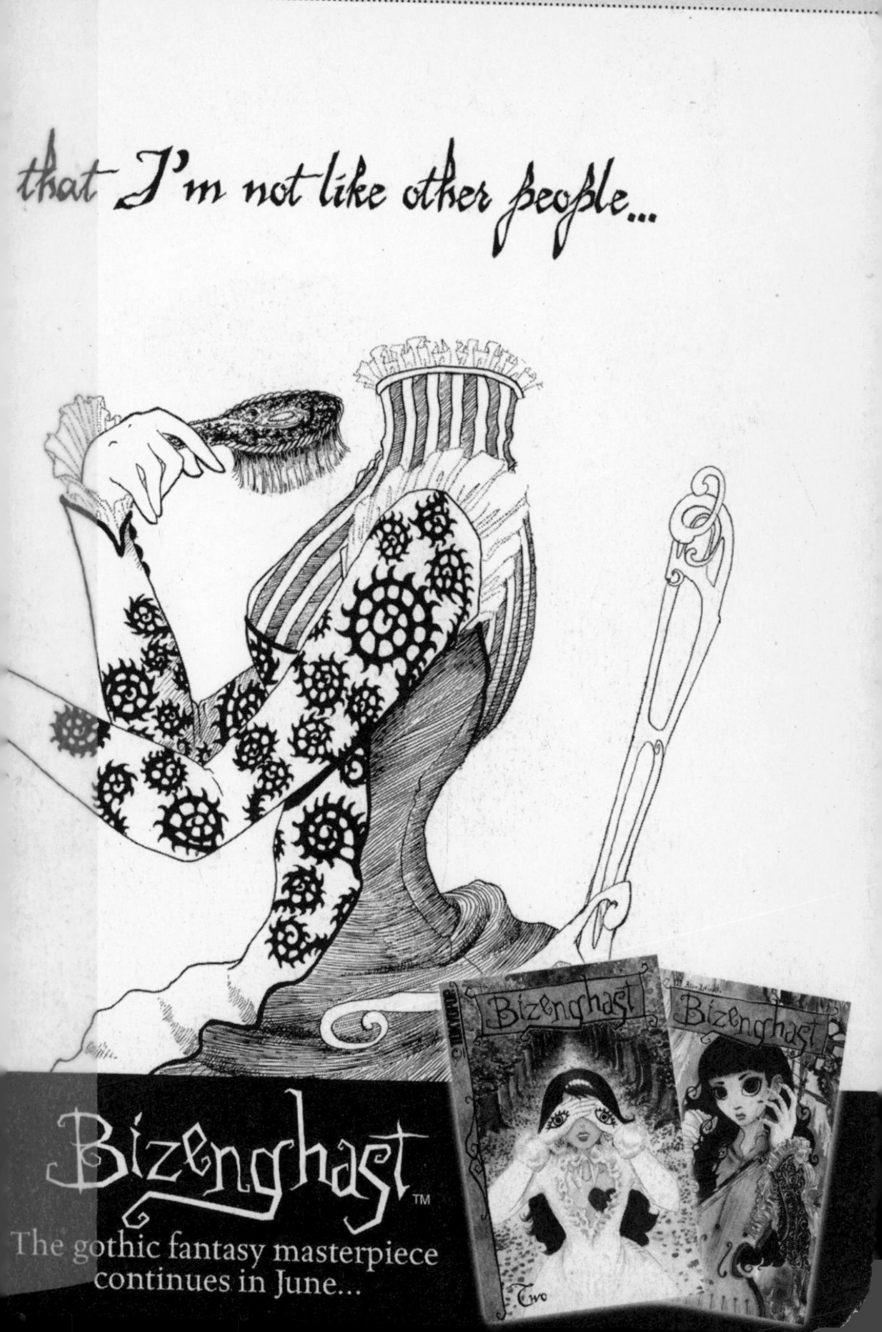
that I'm not like other people...
Bizenghast
Bizenghast
Two
Bizenghast™
The gothic fantasy masterpiece
continues in June...

BIZENGHAST

Dear Diary,
I'm starting to feel

THIS FALL, TOKYOPOP CREATES A FRESH, NEW CHAPTER IN TEEN NOVELS...

For Adventurers...
Witches' Forest:
The Adventures of Duan Surk

By Mishio Fukazawa
Duan Surk is a 16-year-old Level 2 fighter who embarks on the quest of a lifetime—battling mythical creatures and outwitting evil sorceresses, all in an impossible rescue mission in the spooky Witches' Forest!

BASED ON THE FAMOUS
FORTUNE QUEST WORLD

For Dreamers...
Magic Moon

By Wolfgang and Heike Hohlbein
Kim enters the enigmatic realm of Magic Moon, where he battles unthinkable monsters and fantastical creatures—in order to unravel the secret that keeps his sister locked in a coma.

THE WORLDWIDE BESTSELLING FANTASY
*THRILL*OGY ARRIVES IN THE U.S.!

This is the back of the book.
You wouldn't want to spoil a great ending!

This book is printed "manga-style," in the authentic Japanese right-to-left format. Since none of the artwork has been flipped or altered, readers get to experience the story just as the creator intended. You've been asking for it, so TOKYOPOP® delivered: authentic, hot-off-the-press, and far more fun!

DIRECTIONS

If this is your first time reading manga-style, here's a quick guide to help you understand how it works.

It's easy... just start in the top right panel and follow the numbers. Have fun, and look for more 100% authentic manga from TOKYOPOP®!